CLOCKΨORK LIΛES

KEVIN J. ANDERSON
AND NEIL PEART

Illustrations by Nick Robles

ECW PRESS

To Xavier and Theodore, my other two grandsons.
Your lives are going to be epics! —*KJA*

―――――――――――――――――――

To Carrie and Olivia, who make my life anything but "clockwork" —*NEP*

Some lives can be summed up in a sentence or two.
Other lives are epics.

CHAPTER I

As a blue alchemical glow illuminated the rails, the steamliner came into Lugtown on its weekly run toward Crown City, the heart of the land of Albion. The chain of cargo cars and passenger gondolas was suspended by bright balloon sacks, each marked with the loving Watchmaker's honeybee symbol.

The steamliner touched down, steel wheels striking the rails outside of town and decelerating with gouts of steam and showers of sparks. Steam vents hissed, lowering pressure inside the coldfire boiler chambers. The pilot would park at Lugtown for the better part of a day to refill water tanks and take on cargo.

Restless passengers disembarked, the men wearing frock coats and top hats or bowlers; some women wore voluminous dresses, gloves, and button-up black boots; other women wore more casual traveling clothes, or even work overalls on their way to distant job sites.

The steamliner's weekly arrival was extremely disruptive for a person with a schedule to keep and work to do. Standing impatient and then trying to make her way around the crowd, Marinda Peake watched the travelers' expressions shift from optimism to disappointment, apparently not impressed with the little village of Lugtown. They were on their way to Crown City or to parts unknown—and Marinda had her own business here.

She had often considered shifting her regular supply trip into town to a different day of the week, but she had always come on Wednesday, and it would be too unsettling to change. A well-established routine served a valid purpose.

The steamliner pilot emerged from the front motivator car, which was connected to a passenger gondola and smoking compartment. Marinda held a long-dampened resentment toward any steamliner pilot, since her mother had run off with one such pilot when Marinda was just a girl, mesmerized by his stories of far-off places, the freedom, the flexibility to travel. Elitia Peake was never heard from again, and Marinda's father rarely spoke of his long-lost wife, except with a wistful smile and few details. That had been more than twenty-five years ago. . . .

Marinda did not bother with memories of her mother, though. The woman was never coming back, so there was no sense wasting time or mental energy thinking about the faithless woman. She had other things to do.

Now, the barrel-chested pilot barked commands to his crew, and they hooked up water pipes to refill the boiler chambers for the long journey into Crown City. Cargo workers swung down from their drab bunk car to unload merchandise. Villagers came forward, eager to see what interesting items were available for trade, but Marinda had no interest. Such fripperies were a waste of time and imagination, and she and her father already had what they needed.

The people brought wagons and chugging carts loaded with their finest craftsmanship, which they would ship to Crown City. Lugtown was primarily known for burls from local oaks that were twisted and distorted by a perennial fungus. In keeping with the tenet of the Clockwork Angels that "even the ugly can be made useful, possibly even beautiful," Lugtowners carved the burls into furniture, decorative accent pieces, and fantastic sculptures—particularly carvings of the angels. Every house in town had burl tables, burl chairs, burl countertops, burl bowls, even clocks framed with burlwood.

The carvers sent their work off on the steamliner, but none of them bothered to go to Crown City to see their art displayed in galleries. When Marinda had asked a woodcarver about it once, he'd responded with a baffled look. "Why would I want to do that? The Watchmaker granted me the gift to be a sculptor, not a traveler. Should I diminish something I *am*, for something I am not and do not want to be?" Marinda found that logic eminently reasonable.

A local quarry also produced many thunder eggs—agates—which the Watchmaker supposedly found beautiful. The polished stones went off to Crown City in crates neatly separated from the burlwood items.

Showing no inclination to hurry, since the steamliner would be there for hours, the villagers loaded their outbound cargo and perused the new shipments of supplies. Marinda bustled past them, away from the steamliner station, and made her way into town. Fortunately, with so many townspeople gawking at the inconvenient disruption of the steamliner's arrival, the local businesses would have fewer customers, which made for easier shopping on her part. That allowed Marinda to complete her errands more efficiently.

Lugtown was laid out on the same general map as all of the villages in Albion; the Watchmaker had standardized the whole land more than two centuries ago when he imposed his benevolent Stability. Thus, Marinda adhered to the philosophy that if she'd seen one town in Albion she had seen them all, and it was a lot easier just to continue seeing this one.

With measured steps, she walked down the main street, past shops, clerks' offices, the local newsgraph station. A cloud obscured the sun, and the wind whisked by. Marinda reached up to touch her brown hair, done up in an efficient bun so the strands would not be blown astray; they all remained firmly in place. Marinda believed in stability in her hair arrangement, as with all things.

Though she was only thirty-two and her skin was still smooth, she had already adopted the persona of a much older woman. In that, Marinda was ahead of schedule. The hours ticked away. She ticked away . . . and her father was ticking away even faster than the rest.

She reached into the pocket of her gray wool skirt to withdraw her list, reviewing the items she needed to purchase. Today, she had to make a special trip to the apothecary for unguents, prescription powders, and ophthalmic salves, though all of those curatives had less and less effect as her father's health continued to decline.

As she walked past the solicitor's office, the door popped open, startling her with its jingling bell. Benjulian Frull was Lugtown's only lawyer, a master of the fine art of legal language, obfuscation, and loopholes. The fact that he had no competition in Lugtown made it difficult for any legal disputes to become contentious, because Benjulian Frull, Esq., represented both sides, quoting chapter and verse to each party until the matter was resolved.

"Ah-hem, Miss Peake! I saw you passing by, which is quite fortuitous. I need to discuss a matter with you." Frull stepped out to join her on the street. He was a man with a round face and a round belly; in contrast, his arms and legs were quite spindly so that, in summation, he was an average-sized man. "And how is old Arlen doing?"

"The same as always," she said. "Poorly. His eyesight is mostly gone, and he is in constant pain, but he dabbles with his inventions and keeps his clockwork Regulators functioning, although they don't work as well as he thinks. I believe he's much more ill than he lets on." She put her hands on her hips. "*My* eyesight is perfectly good, and I can see his condition."

The solicitor frowned. "But how is Arlen's *mind?* Ah-hem . . . can he still think clearly? The wheels still turning smoothly?" He tapped the side of his head.

"His body may be failing him, but his mind is not. My father can still daydream, and he likes those silly stories of his more than ever. He wants me to read aloud for him every night."

"Good," Frull said. "I just wanted to verify that in your opinion he is of sound mind? He seemed quite clearheaded when he engaged my services last week, but I wanted to make sure."

Marinda raised her eyebrows. "But he never leaves the cottage. When did he talk to you?"

"Arlen sent one of those clockwork contraptions marching into town while you were away on your weekly errands, summoned me to the cottage. I went out and spoke with him for hours."

Marinda was surprised. "Well, he didn't bother to mention it to me." She knew her father had plenty of secrets, but she didn't realize how much he kept truly private from her.

"It was legal business, a redrafting of his last will and testament. He needs to make certain that you're taken care of. He wants what's best for you. You're aware that he amassed a significant nest egg from his time in Crown City?"

She hardened her expression. "That's all just so much nonsense. People say he has a secret stash of the Watchmaker's gold. If that's the case, he certainly hasn't used it to make our lives easier, and he refuses to speak of whatever he did back then." Some even said that Arlen Peake had once worked for the Watchmaker himself, a long time ago. . . .

Marinda wasn't actually interested in pampered luxuries; she was content with her quiet, perfect life, setting her ambitions low enough so that she met every single one of them. Even if her father did have unimaginable riches from his secretive past, she wouldn't know what to do with wealth.

Benjulian Frull clucked his tongue. "Arlen had me draw up the documents, which are signed and notarized. Although his wishes seem strange, I believe he is in full possession of his mental capacity. I'm glad you agree. He is preparing for the day when he is no longer with us."

Marinda felt uncomfortable with the subject. "I've tended my father for years. Sometimes, he's prone to overreacting." She pulled out her list of items for the general store and the apothecary. "I need to pick up these supplies and get back to my father in time to prepare him dinner. Good day."

Nodding, the solicitor stepped back inside his office.

Camberon Greer, the round-faced and jovial grocer, knew that Marinda came in every Wednesday, so she never understood why he didn't just have her order packaged up and ready, so as not to waste her time. The grocer didn't have the same respect for time as Marinda did—he never had. Marinda wondered what she had ever seen in that man. If circumstances had been different . . .

Much to Marinda's surprise, Greer was closing up his store just as she arrived. She frowned up at the nearest clock tower, looked at the smaller clock mounted on the corner of the building across the street, and frowned again. The sign above the door said *Camberon Greer: Grocer, General Store*; the hours were prominently marked, and they did not match what she was seeing with her own eyes.

Camberon grinned as he pulled the door shut. "It's Miss Marinda! Happy to see you as always. You're looking lovely." He said that to her every time; she knew he used to mean it, but now it was just a habit for him, and a bittersweet reminder for her.

Marinda pointed to the hours. "You're supposed to be open. I need to purchase my weekly supplies."

"Sorry, but today is special, Miss Marinda." *Miss* Marinda. Did he always have to remind her of that? "It's my youngest boy's birthday, and we're closing down so we can go crack thunder eggs at the quarry. We might get lucky and find a pearl of quintessence!"

The door popped open again, and three rambunctious boys ran out laughing and harassing one another. They were all redheaded, freckled. *Unruly ragamuffins*, Marinda thought. They were named Oberon, Albert, and Tom—definitely not the names she would have chosen if she and Camberon had had children. She stopped herself from thinking like that.

"But you're supposed to be open," she repeated. "I need supplies."

Camberon continued cranking down the awning and closing up crates of items on display. "Sorry, it's a special day." He cocked his eyebrows at her. "And I know you and your father have plenty of supplies for another week."

"But . . . my list." She pulled out her paper from the pocket in her skirt.

"We're going to see the steamliner," said one of the boys—Albert, she thought, though she never really paid attention. They weren't her children, after all.

"Then we're going to the quarry," said the youngest boy, Tom, the one with the birthday.

"The quarry is always there," Marinda pointed out. "And the steamliner comes every week."

"But today's my birthday," said Tom, "so it's special."

Camberon tousled the boy's hair. "Is your mother coming?"

"She's packing lunch," said Oberon.

Marinda frowned at the inconvenience. It was Wednesday, and she always got groceries on Wednesdays.

Camberon saw her consternation and gave her an understanding smile. "We'll open again at sunset. You're in town, why don't you relax, walk along the stream, go to the park, read a book? There's no hurry, is there?"

Marinda wasn't even tempted by such diversions. She had to get home and care for her father; the words of the solicitor had unsettled her. Old Arlen was not well, and she needed to be there to watch over him. It was her responsibility. She had given up so much to take care of him, year after year.

Camberon's wife, Jasselyn, came from around the back of the store carrying a picnic basket. The three boys jostled, wrestled, and ran forward to cling to her arms. She endured it all with a smile, and Camberon grinned.

Jasselyn had long brown hair like Marinda's, but she kept hers loose, sometimes tying ribbons in it, sometimes adding flowers, other times just curling it into an unexpected mane. She looked much younger than Marinda—which was unexpected, because one would have thought that three busy children would wear a person out. "Hello, Miss Marinda." She sidled up next to her husband, and the children gathered around.

Camberon said, "Please come back at sunset, Marinda. It'll be fine—I promise."

The family walked off, leaving her with unsettling thoughts of what might have been. A long time ago, the Watchmaker had planned that Marinda and Camberon would be married, sending pre-printed engagement cards and everything, and he had been so eager to have children.

But all that had changed when Arlen had gotten sick. Accepting her priorities and responsibilities, Marinda broke off the engagement with Camberon to care for her father.

Planned lives, scheduled happiness . . .

"Have a good picnic," she said, but doubted they heard her as they walked toward the steamliner tracks and the road leading to the quarry on the outskirts of town.

CHAPTER 2

Storytellers might have described Marinda's little cottage, yard, and garden plot as idyllic, but no storytellers would ever write about this place. It was just her home, and it was *perfect* because that was how Marinda chose to define perfection.

Marking the head of the path that branched off to the cottage stood a five-foot-high burlwood angel. This particular angel looked bent rather than majestic; one wing tucked under the other gave the impression that she was flightless. Only perfect burlwood angels were sent to the markets in Crown City, while less successful carvings, like this one, remained in Lugtown like beloved albeit misfit children.

Marinda headed back to the cottage much earlier than expected. But Arlen Peake could be capricious and unpredictable himself, so he wouldn't be overly bothered by the change in schedule.

As an inventor, he was expected to be eccentric. If the rumors were true, the Watchmaker himself had tolerated Arlen's unorthodox behavior—and if the loving Watchmaker allowed it, then the people of Lugtown wouldn't hold it against him (although, truth be told, the eccentric behavior presented its own challenges for Marinda, on top of caring for his other infirmities).

The conversation with Benjulian Frull had troubled Marinda. She knew she had to accept that her father would pass on someday, and then the cottage would belong to her. In the typical blueprint of a life in Albion, Marinda would have settled in that cottage with a husband and a family, maybe three children, maybe even redheaded and freckled boys, but she had deviated from that norm. She would find a profession for herself, do something useful and interesting to occupy her days, and carry on.

The Clockwork Angels said that good work leads to good fortune, and she had no doubt that her fortune would continue, with or without whatever secret gold her father had stashed away from his time in Crown City. Marinda didn't think about it often. *We get what we deserve.* That was what the Watchmaker always said.

In front of the cottage, she saw the three clockwork Regulators that Arlen had built out of spare parts scrounged from mining machinery at the agate quarry, engineering castoffs from the regular steamliner, and specialized components ordered from providers in Crown City. The mechanical Regulators were powered by tiny rock pearls glowing with quintessence, assisted by standard spring-driven clockwork mechanisms.

Arlen Peake had named the three windup companions Zivo, Woody, and Lee, apparently after three Regulator friends he had known back in Crown City. Her father often told wistful stories about the real friends, but he said very little about his time in the Regulator barracks or the Watchmaker's tower. "That is a story you will get in due time, my sparkling daughter," he had said. "All in its time, all in its place." She could accept that.

The clockwork Regulators were four feet tall with metal arms and legs, pulleys and pistons that glowed with the addition of coldfire fuel. Each head was a smooth copper pot painted with a cheery face. They ratcheted about, did their assigned tasks. To prevent overheating, puffs of steam would blast out from tiny vents where their ears should have been. Each wore a downsized uniform just like that of a traditional Regulator, Zivo in the bright uniform of the Red Guard, Woody dressed as a member of the Blue Guard, while Lee served as a miniature Black Guard.

When Arlen Peake had built these three charming companions, he'd intended for them to do household chores and work in the garden. He wanted to ease Marinda's burden of taking care of him, so she could have the freedom to live her own life. Alas, the three artificial Regulators required their own maintenance and supervision, which negated any time savings.

Black-uniformed Lee stood guard on the walkway, as if ruthless bandits from chaotic times before the Watchmaker's Stability might raid the cottage . . . although this clockwork contraption could have done little to defend them.

Woody worked the well pump in the yard to fill a water bucket, since Wednesday was soup night. The Regulator activated the syncopated well-pumping station, a set of gears that spun an engine driven by a few drops of coldfire. He set the wheels in motion, oscillating a piston up and down, and water spilled clear and silver into the bucket.

Meanwhile, his red uniform covered with mud, Zivo used a diminutive hoe to chop weeds in the garden. Unfortunately, his crude visual sensors were poorly calibrated, and he couldn't always tell the difference between weeds and vegetables.

"Hello Lee," she said, as she always did when she returned home. The clockwork Regulator snapped to attention, as if to prove that he took his guard duties seriously.

"Hello Zivo." The mechanical man in the garden swung his hoe right into the center of a thriving potato plant.

"Hello Woody." The blue-uniformed contraption bent his copperpot head in a nod. She took the water bucket from him, and Woody ratcheted off to do other household chores, walking a path around the cottage, circle after circle after circle like a turning clockwork gear.

Carrying the bucket, she entered the cottage. Her father had heard her come up the path, and he smiled in her general direction. The old man sat propped in his calibrated chair, bathed in warm afternoon sunlight from the window. The chair was motivated by a clock that Arlen adjusted for the seasons, which moved the chair at the same speed that the patch of sunlight crossed the floor. He was like a cat soaking up the warmth. Six different clocks set within randomly shaped blocks of polished burlwood hung on the walls, ticking synchronously.

He squinted at her, although he could barely see. "Hello, my sparkling daughter."

At his side Arlen kept an array of magnifying glasses of various diameters and curvatures. On his blanketed lap, he had spread out a map of random lines, some dotted, some bold. She didn't know how he could discern anything even under the highest magnification, but that didn't stop her father from trying.

He was too proud to admit he could no longer do the things he used to do, but he occupied himself with pondering rather than reading. He held up the paper and smiled at her, but his gaze was off by a few degrees. "I've learned a great deal. This is a secret map."

"A map?" she asked, tucking the blanket around his legs. "A map of what?" *And where do you expect to travel?* she thought. *How do you imagine you might get there? You should stay home and think about practical things.*

"It shows the rivers under the Redrock Desert."

"And what good is that? We're nowhere near the Redrock Desert. I don't even know where it is."

"You should know your geography better, my dear. It's on the continent of Atlantis, far beyond the alchemy mines, on the other side of the mountains." He spoke as if he had been there himself. Maybe he had . . . but if so, her father had never told her about it.

"Well, Albion is a long way from Atlantis," Marinda said, activating the efficient coldfire burner so she could boil the soup water. "And my feet are sore just from walking to Lugtown and back."

"You should plan a trip to Atlantis," Arlen suggested. "Book passage on a cargo steamer. Go to Poseidon City."

"Now why would I want to do that? I have you to take care of, I have this cottage, I have everything I need."

"But is it everything you *want*?"

"Yes it is. Now I have to get busy making dinner."

As the pot simmered, she prepared the salves, unguents, and medicinal powders for her father's various ailments. Arlen opened the small bottles and jars by feel, sniffed the preparations. He wiped a gummy substance over his milky eyes; it smelled like almonds and was supposed to increase his visual acuity, a claim that Arlen did not confirm. Other compounds were for his aching joints, his digestion, his heart. The mixtures muddled his thoughts, and her father sometimes preferred to deal with the pain rather than lose his mental sharpness. He told her he still had too many ideas to work out.

The three clockwork Regulators came inside as she and her father ate their meal. The clicking hum of the clockwork Regulators and the hiss of occasionally vented steam added to the comforting tick-tock of the burlwood clocks on the wall.

The soup contained cabbage, root vegetables, and a small amount of minced chicken, accompanied by a loaf of day-old bread she had gotten for a bargain at the Lugtown Bakery. It was a frugal meal, as was Marinda's habit. Her father insisted they didn't have to be so careful with their money, but since Marinda had never seen any sign of his alleged secret gold, she preferred to be conservative.

While Marinda sipped soup and judiciously sopped the rest

with a hunk of bread, old Arlen talked wistfully about the remote alchemy mines on far-off Atlantis and the exotic and dangerous Poseidon City. He had read about such places in books that he kept on his shelf, but once his eyesight had begun to fail, he had asked her to read to him. Marinda did so because she loved her father (although she did the reading reluctantly, not wanting to encourage foolish ideas).

As if he could sense her impatience with fanciful tales, old Arlen tried to bring the stories closer to home. "Since you've never found Atlantis interesting, I'll tell you about wondrous places right here in Albion."

"It sounds interesting enough, Father," she said as she gathered their bowls, wrapped the last of the bread, and cleaned the kitchen. "But Atlantis and even the rest of Albion are too far away for me to bother with."

"Too far away?" Arlen's eyes were still filmy from the salve. "What is the distance of dreams?" He sighed. "I've saddled you with too many responsibilities here, and I apologize. I never should have done that to you."

Marinda clucked. "It's a daughter's duty to take care of her father. If I had gotten married according to the original plan, I would be busy caring for my family, and I still wouldn't have a chance to gallivant off to strange continents and foreign cities."

"Not even the Alchemy College? To Crown City? Everyone should see the Clockwork Angels at least once in their lives."

Marinda moved his chair to the hearth where she added a lump of imported redcoal. It was late spring and the nights were getting warmer, but Arlen was easily chilled. "Maybe I'll get around to it someday, when I'm not so busy."

With a long sigh, her father looked right at her for the first time in months. "I am so sorry for you."

She adjusted his blanket. "As I said, there's truly no apology necessary."

He looked away. "And I'm more sorry that you don't even know what I'm apologizing for."

Night had fallen and the stars were bright outside. On his shelf, her father kept star charts that identified constellations and asterisms. He had often encouraged her to go look at the night sky to understand the clockwork universe. More than once, she reassured Arlen that she would do just that, primarily so he would go to bed in peace, but she hadn't yet gotten around to stargazing.

Tonight, though, he didn't ask her to read to him or step outside to look at the stars. "I think I'll go to bed early, if you can help me?" He just seemed more tired than usual as she took him to the bedroom.

Out of habit, Marinda turned the key in the special antique clock on his shelf, which supposedly commemorated his service to the Watchmaker. Her father sat on the bed and fumbled around the nightstand table, then patted the bedspread, searching. "Where's my . . . thing?"

She knew what he meant. She picked up an unusual helmet contraption of his own devising. "Your sequential optical enhancement device. You invented it—you should remember what you named it."

He reached out for her to hand him the helmet, which he attached to his head. Leather straps and buckles fitted it to the back of his skull, and a visor composed of integrated lenses and prisms, clear lenses, blue lenses, red lenses, covered his face. He made adjustments to the visor, shifted the lenses into place, and lay back on his pillow, letting out a long contented breath.

"I don't know how you can sleep with that on," she said.

"I've gotten used to it. My body presents enough other inconveniences—I can tolerate this one."

She stood at his bedside, frowning. "But why do you need an optical enhancement device when you're sleeping?"

From behind the complicated helmet, he said, "To see my

dreams better, of course. Where is your imagination?" She kissed him on the chin, the only spot she could reach beneath his helmet contraption. "May your dreams be pleasant ones, my sparkling daughter," he said. "Always."

She dimmed the lights in his room, even though he couldn't see anything with the optical contraption over his eyes. "Good night to you too, Father." It did not seem to be the acknowledgment he was looking for.

Marinda dampened the motivator engines of the three clockwork Regulators, shutting them down for the night, so that the only sound she heard was the ticking of the numerous clocks. She stayed up by herself in the main room, reading by coldfire light.

Bookshelves filled one wall, and Marinda glanced at the novels, legends, fanciful stories. She had never paid much attention to the titles or subjects. In recent years, she had read some of them aloud to her father, at his insistence, although she never understood the charm of fanciful fiction.

This night, she worked on the household accounting instead, then she extinguished the remaining redcoal in the hearth and went to her own room where she slept soundly, assured that the budget was in order.

———————◆◆◆————————

Next morning, she awoke, started the coldfire stove, and put on a kettle to boil for their morning tea. She reactivated the three clockwork Regulators and went in to wake her father. Although he usually stirred before she did, sometimes he chose to sleep in.

She entered Arlen's room to find an odd silence and she realized that the special clock from Crown City had run down. She frowned. What had her father called that gift from the Watchmaker? A Lifeclock. Well, apparently it wasn't good for much of anything.

Arlen Peake lay in bed with the optical contraption still covering most of his face, and when she tried to shake him awake, he did not respond. He wore a smile on his face as if the strange helmet had actually sharpened the visual acuity of his dreams.

He had died in his sleep.

CHAPTER 3

The teakettle boiled dry, and Marinda barely noticed the whistle. Stunned into an instinctive response, she tried to utter the Watchmaker's benediction, "All is for the best," but the words would not come out of her mouth. A small voice in the back of her mind said that she should have prepared herself for the imminent, inevitable reality. Now, Marinda had no plan to follow.

She stood in her father's room for an incredibly long moment, just staring as time stood still. The clockwork Regulators marched into the room and stood at respectful attention. Because their faces were merely painted on their copperpot heads, the mechanical companions could express no overt sorrow, but their demeanor had changed, as if sadness now flowed through their hydraulics.

All Marinda could hear was the ticking of clocks out in the main room and the whirring machinery of Zivo, Woody, and Lee. The shrill screech in the background had fallen silent . . . and she finally realized that it had been the teakettle on the stove. She would attend to that later.

Marinda shed tears, but wiped them away because she had much to do and many things to deal with. It was time to be stoic. Methodical, she went to the kitchen and the writing desk, from which she removed a sheet of paper, then a fountain pen, the same one she had used to balance the household accounts . . . the same fountain pen her father had used to sketch his inventions and to write notes to himself. She sat at the same table where they had eaten the frugal meal of soup and day-old bread the night before.

The clockwork Regulators stood at attention as she wrote out a brief note for Benjulian Frull, informing him of her father's death and requesting instructions as to what she should do. Since this important mission should be entrusted to a member of the elite Black Watch, and Lee with his black uniform was the closest option at hand, she handed the note to him. His articulated fingers closed around it.

"Take this note to Lugtown and deliver it to Mr. Benjulian Frull. He will return with you."

With humming gears and a burst from the steam vent by his ear, Lee left the cottage and marched down the path. The other two clockwork Regulators waited for instructions, but Marinda gave them none. Instead, she returned to her father's bedroom, looked at his motionless form. Angry and helpless, she turned the key in the Watchmaker's Lifeclock, trying to start it working again, but the mechanism was broken.

Needing to see her father's face again, she gingerly removed the straps and buckles, lifting away the helmet contraption. Arlen's expression looked content with whatever he had seen inside the ocular enhancement device.

Feeling a large hole in her heart, Marinda realized she would never know the real story of his years in Crown City with the Watchmaker and the Clockwork Angels. *In due time*, he had said . . . but time had come due for him, and the opportunity was missed. She wondered what her father had been looking at in his dreams, if he could see anything at all.

She had never tried on the helmet herself, since her eyes functioned just fine, but now she needed to see what he had seen. She owed it to him. With some trepidation, she lifted the helmet, adjusted the visor, and noticed that it contained two images. Arlen had been viewing the second one when he died, but because Marinda chose to do this in an orderly fashion, she reset the optical projector, moved the visor in place, and activated the chronograph.

An image appeared with an intensity that exceeded reality: a moment, a person frozen in time—a mysterious and beautiful woman with a distant gaze and an aloof smile. Marinda realized she had seen this woman before in her father's old scrapbooks, the ones she had never seen him browse, even when his vision had been perfect.

This was her mother, Elitia Peake. Marinda barely remembered the woman who had left them when she was just a little girl, and yet Arlen projected her image into his dreams every night.

But that wasn't the image he'd been viewing when he died. The second chronograph contained her own face—a young woman in her late teens, someone who looked beautiful and happy. In the chronograph, Marinda was smiling, her hair loose. It was an accidental moment, just the briefest glimpse of how her life might be. . . .

She couldn't remember when that chronograph was taken, yet her father had captured it somehow. How had he known to be there to see that small carefree moment? Or maybe such moments had happened more often than Marinda herself had noticed, years ago.

She didn't bother to switch back to the chronograph of her mother, since Elitia had left them long ago. Long ago, Marinda had decided to pack up the rest of her anger toward her mother, lock it in an imaginary box, and store it in a place deep inside herself. Her father had refused to speak ill of his wife, insisting that Elitia must have had her reasons. That woman was no longer relevant to either of them, and Marinda and Arlen had made a very acceptable life for themselves.

And now Marinda was alone.

Far more interested in how her father regarded *her*, she continued looking at the image of herself for some time. Was this how Arlen saw his "sparkling daughter"? She would never question the accuracy of a chronograph, but it seemed a paradox to her. When she held the images, both of these people seemed like strangers to her.

<hr>

Fortunately, the solicitor knew exactly what to do. Through long experience, he already had a plan in place.

He accompanied the clockwork Regulator back to the cottage two hours later—two of the longest hours in Marinda's life. Frull's round face bore a look of deep concern. "I am deeply sorry for your loss, Miss Peake. Arlen loved you very much, but all is for the best."

"All is for the best," she managed to respond. "But . . . what do I do now? How do I arrange a funeral? How do I transfer ownership of our property? I assume there are efficient and established ways for a person to get her life back to normal?"

"There are ways," Frull said, but he looked troubled. "As soon as I received the message from your representative"—he looked down at the black-garbed Regulator, who stood ticking and whirring in place—"I began to take care of matters. Ah-hem, since Arlen had previously informed me of his wishes, to save you the trouble, we had already filed a plan with the undertaker."

Marinda felt a wash of relief. "Thank you." Naturally, there would be a standard routine for such things, not just in Lugtown but across Albion. The Watchmaker himself might be nearly immortal with more than two centuries of the Stability, but normal people died, and it reassured her to know that everything would be taken care of.

Marinda had not yet grasped the ways in which her life would change, though—what this cottage would be like without her father's presence, what she would do with all his unwanted books and contraptions. She did not know how to maintain the three clockwork Regulators; no one in Lugtown did. The apothecary and the physicians had tried to fix Arlen Peake, and they had not been successful. She supposed that even clockwork Regulators must wind down and die.

"I've already contacted the Lugtown newsgraph office to send out announcements," said Frull. "You, meanwhile . . . it would be best if you just stayed here, enjoyed your cottage for a little while longer."

She sensed something behind his words, something he wasn't saying, but Marinda's heart was too heavy to consider it. She lifted her chin and drew a deep breath. "It will never be the same here without my father, but I will try my best to get back to normal."

On the morning after the funeral, Marinda had an appointment at the solicitor's offices, where he would read her father's will. When she arrived, Benjulian Frull was waiting for her behind his desk. He wore a formal brown jacket and a gray vest complete with pocket watch. His expression was serious—which Marinda appreciated, because this was no light social call. A neat stack of stamped and notarized papers rested in front of him on the desk blotter. Glancing at the top sheet, Marinda saw *Last Will and Testament of Arlen Peake.*

She took a seat primly on the other side of the desk and folded her hands in her lap. Without bothering with pleasantries, Frull picked up the papers and studied them as if searching for something he knew wasn't there; he was more than familiar with the document, since he had written it himself in close consultation with her father. He cleared his throat. "I have to warn you, Miss

Peake, that this is, ah-hem, not what you expect."

Marinda was impatient. "You're going to tell me that my father did not actually have a stockpile of gold, and that all those stories about working for the Watchmaker were just fanciful tales like the ones in his books. Well, I loved my father regardless, and I managed to run my household all these years without any extra bricks of gold. I'm sure I can manage now."

The solicitor looked up at her. "Oh, it's not that, Miss Peake. Not that all. Your father did indeed have substantial wealth locked away in the Watchmaker's Bank, and to the best of my knowledge—though I can't prove it—he did spent his early years in Crown City before he retired young and moved to Lugtown, made a home, married your mother and"—he shuffled the papers awkwardly—"well, you know the rest."

Marinda frowned. "Then what is the problem?"

Frull searched among the papers, withdrew one. "Ah-hem. Perhaps I should let Arlen explain it in his own words, which he dictated to me. We had several private meetings so he could get his last letter just right."

He handed her a brief document, which Marinda read while he fumbled with the lock on his large burlwood desk.

My sparkling daughter, it seems the only thing I can do in these last years of my life is sit and think deep thoughts, and many of those thoughts are about you, the life you have and the life you should have had. Your mother disappointed us, but that was so very long ago. I am more concerned with how I failed you. And now that I have passed, this is the way I can make it all up to you. Trust me, I have considered every detail. All is for the best—and I want only the best for you.

Marinda looked up at the solicitor, her brow furrowed. "What does he mean? This isn't a time for ambiguities."

"Oh, he was very clear in his wishes."

Marinda kept reading.

Because I made you abandon the life you should have had in order to care for me, I give you the gift of many other lives. I want you to see the things that might have been, the people you should have met, the experiences that could have been part of your own story—and still can be. Therefore, I have arranged for you to have all the journeys of a great adventure—and in doing so, you will live your own life as well. I wish I could have joined you.

At first you will hate me for this. Then you will love me for it.

Your father.

Frull opened the wooden desk drawer and lifted out a large burlwood showcase box, which was also locked. He removed the pocketwatch on his vest chain and used a gold key dangling from the fob to open another locked desk drawer, from which he withdrew a second key and finally unlocked the burlwood case. "Important things must be kept under lock and key."

He lifted the lid and removed a leatherbound book with an oxblood red cover stamped with clockwork gears and inset with alchemical symbols. Next, he pulled out a small crystal vial that contained a thimbleful of blood, sealed tight, and set it on the desk. Finally, fumbling with the spine of the book, he plucked out a long golden needle that had been inserted into the binding, its head crowned with a dull, rough diamond that looked like the result of a failed alchemical experiment.

Marinda had no idea what he was doing.

The solicitor cleared his throat and recited, "By the direct and clear wishes of Arlen Peake, who was of sound mind when he gave me his instructions, you are to be removed from your home in five days' time, and the cottage will remain vacant until certain conditions are met. All of his financial accounts are also frozen, and you, his daughter, will have no access to any funds except for a very specific stipend."

He slid the tome closer to Marinda. "He did however leave you this book."

Marinda couldn't believe what she was hearing. "I don't want a book. I have plenty of them on our shelves already. What about my home?" Flustered, she opened the cover of the volume, to find that the title page said *Clockwork Lives*. She turned the page, but the paper was empty. She flipped to another, and another, then through the entire volume. "There's nothing written here. It's blank."

"Nothing yet." Frull looked at her intently. "This is a special volume, created just for you, each page impregnated with the most complex alchemical infusions."

Growing more and more upset by this nonsense, she said, "A magic book? There's no such thing as magic."

"Not magic—*science*. Alchemy. Your father was quite a genius."

"This is absurd, Mr. Frull. You know that."

"What I know is that your father left no room for doubt when he explained his wishes to me." Frull picked up the papers again, straightened them, and handed them to her. "There are instructions. This book is designed to collect stories. The pages are alchemically treated to react with human blood in a very specific fashion." He nudged the golden needle closer to her. "Collect a blood sample from your volunteers. One drop of blood will spread out on the pages and record that person's story."

He touched the tiny crystal bottle of blood, gave her a wan smile. "And this is a sample your father preserved for you, his own story. To get you started."

Though Marinda sat frozen, he was finished with the meeting. "I am not allowed to release your inheritance until you have filled this book with other lives—a full spectrum of people, interesting characters from all walks of life."

"But . . . but this is entirely irregular," she said. Since she had spent her adult years tending for her father, Marinda had no money of her own; the household possessions, furniture, financial accounts, everything but her clothes and a few personal items technically belonged to Arlen Peake. As the weight of the pronouncement pressed down on her, she began to feel a sense of desperation. "I will contest it."

"You can try to contest it, but since I am the town's only

licensed solicitor, I must advise you that you are not likely to win."

"But why would he do this to me?" Marinda felt lost. "Didn't I already give up enough to care for him? What did I do wrong?"

"Ours is not to understand. Arlen's reasons were sufficient to him." He handed her the book, shaking his head sadly. "You have five days to vacate your residence. If you refuse to obey these instructions, you will be forcibly evicted. Your father's funds and possessions will be placed in safekeeping in the meantime. I suggest you spend the time planning." He smiled and said in a bland, rote voice, "All is for the best."

Marinda gathered the will, the book, the vial of blood, and the golden needle, then left the solicitor's office, stepping out into a world where she had been cast adrift.

CHAPTER 4

First you will hate me for this.
    Then you will love me for it.

Marinda did not and would not hate her father, but his prediction certainly disturbed her. She was at a loss, confused, and dismayed at what had happened to her. All was definitely not for the best. The shock inside her was slowly suffused with anger and a sense of injustice.

Life in Lugtown was carefully balanced, perfectly ordered. Everything in its place and every place with its thing. Marinda had always done what she *should*, not what she *wanted*. But now, thanks to a piece of paper, Marinda had to leave her home and go on a silly mission for no real purpose that she could see.

Should she just ignore the whole fool's quest? She was strong, competent, intelligent, hard working—given time, she could easily find a profession and make an adequate living for herself, even without her inheritance. But her entire life up until this point had been focused on her father. She would be starting entirely from scratch, and with no money. The modest stipend Benjulian Frull was allowed to grant her would cover few expenses. Even with her best intentions and determination, she could not create an entirely new existence for herself in *five days*.

How was she supposed to plan for that? Where should she go? She had the empty book—the foolish "magic" book, but an alchemical collection of self-written lives seemed too far-fetched to be real. Why did her father believe this would benefit her? *How? What were you thinking?*

She looked at the large book, the thimbleful of blood—her father's blood. The best place to start, she thought, would be with his story . . . if the alchemically treated pages worked at all. Since the papers were all blank, obviously her father hadn't tested the tome.

She knew exactly where she wanted to be when she tried this for the first time. Arlen Peake's gravestone was carved from a square block of polished burlwood, cut to perfect conformity with all the other burlwood headstones in the Lugtown cemetery, which stood on a hill above the agate quarry.

She took the book and the blood sample, and made her way to the well-organized cemetery. Trees surrounded the graveyard, some of them bent over with the affliction of burls, while others stood straight. All the wooden headstones were laid out in a perfect grid, each identical, each grave plot marked with appropriate boundaries, for the Watchmaker insisted on stressing absolute equality in death.

She located Arlen Peake's grave, the newly packed dirt planted with fresh grass, the flowers propped in vases. Marinda found a place to sit on the grassy plot adjacent to her father's, whose occupant had died ten years ago.

She read his name on the polished burl grave marker and shook her head. With tears burning her eyes, she said in a scolding voice, "You could have asked, and I'd have told you this is not what I wanted! I know you meant well, but your silly dreams are not mine. I wanted a quiet life." She sniffled. "I earned it!" She felt the sting of tears, the anger of disappointment, and the unsettled abandonment of confusion.

Supposedly, the answers lay in her book of *Clockwork Lives*, as yet unwritten. All the words were stored in that tiny sample of blood her father had left. The alchemy would release it.

Or so he said.

The little crystal vial glowed red in the afternoon sunlight. This was her father's blood, his *life's blood*, which contained the story of his life. And the alchemy would write it for her.

She removed the cap and paused. Her father had stored the blood when he was alive. He had wanted her to do this. Marinda chastised herself for worrying too much over things that could not be changed, so she tilted the vial and held it over the first blank page of the volume. A book without stories . . . and it was about to have one.

The crimson droplet fell from the lip of the vial and splashed on the paper. The redness soaked into the fibers . . . and Marinda wondered what she was supposed to see.

Then the blood started to shine as if illuminated by its own fire. It seeped out like spider veins, bending at angles, zigzagging as if flowing through a maze. The lines began to form letters, words, drawn out in the rush of a frantic, inspired calligrapher.

Arlen Peake's life story filled the blank space, and Marinda turned the page to watch the words continue on the opposite side, line after line. The words filled a second page, and a third. All the things her father had lived. All the things he had wanted to tell her in his story.

Marinda's pulse raced, and she felt a thrill of wonder. She had never known the feeling. Was this what Arlen experienced every time he saw new things?

When the blood was spent and the letters finished scribing themselves, the pages were covered with line after line. Her father's story.

Sitting in the Lugtown cemetery beside the fresh grave marker, she turned to the first page and began to read.

THE
INVENTOR'S TALE

It may surprise you, my sparkling daughter, that I always wanted to be a Regulator.

As a boy in Crown City, I would watch the Watchmaker's uniformed guards moving about with perfect precision: specially chosen, specially trained troops, all so punctual . . . just like human machines.

I would see the Blue Watch patrolling the streets on a schedule that did not deviate by so much as a minute per day. Or the Red Watch, who stood like vigilant statues outside Chronos Square, the Watchtower, or anyplace else that was important enough to be guarded by the best. Or the Black Watch, elite Regulators who observed the people of Crown City and even conducted secret missions to enforce the peaceful Stability across Albion.

They seemed as perfect to me as the Clockwork Angels themselves—but the Regulators, at least, were *human*, and they were something I could aspire to.

Only the best were chosen to be become Regulators, though, whether Red, Blue, or Black. Even as I played in the streets with my three boyhood friends—Zivo, Woody, and Lee—we would dream of joining the Regulator corps when we grew up. What could be a more marvelous goal?

Alas, I had a fundamental flaw that made me unfit to be a Regulator. I was never on time.

My friends and I devoted ourselves to turning our dreams into reality. As boys, we trained and practiced and drilled together—it was just a childhood game, but we wanted to be ready for when we were old enough to submit our applications to the recruitment offices. We found empty alleys and marched up and down, marking off precise steps. We timed one another with a metronome that Woody had borrowed from a music teacher who insisted on exact rhythm from his students.

While my friends all moved with clockwork precision, I would often stumble or miss a step. I was the dissonant note, as the music teacher would say. Lee, Zivo, and Woody made it seem so easy, as if the gears turned smoothly in their minds and bodies, while mine were jammed up with grains of sand. No matter how earnest I was, I could not keep time to the exacting standards of a Regulator. Even so, I did not give up on impossible dreams.

———◆◆◆———

You probably have many questions, my sparkling daughter. Since this is the very first tale you will collect in your book—the first of many enjoyable and enthralling stories, I expect—let me explain how the special alchemy on these pages works, and also how the magic of storytelling works . . . a magic that you should be familiar with, but I suspect that you paid little attention when I compelled you to read all those books aloud to me.

Chronicling a person's life does not entail including every tedious moment of it. By design, the alchemy left many gaps in this tale. How was I born? What about my years as an infant, as a toddler? Where did we live? What did my parents do? How did I meet these three friends, and what made us so close? What happened to them after they played their role in my story?

The fact is, dear Marinda, those parts aren't *relevant* to this particular tale. The magic of a story is to take the totality of a life and winnow it down to the important events, strip out the dull everyday existence, assess the side notes and determine whether they are vital to the core of the tale or merely interesting tangents. My memory has a second sight. The alchemy in this volume has a very selective reactive mechanism, a filtration effect that hones the story down to a fine gem. And through special alchemy, I have fine-tuned this particular tale to my genetics.

One would never want a life story to be *boring*.

And this is not my entire life story, daughter—not by any means. It is just the story you don't already *know*.

When we reached the proper age and all the forms had been filed, my friends and I were assigned to Regulator training. I know now that some of the qualification fields in the submission documents may have been exaggerated slightly in my case, but after I'd been approved, no one would question my legitimacy, because errors simply did not happen in the Watchmaker's Stability. Who would even consider that some Crown City bureaucrat could have improperly assigned me?

Zivo, Woody, and Lee supported me throughout our basic training. They helped me and—more often than I like to admit—covered for my mistakes. We moved into the Regulator recruit barracks, received Gray Watch uniforms to show we were trainees, and settled into our proper subdivision in the ranks. We began our new lives.

And I failed miserably.

Even the bonds of friendship could not overcome imperfect punctuality where the Regulators were concerned. When I marched with the trainee ranks, I was out of step. When we practiced complex formations on the parade ground, I stumbled and thereby entangled the performers.

Before long, I was deemed unacceptable for Blue Watch patrols, and with some consternation our training captain transferred me to the Red Watch recruits. If I could not keep time or march with perfect rhythm, I should at least be able to stand motionless and alert, on guard like a human statue.

But I was too fidgety for that, and my mind wandered. Rather than staring fixedly ahead, I would daydream, look at passersby, or even just gaze into the sky as ideas struck me. After only a month, the trainee captain removed me from Red Watch duty before anyone could notice my failings or his embarrassment.

Discharging me from the training corps, however, would also be unacceptable, because all the properly approved forms showed that I was *supposed* to be in the Regulator barracks, and mistakes were simply not made. Therefore, I needed to make myself useful in some way. I had to demonstrate proficiency in some necessary career, and then all would be for the best.

My three friends were sad for me. Their training was going well, and they had a bright future in the Regulators. While they sailed ahead down the main current of their careers, I got caught in a side eddy and drifted in a backwater.

Angry at my failings, I became obsessed with the machinery of time. What did I lack? The internal perfection of fitting my life's gears with all those others! The fact that I couldn't keep time made me even more intrigued by it. And when I noticed that three of the twelve clocks inside the trainee barracks were off by as much as two minutes from the city's primary Watchtower clock, I determined to fix them.

I discovered I had quite an aptitude for the delicate mechanisms, the wheels within wheels, the hair-fine springs. I adjusted those barracks clocks and made them perfect. Better still, I impressed the

Regulator captain with my work. At last, I had something useful to do! The captain dispatched me to assess, calibrate, and maintain the various clocks in the other barracks.

Guarding the accuracy of time was a heady responsibility, touching on the same ethereal territory the Watchmaker had claimed for his own.

Each day, while the Regulator trainees practiced, I would busy myself in a makeshift workshop, dismantling decommissioned clocks, studying how they worked and—dare I even suggest it?—discovering ways to *improve them*.

Tick-tock.

Zivo, Woody, and Lee finished their basic training, perfectly synchronized, as expected. All three of my friends received Blue Watch uniforms so they could patrol the streets of Crown City and protect the schedules of all good citizens, while I kept my gray uniform as a trainee—a perpetual trainee, apparently. Since I had been removed from the regular routine, I had no hope of graduation. I simply fixed the Regulators' clocks.

As my reputation grew, others brought me problematic timepieces, and I worked miracles to align them with time again. Some were unsalvageable, so I kept the spare parts, the gears, springs, bushings, and crystals. Since the Clockwork Angels admonished those who waste, whether it be time or resources, I kept those pieces, hoping they would someday prove useful.

On the night that we celebrated the graduation of my friends and their class (which would have been my class), we heard a commotion outside the barracks, and we emerged to see a wandering pedlar standing in the darkness. The trainees who had just become Red Guards stood at attention and pretended not to notice anything out of the ordinary. The full members of the Blue Watch on duty did not deviate from their routines. But because I had no set schedule, and because Zivo, Woody, and Lee were still celebrating their promotion, we all went outside to stare.

The pedlar had an overburdened cart, a steam boiler that glowed blue with coldfire, pistons that huffed inside brass-encased cylinders. Everything was adorned with gold, which was very common in the Watchmaker's land. His cart was loaded with interesting paraphernalia, secret packages, decorative glass spheres, vials of alchemical substances, trinkets, lamps, pots, coldfire batteries, even a selection of ornate music boxes.

The objects were less interesting than the pedlar, though. He was an old man with tangled locks of gray hair beneath a black top hat. He wore an overcoat, a beard, and an eyepatch that made him all the more mysterious. He paced alongside his self-motivated cart that chugged along at a slow pace so as to display his wares for potential customers.

Even more interesting, he was accompanied by a black-and-white spotted Dalmatian. Since dogs did not adhere to plans or schedules, they were a rarity in Crown City, but the pedlar's dog moved as if it were part of a clockwork caravan, keeping pace with the chugging cart and the plodding pedlar. The Dalmatian had a strange cockeyed gait, as if it had injured its foreleg, but it soldiered on, wobbling but never pausing. It seemed very old, but I couldn't guess its age, because the clocks of Crown City are not calibrated in dog years.

The pedlar called out as he passed. "What do you lack?" Since the Regulator training barracks were on the outskirts of Crown City, there was little casual pedestrian traffic, so the arrival of the pedlar was a matter of some note. With his one eye, he looked at Zivo, Woody, and Lee, then his gaze finally settled on me. "What do you lack?"

"We are all trained Regulators, sir," said Zivo. "The loving Watchmaker has provided for everything."

Woody added, "We have our barracks, we have our uniforms, we have our duty."

Since I had found my purpose, even I didn't lack anything. The old man's gaze lingered on me, but I was more interested in the limping but persistent dog.

I bent close to the serene, focused animal to study its obvious limp. I was astonished to discover that the Dalmatian was an *enhanced* dog. Beneath the smooth skin, I could see delicate machinery, pistons and tubes covered by spotted fur. I found a hairline crack and realized that a portion of the fur on the dog's back was hinged . . . an access plate.

"This is no ordinary dog," I said.

The pedlar looked at me. "Indeed not. Martin is quite an extraordinary dog."

Thinking of the mechanisms, the delicate timepieces, the precision gadgets that I had disassembled, reassembled, and (sometimes) improved, I touched the now-stationary dog, ran my fingertips over the pelt, and assessed the clockwork mechanism beneath the skin. "He could use some adjustment," I said.

"Martin has been my companion for some time, and he suffers from the perennial flaw in biological machinery. We tick away, and alas, some of his mechanisms have worn down."

Zivo, Woody, and Lee watched me, curious, but they had always been good enough friends to tolerate my unorthodox behavior. I touched the interconnected framework while the dog endured my probing ministrations. I could feel the fine-gauge gears, the pulleys, the thin pistons, and uncovered a lump—a set of interconnected gears slightly out of alignment.

Recalling my workshop inside the barracks, I said, "I've found what seems to be wrong, sir. If I understand how your extraordinary pet is put together, it's a simple enough fix, given the proper parts—and I believe I have the proper parts."

He raised his eyebrows. "How is that so? Martin is one of a kind. I would not expect a Regulator trainee to have components even remotely resembling what a clockwork dog would require."

With some embarrassment, I was forced to admit that I was

an inadequate Regulator trainee but quite skilled in repairing and adjusting timekeeping mechanisms. I explained my tinkering, my innovations, and my instinctive understanding of precision machinery.

The pedlar was intrigued. "I will allow that. In fact, I would appreciate it very much—and so would Martin."

While the newly graduated members of the Blue Watch and Red Watch observed me, I returned from the barracks with a basket of assorted spare pieces as well as delicate instruments, calipers, repair tools. I set to work under the pale blue illumination of the coldfire streetlamps, fixing and lubricating the unique machinery that animated the clockwork dog.

When I closed up the hinged access plate again, the dog paced back and forth smoothly, rejuvenated. His tail wagged in a way that reminded me of the metronome we four had used to practice our marching when we were just boys.

The old pedlar patted his dog, then he looked at me with genuine gratitude. "Thank you, young man. You may choose any item from my cart. It is the only reward I can offer."

Many of the odds and ends looked intriguing to me, but they had no real place in my work at the barracks. "As I said before, sir, I lack for nothing. I am happy to help. Truly, I need no reward."

"We get what we deserve," the pedlar said. "Are you certain you won't take anything?"

Again, I shook my head. "Happy to be of service." I patted the dog's head, and the pedlar moved on into the city with his chugging cart and his pet Dalmatian, who now trotted along smoothly and happily.

———◆———

Two days later, unexpectedly, I received a transfer and promotion from the Regulator barracks. I was given the unprecedented assignment of monitoring, regulating, and maintaining *all* of the primary clocks in Crown City.

Since the order came from the Watchtower itself, my Regulator captain accepted the transfer with good grace and without questions.

For my own part, I had plenty of questions but no regrets. This seemed the perfect career for me. I could impose the blessing, or tyranny, of time throughout Crown City. I could study, repair—and, yes, improve—the giant clocks in the tall towers throughout the city. I understood how each pendulum swing, how each gear moved, like a slave master whipping one second after another into line. I gloried in the tops of the towers, standing on the back side of the clock face, as if I stood behind time itself. As the giant gears turned, I felt like I was part of the machine.

Each clocktower had its official resident clockkeeper, a mostly ceremonial position, a man or woman who lived at the base of the tower and performed basic regular maintenance, but I was the Official Regulator of Clocks. I performed the delicate adjustments. I had Time on my hands.

Over the next year, I got to know all the clockkeepers and all the clocks, every gear and pendulum. And though I was not punctual enough to qualify as a Regulator, I kept the main clocks in Crown City accurate to within a few seconds—good enough even for the Watchmaker himself.

———— ✦ ————

Two years into my duties, as I emerged from the Neptune Tower—an ethereal tower named after a distant planet that no one but astronomers had seen—a Regulator intercepted me, a member of the Blue Watch. With brisk angular movements, he handed me a sealed card embossed with the Watchmaker's honeybee symbol.

A young man with as little punctuality and habits as eccentric as myself was startled to receive a direct communication from the loving Watchmaker. I was so taken aback that I didn't at first realize the Regulator was my old friend Woody! He looked prim, professional, and identical to all the other members of the Blue Watch patrolling the streets.

I met his eyes, and he did his best to become a human statue as Regulators were taught to be, but I saw the glint in his eyes, the quirk of a smile. I took the document from him. "Woody? What is this about?"

"The Watchmaker has summoned you." He nodded toward the sealed letter. "That card contains all the information you require."

I broke the wax seal and opened the folded message. Apparently, the Watchmaker had taken note of my skills, and he had a special task for me, an important assignment regarding some confidential maintenance within the Watchtower itself. My heart beat a wildly asynchronous rhythm. Did he want me to calibrate and adjust the primary clock in all of Crown City, the most important timepiece in the land of Albion?

"Follow me, please." Woody turned on his heel as briskly and precisely as if he were a clockwork construction, just like Martin the Dalmatian dog—or the awe-inspiring Clockwork Angels themselves.

Because I'd grown up in Crown City, I had been to Chronos Square many times. I had attended solstice festivals. I had watched the Regulators perform in their precision parades, I had seen the traveling carnival extravaganza with all of its wonders.

And of course I had observed the Clockwork Angels many times. Every citizen of Crown City received tickets to watch the wondrous statuesque creatures ratchet forth from their alcoves high in the Watchtower and issue their words of wisdom to adoring crowds.

But I had never been inside the Watchtower, the home of the Watchmaker himself! When Woody delivered me to the tower's closed door, he turned about and marched away without bidding me farewell, though he did cast a curious glance in my direction.

I stood holding the Watchmaker's invitation, and before I

could ask what to do, the door opened to reveal a member of the ominous Black Watch. "Arlen Peake," he announced, as if I had forgotten my own name. "You are expected. Climb the steps, and you will find the Watchmaker."

I climbed a staircase like a wound-up watchspring, and at the top I found another black-uniformed Regulator waiting to receive me. He opened the door and allowed me into an expansive laboratory that also served as an office. There were easels, blueprints, engineering plans, and a desk covered with stacked papers. Lamps glowing with blue coldfire levitated near the ceiling.

The Watchmaker stepped forward, moving stiffly, no doubt because he was so old. *So old!*

I knew, of course, that the Watchmaker had imposed his Stability more than a century and a half earlier, so he had to be an unnaturally ancient man. And as I looked at him now, I felt all those years. The Watchmaker had sallow cheeks, papery skin, and wispy gray hair plastered across his skull. He wore a formal jacket, trousers, a vest. His sleeves were pulled down all the way to his hands, held in place by golden cufflinks.

"Welcome, Arlen Peake," he said in a portentous voice. "Unsuccessful Regulator, yet highly skilled perfector of clocks."

Something about him looked familiar, but I stood in such awe of being in the Watchmaker's presence that I couldn't place it. Then I noticed, hanging on a peg on the wall, an old black top hat, an overcoat, a wig of tangled gray hair. And an eye patch.

"I remember . . . " I began.

A spotted dog emerged from a side room with fluid steps, a clockwork dog that hadn't changed at all since I had repaired it beside the pedlar's cart outside the Regulator training barracks.

"You helped Martin when he needed it years ago," the Watchmaker said, "and I watch how well you take care of my clocks. Now I need your help again. This time I hope you will accept a reward for your services."

I stammered an answer that was embarrassing in its impreci-sion. Even so, the Watchmaker took it as a Yes.

"Come with me." He led me through another door in the back of his laboratory—a door that led to another set of steep stairs. "I have prepared everything for you. I have all the tools and spare parts you will require."

Dumbly, I followed him, and the clockwork dog trotted after us. My repairs must have done the trick, for the dog still moved as smoothly as if he were a clockwork puppy.

I was awestruck in the presence of the Watchmaker, but when we stood inside the top-floor mechanical room of the primary clock, I felt even more overwhelmed: the gigantic toothed gears seemed as large as planetary orbits. The pendulum ratcheted back and forth, extending down through many floors of the tower, each arc advancing time forward by one increment. I was a keeper of clocks, the master of the mechanism, and this was the most mag-nificent clock in all the world.

"You—you want me to make adjustments here, sir?" The Watchtower could not be out of alignment! This clock defined time itself, as far as Albion was concerned.

The ancient Watchmaker looked at the ratcheting gears, as if distracted. "No, not that."

He went to tall closed doors at the outer wall and rolled them aside to reveal four beautiful Titans, stone female figures whose beauty was legendary, whose wisdom was indescribable. Every inch of their bodies was made of a pure white substance halfway between flesh and stone. And their wings! Arched wings curved against their perfect backs, layered with feathers, each one as long as a sword. The Clockwork Angels were motionless statues, not alive . . . and yet they were.

"These are what I need you to fix," said the Watchmaker. "I created them long ago to replace something I lacked. They are far better crafted than Martin." He absently patted the clockwork

Dalmatian. "Far better than . . . other experiments of mine. The Clockwork Angels are the pinnacle of my achievement. They are perfection itself."

"Every person in Albion knows that, sir," I said.

"Indeed, but it seems that even perfection has a time limit. I have endowed the four of them with quintessence. I have given them all the care that it is possible for one man—even me—to give."

He handed me a wrapped leather case, which I opened to find a full set of delicate and intricate timepiece repair tools. "Something is wrong with their hearts. See if you can fix them . . ." The Watchmaker's voice hitched. "See if you can make them remember how to love me again."

The Watchmaker left me in the high Watchtower room with my tools and with the Clockwork Angels. He locked the door, and a member of the Black Watch stood outside to prevent me from leaving.

———— ·•·•· ————

I worked in the locked room.

As I touched the Clockwork Angels and accessed their internal workings, finding the spark of quintessence and the complex machinery of their delicate yet eternal—and artificial—hearts, I was afraid: I knew that I was seeing things, learning things that no human was meant to know. The Clockwork Angels were sacred, symbolic foundations of the Stability. All of Albion worshipped them, gathering in Chronos Square to see the figures emerge from the tower. They would chant and swoon and raise their arms. The Clockwork Angels . . . no one could know that there might be a flaw, that anything could possibly be wrong with such perfection.

I swallowed hard and focused on my work.

I used all my skills, studying each component under magnification. The Black Watch delivered meals for me, but I was not allowed to leave.

I tinkered and adjusted for days, but before long, I came to real-ize that the fundamental flaw was nothing I could ever fix. And with great sorrow, knowing that I had failed our loving Watchmaker, I summoned him and hung my head as I gave my report. "I strived to the best of my ability, sir. But try as I might, I cannot make the Angels love you. It is not something I can adjust."

The ancient man looked at me with intense sorrow that seemed more despair than disappointment. I had not failed him—I had destroyed his last vestige of hope.

I feared he would react with anger, that he would throw open the alcove doors in the high Watchtower and hurl me out for a final flight down to the flagstones of Chronos Square far below. Instead, he did something different. The ancient Watchmaker used stiff fingers to remove his gold cufflinks and unfastened his shirt-sleeve, which he rolled up to expose a thin, withered forearm.

But it was not just an old man's arm. I saw the pale blue of cold-fire, thin tubes, and well-lubricated hydraulic pistons implanted beneath parchment-like skin.

Martin the clockwork dog stood next to him, as the Watchmaker extended his not-quite-human hand and flexed his fist so that I could see the coldfire hydraulics and the enhancements had made to his own ancient, near-immortal body.

"Then," he said, "you must do what you can to fix *me*."

———— ❧ ————

Two days later, I had done what I could for him. I knew more about the secrets of the Clockwork Angels and the Watchmaker himself than any man could ever be allowed to know and live, and I guessed the Watchmaker might execute me. When I saw his face darken, I knew what he was thinking: a man so ancient, with so many lives in his grasp, might have only a measured amount of compassion and a limited time for mercy.

But he patted his clockwork Dalmatian with great fondness,

and a flicker of gratitude crossed his expression. He called for the Regulators, and when they arrived and stood before him in silence, the Watchmaker said, "We get what we deserve. I offered you a reward before. Take it now."

He seemed frightening and angry, but I also realized that he was embarrassed by the terrible things I knew.

"I'll give you a great wealth of gold, which any man would consider a tremendous treasure . . . though gold means little to me, since I can always make more. It is everything you will need—but you have to go. Leave Crown City. Travel far away . . . and tell no one of this for as long as you live."

<hr />

And so, my sparkling daughter, that is why I left and traveled to the far end of Albion, where I found a small, quiet village called Lugtown. Still a young man, I found a wife, settled down, and was left to invent things and dabble with my knowledge. Although my marriage did not follow the plan I had envisioned, you were the greatest part of the rest of my days. I had a great treasure and an even greater secret. I kept this secret to the end of my days, as I promised, but it is yours now to do with as you will.

My life story does not end there, as you know, but *this* story does, and now the rest is up to you. I ache for the radiance I saw in you as a little girl, such hopes and dreams I had for how your life might be. To see that light betrayed, first by your mother— how terribly abandoned you felt—then to watch helplessly as your horizons narrowed to the dutiful care of a failing old man. It is unbearably sad. I can never repay you, never atone, but I can try to give you one last gift. For it is no simple thing to say that the true gift of life—is living.

At first you will hate me for this. Then you will love me for it.

I hope you find many more tales to fill your book of *Clockwork Lives*, and I hope you come to understand what I have done for you.

CHAPTER 5

Marinda stared at the flowing words that were distilled out of her father's blood, Arlen Peake's mysterious early years wrung out of the alchemically treated pages. She had lived with the man all her life, had remained with him in the lonely years after her mother ran away; she had read him stories as he grew more infirm, kept him company, tended him, but she had never imagined the secret tale he kept inside.

Marinda found it bittersweet, yet gladdening, that her father had burdened her with some of the answers and a foolhardy quest she had never wanted. Unlike her father, though, she valued contentment over adventure, stability over recklessness. Well, there was nothing for it but to do the task he had set her. The sooner she filled this book with its life stories, the sooner she could be back to her normal schedule. Yes, that was what she would do—if it meant so much to her father. Best to get on with it.

She closed the tome and rose from the graveside, brushing grass off her skirt. Her knees were stiff from sitting so long in such an awkward position. In deepening twilight she hurried back to her cottage. She wished she had brought a coldfire lantern, but she hadn't expected to sit so long in the cemetery reading. In fact, she hadn't expected the book of *Clockwork Lives* to function at all. Even though the book's magic had edited out all of the tangential information, her father's tale had been quite a long and—yes, she admitted—engrossing story.

Back home, where she was all too alone despite the company of the three clockwork Regulators, her mind was filled with thoughts that had not yet crystallized into definite plans. Though Lugtown had not changed, and likely never would, her own future was in turmoil. It reminded her of the anarchy Albion had endured for so long before the arrival of the Watchmaker.

That night, by the light of a coldfire lamp, Marinda read the story again, aloud, to Zivo, Woody, and Lee. It reminded her of when she would read to her father. The clockwork Regulators stood at attention in their bright uniforms, listening to her every word, although their painted-on expressions never changed. Their only response was an occasional hiss of venting steam from the valve flaps in their copperpot heads.

When she finished the tale, she found herself wondering about all those other aspects of Arlen Peake's life that he had chosen not to chronicle, particularly his love for her mother and what had gone wrong, why Elitia Peake had found him lacking as a husband and, presumably, Marinda lacking as a daughter. Or maybe Elitia had found her own life lacking, and the hurt she had done to her family was simply collateral damage. Marinda didn't know, wasn't even sure she wanted to read that story.

But her father's tale filled only ten of the blank pages in her thick volume. She had a lot of work to do, so she went to bed for a good rest, determined to get an early start the following day. She would have only four days to have the book completely filled before she'd be evicted, and she did not want that inconvenience.

She wondered what other interesting and unexpected revelations she might receive from the townspeople she had known all her life.

Next morning, she got dressed while a happily whirring Woody used the clockwork pump outside to fill their spare teakettle, since the other one had been damaged on the morning of her father's death. She chose the clothes she usually wore for her regular Wednesday trip into town, even though this was only Sunday. Her schedule had been knocked completely off the rails. Letting Zivo, Woody, and Lee tend to the routine household business, she tucked the alchemical book under one arm and set off.

Even though she had a lot of lives to collect in the next few days, Marinda was confident that if she simply set about the task in a methodical and diligent way, she could fill the book. Now that she knew what was expected of her, she formulated a plan.

First, she went to the solicitor's office to claim her stipend. As she arrived at Frull's office precisely on time, Marinda looked at Lugtown's public clocks, all of which were said to be accurate to within a minute. With her father's poor health and failing eyesight, Arlen Peake had been in no position to maintain the local clocks. She wondered who fulfilled that function now.

Benjulian Frull sat at his desk waiting for her, and Marinda was all business. She opened the *Clockwork Lives* volume for the solicitor to see. "I admit I was skeptical, but this book works exactly as my father said it would."

Frull looked down at the crimson letters that wrote out Arlen Peake's story. "Your father was a man of many surprises." He ran his fingertips along the writing. "I'm sure it's a fascinating story."

Marinda took the book back from him before he could read the tale, which she wanted to keep private, at least for now. "I've decided to get started on the work he set me to do. I believe you have a stipend for me? No doubt I will encounter some unforeseen expenses before I am finished."

She would ask many people for their stories, but she might have to pay some of them to fill a few more pages of her volume. And if she couldn't finish before Wednesday, when the eviction order took force, she might have to pay for temporary lodgings just to wrap up the last few pages in the book.

The solicitor unlocked an embedded safe from which he withdrew a stack of gold honeybee coins. He counted them out carefully. "That should last you for some time, Miss Peake, provided you are frugal."

"I am quite familiar with frugality." She tucked away the money, then slid the tome across the solicitor's desk, turning to the blank page after her father's story. She withdrew the golden needle from its place in the binding. "Mr. Frull, I would like to add your story to *Clockwork Lives*."

Frull was surprised, then he chuckled. "Of course, although I don't know why you would be interested in my simple story."

She waited for him to present his fingertip. "I am not interested in collecting anyone's story, yet that is what I have been tasked to do, so I will do my job. Good work always leads to good fortune."

He let her prick his skin with the sharp needle, then milked his fingertip until a blood drop formed and dropped onto the blank page. The red splash spread out into furiously scrawled words written in perfect alchemical penmanship. The solicitor watched the process with fascination.

His blood wrote one paragraph, then another, and finally a brief third paragraph before stopping. The words didn't even fill an entire page. One drop of her father's blood had been enough to cover ten complete pages of his life story, even condensed and edited.

Benjulian Frull's life generated only a few paragraphs?

"Maybe it needs another drop of blood," Marinda said.

But when the solicitor scanned the lines in the alchemical book, he smiled. "Quite an extraordinarily concise and efficient summary of my life, without the flowery convolutions of legal language."

Marinda read the paragraphs and found that Frull's whole tale could indeed be summarized in those few words; the story was complete, as written. The alchemically treated pages filtered out the dull parts and polished the man's life down to its essence.

Frull had grown up in Lugtown, studied his law books, took the standardized test issued by the Watchmaker's Ministry of Solicitors, and after he was accepted, he set up his offices, worked his cases, and did what was expected of him. End of story.

The solicitor read it again with a broadening smile. "Yes, that is quite good. Everything in a nutshell."

Disappointed, Marinda closed the book and retrieved the golden needle. She looked at the time—10:00 a.m.—and decided to get moving. She had an entire book of lives to fill, and that was going to be difficult if each person's life comprised only half a page.

She walked down the town streets, looked at the shops and offices. Everyone went about their business just like every other day. The old apothecary peeped out of his shop, expressed his sympathy to her, and thanked Marinda for her business over the years.

She paused to explain about the alchemical book, and out of respect for her father, the gaunt old man agreed to give Marinda what she wanted. A pinprick, another splash of blood . . . and the words scrolled out, sentence after sentence.

The apothecary's tale described how he had always hoped to be an alchemist, dreaming of a scholarship to the Alchemy College in Crown City, but found that he had more of an aptitude for medicinals. He studied botany, pored over books on natural science. He experimented with medicinal plants, identified formulations and concoctions after annotating countless home remedies and local treatments. He submitted some of his best discoveries to the Apothecary Board, hoping they would become standardized treatments.

But because the man used himself as an experimental subject, testing countless herbal treatments, medicinal substances, and even marginal poisons, his life story was told in disjointed, fragmented sentences. Sometimes they ran on; sometimes they stopped abruptly without reaching a point. The apothecary's tale filled the rest of the page beneath Benjulian Frull's life and ran onto a second page before petering out.

Another story down, another page filled—but it was one more hour gone and she still had hundreds of pages left to go, in only a few days.

Marinda began to feel disappointed and frustrated. She walked past the general store, where she saw the three rambunctious redheaded boys playing out front. The grocer took fresh apples out of a crate shipped from Barrel Arbor. He waved at her, then polished one of the apples on his sleeve before stacking it on the display.

She could ask Camberon for a drop of blood. His story might fill pages . . . but she felt reluctant to do so. She didn't really want to know about his happy life.

Once the alchemical magic distilled his biography, she wondered whether she would even merit a mention in it, if their betrothal and possible life together had even made an impact on him . . . or if all of their hopes and dreams together would be an extraneous storyline that the alchemy would edit out for improved focus and pacing.

Marinda decided there were other tales she would rather have in the book.

She went to the agate quarry in search of other volunteers. She found an ancient, bent man sitting outside on a bench staring toward the rock terraces. The crews worked like termites in stone, digging out thunder eggs and also quarrying mundane stone to be used for construction purposes. The very old stonecutter had retired, but he still sat and watched, listening to the musical clink of rock hammers as they carved away the stone.

Marinda stepped up to his bench and offered him one of the gold honeybee coins. "I would like a drop of your blood," she said, "for your life's story."

The old man perked up and took notice, as if he had cracked open an average-looking thunder egg and found a pulsing rock pearl. He didn't understand her request, but he understood the coin, and he slowly unfolded arthritic hands that were damaged from years of gripping a hammer and striking hard rocks. The calluses on his fingertips were so thick she had to prick him twice with the golden needle before a tiny droplet spilled out.

Despite his long life, the old quarry worker's story filled just three lines on the page: "Grew up at the quarry, worked in the quarry, got married, had a son who works in the quarry. Found a very large thunder egg once, beautiful agate which I polished and then sent off to Crown City, but never heard anything back from the Watchmaker. I worked in the quarry some more, but now I'm too old, so I rest and I watch." His story ended there.

Marinda read it with disappointment. "That's all?"

"What more is there?"

A middle-aged stoneworker came down the gravel path to join them, and Marinda realized this was the old man's son, who was curious to see her there. The retired stoneworker held up the golden coin. "It's Marinda Peake—just as odd as her father. She'll pay you a gold coin if you let her prick your finger."

"I could use a gold coin." The worker extended his finger without hesitation, so Marinda took the proffered sample. His droplet spelled out a biography even more curt than the old man's: "My father taught me to work in the quarries. Our family has an affinity for thunder eggs. We find them better than others do. I work in the quarry like he did, and now my own son is trained to crack thunder eggs."

Marinda blinked at the story, surprised that this man, and his father, had nothing more to tell.

"Hey Gero! Come here." The father shouted to a group of children who huddled over piles of round stone cannonballs extracted from the shafts. The children wielded small hammers and had grown quite proficient in cracking open the agates. One of the boys, who looked remarkably like the middle-aged man, jumped to his feet and scrambled up the rock steps to join them. "Hold out your finger, boy. You'll get a gold coin for it."

"What do I have to do?"

Marinda cautioned, "I'm not certain that it's worth—"

But the father encouraged the boy. So as not to go back on an implied promise, Marinda handed young Gero a honeybee coin, then pricked his finger with the needle, startling him. He yanked his finger away, but Marinda caught his hand before he could suck on the droplet. "I need that." She squeezed the blood onto the paper, and the boy's indignation of having been pricked vanished as he watched the magic words scrawl across the paper.

"I want to be just like my father."

That was all.

By the end of the day, Marinda was discouraged. She had gathered eight more lives from Lugtown, but filled only three more pages. She looked at the book in her hands as if it had betrayed her. "At this rate, I'll run out of stipend money long before I fill the book," she muttered. It didn't seem possible that all these people in Lugtown, combined, had lived half as many pages as the abridged, condensed life of Arlen Peake.

At sunset on the second day, she passed by the solicitor's office as he was closing up for the evening, and she confronted him with the alchemical book. "Mr Frull, there seems to be a flaw in the plan!"

He clucked his tongue. "Oh, I doubt that, Miss Peake. A properly executed plan can have no flaws."

She showed him the few pages cluttered with brief, uninteresting lives, and he drew his brows together. "Hmm, I'm not surprised. You already know these people, and you know this life. Perhaps you need to look elsewhere to find the epic lives you seek? I believe that may have been Arlen's intent."

Marinda had been thinking the same thing, but not yet willing to consider it. She might have to leave her familiar surroundings. No doubt, her father intended to nudge her out of the nest, to make her go beyond her comfortable boundaries of a sleepy little town.

"Very well. The steamliner comes on Wednesday, and that's when I have to be out of the cottage anyway. I will purchase a ticket to Crown City, where in short order I'll be able to find far more stories than I require." Under such uncertain circumstances, that did seem the most efficient solution. "I'll be back before you know it."

He fiddled with his lock and key. "I am sure you will be. In the meantime, after you leave your cottage, I will make sure all of the items remain safe and preserved, ready for you to claim them." He tipped his hat. "Good evening, Miss Peake."

The solicitor walked away, brisk and content, for he had his own quiet, perfect life to go back to.

CHAPTER 6

The steamliner arrived on Wednesday, precisely on schedule, drifting in with its chain of levitating gondolas and cargo cars. The townspeople, also on schedule, came out to greet the steamliner. They were accustomed to seeing Marinda there on her weekly errands, but everything was different now. This was by no means a normal Wednesday. Not at all.

Albeit reluctantly, she had purchased a steamliner ticket and stood outside the station, waiting to board. Marinda held a battered valise she had found among her father's possessions. She had no suitcase of her own—when had she ever needed one? Her father had been forbidden to travel, by order of the Watchmaker, and she guessed that this was the very valise that young Arlen Peake had carried with him when he was exiled from Crown City. Or maybe it had belonged to her mother and been left behind when she'd run off. Marinda got the impression that Elitia had done little planning when she tore up the neat blueprint of her life and flitted away from Lugtown, never to be seen again.

After the steamliner settled into place, the passengers disembarked, looking around at the village. Marinda had always given such people a wide berth, content with her own life and having no interest in theirs. Now, she *had* to go with them, ride aboard a passenger car through the sky and on the rails. These would be her traveling companions for several days as the steamliner stopped at other Albion villages en route to Crown City.

The steamliner pilot swung down from the main motivator car that not only served as the steamliner's engine, but was also his home. As pilot, Brock Pennrose had served the run to Lugtown and points beyond for at least ten years, as long as Marinda could remember.

The steamliner remained parked while the porters unloaded and loaded cargo and refilled its boilers, but Marinda was ready to depart. She was done with Lugtown until she finished her quest.

While most villagers did not travel, there were always business passengers, traders, bureaucrats, speculators, and occasional sightseers making a pilgrimage to see the Clockwork Angels or to submit supplications to the Watchmaker. Marinda had never before bothered to think about who the travelers were or why they were aboard the steamliner. Now she thought they might have stories to tell, stories that would fill many pages; maybe she would even complete her book by the time she reached Crown City—and then she could turn around and go home. Job done.

Ready to leave, for a while at least, she had closed up the cottage, shuttered the windows, and covered the furniture with sheets. After bidding the three faithful clockwork Regulators a fond farewell, she made them stand at attention against the wall and powered them down. Zivo, Woody, and Lee would gather dust, unattended, but she promised them, and she promised herself, that she would not be gone long. As the last steam blew out of their release valves, the three Regulators sighed into mechanical slumber. For them, time would stand still until she returned.

After she departed, Benjulian Frull would nail a notice to the door, declaring the cottage closed and off-limits, no trespassing. Marinda did not want to see him do that. With the clockwork Regulators shut down, even her garden would grow wild and unruly by the time she came back.

Although she was leaving her home, her town, and her neighbors, none of them seemed to notice she was going. No one bade her a warm farewell; no one waved or cheered her on or wished her well in her endeavors. After accepting another load of fresh vegetables from the outlying farming villages, Camberon Greer raised a hand to wave at her as she stepped up to the steamliner, then went back to dickering over the price of lettuce.

Clutching her ticket and her valise, she boarded a colorful passenger gondola situated just behind the large motivator car. The gondola was suspended by a scarlet levitating sack, and the door and interior had ornate appointments with knobs and filigrees made of solid gold, which was plentiful, thanks to the Watchmaker's alchemy. The gondola looked much too fancy for her, but the conductor glanced at her ticket, punched it, and gestured her aboard.

"On my way at last," she muttered to herself, regretting every moment.

Marinda looked at the strange furnishings, the crowded opulence in the lounge car. When the departure whistle blew, the passengers who had been investigating Langtown came back aboard. A few had bought burlwood sculptures or polished agate slices, but most hadn't found anything worth carrying.

The steam whistle blew again, and Captain Pennrose climbed aboard the motivator car. Soon, the pistons began to chug, the big wheels spun, and the rails glowed blue with inner alchemical fire. Pennrose blew the whistle a final time.

The last passengers hurried aboard, some of them slipping through connecting doors to reserved sleeping compartments in adjacent gondolas. Marinda had not paid for such an extravagance.

Even the gold-appointed community car seemed like too much, but she didn't want to ride in the cargo cars or bunk with the roustabouts and porters (even though some of them might have had interesting stories for her book).

The other passengers relaxed as the steamliner began to move. Marinda was the only new person who had boarded at Lugtown, and her traveling companions, preoccupied with their own invisible worlds, made no overtures of conversation. Obviously, she would have to approach them herself, explain the book and the golden needle, ask for a drop of blood—none of which was within her comfort zone. She had never done anything like that before.

First you will hate me for this. And then you will love me for it.

Marinda pushed back her sadness and impatience toward what her father had done to her. "All is for the best," she told herself.

The steamliner began to move, building up speed. The levitation sacks inflated, the steam boilers came to full pressure, and the caravan of connected carriages raced headlong down the rails until the motivator car lost contact with the ground, lifting into the sky. With a lurch, the rest of the steamliner rose and flew away from the village. Marinda felt disoriented, seasick, and adrift as the steamliner began to fly . . . but she had not felt grounded since the day her father died.

Inside the lounge car, she sat with her valise on the floor and her alchemical book on her lap. She watched two gentlemen playing a game of cards, but they were engrossed in their strategy.

She listened to the nearby conversation of two women in trim business attire, not because she was interested in their words but because they were so loud. They were speculators, women who played financial games of chance with other people's money, making vast fortunes from which they profited—or losing vast fortunes, for which they sincerely apologized and then blamed unpredictable market conditions. They talked about their secret plan as if no one else could hear them. The two were investors in mining futures and quite bullish about the price of silver. They had invested heavily in new mines in the north, and they saw bright times ahead for any visionaries who came in at the beginning.

"What is so special about silver?" Marinda interrupted.

The women lowered their voices, leaning closer. "Why, because the Watchmaker's alchemy can create all the gold anyone wants. But *silver* . . . ah now silver! That is another thing entirely."

"But what use is silver?" she asked.

The second businesswoman said with a sniff, "For all those things where gold will not suffice."

They began to quote numbers—values of silver by the ingot, mine capacity, production maximization, output potential—until Marinda's mind grew dizzy with statistics. The first woman lowered her voice even more, although everyone in the passenger lounge could still hear her. Out of the corner of her eye, Marinda saw some travelers roll their eyes, as if they had heard this supposedly secret conversation before. "Would you happen to have any money to invest, Miss? We could make you a fortune."

Marinda thought of the gold her father had received from the Watchmaker, all those ingots held in trust for her whenever she came back with her book filled with stories. "I already have a fortune, but it's not available for me to invest at the moment."

Hearing that, the two women lost interest, and Marinda thought she understood what their game was.

She lifted the book of *Clockwork Lives* and leaned closer, pressing her own request. "I am collecting stories. Would you two ladies like to participate? Just a drop of blood from your fingertip, and the alchemy will spell out—"

The women closed their portfolios. "I'm sorry, but we have business matters to discuss."

"Matters of a confidential nature," added the second woman, turning away with a sniff.

Although disappointed, Marinda supposed the life stories of

those two business-obsessed women would likely have been dull. Rather than creating sentences and paragraphs, their blood might have written mere columns of numbers.

After she had rebuffed, and been rebuffed by, the two silver speculators, Marinda caught the eye of a mysterious man who sat at the far end of the passenger lounge. He was wrapped in a silence of his own making, but his hawk-like gaze showed that he had been watching everything. He met and held Marinda's gaze.

The stranger had a thin, angular face, a goatee, and significant eyebrows. And though he made no overt invitation, Marinda picked up her book and joined him. The man gave her a hard dissecting look as she set her book down in front of him. The imprinted alchemical symbols and the clockwork gears on the cover seemed to catch his interest. When he reached out to touch the book, she saw that an alchemical symbol had been tattooed on the back of his hand, just like one of those on the cover.

"Are you an alchemist, then?" she asked.

His lips quirked in a smile. "Alchemist? Not exactly the name by which I call myself, although at one time I was a student at the Alchemy College." When he opened the book, Marinda saw that his other hand bore not a tattoo, but the waxy scars of a serious burn. "Circumstances led to my choosing a different career, and yet it all comes back to alchemy, doesn't it?" He ran his fingertips over the pages, looked at the words written in blood.

"What circumstances?"

The man raised his significant eyebrows. "Oh, the more things change, the more they stay the same. After the Alchemy College, I went to many places, many possible worlds, even performed in a carnival, spent time with the Wreckers on the open seas. Good days . . . dangerous days . . . exciting days." His smile had no warmth at all. "And what is this book?"

"My father was an inventor. The pages are treated with a special alchemical substance that reacts with human blood. I am collecting stories, and I would like to add yours."

He glanced at the words on the pages without reading them. "Collecting stories with a drop of blood . . . how interesting." He looked at the other passengers in the compartment, unable to hide his scorn. "So, each one's life is a novel?"

"Or a short story." Marinda glanced down at a few of the other descriptions. "Sometimes just a sentence fragment."

"That's because people are boring. Some of us lead truly magnificent lives while others just waste theirs." He shook his head. "I learned that from the Watchmaker himself. I was his prodigy at the Alchemy College." He gave his thin smile again, as if thinking himself clever. "He had his too-perfect Clockwork Angels, while I was his . . . fallen angel."

Marinda removed her golden needle. Yes, this man must have a significant story—if he could be believed. "Then, if you please, sir, I would love to have your life recorded in my book." She flipped to the next blank page, offered the needle.

Though he seemed amused by the request, he hesitated. Marinda pressed. "Because of the alchemical reaction, this will be a true recording of your life, not fiction. Anyone can *say* he was the Watchmaker's protégé. Your story, in this book"—she tapped the next blank page—"would prove it."

He took the gold needle from her as if it were a toy, then pricked his finger and smiled rather than winced. As a large drop of crimson blood welled out, he turned his finger over so that the drop hung like a tiny ruby, balanced on his fingertip above the blank biographical canvas of the page.

He let the droplet hang there, trembling, as if his heart had stopped beating. Then, just as the drop of blood was about to fall, he snatched his finger away, and the red liquid struck the deck instead.

He handed the needle back to her, and his voice was like an edged weapon. "My story is my own. I don't just give it away." He took a moment to wipe the blood from the deck, then stood. "I have a purpose aboard this steamliner, and it is time to act. Go ahead and collect your stories." He raised his significant eyebrows again. "I have a feeling you will remember mine, regardless."

He stalked off and departed through the connecting door into the long line of passenger compartments and cargo gondolas.

Frustrated, Marinda was even more determined now to get at least one important tale on her journey to Crown City. None of the travelers in the lounge seemed interested in conversation with her, and she did not yet know how to convince likely candidates for her book.

Then it occurred to her that the steamliner pilot traveled from one end of Albion to the other, again and again, from Crown City to the outermost pivot point, and back. Captain Brock Pennrose had seen the whole land, so he certainly had to have a story.

Forgetting the mysterious stranger with his arrogance and his tattooed hand, Marinda went to the connecting door into the front motivator car, the engine, the coldfire boilers, and the pilot's private quarters. The door was marked *RESTRICTED AREA, NO UNAUTHORIZED ACCESS.*

"It is forbidden," said one of card players as he saw her standing before the door. "Rules are rules."

Marinda held up her book. "It says no *unauthorized* access, and I am an author."

And she was, in a way. She was collecting the stories, compiling her book, and she had to choose her subject matter from the material available. She hoped to get the steamliner pilot's tale.

The card player hesitated, then realized that her answer was well considered. He lay down a card, challenging his opponent, more interested in his game than in her possible trespass.

When Marinda opened the hatch she was suddenly buffeted by the loud background noise of engines, pistons, and stray gusts of high-altitude wind. She crossed over the connecting ramp and opened the second door, calling out, "Excuse me! I would like to speak with the pilot."

Hearing no answer, she ventured toward the sounds of machinery, the hiss of steam. She followed a blue glow to a large chamber where the barrel-chested steamliner pilot stood with his shirt off, his trousers held up by a set of suspenders. He grunted, flexing his muscles as he shoveled a load of alchemical crystals into a hungry boiler furnace.

He looked up at her, startled. "Sorry, miss, but this is a hazardous area. You're not allowed." He threw another shovelful of crystals into the furnace, then slammed and latched the door.

She clutched the book. "Could we go someplace less hazardous? I'd be interested in talking with you."

"That is highly irregular."

"I understand. My life has become quite irregular of late. My name is Marinda Peake, and I have a request for you."

Hearing her name, the steamliner pilot swayed before catching his balance, as if he wasn't accustomed to this kind of turbulence. He wiped a grimy hand on his forehead, which only distributed the grime more widely, but even so his face seemed suddenly pale. He snatched his shirt from a peg on the metal wall and pulled it on over his broad chest. "We'd better go where we can sit and talk."

He led her out of the engine room, up a spiraling metal staircase to the upper deck, but he seemed unaccustomed to company. A large framed map on the bulkhead showed the whole land of Albion with Crown City at its heart and roads spiraling outward from Chronos Square; straight lines like the spokes of a wheel showed the steamliner routes ranging from the Mainspring Hub out to the end of the land, with stops at numerous villages just like Lugtown, back and forth, back and forth, like the pendulum of a giant clock.

"I've been the steamliner pilot on this route for well over a decade," he remarked as he saw her studying the map. "But even before that—long before that—I serviced Lugtown."

"Then you must have many stories and many experiences. My father was an inventor. He recently passed away."

The pilot looked queasy, then he turned away. "Poor Arlen . . . I am sorry to hear that."

"Oh? Did you know my father? From Lugtown?"

"In a way . . ."

She held up *Clockwork Lives* and launched into her explanation. "He bequeathed me this book and gave me a quest. You see, after my mother left us when I was just a little girl, my father grew lonely and infirm. I took care of him, as a daughter should, but he felt guilty that I gave up the life I should have had. He concocted a way to make up for it, even though I didn't ask. I have to collect the tales of interesting people I meet."

His shoulders slumped. "I am not sure you want my story."

"Of course I do," she said, all business. "Every page I fill brings me one page closer to completion. I am on my way to Crown City to gather other tales, but the more I accomplish during this steamliner journey, the less work I'll have to do there . . . and the sooner I'll be able to get back home and back to normal."

Pennrose adjusted his compass and set the steamliner on autopilot, so he could talk with her. His voice cracked as he said, "Come back into my private study, behind the piloting deck."

By now it was full night outside, and the steamliner steered across the stars. On the ground far below, evenly spaced like luminous dots on a map, were the regularized villages of Albion. Marinda stared at the view; from up here, the world looked so wide. She knew that was one of the things her father would have wanted her to see.

The pilot looked as if he carried a heavy burden. He gestured her to a comfortable reading chair. "Marinda Peake . . . if you will sit, I can tell you my story and answer your questions."

Next to the chair, she saw a shelf full of books that looked well read, including *Before the Stability*, the classic historical account written by the Watchmaker himself.

"Actually, I need a drop of your blood on the alchemically treated pages," she said apologetically. "If you tell me your story *aloud*, that won't help me achieve my goal—although I'm sure it would be fascinating. I need to fill this volume. My father was very specific."

As she settled into the chair, she spotted a chronograph mounted in a frame—a burlwood frame—resting next to the books. The image of a beautiful young woman looked strikingly familiar, with a face that showed some hint of Marinda's own features.

She caught her breath. She had just seen this chronograph mounted inside her father's optical enhancement helmet—one of the two images old Arlen had been viewing on the night he died in his sleep. She stared. Why would an image of her mother be on the shelf in a steamliner pilot's library?

Pennrose fidgeted. "Marinda Peake . . . it's such a beautiful name."

She picked up the burlwood frame and turned the chronograph toward him. "Is this my mother?"

The color drained out of his face—but before the pilot could answer, an explosion rocked the steamliner, an eruption that shook the caravan of levitating gondola cars like a dog killing a snake. The motivator car lurched. Steam blasts vented from pipes that ruptured. Alarm bells clanged. The books toppled from the shelves, and Marinda dropped the chronograph of her mother as she fought for balance.

The deck tilted at a terrible angle, and she realized they were *falling* out of the sky.

As the motivator car spun through the air, Marinda saw that the back half of the steamliner caravan had been severed. Three of the swollen levitating sacks were on fire; two others had burst. An entire cargo car broke away, tumbled and reeled as it plunged toward the ground. The rearmost passenger and cargo cars were falling free with nothing to keep them aloft.

And, astonishingly, through the window she saw the lone figure of a man dropping gently through the sky, suspended by a fabric scoop tied to his shoulders as a makeshift parachute.

"Damn! The engines must be damaged." Pennrose lurched toward the piloting deck. The front motivator car and the next three gondolas attached to it were also dropping out of the sky, but slowed by the boilers and levitators. "The explosion would have caused feedback in the coldfire." He dashed to the spiral metal staircase, flinging himself down to the engine deck below.

Still clutching her book, Marinda ran after him, trying to keep her balance on the shuddering metal steps. "But how could that happen?"

"Mechanical failure—but not likely. The Watchmaker has rigorous maintenance performance requirements." He paused halfway down the staircase. "No, the only time I've seen this happen before was deliberate sabotage."

She followed Pennrose into the engine room, hoping to help, if possible. She knew the other passengers in the lounge gondola would be screaming in panic—if any of them were still alive.

Steam gushed out of the burst pipes like spurting arterial blood. Captain Pennrose threw open the furnace and furiously shoveled alchemical crystals into the combustion chamber. As the blaze brightened, he grabbed a crate that had tumbled to the deck beside the furnace, stomped on it with his heel to smash it open, then poured dense redcoal into the chamber as well.

Coldfire shimmered through the pistons, and the steam built up again, but the large water reservoir was leaking. The gauges connected to the pipes pointed accusingly into the red zones, while other gauges had simply given up. The pilot hammered the side of the furnace with his bare fist, and his flesh sizzled, but he was too angry, too desperate, to acknowledge the pain.

"Come on!" he howled at the boiler. "Build up pressure! Just enough to keep us levitating!" He shot a glance at Marinda. "We are going to crash. The only part up for debate is the matter of degree." He coaxed his engines, even prayed to them as if they were the Clockwork Angels.

Suddenly alarmed for a different reason, he shouted, "Marinda, get to the upper deck—strap yourself in to my chair and save yourself! It's anchored and protected. That may be enough . . . just barely enough."

She was startled. "I should help, if I can—"

"*Go!* There's nothing you can do here." His voice carried such a force of command that Marinda did as she was told. She pulled herself up the metal stairs, gripping the rails to keep herself from being flung down as the steamliner careened through the air. When she reached the piloting deck, the wide window showed them plunging toward the scatter of lighted villages, weeping steam from all the damaged machinery. The ship would never survive.

Behind them, the attached passenger gondola's levitating sack remained intact, and that suspended them somewhat—a small blessing. Maybe the Angels were watching over them after all, working overtime.

The ground was coming up fast. Marinda strapped herself into the chair, as instructed, still clutching the leatherbound book, although she doubted she would ever fill it with tales now. From the engine deck below, she heard the clamor of tools, loud clangs, shouts as Pennrose cajoled and cursed his boilers.

Then the plummeting steamliner slowly, grudgingly began to level off, changing its angle of descent . . . but a hill on the rolling countryside rose up in front of them. The bottom of the motivator car scraped the hillside, gouging dirt and grass while stealing some of their forward momentum, and then the wounded steamliner careened forward again, over the hill and tumbling into the valley.

Belowdecks, the main furnace exploded with a resounding roar, and the shock wave was just enough to shove them into the air, drain away some of their velocity, before the steamliner plowed into the ground. The vessel carved a long divot forward, groaning, spraying, and then rolled over on its side like a collapsing beast of burden.

Marinda expected to be crushed at any moment, but when the steamliner came to rest, with the front window shattered and the bulkheads smashed, she was alive, unhurt, and strapped into the protective chair. Stunned, she released the straps and climbed out. Her ears rang, and colored splotches sparkled all around in her vision.

Then she remembered Captain Pennrose down in the engine chamber.

Dazed, she found the metal staircase, then climbed and crawled and pulled herself forward until she got to the mangled wreck of the engine room. The furnace had exploded as Pennrose wrung out a last bit of pressure to keep them aloft just a few seconds more.

The steamliner pilot was in no better shape than his furnace. The explosion had caught him in his chest, throwing him back into a bulkhead so that he left a large dent in the metal. His skull was cracked, and his arms hung at unacceptable angles. His eyes were dulled, and blood spilled from his mouth, but he sensed her nearby. His lips moved, and he managed to rattle out a sound that was something like "Peake."

Marinda had so many questions, and he had wanted to tell her his story. Why did he seem so guilty, so burdened? And what was he doing with an old chronograph of her mother?

In her confusion she still clung to the book, and as Brock Pennrose slumped there in his last moments of life, she realized that he could indeed tell her the story he wanted to share. Frantically flipping pages, she opened the volume to the next clean sheet of paper and bent over his sagging body where blood dripped from innumerable wounds.

Crimson splashed on the clean white page, and the words of his life story raced out.

THE
STEAMLINER PILOT'S TALE

This is more *her* story than mine, but her story became mine, and I have lived with it for more than twenty years. First Elitia Peake stole my heart—ripped it right out of my chest—and then she went on to steal everything else.

What did I see in her, fool that I was?

I was culpable too—no avoiding that. I played with fire, I struck the spark. I flirted. I smiled at the ladies with the roguish smile that I knew would feed that twist of longing in a certain sort of woman. Elitia was indeed that sort of woman, but she was not the only one.

With their everyday clockwork lives, the Albion villagers think steamliner pilots are glamorous. After all, we travel across the land, guiding a caravan of passenger gondolas, cargo cars full of exotic wares from faraway places. I was dashing and handsome. I commanded the steam engines. I piloted the monstrous vehicle along the coldfire rails and up into the sky. I stoked the fire on the big steel wheels. I was everywhere. I was mysterious.

Some women like that—and I know how to find them.

Albion is quiet and content nowadays, full of peace and prosperity thanks to the Watchmaker's Stability. The people carry on their lives with little desperation and few ambitions. But not everyone sleepwalked through their days in the villages I visited. I would land the steamliner at a station, stopping for a day to visit, to conduct business, and, more often than not, slip in a secret rendezvous. My aloof life was both predictable and exciting.

Then I met Elitia, and a light but illicit game became a tangled trap. It was my own fault. When an alchemist plays with dangerous chemicals, the reaction doesn't always produce gold.

In those days I traveled different routes from the Mainspring Hub, just for the variety. I would take my steamliner into Crown City, then shift to another spoke route and head off to a new endpoint. I would cruise out to far-flung villages, where the townspeople greeted me with hospitality, and the pretty young girls met me with sparkling eyes, whispered invitations, and more. I was there and I was gone—a philanderer, if that's the term you must use, but I saw no harm in it. Neither did the women. If the clock isn't watched, who notices a few stolen seconds?

Truth be told, when I was cocky and playing with fire, I actually preferred married women because they knew the extent of what I was offering, and they knew what they needed; they had no silly dreams of anything more.

Once, I made an error with a flighty young girl who became caught up in unrealistic fantasies, wanting to ride across Albion like a queen at my side, believing herself to be my One True Love. That didn't fit my plan at all, and after an awkward unpleasantness, I had to switch steamliner routes until such time as the girl found herself another One True Love and forgot about me.

For married women, though, I was an occasional ray of sunlight in an otherwise overcast life, just a brief thrill. They rebelled against their predictable lives. I offered them a flash of excitement, and when I departed, they went back to their normal lives, everyone happy (even the unwitting husbands, who were pleased to see their wives smiling more than usual). Married women had no flights of fancy, no dreams of running away.

But Elitia Peake was different. I should have sensed the danger when *I* was the one who began to have foolish dreams of a future with her. I looked forward to Lugtown more than any other destination. We had our fling, and each time was better than the last. I didn't realize how quickly she had me wrapped around her finger.

Elitia was married to Arlen Peake and had a young daughter and what others considered a quiet, perfect life, but that was by no means enough for her. Elitia had a hunger that consumed me and consumed all common sense, until after a scheduled stop in Lugtown, when I stoked the fires and built up the engine pressure, Elitia ran to the motivator car at the last minute. She swung herself inside as the coldfire rails glowed and the cars began to move. She had only a change of clothes and a smile that melted my heart.

"Take me with you, Brock," she said. "I need this. For once in my life, I'm going where I want instead of where I should."

I had no way of knowing how fateful that decision would be, but I also had no way to resist her. I said yes. We left Lugtown and rode off together on the steamliner, high above the world. We traveled to other villages, followed my dreamline compass to the far ends of Albion and then all the way back to Crown City. At night there were stars in her eyes and stars in the sky, and we talked about the future, the routes we could explore, the places we would go.

Once I reached the Mainspring Hub, I could easily adjust my schedule so as to avoid Lugtown, sure I wouldn't be welcome there again. I wasn't the only steamliner pilot who had encountered an "unexpected awkwardness" like that, and we helped one another. Steamliner pilots were interchangeable cogs in the big machine, and the Stability continued.

I gave Elitia exactly what she wanted, what she needed. I was too caught up in it all to think about what *I* wanted or needed. *Elitia.* That was my answer whenever I asked myself the question.

She and I explored Albion and explored each other, and reveled in the happiness we had mapped out in our wistful fantasies for months . . . until even that life became routine. Dreams shine brightest when they remain only dreams, because reality becomes prosaic all too quickly.

Elitia wasn't much of a reader, but during the long hours in my private cabin she would peruse the volumes I kept on my shelf. She was particularly interested in *Before the Stability*, the salacious account of the dark, violent times that had beset Albion before the Watchmaker's arrival more than two centuries ago, how he had learned to create plentiful gold through alchemical means, how he had devised coldfire as a clean and abundant power source, how he had stopped the chaos and put the whole world in order.

But the cautionary descriptions of those lawless times did not have the expected effect on Elitia. She found the descriptions edgy and exciting; her eyes shone with the thrill. Wanting to maintain my hold over her, I revealed to her some of my own family history, which was perhaps best forgotten.

"Back in those days," I said, with what I hoped was a tantalizing grin, "my family members were outlaws—quite infamous." I paged through *Before the Stability*, finding the appropriate chapter and pointing out where the Watchmaker described the mayhem caused by the Pennrose Clan.

Although the book exaggerated those legendary misdeeds to make a point, I did remember my great-grandfather telling stories when I was a boy, describing the adventures of *his* great-grandfather. From the way he told it, the old Pennrose gang was a group of piratical scalawags with hearts of gold as well as hoards of gold. It was a rough-and-tumble time, where being self-sufficient meant that one had to be aggressive—take or be taken.

Elitia read the chapter avidly, and she found it glamorous, the outlaws romantic. Back in Lugtown she had left her dull existence for the dream of an exciting life aboard the steamliner with me. Now, unfortunately, I saw that dream slipping away into the prosaic. After all, Elitia Peake had *me* already, and what kept her going was the desire for something else. How did I not foresee that she would grow as bored with me as she had with her husband? I think she was addicted to the adrenaline rush of new things.

She made the ridiculous suggestion that we should become outlaws ourselves to recapture that exciting and unpredictable time before the Stability. And because I felt I was losing her, I became even more foolish and encouraged such talk, feeding her imagination. Other than what she read in *Before the Stability*, Elitia knew little about what an outlaw was. Neither did I. Yet we were giddy with our plans.

We decided to rob my own steamliner.

My airship hauled levitating cargo cars filled with lumber, grains, construction stone, even livestock. Passenger gondolas carried people from Crown City to the outskirt villages and back. Secure armored cars carried the Watchmaker's gold to maintain the trading network throughout the land.

Elitia became obsessed with the idea of gold. After reading legends from *Before the Stability*, she gave the rare metal an almost mythical quality. Once the Watchmaker's alchemy had made gold ubiquitous—still vital but less precious than before—its value had decreased, but Elitia still fantasized.

So I began to make plans.

Cargo workers and porters traveled in the steamliner's back compartments. They were considered low-class citizens, unruly and unreliable; restlessness made them change their jobs often and move on. Right now, that worked to our advantage, for if we were to become outlaws, then we would need people of flexible morals and ill-defined schedules.

When my steamliner set down at a destination village, Elitia would make a point of striking up a conversation with the cargo workers in the back cars. She gradually developed a list of men and women who seemed amenable to a risky and exciting, but unspecified, plan—and others who weren't. When we reached the Mainspring Hub in Crown City, I already had a good idea of which ones to let go and which ones to keep on. Thus, Elitia and I shaped the character of the crew working aboard my steamliner.

I had many uncertainties, but whenever I voiced them, Elitia would look disappointed—in me. And her overwhelming enthusiasm smothered my doubts. If I grew nervous about the enormity of what we were planning, she would calm me, focus me, and make me think of only the next small step, which didn't seem so insurmountable. We were tiptoeing down the slippery slope.

Besides, the excitement of planning such a great adventure made her a wild and passionate lover, and that would make me forget my concerns, for a while.

Finally, when Elitia was certain she had our crew also wrapped around her finger, we revealed our bold plan. I was sure some of them would recoil in shock, at which point I didn't know what we'd do. But Elitia had dropped just enough hints to whet their appetites, and every one of them agreed, lured by the glory of adventure as well as treasure. They did exactly what she told them to do . . . just as I always did.

Despite my terror, when the time came to rob my steamliner, the escapade was remarkable and exciting—just as she had promised. That night on the pilot deck, I operated the controls, damped the engines, vented the coldfire exhaust, and dropped the steamliner. Many of the travelers were asleep in their passenger gondolas and oblivious to the unscheduled landing until it was well in progress. From flying these routes for many years, I was intimate with the geography of the grasslands and rolling hills. Even though there were no alignment rails to take us on a vector into a particular village, I set the steamliner down on the uninhabited plains of Albion.

It was a rough landing, but Elitia threw her arms around my neck, kissed me hard, and disembarked, tugging on my arm to follow. The cargo workers swung down from their rear compartments and went to work on the passenger gondolas. The steam pressure was still high, and each separate gondola was held aloft by swollen levitation sacks, different colors signifying the class of transport.

The rough crewmembers disengaged the gondolas, breaking the pistons and hydraulic connections, then setting the cars aloft. The levitation sacks carried the gondolas aimlessly upward, without guidance; they would descend of their own accord soon enough, many miles away. For now, passenger cars scattered like colorful soap bubbles on the wind. Awakened travelers opened the hatches, waving their hands and demanding help as they drifted off.

Elitia laughed as she and I marched up and down the line of grounded cargo cars. I already had the steamliner manifest, so I knew that some of the compartments contained cut fieldstone, others had cast-iron rods, sacks of grain, crates of potatoes. We discarded all of those.

One small armored gondola had a yellow levitation sack. "This one contains the shipment of gold," I said, stating the obvious to the crew.

Working together, tense, thrilled, giddy, we attached the motivation engine to the gold gondola, then connected two of the crew compartments, where our co-conspirators would live and sleep and celebrate. I powered up the engines, added coldfire to the furnace. Our abbreviated steamliner flew away into the night with its stolen treasure.

I knew my family history and the charts of our old holdings from before the Stability, so I went there. I landed the motivator car in the rugged empty hills, where we unloaded the stockpile of the Watchmaker's gold—cases filled with neatly stacked coins, ingots, perfect circular rings, thin rectangular sheets of gold foil to be used for ornamentation. Everything glowed with the vibrant yellow of true wealth. An incalculable fortune.

We had become genuine outlaws.

Over the next few months, we robbed six more steamliners.

After slipping in our crew as cargo workers aboard a liner, Elitia and I would travel as wealthy visitors to distant lands, clothed in fine garments with new pocketwatches and jewelry purchased with the Watchmaker's stolen gold.

As we lived free and chaotic lives, Elitia blossomed into an even more vibrant, intense person. She took my breath away; sometimes she frightened me. Our adventures reminded her of the heady days before the Stability, exciting outlaw times with no schedules. We were self-sufficient, clever, and resourceful. We took whatever we could, we lived wherever and however we chose, and we moved across Albion so that no one would find an established hideout. We were becoming a notorious gang of thieves and anarchists.

Bear in mind, all this occurred twenty years ago, long before the current Anarchist who causes the Watchmaker such consternation. Our gang caused far more turbulence to calm and orderly Albion than that atrocious man could hope to do. The Anarchist may be bombastic, but he's not much more than an amateur—one person more interested in ideology than profit, which makes him laughable. Our gang, though, enriched ourselves. We shook up the world—and those were some of the best times I had with Elitia.

But, as before, even the greatest excitement becomes prosaic after a time, and she wanted each new robbery to be more spectacular, more audacious than the previous one. Although Elitia managed to make me agree every time, I felt something hard and heavy gnawing inside me as the months went by.

Some members of our crew took their share of the wealth and slipped away, but our band grew nevertheless, which meant more outlaws to split the profits, more people to implement more complex robberies. At first I knew each man personally, and they gave at least lip-service to the conceit that I was the leader of our gang, since I was the steamliner pilot. But it didn't take them long to see that it was *Elitia* who posed the challenges and made the decisions. It was so easy for her to manipulate me. For a long time, I pretended that I made those ill-conceived choices of my own accord, but eventually I realized otherwise.

Then a dashing and edgy young man named Glendon joined us. He was dark-haired, roguish, and always two days past a clean shave. Elitia recruited him in Crown City, listened to his ideas, and the two of them immediately proposed even greater plans. Glendon inspired the other members of the crew to tackle even more ambitious robberies, just as I was beginning to backpedal, suggesting caution. I worried that the Watchmaker and his Regulators would surely be intent on capturing us to quash the constant disruption of schedules we caused.

But Glendon talked with such grand designs and grand gestures that Elitia was caught in his spell, just as I had been caught in hers. She was enthralled with him, and she laughed off my concerns; at times it even seemed that she was laughing at me.

Again, afraid that she might be slipping away from me, I clung tighter in the only way I knew how—I agreed to everything she wanted, despite my reservations. I went along with what she and Glendon proposed. Elitia clung to me, she reassured me, but I felt a widening gap between us.

During our next raid, when we seized another airship, we were surprised to discover that two members of the Red Watch were hidden inside the armored compartment, assigned to guard the Watchmaker's gold. The Regulators were armed with cartridge-powered rifles that shot golden bullets. The guards were just as startled by our unscheduled robbery as we were to find them there.

I was sure we'd been caught, but Glendon fought like a mad dog. Elitia was at his side, and I tried to protect her, but the battle was over in a few seconds. Both of the Red Watch guards lay dead. Glendon looked exhausted but satisfied. "All is for the best," he said with a mocking sneer. Then he rummaged through their red uniforms and robbed the two dead men.

Unsettled by the dramatic shift, our gang scrambled to complete the robbery and offload the stolen gold. We fled with the treasure, leaving the dead bodies behind. I was sickened, horrified. I didn't know what to do. As outlaws, we had crossed a line that I had not even seen coming.

The worst moment came when I looked over at Elitia and saw that her eyes shone with a bright excitement I hadn't seen since the first time we had illicitly made love. She was flushed, breathing hard, and I could see that she wished she could do it all again.

We made camp in a place where we were sure no one could find us. After we divided up the treasure, four of our disconcerted outlaws vowed that they were leaving the very next day. "Gold is gold," one man said, "but blood is too high a price."

I couldn't argue with them. In fact, I longed to take Elitia and run away, too. We could stop this chaotic, dangerous life, find some place like Lugtown, or Barrel Arbor, or Ashkelon—they were all the same—to settle in and find our own new Stability.

"This has to stop," I said to her when we were alone. "Enough! Two men are dead. We can't ever let this happen again."

Elitia just mocked me. She and Glendon had already begun planning their next robbery, which would be even grander.

By now all of us had more gold than any person could want, but the outlaws decided that they needed more. When Glendon proposed hitting another steamliner only a week later—much sooner than the Watchmaker would ever suspect, he claimed—he asked for a show of hands, and every one of them agreed. What could I do, fool that I was? I cast my vote as well, hoping Elitia would approve, though she rarely noticed me anymore. None of our gang mistook my agreement for enthusiasm.

Because Elitia spent so much time with Glendon, I learned to understand loneliness even when I was among so many comrades. Oddly enough, though I had spent months with these people and committed crimes at their sides, I didn't really know them at all. The vivid memory of those two dead Red Watch members was a more constant companion. The blood that spilled on the ground was certainly more valuable to those guards than any gold.

On the night before our next ill-advised steamliner robbery, I was restless and deeply insecure about the things I feared would go wrong. Seeking reassurance, even if I had to give it to myself, I wandered away from the camp into the dark night so that I could be even more alone than I was with my fellow outlaws. I was tempted to just keep walking, to leave that part of my life behind and reset it like a clock, but I didn't have the nerve.

Until I found Elitia and Glendon together under the moonlight.

They had taken a blanket to a distant hillside, where they lay naked and intertwined, laughing, whispering. Elitia made contented purring noises that I had not heard from her in some time.

I stood in the shadows under the trees, just staring, as if my heart had turned to lead without any alchemical reaction whatsoever. I felt betrayed, dismayed, yet not at all surprised. How could this be unexpected? Elitia had proved herself unfaithful from the very moment she'd left her husband and run off with *me*.

A decisive man sets his own course, but Elitia had made my decisions for me for some time now. And now she made another one for me, although inadvertently. I turned my back, knowing that the two hadn't even noticed me there. If I confronted them, I was sure Elitia would not have shown any guilt, and Glendon would just have been smug. I didn't want to give them that.

I didn't bother to take my share of the gold. I took only my dignity, although few shreds of that remained. I simply walked away, heading across the open landscape that centuries ago had been an unruly wasteland infested with outlaw bands like my own family. Now I was all alone, and I set off, knowing that if I walked far enough in a straight line I would eventually come upon steam-liner tracks.

If I had been a sensible man, I would never have looked back, but as I'm sure my story has shown, I am not a sensible man. I could not disentangle myself so cleanly from the strands that bound me to Elitia. And when I discovered steamliner tracks in the open hills, knowing the outlaws' plan, I had to watch where they meant to strike, even if I didn't intend to participate, even if I refused to stain my hands with any more innocent blood.

I found an outcropping that would give me a good vantage, where I could see the tracks and the surrounding hilly terrain, the small reservoir. Far out here in open country, with no nearby vil-lages, the steamliner would descend to refill its boilers from the lake.

And that was where Elitia, Glendon, and their fellow outlaws would strike.

As with most of our robberies, everything occurred like clock-work. The steamliner arrived overhead with its chain of levitating balloons, its cargo gondolas, the yellow sack with prominent honeybee markings. The vessel settled down on the glowing blue tracks, and the steamliner pilot emerged from the motivator car. His crew disembarked from their living compartments, ready to pump water into the big tanks. I recognized the pilot as an old comrade of mine, a woman with a deep voice who liked to sing to her engines, back when my life had been on an entirely different schedule. She looked older now, but surely I did, too. Her life had ticked away in a precise fashion, and I could have had that life, if I hadn't broken away to become an outlaw. If I hadn't met Elitia. All those wasted years . . .

That was when wild Elitia, Glendon, and six others struck.

From where I sat hidden, I hoped they would succeed without anyone being hurt or killed, although I knew Glendon had a taste for it. I felt both dread and fascination as I watched from my hidden vantage, remembering when I had found our heists exciting, when the outlaw life had made me feel alive and inflamed with love for Elitia. Now I felt like an astronomer staring at alien life on a distant planet. I didn't understand any of it.

As the gang closed in on their prey, the two passenger gondolas burst open, and a full contingent of the Black Watch boiled out, carrying cartridge-powered rifles. It was a trap! As I suspected, the Watchmaker had devoted great resources and predictive abilities to stop our chaotic robberies. After he had imposed his Stability, Albion was supposed to be a place of contentment and prosperity. He could never tolerate a gang of outlaws.

The Black Watch showed no mercy. They opened fire, shooting a rain of golden bullets. They cut down the two foremost gang members who rushed the steamliner. I stared, and my throat went dry as the black-uniformed soldiers rushed out, perhaps trying to capture the outlaws, but just as satisfied to kill them.

Moving as a team, both desperate yet flushed with excitement, Elitia and Glendon fought back. Like an animal, she threw herself on one of the Black Watch guards, startling him. Glendon tore the rifle free from the man's hands and killed him, then swung the weapon around to shoot another Regulator. Then he and Elitia, without even speaking of their plan, rushed the passenger gondola, which was now empty since the soldiers had all emerged.

Elitia dove aboard the gondola as Glendon disengaged it from the steamliner caravan. Separated from the rest of the chain, the lone gondola rose into the sky, borne aloft by its bright blue levitating sack. Hanging out the open door of the compartment, Elitia and Glendon laughed at the soldiers below. They rose higher, out of reach, drifting on the uncharted wind.

From my hiding place on the distant outcropping, I shaded my eyes and stared upward, dismayed. My heart pounded. Even though I knew how faithless Elitia was and what she had done to me—*all* the things she had done to me—my heart still wanted her to get away. To be safe.

Then three members of the Black Guard emerged from another passenger gondola. On the ground, they set up a larger-bore weapon—an alchemy cannon!—aimed its barrel at the sky, and launched a gleaming artillery projectile. Elitia and Glendon saw it coming.

Like a streak of lightning, the projectile struck the blue levitation sack and detonated, transforming the gondola and my faithless lover into a ball of blue-white fire like a new alchemical sun in the sky.

Elitia, my Elitia, vanished in a blaze of glory. And even though I watched in despair, I realized that this legendary death was exactly the way Elitia would have wanted her tale to end.

———————◆◆———————

Defeated and aimless, I found my way back to our now-abandoned outlaw camp, where I gathered the supplies I might need for a long cross-country trek, but I left all the gold.

It took me six days to reach a village on the steamliner path, and from there I made my way to Crown City and the Mainspring Hub, by which point I had concocted a story to explain myself. I would file papers and tell the appropriate officials that I had been held prisoner by Elitia and her bandits all this time. I expected to be bombarded with questions, and I hoped I could find an acceptable way to answer them.

As it turned out, all I had to say was that I had trained as a steamliner pilot, and that I belonged on board, guiding the caravans. Experienced pilots were always in demand, and the Watchmaker's bureaucracy slotted me into the schedule again.

I became a pilot once more, following the straight-and-narrow path of the coldfire rails, returning to a quiet, perfect life that now seemed hollow, but I convinced myself it was enough. I carried passengers and cargo back and forth, back and forth. Prosaic, yet satisfying.

I have served as a reliable steamliner pilot for twenty years. I no longer seek out rebellious women in the towns I visit, although I know they are still there.

And that is why seeing you now, daughter of Elitia Peake, brings all this back to me, highlighting the excitement . . . and reinforcing my regrets.

Now, after the disastrous explosion as my steamliner comes in for what will surely be a horrendous crash, I know the bandits have struck again. I hope I can save you, Marinda, but regardless I will die knowing that at least I am no longer an outlaw.

I take solace in that.

CHAPTER 7

Fire and smoke surrounded her after the crash, and the creaking groans of shattered metal echoed in Marinda's head. She saw the pages and pages of blood-words telling the pilot's story in her book, but she had no time to read the tale now. She didn't want to be trapped in the wreck of the airship. She had to get out, see if she could find any other survivors.

Leaving the bloody body of Captain Pennrose inside the battered, broken body of his steamliner, Marinda found a spot where the hull had split open, and she crawled out into the stunned night. She still clutched her book, and she found her valise, which had been tossed about.

She looked around outside, staring at the disaster. The placid hillsides were covered with dew, and a gibbous moon shone silver light across the grasses. Fires from scattered steamliner cars crackled and smoked. Blessedly, three sleeping compartments and passenger gondolas remained aloft, their levitation sacks still buoyant enough that they drifted gently to the ground.

The detached lounge car had slammed into the ground near the motivator car, and four people struggled out of the wreckage. She saw the men who had been playing cards, one cradling an obviously broken arm. When she peered inside the wrecked car, she saw the others were silent and lifeless, including the two speculators who had been so intent on raising money for silver futures; now, neither of those women had a future of any kind.

Marinda heard shouts, saw figures approaching from the nearest village, silhouettes carrying coldfire lanterns. The villagers would have been awakened by the spectacle in the air and the crash. The breathless villagers huffed and ran, jiggling their lanterns as they searched for survivors. Those passengers still able to move gathered near the wrecked motivator car, not sure what to do, probably in shock.

Marinda moved about looking for the injured, helping where she could. She had tended her sick father for so long, but this was entirely different. Before long, she was covered in other blood, not just Brock Pennrose's. She pressed torn cloth against ragged wounds, helped apply a splint to a broken arm, moving from patient to patient. She saw more dead people in half an hour than she had seen in her entire life.

She could have used a drop of blood from each casualty to fill many more pages in her book, but she dismissed such ghoulish thoughts. Yes, she wanted this nightmare to end, and she wanted to go home, but that seemed entirely inappropriate. Brock Pennrose had wanted to tell her his story, but these others were just . . . victims.

"It was an explosion—a bomb!" said one of the card players, leaning against the tilted gondola on the ground. "And that suspicious-looking man—he leaped out of the steamliner in midair. I saw him jump!" He shook his head. "I thought he meant to kill himself."

"He had a parachute. He's still out there, somewhere."

The villagers were shocked. "Was it the Anarchist?" They seemed terrified that the evil man might still be wandering the landscape near their village.

"He's gone now," said the second card player. "A lot of things are gone."

One of the rescuers shone a pale blue lantern in Marinda's face. "Are you all right, ma'am? Are you injured?" She had been helping out, but paying little attention to her own condition.

She honestly didn't know. She set her valise down on the damp grass and placed the leatherbound book on top of it. "I'll let you know as soon as I check." She methodically touched her arms, her head, her ribs, flexed her legs. She had a great deal of blood on her hands, but it was not hers. "I seem to be. I can still help."

The village doctor came with his kit and a plentiful supply of bandages, all of which were used up within the first hour. The wounded cried out in pain as the doctor set broken bones and wrapped up cracked skulls, but crickets and nocturnal insects eventually began their night songs again, already forgetting the mayhem of the crash.

———————

After an emergency signal went out from the village's newsgraph office, Crown City dispatched rescue vehicles and a team of crack investigators. The Watchmaker announced he would get to the bottom of the disaster, though by the time the first response teams arrived late the next morning, most had already concluded this was the work of the Anarchist, a violent freedom extremist. Even here, in perfect Albion at the heart of the Stability, no one was safe.

The survivors were cleaned up, given blankets and a place to rest. A café provided hot tea, biscuits, and comfortable cushions while they waited. Marinda was so shaken she could barely think. She longed to be back home in Lugtown, completing her daily chores, ably assisted by the clockwork Regulators.

Had her father realized what risks she would face in order to complete the silly quest he had given her? Placing herself in such danger just to gather *stories*? She conjured up Arlen's image, wishing she could speak with him, demand answers. "What is the meaning of this? What are you trying to do?" But she got no answer.

Instead, she huddled in her blanket, sipping her tea and thinking about the steamliner pilot who had so bravely fought with the doomed airship to keep her alive. The framed chronograph of her mother had been lost in the wreckage, but she did have his story. And she was eager to learn it.

As the conversations droned around her and her tea grew cold, Marinda opened *Clockwork Lives* and, ignoring other distractions, she finally read Brock Pennrose's tale.

When she finished, Marinda felt as devastated as when she had walked away from the crash. The components of her life were beginning to fall into place—the gears ground and meshed. She had never really wanted to know such things about her mother or her father. Even though she now had more answers and details than she had ever wished for, none of it made sense. Did her father even know what had become of Elitia?

Marinda closed the book and sat with a heavy heart. She felt no joy in filling so many of the book's pages with the pilot's tale. Rather than looking at the book as a blank canvas on which to tell epic stories, she now began to fear the empty spaces she was still required to fill.

She looked at her fellow passengers around her, knew the tragedy they had just endured, and decided she didn't want to ask these poor people for their stories after all. She would wait until she reached Crown City, where she would have plenty of easy opportunities.

By noon, the Watchmaker's rescue vehicles arrived, rolling

steam cars to carry the injured in an ambulance back to Crown City, mortuary vehicles to deliver the less-fortunate bodies to their proper places, while the intact passengers would ride in a comfortable coach to the city.

Marinda was withdrawn as she climbed inside the vehicle. She held her valise and placed the book of *Clockwork Lives* in her lap. Fortunately, no one else seemed talkative, and she stared at her own thoughts as the steam coach rolled off with a hiss and a chug. The two card players shuffled their deck and engaged in another game, desperate to get back to normal patterns. Marinda finally opened her book and read the two long stories again, still trying to understand.

The countryside rolled by as the coach picked up speed. The cross-country journey took the rest of the day, although far ahead along the arrow-straight road, she could see the shimmering towers of Crown City. Tall buildings, crowded streets, coldfire vehicles, and even steam aircraft patrolling above the tallest structures. And clocks—large timepieces that adorned the towers, precision instruments that needed someone like Arlen Peake to maintain them.

The passenger coach arrived in the heart of the city during the colorful fanfare of sunset. When the hatch opened and a steward extended his hand to help them disembark, the survivors emerged into a bustling terminal—the Mainspring Hub, where all roads came together and all steamliner tracks converged.

Vented steam and the rattle of gears filled the air. Conveyors shouted to one another as they hauled crates of cargo, while helpful young porters grabbed luggage and assisted grateful passengers who emerged from arriving steamliners. Large motivator cars were parked in their berths, ready to set out as soon as the next train was assembled. Colorful passenger gondolas and cargo cars were arranged out in the yards to be collected for the next outbound journey.

Marinda stood with her fellow survivors, with no idea where to go or what to do. She had hoped to arrive uneventfully in Crown City, merely wanting to fill her book of stories and then go home.

A pair of well-dressed Crown City officials converged on the passenger coach, accompanied by blue-uniformed Regulators who stood at attention. "We greatly apologize for the inconvenience," said a man with sideburns so bushy they could never have fit inside a hand mirror's reflection, which must have made shaving problematic. "We assure you that steamliner crashes are most unusual, and the Watchmaker has issued this pre-printed card with his apology."

The bureaucrat passed out cream-colored cards to Marinda and the others from the coach. *Everything is taken care of. Our loving Watchmaker wishes only the best for his citizens.*

The sideburned official gestured to a junior official at his side, a woman in trim business slacks and a tight vest, who opened up a black leather briefcase containing rows and rows of golden coins. The junior official counted out a precise stack of honeybee coins to Marinda and an identical stack to each of her companions. "For your trouble. We hope this will make up for any losses or delays you incurred. Pure gold, made by the Watchmaker himself."

Marinda accepted her coins, which she would add to her stipend. She should have plenty of funds to last her while she filled the rest of *Clockwork Lives.*

"If you will all follow me," said the Blue Watch commander. He swiveled on his heels and marched forward, expecting them to follow. Marinda took her valise and her book and set off after the blue-uniformed guards.

As the group wove through the crowded bustle of the Mainspring Hub, Marinda stared at all the people, wondering why they had come here, what their business was, what their stories were. But she could not lose her efficient escorts, who seemed to know where they were going.

The Blue Watch led them past shops that were being shuttered for the night, then into quieter streets and a line of lodging houses, all of which bore the honeybee symbol. In each, a window sign stated, *Lodgings Approved by the Watchmaker.*

"We have arranged a room for each of you," said the Regulator captain. "Rest well, clean up, calm yourselves, for tomorrow will be a fresh reset, and you can be on with your lives." The Regulators marched away, leaving them to fend for themselves.

An innkeeper opened the door of the nearest lodging house and gestured them inside. "Let me have a count, please."

It was all handled very efficiently. Marinda's room was small but clean, and had one of everything she needed: a chair, a writing desk, a narrow bed, a washbasin and pitcher, and a window.

As full night fell, she sat on her bed and looked out at the streets of Crown City, saw coldfire streetlamps as well as a warm glow that shone from homes. People ate dinner at street cafés, sitting outside in the warm night. Men and women strolled along the boulevards, taking in the night air.

Crown City was a vast, crowded mystery to her, and she found it overwhelming. Despite the tribulations she'd endured to get here, she had reached her destination. She didn't need to ask why she was here; she was *here*.

Sitting on the edge of the bed, she touched her father's leatherbound book with some trepidation and looked at the figures outside, knowing that every person there had a story—some of which might even be worth recording.

CHAPTER 8

Despite her exhaustion from the ordeal of the previous night on the steamliner, Marinda slept only fitfully in her unexpected lodgings. This wasn't her bed, wasn't her home, and it was only the beginning of this part of her task. (Her father would have called it an "adventure," no doubt.) Crown City was the heart of legends, exotic sights, possible epiphanies, almost certain intimidation.

She found herself alone in a strange metropolis, but she had always been able to take care of herself. So far, she had survived the crash of a steamliner and, worse, she had survived the true story of her father and mother. It was time to fill her book with other tales, ones that weren't so personal. Yes, that would be much safer.

At first you will hate me for this. Then you will love me for it.

"We'll just see about that," Marinda said to herself.

After she washed and put on the clean set of clothes from the battered valise, she left at dawn, telling the sleepy innkeeper to keep her room available so she would have a place to come back to. She would need several days at least to complete her task, she knew, and the knowledge that she had a temporary home, no matter what she encountered during the day, gave her one sure point of stability, and her life now had few enough of those.

Leaving the inn, Marinda set off into the cool, hushed streets of Crown City. Coffee shops were just opening up. Bakeries propped open awnings to unleash aromas that struck Marinda as the very essence of bread. Shabby men pushed wheelbarrows full of produce, while wealthy merchant women paced alongside coldfire-powered carts laden with exotic fruits and vegetables fresh from the docks. A butcher hung out smoked hams and sausages on hooks above his window. Clothiers fluffed up garments on their racks. A hat seller set out the latest fashions, primping and arranging them to catch the eyes of passersby, but when he turned toward Marinda she was surprised to see that his own eyes were milky and sightless; the blind man arranged the hats by feel alone.

This was *Crown City*, and Marinda realized where she had to go first. After asking directions, she headed to Chronos Square so she could see the Clockwork Angels—and not just because she knew that her father had worked on them.

The city center was a vast open area of flagstones polished by countless feet surrounded by towers and government buildings. On weekends, Chronos Square was also a market that held vendor stalls and street performers, food carts, and flower merchants. The Red Watch stood before the entrance to the square, but they were merely there for show. Their uniforms were impeccably scarlet, like the blood of Captain Pennrose she had seen two nights before. . . .

The Regulators did not challenge Marinda as she passed through the looming stone arch into the mostly deserted square. Workers in red jumpsuits used pushbrooms to clean the clutter and garbage after the previous night's show.

She looked up at the high Watchtower with its giant clock face, the primary clock of all Albion. She also saw the closed doors at the top from which the Angels would emerge and issue their pronouncements to the crowds below. For those who couldn't hear the words, the latest statements were printed on small leaflets handed out to each visitor before the show. Some of the discarded sheets lay on the flagstones now, dropped by ecstatic and distracted supplicants. Marinda watched the jumpsuited men and women clean up.

The clock struck seven, and everyone in the square paused, as if holding their breath until the bells had counted out the hour, then they went back to work. Years ago her father had adjusted that time-piece, monitored it, made it perfect. Somewhere behind those high shuttered doors, he had also tinkered with the Clockwork Angels, trying to fix them per the Watchmaker's instructions, but unable to repair that particular flaw. She wondered if the Watchmaker remembered Arlen Peake after so many years. . . .

She stopped one of the jumpsuited men, who was pushing a bristly broom. "Excuse me, sir. Does the Watchmaker accept visitors? How can I see him?"

The man stared at her. "He doesn't, and you can't."

"But if he's our loving Watchmaker, doesn't he want to hear what his citizens have to say?"

"He already knows, ma'am. He already knows."

Near the tall Watchtower, a golden statue caught her eye, a teenaged boy perfectly rendered with street clothes and an aloof manner; his face looked absolutely real, as if he were a chrono-graph made out of solid gold. His expression looked either cocky or fearful, depending on the light. No placard identified the statue boy, however.

A jumpsuited woman used a long squeegee and a bucket of paste at the brick walls surrounding the square. She unrolled a colorful poster, slathered the back with paste, and applied it to the wall, aligning the top edge with the perfectly straight mortar lines. *Coming for the Solstice Festival!* The poster showed an amazing assort-ment of cheerful clowns, a raven-haired tightrope walker, a dashing swordsman, a well-muscled strongman, an ancient fortune teller, a bearded lady, and a dapper ringmaster with a top hat and handlebar mustache. *Magnussen's Carnival Extravaganza! See—And Be Amazed!*

Marinda would likely be in Crown City for at least a week; maybe she would visit the carnival. Such extraordinary people would certainly have extraordinary stories. In the meantime, though, she had many other tales to collect, and many opportunities to do so.

She followed the winding streets that spiraled through the city. Each block of Crown City held as much activity as all of Lugtown, even on a busy day. So many people! Daily lives, lived daily. Marinda tried to imagine where they had come from, their wives and husbands, their children, their pasts . . . their interests, their joys, their tragedies. Before her father had given her the book, Marinda would never have considered such things. People were just *people*, each man a mystery to himself, each woman a story kept in a private diary. Now, though, Marinda wondered about them.

In Lugtown, when she had asked her neighbors to give her their tales, their well-confined lives usually comprised no more than a line or two, a paragraph at most. In Crown City, however, surely the people were different, their lives more exciting.

"We go out in the world and take our chances," she muttered to herself, quoting the Clockwork Angels. She set about stopping people in the street, explaining her mission. She showed them *Clockwork Lives*, the first pages filled with dark-red words. Many brushed her aside, until she told them that her father had once worked for the Watchmaker himself, then at least some of them agreed.

Alas, when written out in alchemical letters, their life stories were no more engrossing than the inhabitants of sleepy Lugtown. Oh, these were good people and earnest, doing their best, fulfilling their duties, being the most perfect cogs possible in the Watchmaker's very big machine. They had small dreams, but achievable ones; they satisfied themselves with everyday glory, but they were not heroes or titans by any measure.

At the end of two days, Marinda sat in her acceptable room at her Watchmaker-approved writing desk and read paragraph after paragraph, one tale at a time. Four pages after all that work. That was the methodical, sure solution, but it would take years, half a page at a time, person after person contributing a line or two.

And when *Clockwork Lives* was finished, such tales would make for ponderous reading indeed. Marinda doubted those were the types of lives her father intended for her to experience. Arlen Peake wanted his daughter to see what she had been missing, not the small measures that kept some people content.

Marinda went about her business, still hoping. On the fourth day, she went to the docks at the mouth of the Winding Pinion River where the lazy waters poured into the sea. The river wound through Albion, bearing barges laden with sacks of wheat, corn, and rice. Another flatboat was crowded with pigs being delivered to the stockyards. Tied to the main docks was an enormous cargo steamer that had plied the expansive ocean from Atlantis, distant places that she had heard of only from her father's books.

Swarthy carters unloaded crates, barrels, and sacks of exotic minerals extracted from the fabled alchemy mines. Standing on the dock and peering up at the steamer, Marinda saw sailors with exotic features, bronze skin, long dark hair, clothing of a style she had never seen before. When she learned they were from Poseidon City, she knew they must have stories to tell.

The foreign sailors were pleased to take a gold coin in exchange for being pricked with the golden needle for a drop of blood. Reading their tales later, Marinda learned about long and perilous voyages, families left back home, lovers in distant ports, childhoods spent in Poseidon City, friends and enemies. But although the locale was different and the names had an unusual flair, these tales were not the epics she wanted to include. She filled several more pages during that day and the next, and was glad to mark the progress, but she was left feeling unsatisfied.

Marinda continued to explore Crown City. On a side street she found a two-storey museum with a domed roof. *Official Orrery—the Universe According to the Watchmaker.* She thought that the building seemed a bit small to contain the entire universe, although it might be worth investigating.

Inside the orrery museum, she found a cavernous vault. The walls were covered with numerous posters and star charts. Vitrines contained models of planets and small mounted telescopes. Marinda looked up at the domed ceiling and found a breathtaking contraption mounted above. The stars in the heavens were painted in great detail on the hemispherical dome, points that glowed with alchemical light, while the sun, planets, moons, and minor planets all rode on metal tracks, connected and run by gears, linked by a complex webwork of armatures and pivots.

At the back of the room, three docents wore identical round spectacles, white shirts, gray vests, and black slacks. The men were of varying ages and varying stages of baldness, making them look as if they were the same person taken from different points in his life. Tinkering with a generator and related machinery, the docents looked up as she entered. The youngest of the three hurried over to her. "Welcome to the Universe, madam. Have you come to observe and learn how the heavens work?"

"Does anyone know that? In detail?" Marinda asked.

"The Watchmaker does. Ours is not to understand, but we can observe. And for one mere honeybee coin we can run the machinery for you. You'll watch the big wheels spin, the planets move along their courses."

The middle-aged docent came up. "It's well worth the price of admission."

From the opposite side of the vault, she heard a faint cough. For the first time she noticed a motionless man huddling in a wheelchair, a blanket over his bony knees. The ancient man was sculpted from the same model as the other docents, but he was much older. Gnarled hands grasped the arms of the chair, and thick spectacles poised on his hawkish nose. He wrinkled his forehead and stared longingly at the orrery contraption as if his prayers could make it move.

Curious to see the clockwork universe in action, Marinda handed one of her coins to the youngest docent. After his two companions closed and restarted the engine, he inserted it into a slot in the machine. The coldfire power source brightened, and dials on the machinery glowed as the artificial heavens awakened. After a straining hum, the wheels began to turn overhead with a clack and a clatter of spinning gears and oscillating armatures.

"The stars and the planets take years, even centuries, to move along their courses," explained the oldest docent. "But we have the ability to make time whirl ahead. Observe." He turned a knob on the generator, and the orrery thrummed and rattled, picking up speed.

The moving planets entered epicycles and then returned to their main orbits. Marinda found it captivating, and she watched the heavenly bodies continue through several orbits until the coldfire dimmed, the generator ran down, and the orrery froze back into place.

The three docents also watched the contraption, but they had seen the universe many times before. Marinda heard another cough and remembered the ancient man in his wheelchair. She saw him staring at the orrery, slowly shaking his head.

Marinda turned to the young docent. "Who is that man?"

"He's always here—an old astronomer, paralyzed and unable to speak."

The middle-aged docent added, "We've been told that he's the original builder of this orrery, but he never talks to anyone, just stares at the mechanism. I can't say why."

The oldest docent said, "We tolerate his presence, but no one knows his story."

That caught Marinda's interest. She walked over to the ancient man, who continued to shake his head, staring through thick glasses at the astronomical display. She bent close and extended her leatherbound book. "I would like your tale, sir. I want to know what you've done and what's inside your mind." She opened to the next blank page after so many pages filled with small stories. Not knowing whether he could hear her, she explained about her book, the alchemically treated pages, the lives she had collected so far. "You must have a story to tell."

The ancient man blinked, and a tear leaked out the corner of an eye, trickling through the path of least resistance down his wrinkled cheek. A perfect transparent droplet. Marinda wondered what the alchemy would do if the old man presented a tear instead of a drop of blood. Perhaps the words of his life's tale would be written in invisible ink. . . .

The ancient astronomer's eyes shifted from the artificial stars, the intricate clockwork contraption in the dome of the astronomy museum, and then he looked directly at her. Part of his face twitched while the rest remained motionless, like flesh-colored clay. But his hand twitched, then slowly lifted from the arm of the chair, extending a forefinger toward her.

Taking that as permission, Marinda took out her golden needle, pricked his fingertip, then squeezed a drop of blood onto the blank paper.

The alchemy reacted, and the words of his life spread out like a meteor shower on the page.

THE
ASTRONOMER'S TALE

The heavens hold profound mysteries and, like a nervous schoolgirl with a secret, the universe drops many hints, hoping that someone will guess the truth. The patterns of the stars, the phases of the moon, the convoluted orbits of the planets are those hints, and the universe eagerly waits for someone to divine the greatest secret of all.

I tried to do just that.

The stars are right up there for all to see, arranged in patterns on which people imagined monsters or heroes. Although I memorized every constellation, I never saw those patterns as mythological illustrations. I saw a *code*.

As a boy, I was considered an odd duck—Leopold Sanjay, a boy teased for having his head in the clouds—but that wasn't correct, for clouds are an atmospheric phenomenon, and my aspirations went much higher than that.

Because the other children mocked and teased me, I had few friends—which gave me more time to study the stars. My parents realized I was frighteningly intelligent, although my schoolwork and grades gave little indication of that. I would secretly spend most clear nights outside studying the stars and watching the planets move in their slow courses. Afterward, I would sneak back into my room before dawn so I could catch an hour or two of sleep; thus, I often dozed off in my classes.

I read astronomy books, but I quickly realized that the official texts were fraught with errors, a fact that I found highly disturbing. When I pointed out the obvious mistakes to my teachers, they didn't want to hear it. They scolded me, then reprimanded me, and I learned an important lesson: to keep such challenges to myself while I collected more data. Evidence.

I maintained my own observational records from the time I was ten years old. At first they were crude measurements, but I compared, learned, and improved. I found old almanacs with precise lunar and planetary data that had been kept for centuries. Although anything from before the Stability was considered unreliable, the numbers seemed accurate to me. Using clockwork components and precision tools, I developed my own instruments, refined them, and took more measurements.

An accurate timepiece is vital for accurate astronomical measurements, and the Watchmaker's Albion has countless perfect clocks. I kept logs of sunrise and sunset; I documented the phases of the moon, noting any fluctuation in the lunar orbit. By the time I turned eighteen, I had compiled my own charts and sorted, collated, and digested centuries of measurements. That was enough for me to begin my real work.

I began to suspect that the Watchmaker's universe did not function as accurately as his own clocks. There were errors, faults . . . and I realized the universe was in serious need of adjustment.

Burying myself in planetary orbits, I went deeper into the numbers, analyzing countless columns of measurements taken year after year, decade after decade, century after century. Some might say I became obsessed, and I wouldn't be one to disagree with them.

Even so, my stargazing had to remain a mere hobby, because the Watchmaker had no official, salaried astronomers. I had to choose an approved profession, earn a living. Because of my proficiency for numbers and records, I found a quiet, perfect job as an inventory manager at the Mainspring Hub. I tracked and documented cargo shipments, ensuring that commerce across Albion proceeded like clockwork. I was good at my job but not at all interested in it. The rest of the universe was what fascinated me.

In the usual course of a human life, I courted a woman who eventually became Mrs. Leopold Sanjay. We loved each other, but the stars were my passion, and she knew that. Life proceeded along its inevitable orbit, like the moon and the stars. We had a son and raised him, and we all lived contented lives—and that's enough of that, because it isn't the interesting part of my tale.

By the time my son Zivo went off to be trained as part of the Regulator corps, I received a celestial epiphany from all the planetary data I had collected. *Crack the code.* The nervous schoolgirl of the universe had finally whispered her secret, and only to me.

There was only one explanation for the subtle but incontrovertible discrepancies that had compounded over the centuries: the universe itself was imperfect, and I had the mathematical evidence to prove it.

Obviously, the Watchmaker needed to know this.

On a scheduled day off from work, I gathered my records, my derivations, my conclusions, and I went to Chronos Square. Appearing before the gates of the Watchtower, I spoke to the uninterested Red Guard at the door. "I've brought disturbing records. The Watchmaker needs to know about a brewing crisis. The universe doesn't work in perfect circles as expected. Centuries of data show that the planetary orbits are *ellipses*, not circles. I find this most disturbing, as will the Watchmaker. Once he knows about the error, I suggest that he institute an adjustment to the universe."

Since the universe itself was at stake, the Red Guard took my petition and my accompanying records, as well as my name and address. He promised to present them to the Watchmaker himself.

I heard nothing for six months.

Then a supervisor at the Mainspring Hub informed me that my accounting services were no longer required, that I was to leave my office and go home. I was shocked; even though I was not passionate about my job, I did have a wife, family, and home, and such things required an income.

At home, I found a blue-uniformed Regulator at the doorway—our son Zivo. But he had not come for a family visit. Instead, he bore an official document from the Watchmaker.

Leopold Sanjay, your astronomical records and your conclusions are quite impressive, the Watchmaker had written. *This is only one of many possible universes, and there are naturally variations from one to another, but you may have identified a flaw in this one.*

Before the universe can be fixed, however, I require a working blueprint that accounts for all the orbital shifts and eccentricities you have identified. I, your loving Watchmaker, hereby reassign you to this task—and only this task. You will have a proper building, a workshop, and all the funding you require. Construct an accurate model of my official clockwork universe.

It was as if the Angels themselves had swooped down from the Watchtower, embraced me, and lifted me up to a heaven of my own creation.

———◆———

I set up shop in the domed building that would house my complex orrery. The hemispherical interior surface was a blank canvas, and I knew all the stars belonged there, infinite sparkles painstakingly applied with alchemical paint that shone on its own.

It would take me years just to paint the vault of the heavens, but that gave me time to concentrate, because the stars themselves were more stable than even the Watchmaker's Stability. Yes, they rotated in endless circles around the celestial pole, but they didn't shift among themselves, at least not to a degree that any human instrument could measure.

While I painted the universe on the dome, my mind was designing the wheels within wheels, the gears, the tracks, and the armatures that would be required to tame the universe and restore the orbits to order. I made small working models that turned and whirled, spun, reversed to retrograde direction, and then resumed their courses, everything marching in a gravitational lockstep that would have made the most stringent Regulator commander proud.

But as I built more accurate models and ran them through greater spans of time, errors cropped up again, which required further modifications and even more complex sets of nested celestial gears.

Craftsmen built the components according to my designs, and sometimes their precision was lacking, which required additional adjustments. I refused to let anyone else do the actual assembly work, so I climbed the high ladders, perched on the tottering scaffolds, connected, tested, adjusted. This was my design, my universe, and I had to make it function properly, by the Watchmaker's command.

I made every calculation, tested each component, stood precariously on metal ladders to lubricate the joints; I tinkered and twisted each connecting arm. I moved about on tall scaffolding platforms, creating my celestial machine.

Five years after I painted every star on the celestial dome, after I built machines and gears to simulate gravity, I finally assembled my artificial solar system with all its collected armatures and its perfect metal tracks, its smooth gears, and its illuminated sun at the center of it all. Finished!

The worst punishment one can give an obsessive man is to let him complete his task.

I had been happily working for a long time, doing a job that fulfilled me. I set the wheels in motion, speeding up time so I could watch my private self-contained universe go through its paces.

I possessed exhaustive records of all the planetary movements. I sat in a chair inside my orrery vault, staring at the thrumming orbits, the whirling artificial planets, comparing them to the long-term records, the columns of numbers and positions. I watched the universe for days, and I finally reached a point where I could report success to the Watchmaker. I had constructed an accurate model of how the universe *should be*.

I dispatched a triumphant letter to Chronos Square. I had solved the greatest mystery of all; I had found a fix to an inexcusable error in the cosmos. The Watchmaker's own task would be far more challenging, for he would have to make the real stars and planets conform to the new adjusted model.

And yet, at the end of the sixth day of running my artificial universe, when I was exhausted from my work, hoping only to have a day of rest, I spotted a mistake, a variance. Saturn wasn't where it should be, which put Jupiter in a slightly incorrect position, offsetting Mars by an additional degree.

I stared in disbelief, then checked the measurements. This could not be true! I had already sent my message to the Watchmaker, and soon he would come to see. His Regulators and his bureaucrats would arrive to applaud my perfect orrery. My wife would at last see the finished project that had consumed me for so many years. My son Zivo, now promoted to a high-ranking Captain of the Blue Watch, would tell his comrades that his father, the great Leopold Sanjay, had found a way to fix the universe.

But as I watched the whirling planets and the gliding armatures, the mistake seemed so obvious. I couldn't possibly let anyone see this!

I panicked at first, but as I studied and rethought the chain of gears, the interlocking arrangement of moving components, I saw how I could fix it. An adjustment, a slight increase in the degree of curvature of one of the outer tracks. Yes! It would be difficult to reach, but it could be fixed.

Not sure when the Watchmaker and his representatives would arrive, I retrieved my tall metal ladder, extended it to its greatest reach. I had to hurry. With the orrery completed, I had already disassembled and removed the scaffolding, so this thin ladder would have to do.

I held onto one end of the ladder, straining my muscles, and swung it gently, careful not to damage the universe machine. I propped the ladder against the far wall, brushing the metal legs against the painted stars on the domed ceiling, which caused a small chip in the paint, but for now it looked like another star, and I could always fix that. The Watchmaker would notice the error, of course, but the others would not.

Taking my calipers, wrenches, and screwdrivers, I ascended the ladder, climbing higher as the planets continued to spin along their courses. The ladder swayed beneath my weight, but I had to reach to the fullest extent. I had misaligned the ladder, but if I leaned out, I could reach the component in need of adjustment. I found the proper armature, located my error, realized what needed to be done.

But as I extended my arm with the tool, balancing on tiptoes to make the adjustment, I discovered yet another mistake deep inside the meshed gears.

And making that fix would cause even more repercussions, every one like a ripple in a quiescent pool of perfection. But each one could be fixed, step by step. I felt both exhausted and dismayed by the magnitude of work required, but overjoyed that there was still a solution.

I turned the screwdriver to make the subtle change—and the screwdriver slipped. I grabbed for it, which overbalanced me. The ladder slid, and I lurched out over the abyss.

I fell, tumbling through the air.

The universe is supposed to be infinite, but the hard floor came up swiftly, and I smashed into it like meteor. With a resonance that went through my entire body, I heard my spine snap, my skull crack. There was a wash of pain and then nothing. I lay on my back, barely conscious, barely alive . . . just staring up at the planets as they continued moving.

And all I could see was the error that I could fix, if only I had the chance. . . .

———◆◆———

For years, I have been unable to move and I cannot speak. All I can do is spend my days staring at that wondrous and imperfect machine. I can't even shake my head at the errors that my successors do not even see.

CHAPTER 9

When Marinda left the orrery museum, dusk was gathering over Crown City. The tale of the paralyzed old man had filled several more pages in *Clockwork Lives* in a flurry of alchemical handwriting, and she was eager to read it.

She found a nice café not far from the Mainspring Hub. She took a table by herself and ordered a bowl of turnip and green apple soup. Under the bright light of the café's outdoor coldfire lanterns, Marinda read the story of the poor old man, wanting to know who he was.

When she read about her father or the steamliner pilot, she had done so with a measure of curiosity and dread, not sure she wanted to know the secrets that had remained hidden from her for so long. The other everyday lives in the book, the ones that comprised a simple paragraph or two, had been strictly for information-gathering purposes.

The story of Leopold Sanjay, however, moved her, captivated her. Even after she finished her soup and her bread, Marinda sat in the café and read page after page until she was done. This was more than just the remarkable tale of a man she wouldn't have noticed a week ago. No, there was something special here. The *reading itself* was a kind of alchemy, something Marinda had not felt before.

While her primary goal was to fill *Clockwork Lives* and return home to Lugtown, Marinda also looked forward to reading the other stories she would acquire. Maybe there was more to the task than just the end result.

Now that she knew the astronomer's obsession, as Marinda made her way through the nighttime streets back to her approved lodgings, she paused to look up at the celestial landscape overhead, all the stars and the planets, and she wondered if the Clockwork Angels were watching from above. She saw no intrinsic patterns in the lights up there, no secret universal code.

Back in Lugtown, she had never stopped to look at the constellations before—just another thing her life had lacked, another thing she never *imagined* she lacked. Marinda lay restless and awake for a long time in her room before she finally picked up the book again, started at the beginning, and read the pages to herself until she dozed off.

The next day, as she continued to explore the city, Marinda passed a newsgraph office announcing the day's most important events. She studied the posted stories, particularly noting reports about the steamliner crash that had cost the lives of sixty-eight men and women, including longtime pilot Brock Pennrose. The disaster was being blamed on the evil Anarchist, and all citizens were asked to be vigilant. With a chill, she thought of the man aboard the steamliner with his arrogant attitude and marked hands. It had been him!

A chart listed the time for that evening's performance of the Clockwork Angels in Chronos Square, for "authorized audience members only," and tickets would be provided on a strictly limited basis "for those who deserve them." Whatever that meant.

Port timetables listed the arrivals and departures of cargo steamers; some ships plied the coast of Albion, while others would head off to distant Atlantis. According to the headline, one such steamer, fully loaded with cargo from the alchemy mines, had vanished en route. *Rumors suggesting that the Wreckers sank the cargo steamer are unfounded*, said the newsgraph. *The Watchmaker's destiny calculators offer no probability evidence that the lawless band of pirates was in any way responsible.*

Lastly, she saw a notice, more of an advertisement than an announcement, that the Magnussen Carnival Extravaganza would perform in two nights. Marinda made a mental note to see the show, since the carnival would surely provide enough stories to fill many pages.

With books and reading on her mind, Marinda paused by a streetcorner bookseller outside the newsgraph office. His table was piled with books, but all the same book, a clothbound tome with an embossed golden honeybee symbol. *The Watchmaker's Official Autobiography: My Life Story So Far.* Beneath the honeybee symbol was stamped *As of* _____ and included that day's date.

Marinda paused to look at the volume. The autobiography was over six hundred pages long, with very tiny type. Seeing this, Marinda mused that if she could just get a drop of the Watchmaker's blood, his story would fill the rest of her volume, and she would be finished with her quest.

"Have you read this morning's edition from cover to cover yet?" asked the earnest bookseller, a long-limbed man with a wide nose.

"No. I haven't read the previous volumes."

The bookseller seemed surprised. "Then what have you been reading?"

"Not much." She lifted her book of *Clockwork Lives.* "I'm collecting stories of my own."

The bookseller clucked his tongue. "You really should have

this morning's edition. It covers significant events from yesterday and the day before."

Marinda considered, but she had started reading for pleasure, rather than out of duty, and she decided this gigantic opus might not be the best place to start. "Do you have any other books for sale?"

The bookseller blinked at her. "If you haven't read *The Watchmaker's Official Autobiography* yet, why do you need other books?"

Marinda wasn't sure if she had an answer for that. "Are there other bookshops in the city?"

"Most of them sell the same book."

"Most of them?"

He lowered his voice, as if he wasn't supposed to disclose such a secret. "You might try Underworld Books, a quirky place that caters to unorthodox customers. I am afraid, ma'am, that you appear to be a bit . . . unorthodox."

Marinda wondered if that had been intended as an insult or a compliment. "Where do I find it?"

He gave her whispered directions, to follow a main thorough-fare, past several cross streets, then turn down an unmarked side alley. "At least that's where the shop was the last time I checked. Underworld Books has . . . several locations."

Curious, she thanked the bookseller and promised to buy a copy of the Watchmaker's autobiography someday. She followed his directions and soon came upon an interesting shop, which was definitely off the beaten path.

She stopped outside in the alley. Faded books were displayed in the window, and she saw large-format hardcovers, *A Chronograph Journey Through Crown City* in several different editions, which appeared to show entirely different versions of the city. A small book with ornate type looked like a personal devotional, *Proverbs of the Clockwork Angels*. What caught her attention, though, was a battered volume with a simple tan cloth cover: *Before the Stability*.

The book Brock Pennrose had possessed, the one that had so interested her faithless mother.

When Marinda stepped into Underworld Books, her senses were filled with the musty smell of words and binding, ink and paper. Well-read copies were shelved in a loving order, rather than an alphabetical one, not chronicled in any catalog but organized in a way that true readers would understand.

The bell jingled above the door, startling the lone person inside: a tall, slender woman with a broad face, narrow eyes, and hair pulled back in a prim bun. She was just past her late middle years but not yet to the point where anyone would think of her as "old." The woman seemed tired and a little sad, but entirely in her element.

"Welcome to all the stories of many possible worlds. First-time customer?" When Marinda nodded, the bookseller said, "I am Mrs. Courier. I see you brought your own book—have you come to sell or trade?"

Marinda held the *Clockwork Lives* volume close. "No, I couldn't part with this. But I'm looking for stories."

"Then you've come to the right place. We have books from all across Albion and even special imports from Atlantis, a wide selection from writers in Poseidon City, though if you ask me they don't seem quite so poetic there." Mrs. Courier lowered her voice. "And for those with discerning tastes, we have a wide selection of special editions from alternate timelines."

The bookseller stood at an oak table on which she had been tallying inventory. Behind the main desk, through the door of a cluttered back room, she saw a large rectangular mirror such as might be found in a woman's dressing room. It looked like a valuable antique, with an ornate gilded frame, but as a mirror it was a failure, for instead of a silvered glass the frame contained a sheet of pearlescent moonstone. While the odd mirror was certainly beautiful, it was not at all adequate for conveying a person's reflection.

On a shelf at the back wall, Marinda spotted several spine-out clothbound volumes of *The Watchmaker's Official Autobiography*, but they looked old, as if they had been in the store for some time. Marinda was also surprised, since Mrs. Courier seemed to be such a meticulous woman, that she had mistakenly filed the Watchmaker's autobiography under "Fiction."

Displayed on one table were more copies of *Before the Stability*, but each one had a different cover design, and they varied greatly in length. She picked up one of the volumes. "What's the difference? They all have the same title."

"Yes, but different versions of the story. From different Albions."

"What do you mean by different Albions?"

Mrs. Courier raised her thin eyebrows. "You don't believe this world is the only one that exists? All the writers with all their imagination have only pondered the smallest fraction of the possible variations." The bookseller glided along beside her, as if glad for the companionship. "You've sparked my curiosity. May I see your special book?"

Marinda hesitated, then set *Clockwork Lives* on the oak table. Mrs. Courier ran her fingers lovingly over the alchemical symbols and embossed gears on its cover. She opened the volume, quietly remarked on the neat writing, the dark red ink. With a quick summary Marinda explained the purpose of the book.

Mrs. Courier was intrigued and delighted. "So you're gathering personal stories in much the same way as I expand my collection here."

"Yes, but when my book is finished, my quest will be over and I can go home."

"Ah, but will you want to?" Mrs. Courier asked.

Marinda blinked. "Of course." She had never imagined otherwise.

"Since we are both avid collectors of stories," said the

middle-aged but not-quite-old woman, "I would be happy to share mine with you." Her voice took on a wistful tone. "I've always wanted to tell someone else, but I didn't have the heart to write it all down."

Marinda agreed, though she couldn't imagine what sort of adventurous life a woman sitting in a bookshop could have had. She slid the golden needle out of the spine of the book, and Mrs. Courier held it up, staring at the sharp tip. "And all it costs me is a slight prick and a drop of blood? Writers have agonized and labored over creating their literature—this makes the task seem all too easy."

She let a drop of blood fall onto the page, and both women watched as the story spun out.

THE
BOOKSELLER'S TALE

I was in love with more than just books. My husband and I share a passion for reading, and that common tie bound us together with a passion for each other that made us perfect companions, like matching bookends on an infinite shelf of favorite stories.

Omar and I first met in a library under the glow of coldfire reading lamps, both interested in the same book, and rather than let one of us go home disappointed, we took the volume to a coffee shop and read to each other. We met again and again for days. We enjoyed the activity so much that we decided on another book when we were finished—both of us choosing the same title without any hints from the other.

People tend to view the past through tinted lenses, a halo effect, remembering only the ideals that we wanted to see, but I'm not deluding myself. Omar and I did indeed have a love and a partnership that rivaled anything in a classic romantic novel. We were giddy with each other.

And that is what makes my tale all the more poignant, all the more sad. With our intimate knowledge of literary tropes and the expectations of a story, Omar and I should have been well aware that a great romance requires a *separation*, a loss. No masterpiece follows the storyline of "They fell in love, they remained happy, and lived out the rest of their days in companionable bliss. The end." The quest for the unattainable is a far more compelling story than a simple happily-ever-after.

Fortunately, my story is not yet over, and I am waiting to see how it all ends. . . .

———◆◆◆———

After Omar and I were married, it seemed like the guiding hand of Fate when we discovered a small bookshop for sale. A curious establishment far from any main commercial thoroughfare, it was cluttered and disorganized, filled with countless oddities. The owner had mysteriously vanished, leaving no heir and no instructions.

It was wonderful.

Omar had a good salary as an assistant manager of a gentleman's clothing shop, and the Watchmaker had given us one hundred gold honeybee coins as a congratulatory gift to start our collaborative lives, as he gave to all newlyweds. We counted our coins, stretched our finances, and saw that we could barely afford the purchase, but Omar and I didn't really have to discuss the question. Both of us knew that the shop was destined to be ours. That was as predictable as a plot twist in a clichéd penny-dreadful novel. We dickered with the property agent who represented the sale of the abandoned bookshop and came to an agreement. We signed the deed, and Omar and I became the new proprietors of Underworld Books.

The doors had been locked before our purchase, and the property agent had only allowed us to look around briefly, but now that we owned the shop, we could explore it all, read every volume if we desired. Neither of us cared about the profitability of selling those obscure books—we just wanted to peruse them to our hearts' content. That made us lackluster business owners, but well-satisfied readers.

On the first day, I cut an apple into wedges for each of us to eat while we explored our store. We looked at the shelves, the overstuffed chairs where readers could enjoy books the way they were meant to be enjoyed.

Behind the front desk in a back room was a peculiar framed dressing mirror that had no reflecting glass, but rather an opalescent surface like rainbows mixed with pearls. On a small curio table next to the moonstone mirror was a volume showing an etched silhouette of the looking glass and the plain but intriguing words *User's Manual*.

The manual contained complex and incomprehensible graphs and tables, explanations of dimensional trigonometry, calibration logs, and activation instructions. The mathematical symbols and derivations meant nothing to us, but on the last page, handwritten words—the former bookshop owner's?—gave advice: "Be careful, but enjoy. There are more stories than one world can contain or produce, but they should be made available to all."

Neither of us knew what to make of this, but Omar and I followed the activation instructions in the book, the patterns and paths marked on the gold frame, curious to see what would happen. We discovered that although the reflective moonstone film made a very poor reflecting glass, it turned out to be an excellent *doorway*.

With an ease that we did not entirely understand, Omar and I passed through the moonstone mirror—and found ourselves in exactly the same place. But not exactly the same. It was subtly different.

Yes, we were still inside Underworld Books, but I realized that the stacks of books were arranged differently, the smell in the air had a faint tinge of oranges, and I saw a plate on the oak desk with a sliced orange, half eaten. But Omar and I had been sharing a crisp *apple* before we toyed with the moonstone mirror.

"One of many possible worlds . . ." I said. "This makes no sense."

Omar picked up a book on the table, a new volume that I was sure hadn't been there a moment ago. He read the title aloud: "*Going Where I Want Instead of Where I Should: My Adventurous Life,* by Hanneke Lakota." He began to read the first page. "The best place to start an adventure is with a quiet, perfect life . . . and someone who realizes that it can't possibly be enough."

I looked at the moonstone mirror, next to which was the same *User's Manual* open to the same page. "Something's different here."

Omar closed the book by Hanneke Lakota and took it with him. "Let's go back to our shop." He and I both agreed, and we stepped to the activated mirror, touched the calibration.

Once we passed back through the moonstone, we were in our bookshop again, with the books arranged as I remembered them, and with the sliced apple on a plate, still so fresh it hadn't even begun to turn brown.

Omar held up the Hanneke Lakota book he had brought with him. "We know that other place existed—and there were so many books."

According to the *User's Manual,* the mirror had many settings—infinite settings—with countless places to explore. The slightest change of angle led to a different endpoint.

We couldn't have been more excited. Not only did we have a full library of books to read in our own shop, we apparently had an infinite number of shops to peruse as well. . . .

—◆—

Even with the distraction of the moonstone mirror, Omar and I still had to take care of our shop, arrange the shelves, check prices, develop an inventory. As business owners, we had to be open for our customers. We posted our hours of operation, and we served our clientele properly.

But each evening we closed promptly at 5:00 p.m. when all the clocks around the city struck their resonant chimes. We locked the door, drew the windowshades, and Omar and I went exploring through the mirror.

Each time we adjusted the looking-glass frame, we emerged into a similar version of Underworld Books. Each time, the place was empty, as if the legitimate owner had just stepped out—or stepped *away* to somewhere else. Each shop had many of the same books as well as different ones, altered editions, versions with the same titles but strange stories inside.

We found previously unknown sequels to famous novels. Omar was pleased to discover additional journals from the adventurer Hanneke Lakota, a simple woman from the quiet town of Barrel Arbor who had sailed across the seas, found lost cities, adventured with pirates, and had done as much as any one life could hold.

Each time we returned to our shop, we brought interesting volumes back with us.

Strangely enough, when we came back to the familiar yet slightly disorienting reality that belonged to us, I felt a strange tingle on my skin, as if someone else had been in *our* bookshop for a time and was now mysteriously gone. Since the store was still new to us, our books were such a clutter, without a full inventory, that we never knew whether any titles were missing. . . .

Underworld Books began to attract a sophisticated clientele, readers who wanted special editions, books that looked the same on the surface, but discriminating readers knew that the words were unlike anything available elsewhere in Albion.

Every bibliophile had heard about a classic insightful study of human psychology, a series of four volumes with the overall title of "Fear"—but the fourth volume had been lost in a fire more than a century ago before its publication, and the other three volumes had been released in reverse order. But in one of those alternate bookshops, I discovered the missing fourth volume of "Fear." I froze, just staring at the cover for a long moment, before snatching it, thrilled to be able to complete the set.

Omar discovered a children's book with lavish illustrations, each one handpainted; the volume itself belonged in an art museum. It was a fairy-tale of good and evil, a battle of the overworld and the underworld, fought by a ferocious black wolf against a snow-white dog.

Our alternate bookshops held so many marvelous secrets that we had little incentive to explore more widely outside the door, but as we adjusted the mirror by greater degrees, tilting the angle more and more, the differences between our worlds became more dramatic.

Once, I finally opened the door of the alternate bookshop and looked out at this parallel Crown City, astonished to discover that the buildings were wrong, the clocktowers in unexpected places, ornamented with highlights of silver rather than the gold that is so prevalent in the Watchmaker's Stability.

Each one of these worlds was another place for us to explore, but Omar and I were not adventurers like Hanneke Lakota. We were readers, armchair explorers—we would let other risk-takers do the adventuring for us.

At a certain point in a story, the plot must take a sudden turn to meet the expectations of dramatic tension, something neither the character nor the reader expects. Unfortunately for us, life imitated art.

Omar and I traveled through the moonstone mirror, exploring yet another version of our universe. Although we left our world with sunny skies and the bright colors of sunset, this one had dark gray clouds and a gloom setting in for premature nightfall. The alternate bookshop was closed and full of shadows; we had to turn on the coldfire lamps in order to look around the shelves and see what interesting titles this shop had for us.

The bright lights must have seemed unexpectedly welcoming in the shadows of the alley. We heard a frantic rapping at the door, then the figure of a woman appeared at the display window. She pressed her palms against the glass, peering in, desperate to see if anyone was inside. She pounded on the door again. "Let me in! You have to help me." Her voice came softly through the wood, tinged with urgency.

Omar glanced at me. We had no choice but to help her. He unlocked the door, and the woman burst through the entry carrying a book. She had long dark hair and loose sweat-damp curls in disarray. She plunged deeper into the bookshop and slammed the door behind her.

I suddenly recognized the woman from the chronograph tipped into the back of many books. "You're Hanneke Lakota!"

"That's correct—and I'm in trouble." She thrust the book into Omar's hands. "Here's another diary. I finished it, but someone spilled my whereabouts. I'm on the run. The Green Watch is right behind me." She turned and looked in alarm at the closed door and the dim alley outside.

"The Green Watch?" Omar asked.

"I just need you to stall them." Hanneke looked frantically around the store. "Take the book and hide it. Publish and distribute it, as you did all the others. But if the Green Watch catches me . . ."

We heard the echoing sounds of boot-heels in the alley. Armed and uniformed men—men wearing *green* official uniforms instead of the familiar red, blue, or black—marched up to the door of Underworld Books.

Hanneke looked toward the back of the shop. "That's your exit, right? Just hold them off. I can lose them in the alleys. I know

Crown City even better than they do." She laughed and bolted back there before we could answer. We heard the bookshop's rear door open then shut as the woman fled out into another street.

Omar had a sparkle in his eye as he thrust the new adventure journal into my hands. "Go through the mirror—I'll be right behind you. Let's give Hanneke a little more time."

I didn't argue with him, since it made perfect sense. I activated the moonstone mirror, as Omar reached the door, throwing the deadbolt just as the green-uniformed Regulators began pounding on the door. "Open up, in the name of the Watchkeeper. You are harboring a known fugitive!"

Watch*keeper?*

The mirror surface rippled with a rainbow pearlescent shine. I heard glass smashing. The Green Watch broke their way through the bookshop door, despite the deadbolt. Abandoning his barricade, Omar rushed toward the mirror, following me.

My pulse was pounding, my heart filled with this great adventure we had inadvertently stumbled upon. I plunged into the mirror—and in my hurry to get through, I bumped the frame on the other side . . . not by much, just the tiniest fraction. But in an infinite number of possible universes, even the tiniest fraction can be split a million ways. I changed the angle of the dimensional reflection.

I emerged into my world, *my* Underworld Books—but Omar, following only seconds behind, arrived someplace slightly different, a universe not quite the same as this one.

Though I waited for him all night, he never came back through the moonstone mirror.

❦

I had to find my husband, and I knew exactly where to look, but finding a needle in a haystack would have been child's play in comparison.

I readjusted the moonstone mirror and dashed back to another Underworld Books, frantic to find him, calling out his name. But I encountered only shelves of silent books and endless stories—stories that I was no longer interested in reading if I had to read them alone.

I tried another universe, and another, sure I was close to where I had left Omar. Each bookstore, one after another, looked the same. I was excited when I found one with shattered glass and a broken doorframe, where the unexpected Green Watch had come chasing after Hanneke Lakota. But Omar was no longer there—if he had ever been there.

Then I understood. While I had gone through the moonstone mirror trying to find him, Omar must have gone looking for *me*. And our paths didn't cross.

I passed through the mirror countless times, month after month after month, never giving up, and it all grows hazy now. I'm not sure I even know which one is my original home anymore.

Then one time when I returned through the glass, I found a note left for me on the curio table that had held the *User's Manual*—a piece of fine stationery with *Underworld Books* as its header and rushed handwriting that I recognized as Omar's penmanship. "I am looking for you, my love. Don't give up hope."

The joy and relief I felt as I held that piece of stationery was indescribable. I knew Omar was out there and safe! I knew he was still searching, and I would keep searching, I didn't think about the probabilities, going for broke. If there was even a ghost of a chance, I would find my love. . . .

I went to the bookshop desk, found a fresh sheet of stationery and wrote a note of my own, promising Omar that I was here, and I was elsewhere—and I would not stop looking for him.

I went through the mirror again to another Underworld Books, calling his name. And then another.

How do you measure progress when you have infinite possibilities? Desperation soon leads to exhaustion, and I realized I could not flail about through alternate worlds forever.

If Omar were here, he would have helped me to study the problem, convinced me that all is for the best. But if Omar were *here*, then I would have no problem at all! I tried to imagine how he would think, where he would go, how he would search for me, but we really had no common data point.

I ranged farther, exploring other worlds, deviating from the norm of my usual existence. My chances of finding him this far out of alignment were vanishingly small, but it was also part of an adventure. I think he would have been proud of me.

As I searched, I found worlds where Albion was not the green and idyllic place I knew so well, but had a grittier and more industrial incarnation. Instead of watching over his people from the high clocktower in Chronos Square, the Watchmaker lived in a lighthouse in the clouds, and rather than efficient Regulators, he had simpering gnomish attendants that did not seem efficient at all.

There were bizarre worlds, where the coldfire was red instead of blue, where alchemy itself operated on different principles. Even wilder incarnations, where our bookshop was dark and abandoned, the windows shuttered, the door barred—and outside, visible through smoke-grimed window glass, I could see pyramids and temples instead of clocktowers. And the dusty long-undisturbed books on the shelves bore a prominent symbol not of the Watchmaker's honeybee, but of a bold red star. . . .

Years went by, measured by countless slightly different calendars. I still owned the bookshop, and so did Omar. I still ranged through the moonstone mirror as often as I could. I left him notes, and occasionally I found his letters back to me. Once, he had written an entire diary for me, a treasure trove of love and information, telling of all his adventures, all the places he had visited . . . which seemed remarkably like the places I had visited. We had been in the same place, and I could sense his presence, but it wasn't at the same time.

Yet.

I would keep trying.

He continues to look for me, and I keep looking for him—and oh, the places I have seen along the way! It has been thirty-two years since last I saw Omar.

But what does time have to do with anything, when there are infinite possibilities? My story is not over yet.

CHAPTER 10

Marinda sat in the bookshop, in a comfortable chair reserved for readers. Mrs. Courier had made her a cup of piquant peppermint tea that she drank as she read the story. Compelled, Marinda absorbed the entire tale, and when she finally looked up, she felt a stinging moisture in her eyes.

The bookseller was smiling at her with a wistful expression. "One does not give up hope," Mrs. Courier said. "I, for one, believe that some tales do have happy endings." Then she showed Marinda another scrap of paper, covered with handwriting. A man's handwriting.

Omar had written, *I will* find you, my love. Someday.

Mrs. Courier reread the note that she had obviously read countless times already, then she smiled at Marinda and said, "I know this is a true story." She folded the sheet away and tucked it close to her heart.

Before leaving Underworld Books, Marinda purchased one of the old copies of *Before the Stability* and, because she felt it was necessary, *The Watchmaker's Official Autobiography*. After she brought the books back to her approved lodgings, she realized that she had taken her first steps toward building a library of her own. When she returned to her cottage in Lugtown, she could place those books next to the ones her father had lovingly collected throughout his lifetime.

Instead of reading the new books she had purchased, however, Marinda leafed through *Clockwork Lives* again. Previously, she had despaired of filling all those blank pages, but now, rather than seeing her task as a marathon with no end in sight, she found herself looking forward to the other tales that awaited her.

The stories gave Marinda a new perspective on her own mission. She was inconvenienced by the quest, certainly, but other people had far more noisy and less perfect lives than hers, and *they* managed to hold on. Marinda could do no less. Her father had not doubted her abilities.

She decided that this special book should contain stories that were *worthy* of being told. She wanted it to be a *good* book, not just a *full* book.

In the bright morning, the next story caught Marinda's attention with a clash of cymbals and a swirl of rhythmic taps and pounding. A dapper man with dark hair and a mustache, black suit, and a bowler hat used a polished walking stick as a pointer, drawing attention to the source of the noise.

"I know what you lack, my friends—music! The Watchmaker has given us plenty of gold, but not enough songs." With a drumroll and a swish, his contraption began to perform. "I am Professor Russell, and this is my fabulous percussor."

The man had built an artificial creation that made her father's clockwork Regulators look like simple toys. The percussor had a burnished brass body core and a polished oblong head, but its most prominent features were its articulated arms, each of which had an excess of joints. Each "hand" held a drumstick, precision-aligned. A host of different-sized drums surrounded the main body, tilted at various angles, as if it were all one unit, drummer and drums. Coldfire pulsed through the device, and steam vented out as the clockwork percussor began to move, swinging one stick down, then another, building up a rhythm.

At first Marinda was just curious, since she had never really listened to a drum performance before, but soon she felt something more than just the obvious beat—the rhythm's physical insistence *affected* her. It made her off balance, yet at the same time grounded her.

Objectively, she could hear a single drum pattern repeating on top of another, then interlacing with a third, all of which added up to something more. Marinda felt the deep notes throb inside her, while middle-range beats resonated in her chest. Rapid-fire patterns tapped across her skull, electrifying her mind and body, and something about the combination—the cadence, the lilt, the syncopation of the rhythm—set her arms and legs twitching. Indeed, some of the children and young people around her were smiling and waving their arms and legs to the beat. Then there was the *geometry* of the performance—some of the sounds appeared in midair or sparkled off over her head, while others seemed to echo from faraway streets.

The dapper man stood back, holding up his walking stick like a referee's baton. Marinda noticed that his hand trembled in a manner that had nothing to do with vibrations from the machine's frenetic drumming.

His amazing percussor vented steam, and the inner coldfire glowed brighter as the drumming grew louder, faster, more intense. The crowd stomped and clapped and stared in delight. With a flourish and a rimshot, the contraption finished, then lifted its multiple drumsticks and articulated arms, as if for a round of applause—which the audience gave.

The professor doffed his bowler hat and placed it on the ground before him so that satisfied customers could toss in coins. Marinda added one of her own, then stayed behind as the people dispersed.

Professor Russell fiddled with the valve controls, checking his clockwork percussor to make certain that it had not somehow damaged itself during the exuberant performance. Glancing up at Marinda, he gave her a surprised smile. "Thank you for your generosity, miss! I saw you donate a full gold honeybee, and that allows me to add new components, maintain my percussor, even expand his drum kit."

"It's very fascinating," Marinda said. "In fact, I find you fascinating."

He chuckled. "The percussor is my masterpiece. He's far more interesting than I am."

"Yes, but you built it. That must make you fascinating as well."

He reached out a hand to shake hers, and she felt his nerve tremors seemingly down to the bone.

"If I could ask something of you, sir? It's an odd request, I know, but I hope you'll indulge me."

"Odd requests are more interesting than routine ones," he said. "What can I do for you?"

She took out *Clockwork Lives*. "I would like to include your tale in my book, and I have an unusual way of obtaining it."

The percussor's multiple drumstick arms lowered as the last steam vented out. Professor Russell chuckled. "Believe me, I've had enough experience with being unusual."

Marinda removed her golden needle.

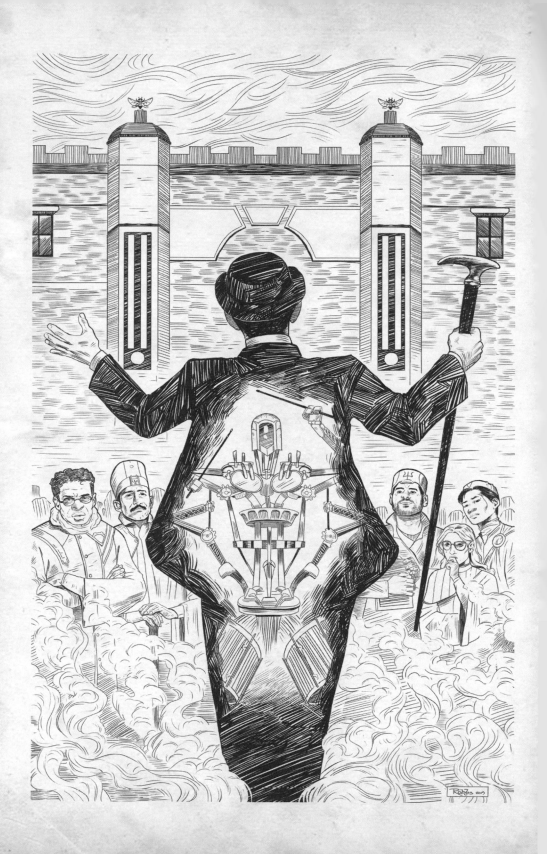

THE
PERCUSSOR'S TALE

The first time I saw the Clockwork Angels, they inspired me. I had just moved to Crown City to become an instructor at the Alchemy College, and the city was full of strangers. When thousands of people crowded shoulder to shoulder in Chronos Square to see the Angels, I felt a sense of community, a sense of anticipation.

After full night fell and the stars appeared overhead, the people filled the city square, muttering with excitement and love, vibrant with anticipation. Wisps of sweet-smelling smoke wafted from vents in the ground, vapors exhaled from the underground coldfire nexus that powered Crown City. The fumes made us dizzy, disoriented, but also euphoric—ready for the Angels. Globes of coldfire light hung suspended around Chronos Square, bathing the crowd in angelic illumination. The Watchtower, with its great clock, stood over the crowd like a fortress of benevolent time and order.

As if from an invisible signal, we all held our breath, turned our faces upward, and watched the high tower doors ratchet open like curtains drawn back on a cosmic play. The immense Angels glided forward on smoothly oiled gears, four beautiful, ethereal figures carved from permanent stone, the most perfect machinery, animated by quintessence. They were flawless.

They spread their clockwork wings, and one after another they dispensed pearls of wisdom that might have seemed like platitudes when read in skeptical daylight. Even now, that night's recitation is engraved in my memory, spinning out in the unearthly voices of the Angels in turn—"*Be kind, for everyone you meet is fighting a hard battle.*" With the dizzying smoke around us and the euphoria of the crowd, though, the words penetrated our hearts as well as our ears. "*Beginning a task is hard. Finishing a task is harder still, but far more satisfying.*"

The people gasped. Some of them wept. And when the Angels raised their wings, we all lifted our hands in a fruitless attempt to reach them.

It was amazing. It was a miracle . . . and yet I realized the performance was missing a fundamental element. I was inspired then. I *knew* what I had to do, why I had been brought here to Crown City.

The Clockwork Angels captivated us all—but there was no music. I could improve on that.

Although it had no bearing on my career assignment, I'd always had perfect rhythm. I could keep time with absolute precision, like the unwavering pulse of a sleeping infant. I could feel the beat of everyday activities. Tick-tock. I needed no metronome. When I couldn't sit still, I would tap out an impatient beat on a tabletop or on my leg, which annoyed nearby people. They didn't hear the same intrinsic beat of the world. They called me restless, fidgety.

I was a respectable man from a respectable family in a respectable town on the outskirts of Crown City. I studied to become a professor, learned the basics of alchemy. My family paid the appropriate fees, and after I passed the appropriate tests, I was brought in as an instructor to the Alchemy College, which should have been enough for any man.

I settled into the instructors' dormitory, comfortable in my new rooms and ready for a new school year. I pattered out my satisfaction on a tabletop, prepared my lesson plans, and—now that I'd been inspired by the Clockwork Angels—considered adding music to the curriculum. Did not an adept drummer "keep perfect time"? And wasn't that exactly what the Watchmaker wanted?

My classes were like all the other first-year classes, with my novice pupils performing standardized experiments, testing reactant powders and metals, growing crystals from saturated solutions, dissolving organic substances in the most potent acids. I taught them how the world's basic elements could be assembled and reassembled into any imaginable substance. The movements of molecules had their own rhythm.

Throughout my first semester, there was very little music at the College, save for the drumbeats I heard in my own head. Music wasn't forbidden in Albion, but neither was it encouraged. The common people had their own instruments, their own songs, but the Watchmaker himself would never express his happiness by bursting into a tune. He simply considered music irrelevant.

When poring over old class records, I was surprised to discover a forgotten part of the curriculum, a discretionary class that no professor had taught for some years, and thus it had fallen into obscurity. "Fundamentals of Music." It was perfect! I immediately contacted Professor Gruber, the chief alchemist-priest, requesting permission to teach the music course, saying that it would broaden the students' experience and knowledge.

Professor Gruber was skeptical and, above all, curious. He summoned me to his office. "There must be a reason this course is no longer taught," he said.

I had to force myself to sit respectfully still and not tap out a beat on my leg. "Perhaps because there was no qualified teacher, sir. I studied the old syllabus, and I believe I have the proper knowledge."

The chief priest frowned down at the papers. "I'm not sure, Professor Russell. Such a class might distract the students from more important pursuits. Music in the abstract? Think about the average person. What use would they have for rhythms and melodies? At the Alchemy College, we focus on science."

"Then I will teach the *science* of music, sir," I said. "Don't you see? Music *is* mathematics—so many intricate systems, the orderly arrangement of notes and chords like formulas, the logarithmic interrelation of harmonies, the geometric patterns and structures of the orchestration—aligned to a strict physical premise of *time*. Surely the Watchmaker would approve.

"The conductor's tempo is the clock, unwavering and unstoppable. Like a grand-complication timepiece, each instrument in the orchestra must play its part in synchrony, each musician meshed in that perfect, ticking pendulum. And there is the emotional resonance in the listener—like *alchemy*." I paused, saw to my dismay that much of my excitement was lost on him.

"It still sounds like only a metaphor to me," said my superior, but he indulged me with a long sigh, signing the paper so that I could prepare my class. "We will consider it an experiment."

My first class was small, only eleven students, and five of them were there as their fourth choice since they had not qualified for the topics that interested them. But I was happy because the class itself allowed me to study and refine my own knowledge, quantifying the things I knew by instinct and giving names to the rhythms I could sense in the universe around me.

And it established a precedent, giving me opportunities for more advanced classes.

But I needed the devices to create music. I discovered that if I described a musical instrument to my colleagues as a *scientific* problem—a resonant cylinder of a certain fundamental note, a membrane with tunable qualities, a soundbox with certain harmonics—the younger alchemists would take it as a technical challenge appropriate for the higher-level classes.

Soon I had invented and assembled an orchestra's worth of tuned drums, chromatic bells, steam-powered horns, and more. Long strings stretched across whole rooms, each one plucked by rotating plectrums driven by coldfire steam.

But I had to teach my students something the Alchemy College considered "worthwhile." Those grand designs I heard and visualized would have to wait until I could express them in some greater arena. An audience. But that day would come. Surely it would be perfect enough for the Clockwork Angels.

So I instructed my students in harmony and melody, but the study of *rhythm* excited me most of all. At the front of the classroom I set up an arrangement of drums, and I would start each class with one big *boom* on a mounted bass drum. Having attracted their attention, I silently counted a slow three bars, then hit it again. *Boom!* After the same interval, I struck the drum a third time, and by then we could all feel a pulse.

As the students listened, I added a counterrhythm on a small, snappy drum, with the bass drum still punctuating every third one. A foot pedal activated a drone with rippling harp-like harmonies, and I brought in quick flurries of "rat-a-tats" on small melodic drums. Seemingly out of time, they slashed across the pulse in a jagged onslaught that raised my own adrenalin.

Some of my students showed a genuine aptitude for the subject, but most exhibited a just-as-genuine lack of interest—not hostile, merely perplexed.

After all my labors and my technical successes with the new instrument designs, I was surprised to become an object of scorn and ridicule among the faculty members. Some of the senior professors mocked me for wasting time with something as esoteric and useless as music—"corrupting our youth" they said, "distracting them from more practical matters when they should be trying to strengthen the Watchmaker's Stability." I defended myself by presenting the mathematical basis for musical theory, but they just sniffed, calling music a mere "pseudoscience," unlike the rigorously proven science of alchemy.

After much justification and debate, I convinced Professor Gruber to extend my class for another semester. I was so pleased with his answer that I felt jittery.

But when the jitters continued throughout the next month, I sensed that something entirely different might be wrong—with *me*. I held out my hand and watched it shake and tremble, as if my nerves were fighting against a thousand clashing drumbeats. It frightened me. I could make the tremors stop by sheer force of will, but they would return. I told no one, but my fear increased as the dread realization began to dawn on me.

I was losing my rhythm.

Though music was my passion, most of my teaching was in basic alchemistry. I would walk among the laboratory tables and watch as the students crushed mineral powders, dissolved salts, and burned crystallized distillates. I made my students perform each step themselves, and, in that way, I could hide my tremors.

It was some kind of degenerative nerve disease. When I saw the best physicians in Crown City, they had no cure for my malady. They gave me potions to counteract the tremors, but the drugs only made me logy, my tongue thick, my vision blurred. I don't know if the tremors stopped, but I was too lethargic to notice them. I decided that was not an acceptable cure at all.

Yet without the potions, my condition grew worse. When I tried to perform interlocking counterrhythms with my connected musical instruments, my fingers, hands, and feet betrayed me—lost their rhythm, lost their time. The tick-tock of my life had slipped a gear tooth. I could no longer control what I needed to do. My sadness increased. How would I ever present the Watchmaker with my grand dream of music for the Clockwork Angels if my own body was an asynchronous wreck?

In my private offices I had a metronome that kept perfect time, swinging back and forth, clicking off the beats. Always before, such devices were superfluous to me because I could hear the rhythm so perfectly in my head. But as I sat by myself holding my wooden stick and trying to match the beats, my hands trembled so much that I kept missing time.

Few of my students could hear the intrinsic beat as anything more than theoretical—they didn't even know what they were missing. But I had always heard that constant tick-tock drumbeat, as reliable as the pounding of my own heart. And now that I was losing it, I found the idea far more heart-wrenching than never to have known it at all.

It was terrifying.

But fear can either destroy a person or make him rise to new levels. I went out to see the Clockwork Angels again, and as I raised my hands with all the others, dizzy from the sweet smoke in Chronos Square, their words poured into my mind. *"All is for the best in this best of all possible worlds."* At first the tears streaming down my cheek were hot and bitter—all was not for the best in *my* world— but soon I wept for a different reason than all those other ecstatic worshippers. I had been inspired again! I still knew what I wanted to do, but I would have to achieve it in a different way.

The Angels, those perfect clockwork goddesses built by the Watchmaker, had surpassed what he himself could do. Though the loving Watchmaker was himself slightly more than human—we all knew that—the Clockwork Angels exceeded even him.

Now that my body had demonstrated its frailty, its unreliability, maybe I could create a substitute as well. Something better than myself.

If every clock ticked out a perfect beat, then perhaps a clockwork mechanism could be expanded into a machine to keep time with the music I felt in my heart, a clockwork drummer whose very existence was to demonstrate the mystic rhythms of the universe for everyone to hear. Not just a metronome's mathematical perfection, but shifting rhythms that pushed and pulled like gravity, tides, or solar winds.

A rhythm could drive forward with intense energy, or relax into a gentle cadence. And oh, the tension when two such rhythms were combined, the upbeats straining against the downbeats. Sublime! If I could not be that drummer to teach the students and show the Watchmaker, then my artificial percussor could do so in my stead.

I went to the chief alchemy priest to give him the sad news that I no longer felt adequate to teach the rhythm and music class. "My health is deteriorating, sir. I have seen several physicians already. And it would be best if . . ."

Professor Gruber made an annotation in his logbook, but didn't seem the least bit disturbed. "All is for the best, Professor Russell. Take each day and use the extra class hour to rest and recuperate."

Yes, I needed the free time, but I didn't choose to rest. With maddeningly shaky hands, I designed my creation, assembling a thousand small pieces of basic steam technology, hydraulic engineering, interlocking clockworks, based on all those instruments and mechanisms I'd asked the engineers to design for my first music class. Wheels within wheels motivated armatures, pistons, ball joints, spiral arrays that ratcheted down to finer and finer movements.

It would be perfect, exactly what I needed the Watchmaker to see.

During the intricate assembly process, I had to fabricate stabilizing tools because the tiny screws and bolts fell from my shaking hands. But those who live with adversity are forced to learn either patience or despair, and I refused to despair as I saw my beautiful percussor take shape before me.

I used muffled caps on the drumsticks so the racket would not disturb my fellow professors—or even alert them to what I was doing. I added coldfire to the small boiler inside the torso chamber, powered up the mechanism, and set the articulated arms in motion: smaller gears for faster tempo, larger pistons for heavy bass drumbeats. Making adjustments, I felt a growing delight despite the fact that my own tremors increased, possibly due to exhaustion or stress.

The percussor was my surrogate rhythm keeper. He could do what I could no longer accomplish, and he kept perfect rhythm. I knew he would exceed even my best.

Seven months later the artificial drummer was complete. I had tested and programmed for all possible tempos and counter-rhythms. Clockwork controllers allowed every rhythmic subdivision or polyrhythm, and could trigger any number of sound producers—drums, horns, strings, and cymbals, all of my own invention. Ah, if this could be integrated into the Clockwork Angels!

But the percussor still wasn't ready for his debut. He had the programming and the well-oiled intermeshed gears, but he was missing one thing. While music is a science, as I had demonstrated by deconstructing it into pure mathematics, music is also *art*—and for that my percussor needed a soul.

As a professor of alchemy, I had access to forbidden materials, including the College's well-stocked chemical vault, and I had the authority to requisition any items I needed. The Red Guard stationed at the door knew me, and he assumed I must be preparing for another laboratory class. I knew exactly what I needed.

Inside the vault, the well-labeled shelves were stacked high and stocked well with all the known combinations of elements, arranged according to a rudimentary periodic table. But what I needed rested on the highest shelf in a sealed case marked with a honeybee symbol—precious, immeasurably valuable, and so misunderstood.

I climbed a ladder to reach the high shelf, set the tumblers of the lock with the proper combination that only alchemy professors were allowed to know, and opened the container with hands shaking even more than usual. Bathed in the pale white light that was life itself, I removed a tiny fragment of the stored *quintessence*.

That was exactly what my percussor needed.

When I prepared my demonstration for important faculty members, I invited the Watchmaker himself. The other professors thought it was just a courtesy, never expecting him to come, but I claimed that this was a most vital exhibition, something of importance to the Clockwork Angels. I needed to show him for myself—how else could I make my case?

I felt weak with relief when the ancient man arrived accompanied by three members of his Black Watch and the highest-order alchemist-priests, as well as Professor Gruber. Even if I hadn't suffered from the degenerative palsy, seeing the Watchmaker in person might have set my entire body shaking.

But I was ready. The precious quintessence had the effect of strengthening me as well, energizing me, and I felt more in tune with my own rhythm. At least temporarily. I would have used more of the substance myself for such a crucial event, but I didn't dare. My percussor needed it.

For the demonstration, I had set up my clockwork drummer in one of the empty auditoriums. The percussor was all brass and copper, bright with coldfire, venting trickles of steam as the boiler built up to optimal energy levels. Regardless of my own anxiety, the mechanism would drive through the performance without a flaw. My multi-armed percussor ratcheted into its initial position, articulated arms bent, drumsticks raised, all components of the kit arrayed around the central torso. Hidden within, the quintessence burned bright.

My job was to introduce the percussor and then wait nervously as my creation performed. Would the Watchmaker hear the rhythms and see what was missing in his Clockwork Angels? I could only hope!

"My gracious observers, at this college I have taught a class in the mathematics of music, the mystic rhythms of the universe, the clockwork beat that ticks away inside all of us. But my own human frailty makes it impossible to achieve the perfection that existed only in my imagination. The best part of being human is that we can strive to create something better than ourselves." I nodded toward the great man. "Just as our loving Watchmaker created the Clockwork Angels, which embody more grace and beauty than any mortal can hope to achieve, this device can add even more grandeur to the Clockwork Angels, fill the silence that accompanies each performance, and make them *better*."

The Watchmaker looked at me fixedly, as if I had insulted him, then turned his attention to the clockwork percussor. His ancient parchment skin was drawn tight across his face. I had hoped for a paternal smile.

I felt the tremors returning, and I badly wished I had another bit of the quintessence, just a small dose, to calm my nerves, but right now all of the precious substance was inside the percussor.

I stepped back, swallowed hard, and activated the percussor. My heart was pounding louder than any drum I'd ever heard. "This piece is titled 'Exaltation.'"

Just as I used to begin my earliest classes at the Alchemy College, the percussor seized their attention with a single deep *boom!* The silence that followed seemed to hang heavy, expectant, impatient. Then came the next loud *boom!* as the bass drum continued to repeat in slow pulses.

Other instruments joined in—rhythmic slashes and melodic bursts, expanding chords and flourishes of bass notes. The percussor was a melody of mechanical movement, smooth joints, gliding pistons, all in perfect rhythm. My amplification chambers could project a sound across the room or make it hover in midair above the listeners' heads. I smiled to watch them swivel in unison when their eyes were drawn by the acoustic illusion, as if they would *see* the sound I had manifested there. Even the Watchmaker turned his head.

I even dabbled with how to create color in the sound—just tinges so far, but I hoped some of my listeners—especially the Watchmaker—might sense an azure chord, a prismatic arpeggio, or a harp gliss that sprayed out in golden sparks. With coldfire steam that emanated from the mechanism I created sensations of cold and heat, damp or arid air, which further amplified the music's power.

The themes were based on the Angels' symbolic identities, the first four movements titled "Light," "Sea," "Sky," and "Land." My music sparkled and glowed, and then waves of sound receded to the back of the auditorium, even as gentle zephyrs swept down like waterfalls from the corners. A pounding whirlwind built to a peak of tension, then I triggered a release—a long sustain into a slower tempo, a softer dynamic, in subtle variations of minor chords.

I created monumental landforms out of sound so that the listener sensed immense chasms, towering mesas, and vast formations of red rock. I built fantastic landscapes from tales of the great deserts overseas and the legendary lands of the far north, Ultima Thule—a mirage of tremendous glaciers under dark skies that danced with shifting veils of colored light, then a tower of sculpted rock, solitary and eternal, with stars wheeling around its upraised finger.

Gradually, I raised the percussor's pitch and the tempo, and the music raced faster, louder. I created darkness, a chill, then slashes of white heat. This began the fifth and most important movement of my symphony: "Quintessence," and its musical language and images might only be understood by the Watchmaker. Chords swirled around the room like desert dust devils, while frantic bursts of notes flashed like lightning. Volleys of drums thundered, while others beat down like heavy rain, or dripped from imaginary eaves. A chorus of ethereal voices seemed to cry out against the tempest.

Forgetting myself and my audience, forgetting everything but the music, I had programmed the crescendo to the very edge of restraint and control, then the percussor concluded with a massive chord that faded away into a flicker of purple fireflies before diminishing into a dark blue forest and the gentle fall of diamond snowflakes.

As the last vibrations fell silent, I stood dizzy, with shaking joints. I knew it had been good. I turned to look at the faculty and, more importantly, at the Watchmaker. Surely he had experienced and understood! Some of the other professors were smiling, but most remained stony-faced. The Watchmaker himself sat erect with a slightly puzzled frown. No one spoke. Everyone waited to hear the Watchmaker's assessment.

Finally, he said, "It is an admirable example of clockwork motion and the intricate synergy of components, but I fail to grasp the purpose. What does it do? How would you add this to my Angels? And why?"

"It is . . . *music*, sir. Rhythms to touch an audience, to move them. Imagine it in Chronos Square, with the Angels watching from above."

The Watchmaker sat still. "I've never been fond of music, though over the years I have come to tolerate it. I realize that some of the lower classes take comfort in it, however, and to deny them that small pleasure would be counter-productive to the Stability. But I would expect the students in my Alchemy College, and my professors, to be more concerned with important matters. I fail to see how this would improve the Clockwork Angels at all."

The Watchmaker stood up along with his black-uniformed Regulators, preparing to leave. "Your grasp of clockwork engineering is indeed impressive, Professor Russell, but we will not be using this device to accompany my Angels. I would suggest you devote your efforts toward something more tangibly useful to my Stability."

He departed, leaving the other professors to mutter amongst themselves, reaffirming what the Watchmaker had said, now that he had said it. They all departed, leaving me alone in the echoing lecture hall with my magnificent but supposedly useless clockwork percussor.

———◆———

Despite my disappointment, I took heart from the smiles I had seen on some of the faces. While many were deaf to the rhythms, others did hear and enjoy them. But my music would never be a part of the Clockwork Angels.

The Watchmaker's lukewarm response was a crushing blow, but he had not *forbidden* any further performances of the percussor. In fact, he had complimented me on my design and engineering skill. Maybe the students would learn something from the mechanics of my demonstration device, even if they couldn't hear the drumbeats for what they were.

I decided to move my grand mechanism and let others see for themselves.

But my body had not stopped shaking, and I felt weak. I couldn't complete my mission unless I controlled myself, and again my best recourse in this difficult situation would be to rely on artificial means. I wanted to move quickly, before word spread throughout the College.

I returned to the alchemy storage vault, presented my standard authorization to the Red Guard. "I require another sample of quintessence for a very important experiment." He didn't question me; the Red Guard had never questioned me. My legs were wobbling as I climbed the ladder to the high shelf. Even the Alchemy

College had only a limited supply of quintessence—but I had my needs, which I considered sufficient.

The marvelous, shining substance felt warm and effervescent as I removed a droplet the size of a pearl, and applied it to my trembling hands, my arms. I felt immediate relief. I was steady again, seemingly younger, and ready.

But even quintessence couldn't last. I would accept what I had now, and I would make it count. I hoped that more of the students would feel and recognize the rhythms.

I reassembled my clockwork percussor in the courtyard between the student dormitory and the looming laboratory building. The process took hours, during which time curious observers watched me, muttering about "odd Professor Russell." I ignored them as I tinkered and adjusted, calibrated the articulated arms and ran my trembling fingertips across the percussor's smooth copper head, the rounded cylinder of the torso that contained a tiny fragment of quintessence. I felt a greater stamina now, and I kept going without rest.

"What is it, Professor?" asked one of my students from the second-term mathematics of music class. "An industrial machine? A device designed for the manufacturing lines?"

"Not at all—something much better."

I hadn't summoned a crowd, but they came anyway, hundreds of students ranging from the freshest novices to the elite graduates. They all watched me as I prepared the percussor, tested the pressure gauges, and finally turned to survey my audience. I gave no introduction this time. I would let the drumbeats speak for themselves.

Pounding out a long sequence of irresistible rhythms, my percussor performed so magnificently that I was swept away in the beat, feeling my pulse increase. Even my returning tremors matched the tempo—the music made me feel as alive as the stolen quintessence did. Some students joined the rhythm, patting their sides with their hands, tapping their feet, but most looked disoriented.

When the percussor finished its intricate programming, the last of the steam vented out, its armatures reset themselves and folded the drumsticks close to the central torso. Silence rang loudly in the air.

There was some applause, but it died quickly. I looked around to see a gathering circle of frowning alchemist-priests. Behind them came a group of uniformed Regulators, and my heart sank.

———◆———

I was stripped of my professorship, my classes assigned to other instructors; my recalcitrance was bad enough, but when it was discovered that I had fraudulently procured some of the vital quintessence, I was told to pack up and leave the Alchemy College.

Even with my disgrace, however, I didn't let myself fall into the depths of despair, knowing the great—even impossible—thing I had achieved. In one small measure of mercy, the Watchmaker did allow me to keep the core of my clockwork percussor. His cryptic message said, *My alchemists and my Regulators have no interest in your device, but the average may have some use for it. I only regret that your obvious talents could not have been directed toward something worthwhile.*

Worthwhile . . . If only the music could have joined the Angels high above the city square.

———◆———

Years have passed, and only this remains. A much smaller device than my original elaborate construction, not much more than a sideshow act, really, but it is the best I can do now. And my percussor is still very good. When the people come to see each performance, some of them can hear what I hear.

The Regulators do not bother me as my device performs to crowds in the streets. Despite the degeneration of my own nerves and muscles, the percussor rolls out the rhythm perfectly, every single time, never missing the tiniest beat, exactly the perfection I had intended to create. It has become more and more difficult to obtain the spark of quintessence my percussor needs—that *we* need—but we manage.

I can still program my percussor, change his performance, add new complexities to the drumming, but he does more on his own—marvelously so. Perfection in the mathematics of music requires two things, both passion and precision. Because the heart of his mechanism still has that fragment of quintessence inside, that tiny bit of soul, now he can *improvise*.

CHAPTER 11

The next day, the Magnusson Carnival Extravaganza was ripe with stories—Marinda could tell by the smell in the air, the sound of the roustabouts setting up in Chronos Square, the colors of the tents, the exotic people intent on incomprehensible tasks. She also saw smiles of anticipation on the spectators who came early to watch the carnies prepare for their Solstice Festival exhibition.

She counted her remaining money. Marinda was always frugal, but she had no idea how to budget for the task of filling her book with tales. But as she looked at the marvelous carnival, she considered the price of admission a worthwhile investment.

A woman in a lavender polka-dotted dress sold tickets at the gate. Lavish brown hair fell past her shoulders and a just-as-lavish brown beard covered her cheeks and chin, accentuated by bright ribbons tied in perky bows. Marinda was fascinated by the sight of the bearded lady. Oh yes, the carnival must surely be full of tales, although the mere existence of interesting facial hair did not guarantee an interesting story.

The bearded lady responded to her stare with a good-natured laugh. "I'm just the first of many sights you'll see inside there."

After buying her ticket, Marinda hesitated and turned back to the bearded lady. "I'm collecting stories to fill my book." She was about to explain about the golden needle, the drop of blood, the alchemically treated pages, but a queue had formed behind her, impatient people eager to see the carnival.

The bearded lady's gaze flicked past her. "You'll find plenty of tales inside. Go seek them out."

The carnival was a colorful and entertaining show that came in with a noisy splash of excitement and then went away again, leaving ripples of delighted people who got back to their normal lives. They had been touring Albion for nearly two centuries, since shortly after the Stability.

Spread across Chronos Square were tents and steamwagons, a giant Ferris wheel that looked like a clock gear, and games of chance. Marinda saw an enclosed booth painted a cherry red, in which sat an ancient crone who told fortunes. A rail-thin, spread-eagled woman spun on a large wheel, riding around and around as a blindfolded knife thrower hurled daggers at her, barely missing her each time.

A man ran a fast-paced game of chance, moving shells across a checkerboard table covered with pictures of snakes and arrows. Finding him momentarily without a customer, she set her book on his gameboard and explained her quest, but the skeptical carny considered the whole idea a scam, and not a very good one. "Believe me, I know scams. You'd best be on your way."

Three goofy clowns in bright pantaloons and ridiculous costumes poked fun at the audience members and performed pratfalls. She spoke to the clowns, but they pantomimed horror at the suggestion of being pricked by a needle. Other carnival attendees were leery of her when she asked for a drop of blood.

Then she heard the loud clang of a bell and the laughter of children. She wandered toward the sound and saw a hugely muscled man with dark hair, chocolate skin, and a bemused smile. He wore a striped exercise shirt that covered his torso but left his arms bare to show his bulging biceps. The strongman stood next to a high-striker game; he had just rung the bell by slamming a gigantic mallet onto the base and accelerating a puck up to the bell.

He placed his hands on his hips and watched as three of the children struggled with the giant mallet, but even together they could not lift it. A banner near the large man named him Golson, "The Strongest Man in the World." Next to his small yellow pavilion she saw a barbell and impressive stacks of round iron plates.

"Come on, you can lift it, lads!" he encouraged, and the three boys strained to pick up the mallet. In unison, they lifted the oversized hammer and let it fall onto the base of the high striker, using gravity more than their scrawny muscles. When the mallet hit, the puck lifted only a disappointing foot, then dropped back down to the ground.

"Let me show you how it's done." Golson seized the wooden handle of the mallet and raised it over his shoulder. When he saw Marinda watching him, the strongman gave her a wink and let out a mammoth grunt as he swung the mallet as if he meant to crack the world in half. The mallet slammed into the platform with the force of an earthquake, and the puck rocketed upward.

The resounding clang and the instantaneous laughter from the boys did not drown out the loud wooden *crack* of the mallet handle as it split along its length and shivered into sharp wooden splinters. The handle came apart in Golson's hands, and the mallet head went spinning off in a lazy pirouette to crash into his pavilion.

The children gasped, and Golson dropped the shattered handle, reeling away. He looked down at his huge hands, which had begun to bleed, as if he couldn't believe what had just happened.

"Show's over for now." Marinda shooed the boys away as

she hurried toward Golson. "It seems you don't know your own strength."

He shook his head, looking baffled. He spoke in a deliberate voice, as if he had to lift each word like a small weight. "Oh, I know my strength—I measure it every day. But I misjudged the strength of the mallet handle."

"Let me see that." She took Golson's bleeding hand, plucked splinters from his palm, and led him to his pavilion, where he kept several cloth headbands. Marinda used one to dab at his bleeding, but minor, cuts.

The strongman sounded disappointed. "Sore hands will make it hard to lift the full weight on the barbells."

Marinda looked at the stacks of cast-iron weights, trying to imagine how immensely heavy they were. She doubted she could have lifted a barbell with even one plate on each side. Beside the stack of plates, one set was bound together with a chain and padlocked through the central hole. "Why are those two kept separate? Are you unable to lift them?"

"Maybe I could, maybe I couldn't." Golson shrugged. "I'm satisfied with my abilities and with who I am. I keep them locked like that so I don't lose track of my limits. I'm already the strongest man in the world—isn't that enough? Why do I need to be stronger still? The chain makes sure I don't put too many plates on."

"That's quite an unusual conclusion. How did you come to it?"

Golson gave her a sad smile. "That's a long story."

Marinda looked at his injured hands where the bleeding was not yet staunched. "I would love to have your story." She opened *Clockwork Lives* to the next blank page after the Percussor's Tale. "And I have a very efficient way for you to tell it to me."

THE
STRONGMAN'S TALE

It started on a road to a neighboring farm—a rival farm—with a cart that was loaded with rocks—*overloaded with rocks*—and a wheel that couldn't carry the burden it was supposed to carry.

My father sent me out from our farm after dark, even though a nasty storm was brewing. The rain didn't bother him, so he said it shouldn't bother me, even though I was the one out on the road. The air smelled wet already, and the rumble of thunder warned me not to go. Flashes of chain lightning across the sky made me uneasy, but when I asked if I could wait until the storm had passed, maybe leave just before dawn, my father and brothers sneered. My oldest brother Seth punched me in the shoulder, hard, and not at all playfully. "We all have to pull our weight for the family, Tam," he said. "This is your job, and you have to do it."

The job always had to be done at night, so old Farmer Sheckel wouldn't see me. If he did, then I would really be in trouble. Farmer Sheckel suspected what we were doing with those cartloads of rocks, but could never prove it was us. Some nights when the moon was bright, the old man would wait outside his farmhouse with a shuttered coldfire lantern, trying to catch me, but I was always careful. If he did catch me, I would pay for it—and then pay even worse when my father and brothers punished me because I had embarrassed the family.

My brothers charged the engine in our rickety old steamcart, filled the boiler, and then loaded the bed with the boulders that we had spent days excavating from our stony cropland, clearing more acreage so we could plant larger fields. Just removing the big rocks wasn't the end of the story, though. We had to dump them somewhere else.

I was the fourth son of six, all of us strapping lads, and I was the largest of the brood (but not the brightest, as my father and the rest of my brothers often reminded me).

Old Farmer Sheckel grew fields of corn, and when the ears were ripe, my mother and two sisters would climb the stone fences at night and slip into his fields, harvesting ears of corn carefully spaced throughout the rows so farmer Sheckel wouldn't notice any of his crop missing.

On our own farm, we grew cheerful sunflowers. The giant blossoms were like a splash of alchemical gold, staring up at the sky, turning their heads from east to west, morning to night. When it was time to harvest, we would all go down the rows, each carrying a curved sickle, and chop the heads off the sunflowers so we could scrape out the seeds and press the oil. Harvest was supposed to be a time of joy, but I found something sad about it. I thought the big drooping flowers looked gruesome, like the severed heads of enemies killed in the bloody wars before the Watchmaker's Stability. . . .

But right now it was the rainy season, and we had a lot of inconvenient boulders we had extracted from our land. It was my job to dump them on a rival farmer's land in the middle of the night, during a rainstorm. My brothers piled the boulders high in the steamcart until the work-worn vehicle was ready to collapse before it moved a foot.

I shook my head dubiously at the mountain of rocks. "That's too much, Dad. It's too heavy."

Seth let out a snort. "It's exactly the same number of boulders as the last two times."

"Would you like to count them yourself?" My father looked at me with great disapproval. "Or can't you count that high, boy?"

I wasn't sure I could, and I didn't want to prove the matter one way or another. "You know best," I muttered.

A crack of thunder roared across the dark sky, and the first cold drops of rain splattered down. "Better hurry, or you'll get wet," my father said.

I put a wide-brimmed leather hat on my head and activated the coldfire engines that heated the boiler. With a disapproving snort of steam, the wheels turned, the pistons chugged, and the boulder-laden cart huffed along the road. I had miles to go through the dark and the rain along the Watchmaker's road.

The workhorse engine kept pushing the enormous load, but the cart's suspension, axles, and wheels were not as strong. I could hear disconcerting groans of metal joints stressed to their limits. It sounded like an arthritic old man trying to climb the steps in a high clocktower.

Sheeting rain ran off the brim of my hat and drenched my coat as I trudged alongside the cart. The wheels left deep ruts in the Watchmaker's approved, and improved, road. I feared the vehicle would get mired—and how would I explain myself with a load of unwanted boulders on the way to Farmer Sheckel's fields late at night?

For the first mile, the rolling hills alongside the road were covered with sunflowers, but as the vehicle climbed a rise, the crops changed to rows of knee-high corn shoots. As the steamcart strained to get up that hill, the engine overheated, and the boiler's pressure gauge edged into the danger zone.

With a dismaying shriek of metal and a snap of broken bolts, the left rear wheel broke from the axle, and the cart crashed down in the middle of the Watchmaker's road, right on the edge of Farmer Sheckel's cornfields.

In a way, the storm was a blessing, because if it had been a clear night, old Farmer Sheckel might have been out watching for me. But I was alone and drenched, cold, exhausted, and I didn't know how I was going to get the broken cart back home at all, with or without the rocks. I had to solve that problem . . . but I've never been good at solving problems—at least according to my father and brothers.

Like a miracle, as if the angels were rewarding me for good work, the rain cleared, and a brisk breeze blew the clouds away. It was actually a fine night to be outside, if not for the broken cart and an illicit load of boulders. After thinking hard, I decided that the first task was to unload the rocks. All of them.

I picked up one of the heavy rocks and used all my strength to heave it out of the cart. It bounced down the embankment and crashed into the edge of Farmer Sheckel's cornfield. If I unloaded the whole cart, I thought I might find a way to reattach the wheel, or maybe even drag the cart back home. No doubt my father would still scold me for the damage to the family's valuable equipment.

I heaved another boulder off the side of the road, and then a third. The night was chilly, but the work kept me warm. I did not count the boulders in the cart, simply did my work.

Hearing distant sounds, I looked up to see the lights of some kind of caravan in the distance, heading toward me. Though it was the dead of night after a heavy rainstorm, I was, after all, on the Watchmaker's road. I stared at the long trail of flares under piercing stars. My broken cart was blocking the way, and I realized with a flash of panic that I would be caught. On the other hand, this might be a rescue, for whoever was in that caravan might help me out.

Not knowing what else to do, I managed to lift two more boulders from the cart; now it looked only as full as it should have been in the first place.

Then the carnival arrived: steamwagons, flatbed haulers carrying the components of midway rides, habitation trailers, and other equipment. Everything was colorful, cheerful, and crowded with a group of interesting, friendly people. Even though they surely had a schedule to keep—as does everyone in Albion—they didn't grumble at me for blocking their way. They merely swung down from their vehicles to see what the problem was.

I met a middle-aged woman with dark hair and a slender build who introduced herself as Cassandra, the carnival's acrobat and trapeze artist; and a fawn-eyed girl with the most startling, yet beautiful, cornsilk covering her cheeks and chin; and an older man who introduced himself as Cesar Magnusson, the leader of the Carnival Extravaganza.

I was most interested, however, in a huge bald man with an extravagant handlebar mustache, heavy black eyebrows, and arms as thick as most men's thighs. He exuded strength, but in an impressive way, not an intimidating one. "Looks like you could use some help lifting, young man."

"Yes, I could," I said. "I'm trying to get rid of all these boulders."

"My name is Levi—short for Leviathan." The name certainly fit.

"My name is Tani," I said.

Seeing where I had thrown the other rocks into Sheckel's cornfield, Levi grasped one of the boulders from the cart and raised it completely over his head. His biceps bulged as if they might erupt with additional muscles, and then he hurled the rock like a meteor. It landed twice as far away as any that I had thrown.

"I've been sitting in the wagons all day and all night," Levi said with a chuckle. "I could use some exercise." He picked up another boulder and hurled it just as far as the first. The other carnies seemed insufficient for the task, or at least more interested in watching Levi and me unload the rocks. "We'll have this unloaded in no time."

I threw another boulder, which barely rolled down the embankment. With a great grunt like a roaring lion, Levi flung the next boulder all the way to the middle of the cornfield. "Why would you dig these rocks out of the ground if you're just going to throw them back on top of it?"

"My family wanted the rocks in a different field instead of where they found them."

"Fair enough," said Levi and threw another stone.

Toward the bottom of the cart bed was a particularly large boulder. I wrapped my arms around it, straining. "Could you help me with this one?"

The strongman looked at me, looked at the rock, and shook his head. "If I help you with it, then you'll never know whether you could've done it yourself. I have faith in you. Challenge your abilities."

I strained until my arms were about to explode. I clenched my teeth, and I managed to lift the great rock over the edge of the cart, staggered two steps to the side of the road. Instead of hurling the rock, it was all I could do just to let it roll down the slope. Panting, I leaned against the cart.

Levi laughed, and while I caught my breath, he casually threw the rest of the boulders out of the cart. The strongman clapped me on the back with a good-natured blow that almost knocked me to the ground, but it felt more welcoming and appreciative than the punches or blows my brothers gave me. "I knew you could do it—I'm proud of you, Tam. You always have to strive harder. You'll never know what you can do if you make up your mind that you can't."

The steamcart was empty, but the wheel was shattered, the axle bent and broken. Even without the weight of the boulders, the cart would need serious repairs, and my father wouldn't like to see the damage—he wouldn't like it at all. Just as bad, I was going to arrive home late, which would spark yet another round of complaints.

Old Cesar Magnusson came up to me, his hands on his hips. "Now that Levi helped you unload, we can push the cart off to the side, and our caravan will proceed. We're on our way to a scheduled show in Winding Springs." He gave me a hard look that cut deep into my life. He seemed to understand me in a way that I'd never bothered to think about. "It's not for me to get into a feud between two neighboring farmers, but I know what you're doing, Tam. I've seen young men like you, and I know how they turn out. Are you the oldest son?"

I shook my head. "Number four of six."

"So, a spare, then. And is your father a happy man?"

I shook my head again without bothering to think about it.

"And your other brothers? The farm? Is that the life you want?"

I shrugged. "It's what I was born to. They're my family."

Levi came forward. "If you stay with them, will you ever push the limits of what you can achieve?"

"It's my life. All is for the best, I suppose."

"But will it allow you to *be* your best?" Levi asked.

I shrugged again. "I have nowhere else to go, no other prospects."

He reached out and surprised me by squeezing my arm. He gave an appreciative grunt. "I see potential there, young Tam. I'll push you, and you'll be amazed at what you can do."

The members of the Carnival Extravaganza gathered around me, and I was baffled. "What do you mean?"

"Join our carnival, start a new life with us," Levi said. "I can't be the strongman forever. I have to think ahead."

"You mean just . . . go with you?"

"To the show in Winding Springs at first," offered Cesar Magnusson. "After that . . . however far you wish to go."

I thought of what lay behind me at the farm. I thought of what my father and brothers made me do. I even thought of all those poor sunflower heads, drying in the big wire crib, and I realized I didn't like it. I wasn't satisfied.

But when I considered what might lie ahead of me with the carnival, it felt like a compass pulling me to magnetic north. I turned to Levi and gestured toward the broken-down steamcart. "Help me with this." We pressed our shoulders against the cart and shoved it sideways until we were at the edge of the road. Though the way was clear enough for the carnival caravan, we kept pushing and knocked the cart down the embankment, where it crashed among the discarded boulders. My father and old Farmer Sheckel could argue over the wreckage all they wanted.

I climbed aboard one of the carnival's flatbed haulers, and we set off. I rode beside Levi, dripping wet with rain and perspiration. I never looked back.

———◆———

I didn't become the carnival's new strongman right away—not for some time, in fact—but because of my strength, I was allowed to set up the rides, lift the heavy equipment, pound the stakes, raise the tentpoles, and then tear it all down again as we moved to the next town.

I had never seen a carnival before, and the Winding Springs performance was a wonder to me. Cassandra, a dark-haired beauty, strolled along a high-wire as if it were as wide as a village street, while her young daughter Francesca watched, clearly wanting to be just like her mother someday. There were games, rides, a fire eater, a knife thrower, a sword swallower, miracles well beyond my ability to count.

The carnies made me feel welcome. This new family was more supportive and warm-hearted than my old one, and when they asked me to do work, I did it out of love and respect rather than guilt and responsibility. Though my muscles ached from the hard work, that was just the beginning, because Levi had it in his mind to make me as powerful and muscular as he was. He had his barbell and heavy iron plates, and he procured another set for me, although my stack of weights was much smaller. "We can always acquire more," he said.

Levi took me under his wing, straining me and training me. He had me swing the mallet on the high striker, adjusting the tension harder and harder so that I could *almost* succeed in making the puck hit the bell. "You need to push yourself," he said, "and realize that you are truly capable of more than you think you can do, even just a little bit. That's how you get better."

So I swung the mallet harder, and when I finally rang the bell, he gave me a heavier mallet which was harder to lift—at first—but as I trained, week after week, I swung the heavier mallet just as easily. When the puck struck the bell for a second time, Levi adjusted the tension a little bit higher.

In order to prove the high striker game wasn't a trick, Levi would call for volunteers from the audience —the strongest men there, or at least the ones who considered themselves strong. After everyone had tried to ring the bell, Levi would casually pick up the mallet, swing it with one hand as if it were no more than a baton, and send the puck to the top every time.

For his barbell, Levi would stack on so many iron plates that I couldn't count them all. No one could even lift it an inch off the ground, not even me, but Levi managed it. He would strain, his face would grow red, the tendons would stand out in his neck. He heaved the barbell to the level of his chest and then with great effort raised it above his head. His thighs looked like trees anchored but trembling in a storm.

Meanwhile, my hard training made me atrociously sore, and every muscle was a nightmare, but I kept trying until the burn became an ache, and the ache eventually felt good. I lifted my own barbell with far less weight than Levi's, and when I could raise that bar over my head, I basked in my victory. Then the strongman added one more plate to each side. "Always do more than you think you can do. That's how you get better."

I knew I had reached a certain level of achievement when my proud mentor gave me one of those crippling claps on my shoulder. "Tam, it's time for you to pick another name—a *strongman* name."

"What's wrong with my own name?"

"Plenty. *Leviathan* is a strongman name. But Tam . . ." He shook his head. "It sounds like a hat."

"But how do I pick another name?"

"Think of the strongest men in history and legend. The two that come to mind are Goliath and Samson, so let's make your new strongman name a combination of the two." He paused in anticipation. "*Golson*—and that's a very strong name indeed."

From what I recalled, neither Goliath nor Samson had ended well, but I could not argue with Levi. He announced my new name to Cesar Magnusson, Cassandra, the beautiful girl with the cornsilk on her cheeks (her name was Louisa), and everyone else. They applauded and cheered. And the name stuck.

I had never met a bearded lady before, and though the hair on her face wasn't lush enough—yet—to make her a star in the carnival, Cesar Magnusson (and Louisa herself) had high hopes. She was confident, smart, yet shy at the same time. Her exotic beard fascinated me, and I didn't find it freakish at all. Somehow, it looked just right on her.

Levi worked me hard and served as my mentor, but Louisa became my friend. She watched me, always impressed when I lifted an extremely heavy barbell. After each show, late at night, she would go inside the office trailer and sit by the light of a coldfire lantern to do the accounting. Cesar Magnusson would tally up the honeybee coins from general admission tickets, then add in the take from each game, each ride, each act. His daughter Cassandra was the tightrope walker and trapeze artist, and he taught her the business of running the carnival. The actual *accounting*, however—the tedious bookkeeping with column after column of dizzying numbers—fell to young Louisa.

I was in awe as I watched her add columns of figures and arrive at sums which she then divided, put in different columns, and categorized numbers that all looked the same to me. I practically went crosseyed. "How can you do that?" I asked. "I've never been good at numbers. I can count up to twenty because that's where my fingers and toes stop, but after that I just lose track. And I'm not good at letters either."

"We each have our abilities," Louisa said. "Our previous accountant was an ancient man with thick spectacles, and he could barely see the numbers anymore. He made too many mistakes, which frustrated Mr. Magnusson to no end, and then he died. Since the carnival had no one else to do the numbers, I agreed to try. Mr. Magnusson was very patient." She smiled at me, and I felt as if my heart might melt.

My arms and legs were sore from all the weight lifting, but my mind was sore just watching Louisa compile the figures. She inspired me to go back to the set of weights resting outside my tent. I stared at the iron plates, drew a deep breath, gathered my strength. Levi had put an extra plate on the bar earlier that day, and I hadn't been able to lift it, but maybe I could do it this time if I pushed myself.

Without calling Levi, just doing this for my own satisfaction, I strained, lifted the bar to my waist, sucked in a breath, then swung the barbell up to my chest. I rocked, poised, afraid to move. My legs were shaking.

But I wasn't done. I had to push the weight higher. And with all my concentration, everything focused on the fibers of my muscles in my arms, stabilizing my legs, and straightening my back, I *urged* the bar higher—until I stood there with the bar above my head, trembling and victorious. It was more than I had ever lifted in my life.

But I couldn't hold it long. When I dropped the barbell, it crashed to the ground. I swayed, then slowly my knees buckled, and I sank to the grass next to the weights, my heart pounding, my lungs burning . . . and my lips smiling.

I heard applause and lifted my head to see Louisa clapping for me. "Bravo! I knew you could do it."

She brought me dinner, and we ate together before she went back to her accounting books in the wagon by the coldfire light.

I got stronger as I traveled with the show for the next year. Levi was still the great strongman, but I became his sidekick to warm up the audiences, impressing them with how much I could lift and how I could ring the bell on the high striker. Afterward, Levi would come out and impress them even more.

He could see how rapidly I was bulking up, how much more I could lift now . . . and I realized that *he* was pushing himself harder, too. Levi put so many plates on his barbell that I couldn't even count them. I couldn't understand why he pressed himself like that, since he was far stronger than I would ever be.

Finally, at one show in a small town that looked just like all the other small towns in Albion (I forget their names just as easily as I forget numbers), Levi was preparing to perform. He seemed overconfident, even edgy. Something had changed between us, but I didn't know why. He viewed me as a rival, and that puzzled me. He would always be Leviathan, the strongest man in the world—I don't know what he felt he had to prove.

Before the show, he warmed up, flexed his arms, and glanced at me with an odd gleam in his eye. Then he looked down at his barbell loaded with more iron plates than I could ever hope to lift. "It's time, Golson." He cracked his knuckles and nodded toward the remaining stack of iron plates on the ground. "Put them all on. I want to test myself—and I am going to succeed."

I wasn't sure that was a good idea. I tried to caution Levi, but he wouldn't hear it, so I helped him slide the plates onto the barbell, one after another. I didn't have to keep track; I just put them on until there weren't any left.

When she saw what we were doing, Louisa was concerned, but Levi gave her a brusque nod. "This is what I need to do."

The nightly crowd gathered, thinking this was a show just like any other, but the carnies also came to watch—for Leviathan, the strongest man in the world, had never lifted so much in his life.

I warmed up the crowd as always. I swung the mallet and rang the bell. I lifted my own barbells. I had to feign my proud swagger as I flexed my muscles and showed off my physique.

Then Levi came out to stand in front of the overloaded bar-bell, which seemed to thrum with intimidation. It looked *impossible*, but he stood next to it, flexed his arms and his hands. He grinned at the audience. In a more intimate moment, he flashed me a con-fident grin and said in a low voice, "I can push myself more than ever before. That's how I get stronger."

He seized the bar, squeezed his hands, and seemed to be com-muning with the iron in the way that an alchemist understands gold. He flexed and strained; his muscles rippled. As he gathered his nerve, I could feel power building up in his body like an electri-cal storm in his veins.

Levi raised the bar off the ground, then heaved it up to his waist. The audience gave a little gasp, but the strongman paused for only a fraction of a second. He curled his arms, lifting the mam-moth weights up against his broad chest. His face was drawn back, his neck tense, his eyes squeezed shut, and he *pushed*, summoning all the strength he could wring out of his muscles. He lifted the bar again, raising it over his shoulders. He wobbled, nearly fell, then pushed the bar even higher.

A groan exploded from between his clenched teeth. Tears poured from between his shut eyes, and with a great cry of defiance he extended his arms and lifted the bar over his head, holding it there for just a second, a moment of glory. His face was red, the tendons in his neck standing out like steel cables.

The audience held their breath.

Suddenly, Levi looked poleaxed, and his face fell. A blood vessel burst in his temple—and the strongman simply crumpled. He fell as if buried under an avalanche. The heavy barbell crashed on top of him, driving him down like a mallet striking the bell platform. I heard the horrible sound of bones snapping.

Someone screamed, and I bounded forward, grabbing the barbell, trying to lift it off of the crushed body of my mentor and friend . . . but even I couldn't lift so much weight.

The other carnies swarmed to help, all of them straining, and we lifted the bar enough that Louisa could snatch one of the plates from the end, then another, until we could move it away.

But Levi was broken. Blood trickled from his nose. His slightly open eyes were crimson from hemorrhages. He may have been dead from the burst blood vessel even before he fell—I don't know. I don't understand those things.

Cesar Magnusson pushed away the shocked audience. The other carnies were sobbing, and I stood next to Louisa, stunned and wondering why Levi had done that when he certainly hadn't needed to.

It took me a long time to realize that I was now the carnival's strongman.

* * *

I have been with the Magnusson Carnival Extravaganza for many years now—just past the point where it's more than I can count. I am the strongest man in the world, supposedly, but I don't need to prove it to anyone. I've seen what happens when you push beyond your abilities.

Oh, I do my absolute best, I stay strong—and I am satisfied. I don't have the pride that Levi did. Striving is one thing, but you have to be willing to accept what you can accomplish, and what you can't. Did that one last plate really matter so much that it cost Levi his life? I was already impressed with his abilities, as was everyone else.

To remind myself, since counting those plates is difficult for me, I chain the last two of them together. The padlock is always there, and I have lost the key so I will not be tempted to go beyond my ability. Any man should be satisfied with that.

CHAPTER 12

After Marinda wrapped Golson's cut hands in one of his cloth bands, he assured her he was ready to perform again. "They were just splinter cuts, and this is our big Solstice Festival show for the Watchmaker. It's a great honor, and I won't let the carnival down." He thanked her, and she went on her way, anxious to read his story.

By now, the crowds had grown thicker in anticipation of the night's show. The tightrope was set up, the carny games were busy, the giant clockwork Ferris wheel turned.

So much to see and experience, so many stories, but Marinda found a quiet place where she could skim the strongman's tale. Her eyes widened in astonishment, and she considered going back to talk with Golson. She heard the clang of the high-striker bell, the laughter of the crowd, and realized he was already performing. Instead, she went back to the gate and found the bearded lady waiting to take tickets, even though most of the crowd had entered Chronos Square.

Marinda walked up to her with a determined look on her face. "I know you now. You're Louisa—Golson's friend."

When the bearded lady gave her a curious smile, Marinda opened her book and showed her the words written in the strongman's blood. "I know his story. I know what happened with Leviathan, and why Golson keeps the last two iron plates chained together."

Louisa looked pained at the reminder, but then her face took on an unexpectedly proud expression that was not masked by her lavish, beribboned beard. "Golson is a strong man, much stronger than he allows himself to think. Years ago, Levi's death weakened him, like Samson with his locks shorn off, but the weakness was all in his mind—just like Samson. But I know a secret. Golson *does* keep pushing himself, and he does get stronger—he is much stronger now than Leviathan ever was."

"But the last two plates chained together . . ." Marinda said.

"Seeing them there gives him the confidence he needs," Louisa said. "But the dear man can't count. I see how much he lifts, and I know how strong he really is. As long as he knows those last two plates are chained together, he's convinced he can lift whatever is left." Marinda saw something strange in the bearded lady's smile. "But he doesn't know when I slip an extra pair of plates into the *unlocked* stack. He keeps pushing himself, whether he realizes it or not."

Marinda's eyes widened. "So you fool him? Isn't that dishonest?"

Louisa stroked her beard. "You might have his story in your book, but I have his life in *my heart*. I know what Golson needs. I'm sure he suspects what I'm doing, but he is happier not knowing."

Troubled over things that had never troubled her thoughts before, Marinda walked through the carnival crowd. A young man strutted about waving a sword that he didn't seem to know how to use. As part of his trick, he belched alchemical fire out of his mouth, to the delight of the crowd.

Distracted by the trick fireworks, Marinda bumped into the bright red booth of the gypsy fortune teller. An incredibly old woman sat erect inside, like a theatrical prop. At first Marinda thought the fortune teller was just a clockwork contraption wearing a formal gown—until she saw a gleam of blue light in the rheumy eyes. She realized that the fortune teller was alive and ancient in ways that Marinda had no way of measuring.

A rattling mechanical voice asked, "Tell your fortune?"

Marinda saw the coin slot and a windup key that might or might not have been a mere decoration. The ancient woman looked at her intently. Marinda wasn't sure that she could wring a story from this clockwork fortune teller, but she placed a coin in the slot nevertheless, turned the key, and the faint blue glow brightened inside the chamber.

As the fortune teller became animated, the sounds around Chronos Square increased. The crowds cheered as the main act started. "What does the future hold for you, young woman?" the voice rasped.

"I know my fortune," Marinda said.

"Then why are you here?"

"Because I want to know about you. My father used to work for the Watchmaker and his Clockwork Angels, and he invented this." She held up *Clockwork Lives* and explained what she had been tasked to do.

"Your father worked for the Watchmaker?" asked the ancient woman.

"Yes. Do you have a story for me? I'll need a drop of your blood." Marinda paused. "Do you even have blood?"

"What I have will suit. And I do indeed have a tale for you."

The fortune teller's hands moved, reached up to the tight bun of gray hair on her withered head. She removed a jeweled pin from her hair and stabbed her emaciated finger. When liquid welled out, she touched it to a small pre-printed card—the fortune that had sat ready for Marinda—which she extended through the slot in front of the red booth.

Marinda took the card and found a perfect drop of blood poised on the surface of the card—deep red blood that was diluted with a shimmer of coldfire blue. Behind the droplet, though, she was curious to read the fortune this strange clockwork crone had chosen for her.

What you live is your own story.

Marinda realized that it sounded most appropriate for her.

She opened her book and applied the quivering droplet to a blank page. As the fortune teller's words spilled out in a long tale of a long life, the ancient woman repeated, "I do indeed have a tale for you." She paused, even though she didn't seem to be breathing. "I am the Watchmaker's daughter."

THE
FORTUNE-TELLER'S TALE

I was happy once, a long time ago. Too far away in time, and too brief a time, but I remember it——like a tiny diamond far out of reach, but one that still sparkles.

Yes, I was happy once, until I discovered the trap. And then it took me many years to find simple contentment again. Many years. And I have lived nearly two centuries.

My story started with fire, and fear, and deadly sickness, in the early days before the Stability was complete—chaotic, exuberant, unpredictable, and dangerous times. I was just a little girl, but I remember the joys and wonders of everyday life. For me, it was a time of family and childhood adventures, when storms came full of wind and rain and lightning, without any Watchmaker's Almanac to keep them on schedule. I remember music and dancing, festivals, and laughter in the face of never knowing what might come next.

Even with that everyday joy I saw as a child, every season had its struggles, too: bandits preyed on the weak; crops failed; some people were poor, while others were wealthy. There were more sicknesses than cures. Some days were dark, some nights were bright. But we were free. Even in anarchy people can survive and thrive. They hope, they love, and they live for the best.

Then the Watchmaker came like a precision whirlwind to "improve" Albion, according to his own definition. *Stability*.

But what was a little girl named Charlotte to know about any of that? Other than the pastel colors of those younger years, the first thing I remember is fire—and the sickness that led to the inferno that consumed my town.

Our neighbors caught the fever first, a nice old man and wife. I remember the kindly woman made pumpkin cookies for every Equinox Festival. Her husband carved little wooden angels that he gave me to play with. The waist-high statue of a benevolent angel also stood as a guardian in front of their home.

That old couple died first. By then, the sickness had spread through the streets, and fear spread even farther and faster.

My little brother Martin brought the fever into our household. I remember him moaning, sweating, delirious—so different from the boy I played with every day. My parents tended him until they, too, caught the sickness and grew so weak that they couldn't get out of bed. I tried to help them, but I didn't know how. I gave my brother one of the toy wooden angels the old man had carved for me, and Martin clutched it in his sweaty hand. I made them all soup and tried to feed them, because even at seven years old I knew that soup was for the sick. But my soup didn't help them, nor did the wooden angel, and they all died. So did the rest of the neighborhood.

Other townspeople barricaded our section of houses, closed off the streets, and refused to let anyone in or out, turning deaf ears to the wails of the sick and dying.

I didn't catch the fever, though. I was immune. Even then, I was a freak of sorts, but in this case it was a good thing—until the terrified townspeople started to burn the homes.

When most of my neighbors were already dead, the fearful villagers torched our streets, hoping to burn away the scourge, to turn the fever and the bodies into purified ash, along with anyone else who happened to be trapped there—like me.

Flames sprang from building to building, consuming homes that remained silent, because everyone inside was either already dead or too fever-weak to crawl away. But I ran, desperate and frightened, until I came upon the barricades, the pointed farm implements, the makeshift spears that kept me away. Grim people who didn't even know my name poked their weapons at me and drove me back toward the blazing homes, their features distorted in the flickering light.

"All plague victims must be burned," said one farmer. I had seen him once or twice in brighter days. He wouldn't let me pass.

"But I'm not sick!" I held up my hands. I clutched one of the small wooden angels, but even that elicited no sympathy. "Look!"

But his fear was greater than his compassion, and I had neither the life experience nor the vocabulary to convince him otherwise. My panicked pleas went unanswered. . . .

At the time, I knew nothing about the Watchmaker, his armies, and his new efforts to impose Stability and order across chaotic Albion. All I remember is that *he* suddenly appeared like an avenging angel, a brave hero, a savior. The Watchmaker and his troops marched in perfect formation, coming to our poor village to see the flames. Even then, I sensed something different about him.

The fire rose higher, and the heat was unbearable. The people guarding the barricades shielded their eyes and cringed back from the rising storm.

"I'm not sick," I wailed as the flames came closer.

And *he* strode in with a stiff, implacable gait, his power based on a forceful personality instead of outright physical strength. "You can't burn the girl alive," he boomed. "Look at her! She's healthy and strong."

He knocked them aside, and his troops protected him as he strode toward the fire. While sparks flew around us like killer fireflies, he swept me up in his strong arms and I melted into his embrace. I held tight as he carried me back across the barricades.

Then we turned and watched in silence as my neighborhood, my home, and my life burned to the ground. The Watchmaker was angry to see the destruction, but more angry at the people and their squalid lives that had made such purging necessary.

His troops surrounded the village to make sure that the fire didn't spread out of control, for the fearful people had not thought ahead. The Watchmaker seemed disappointed in them all. Still holding me, he shook his head at them. "So much work to do." Then he looked down at me and smiled. "All is for the best now. You will come with me back to Crown City. You will have a place. Such a perfect little girl—what is your name?"

"Charlotte." I found my voice. "My father is—"

He cut me off. "That life is burned away. I will be your father now, and you will have a golden life with me . . . my little angel." He plucked the wooden carving from my hands and tossed it behind us into the fire.

I clung to him as he took me away from the dying flames. I felt hopeful, glad, protected. I understood that I had lost everything, but now I had a place again. This was my little diamond of happiness.

That was before I knew him well.

Even in its early years, Crown City was bigger, brighter, and more bustling than any world I had ever imagined. Some people were afraid of how the Watchmaker imposed order and controlled lives "for our own good," while others, especially in times of blight or bandit attacks, appreciated a loving benefactor who could bring Stability. They applauded the flow of gold that poured out of his alchemical industries, reshaping Albion's economy and creating a clean and prosperous civilization.

The tallest building in Crown City was the Watchtower, topped by a gigantic clock, with storey after storey of laboratories, administration offices, storage rooms, and living quarters. And gold everywhere! I had never seen so much gold: the furnishings, the decorations, the statues, the portrait frames, even the basin I used to wash my hands and face—all made of gold created by the Watchmaker himself.

I knew nothing of economics or intrinsic value; I just knew it was pretty.

My new rooms in the tower were lavish and comfortable. When I lay in my soft bed surrounded by plush goosedown comforters and the whispering sound of a fountain in the corner of my room, I wondered if I had died of the fever after all. Maybe this was the heaven my mother had so vigorously begged the angels for as she died on her sagging cot. . . .

The Watchmaker had no wife or children of his own, but he began introducing me as his daughter, his angel, Charlotte. He led me through the wonders of Crown City, showed me the new steamliners he was constructing, explained the coldfire rails that would guide them across the land to create efficient commerce.

My real parents had used wood fires to heat our home and to cook, but the Watchmaker introduced an efficient and plentiful new energy source called coldfire, which he said would rescue Albion even more than his gold would. The Watchmaker wrapped his arm around my shoulder and said, "Your smile generates more energy than my coldfire nexus, dear angel. That is why I have to keep you happy, because your love gives me strength."

I giggled. Though he was a hard and rigid leader to his advisers,

I saw a different man, a personality he showed to few other people . . . one that, alas, died too soon.

The Watchmaker bought me a puppy, a bundle of deliriously happy energy with white fur and black spots, a breed that he called a Dalmatian. The puppy bonded with me instantly, and we played together with such joie de vivre that it had to be its own kind of alchemy. The puppy exhausted me, and I exhausted him. We were perfect for each other, and the Watchmaker was proud of how he *proved* his devotion to me by introducing such chaos into his well-ordered Watchtower. I named the puppy Martin, after my little brother, who had also been full of wild and joyous play—before the fever killed him.

The Watchmaker would let me sit in the corner of his laboratory as he tinkered with new alchemical plans or discussed complex designs with his engineer-priests. He met with his Regulator captains, and together they drew maps of Albion, marking off sections where their Stability was secure and others that remained holdouts of anarchy.

"We are rewriting the economy of the land," he would say to the Regulators. "We must manufacture more gold and spread it swiftly. I need to buy *everything* that remains, so I can stabilize civilization before the economy collapses with a glut of gold."

His alchemists and his advisers laughed at the suggestion. "How can there be too much gold?" My father simply looked at them until they backed down and followed his instructions.

Though he had grand designs of reshaping the land, he also needed to be loved by the citizenry. He wanted his good works to be appreciated. He would convert one village after another, pay them off with gold, and give them coldfire to run their homes and businesses. Then he moved to the next and the next until he had all of Albion in the palm of his hand.

I watched the map for years as I remained with him, going to school, learning what he wanted me to learn. Martin became a full-grown dog, well-trained but filled with unconditional love, just as the Watchmaker expected from me. And I gave it to him.

My father would take me with him as we rode on a golden steamglider through the city streets. We could look up at the tall towers and hear the applause of the crowd. He would pat my arm, point to the buildings, and take pride in telling me that he had created all this out of strife, chaos, and barbarism. He said, "I have brought order and stability at last. It all fits the plan."

And it was glorious. The diamond of my happiness sparkled brighter.

❖

I had everything, but my father wanted more from me—in a good way. I was the Watchmaker's beautiful daughter, theoretically destined to be his successor, even though the great and powerful man never changed, never aged.

When I was thirteen, he took me to the catacombs beneath Chronos Square, where we watched alchemist-priests tend the bubbling, living blood of coldfire that streamed in conduits underground and powered the whole city. As we stood there, he gave me an indulgent smile. "We are only immortal for a limited time. I will need you someday, my angel."

He sent me to the Alchemy College, where I was the youngest student learning the mysteries of acids and bases, dreamstones and redcoal, argent and quicksilver, and exotic substances found only in the distant alchemy mines on Atlantis, far across the sea. I conducted experiments under the close supervision of the instructors and alchemist-priests.

By this time my father's Stability had taken hold, and Albion hummed along like a well-tuned steam engine. My father had discovered the secret of manufacturing gold, and he had unlocked the key to unlimited energy, but he did not rest on his triumphs. He continued his research, always questing for something more important.

"Understanding should not have self-imposed boundaries," he told me. "There is always more to discover, more to apply." He said he was searching for a way to harness the quintessence, the fifth element. Life itself. It seemed impossible, but he had already done many impossible things.

After so many years, I had nearly forgotten my burned village and my original family struck down by disease. Truly, I believed we now lived in a perfect world, thanks to the loving Watchmaker.

But not everything was perfect in this perfect world, and biology doesn't always run like clockwork.

Year after year, Martin the Dalmatian was my constant companion, faithful, warm, loving. I had spent hours studying the pattern of black spots on his back, seeking to find Nature's blueprint, the code that had left a message there in dots to be connected. Although he was still young in dog years, Martin began to slip away. I fed him treats. I loved him. I spent more time with him, but he grew gaunt, he moved stiffly. He slept more often, and he whimpered in his sleep.

One day I sat at a table in my high Watchtower room with the windows open, so I could hear the noises outside while I did my alchemy homework, writing down chemical reactions, studying and replacing symbols. I had just begun an advanced class in the theory and calibration of destiny calculators, but the concept of divining the future remained beyond me. For now.

Martin curled up at my feet as he often did. He heaved a great sigh and went to sleep, then left this life. I was so engrossed in solving my test equations that I didn't even notice the moment the soul flew from his body. Gradually, I realized Martin wasn't moving, and his closed eyes did not twitch with dreams.

I wept as I had never wept before, feeling a personal despair greater than when my family had died, when my neighborhood had been burned to the ground. I wailed inside my room, not knowing what to do, and finally the Regulators brought the Watchmaker to me. He stared at the lifeless dog, clucked his tongue, and then folded me in a strong embrace. "All is for the best, my angel."

"No, it's not! Martin is dead."

He kept holding me, rocking me, but his gaze was directed toward the lifeless dog curled so peacefully on the floor, and he had a very strange gleam in his eyes. . . .

My tower room with gilded trimmings, plush bed, and chuckling fountain seemed entirely empty despite all its treasures. I spent two weeks immersed in sharp sadness, which transmuted into dull sadness, and finally to just an empty ache.

One day, the Watchmaker entered my room as if he had conquered another land. "I brought something for you, my angel. Something I made . . . something that only *I* could make, given my research into the quintessence."

Martin walked beside him—and it was not just another Dalmatian that looked like Martin. After so many years of familiarity, I knew those random spots, the constellations of black against a field of white fur, like a negative image of a starry night. It was *Martin*. He walked with a smoother, more regimented gait than he had shown in years.

I rushed toward him, disbelieving, but I hesitated when Martin didn't react as he should have. The dog stood there at attention, and I saw the sheen of coldfire blue in his eyes, detected the faint hydraulic network of tubes and pistons threaded throughout his body.

"It was a tremendous challenge, but I learned how to animate him," my father said. "A spark of quintessence lives inside his heart now, and the clockwork mechanisms will keep him alive for a long time to come."

I touched my pet with more trepidation than joy. I bent down and wrapped my arms around him, feeling a faint thrumming from inside. This clockwork dog looked like Martin, and it was based on Martin, but it wasn't *him*.

Dutifully, because the Watchmaker expected it, I patted the dog, and just as dutifully, as if following a precision program, his tail wagged back and forth in a perfect arc, like the pendulum of a clock.

———— ❖ ————

I was sixteen, and there was a boy. After gathering the stories of numerous lives in this book, you should know by now that there is always a boy. Or a girl. Without love, or even friendship, there isn't much of a life to tell.

I first met Beneto in classes at the Alchemy College, where his dark hair and dark eyes, his perfect features and his roguish smile distracted me from my studies. He was handsome, funny, and friendly, but he was not a well-accomplished student. His grades were the last thing I paid attention to.

Beneto wanted me to help him with the classwork, by which he meant—I soon realized—for me to actually complete it for him while he flirted with me. I considered it a good bargain. The idea of romance caused unusual chemical reactions inside me, ones that everyone instinctively understood but could not document in any alchemical treatise.

But Beneto meant more to me than just romance. As the Watchmaker's adopted daughter, I was surrounded by smiles and diamonds, all the gold I could imagine. Given that, what did I lack?

Friendship.

Beneto was also a friend, my first and only true friend, other than the unconditional love my dog had given me—but Martin was no longer a friend, no longer a pet. He was just a gadget, and I spent less and less time with him. The Watchmaker seemed more attuned to his own creation than I was.

I made the terrible mistake of telling my father about Beneto, and although he had indulged me in everything else, the Watchmaker seemed troubled by the attentions of the young man.

He asked the alchemy professors about Beneto's performance, and because the Watchmaker had taken a direct interest in this particular student, the teachers discovered his "lack of dedication and originality" (by which they meant that he *cheated*)—and Beneto was ousted from the Alchemy College. I did not learn until much later that the Watchmaker was the cause of it.

My friend didn't say goodbye to me; he simply stopped appearing in classes, and when I inquired about him with growing urgency, I was told simply that he had "moved on to another calling." The brief taste of friendship had merely whetted my appetite for more, and the hint of romance had sparked a hunger in me that hadn't been there before.

Trying to express my independence, I longed to see all of Crown City, and not just in processions and celebratory parades. Regulators escorted me, guided me, and protected me—though from what, I did not know, since the Watchmaker's perfect Stability should have removed all dangers.

For months, alone and friendless, I explored, always looking, always longing. I went to newsgraph offices and bookshops; I saw food vendors, tailors, dressmakers, haberdashers, even street performers. Everyone was a stranger to me and strangers to each other, yet they were all part of a vibrant machine.

Then one day I spotted Beneto, looking more tattered than he had been in the Alchemy College. With his hat placed on the curb in front of him, he stood on a streetcorner and played a guitar, which jangled and twanged as he worked his way through the chords, plucking one string after another, then combinations. He was discovering his talent with mixed success, yet when he inadvertently stumbled upon a melodic combination his delight warmed the hearts of the spectators. He was concentrating so hard that he didn't notice me at first, but my Regulator escorts created enough commotion that he looked up, recognized me, and reacted with such joy that the guitar smacked against his side with a discordant thrum. "Charlotte!"

I hurried to hug him, much to the Regulators' consternation. "I haven't seen you in so long!" I kissed him on the cheek, and he kissed me on the lips, to my astonishment, and right in front of the Regulators and the crowd. I didn't care. I kissed him back, and it was wonderful.

He broke away, laughing, but I was concerned for him. "Is this what you've been doing? Is this what you really want? I thought the Alchemy College—"

He cut me off with a dismissive wave. "The Watchmaker reassigned me. Apparently his destiny calculators showed that this is my true calling in life. Who am I to dispute such a wise man?"

I decided that I would have to review the results from the destiny calculators myself; often, the predictions were open to interpretation. "You look as if you haven't eaten well in a long time, and your clothes could use a washing."

He shrugged. "I'm told that all is for the best."

Lifting my chin and being decisive, as the Watchmaker wanted me to be, I turned to my Regulator escort. "Beneto is my good friend. He'll come back with us to the Watchtower where we'll give him new clothes, good food, and he will keep me company."

The Regulators looked at one another. "This is highly irregular."

Beneto looked very happy. "If the Watchmaker's daughter wishes it, then surely all is for the best."

Beneto followed us back to the Watchtower, where he was astounded by all the gold in my chambers, the golden chairs and golden countertops. I combed my long hair with a golden comb, but I was more interested in Beneto's golden words and his musical laughter, since his limited prowess with the guitar did not provide adequate music.

We practiced kissing again, and it was a very instructive experience.

We spent hours together in my rooms, chatting, eating a

delicious meal served on golden plates, using golden utensils. When he grew restless at last and said it was time for him to go, I offered to find him an apartment in the Watchtower so he could stay nearby, but Beneto brushed the idea aside. "I have my own place to stay." He held up the handful of honeybee coins I had slipped to him, since that was what he seemed to need. "And now I won't ever have to worry about rent again."

"Will you come back?" I asked.

He smiled at me. "Of course—every day. I'll entertain you by playing my guitar."

"You'll entertain me while I watch you *try* to play." And I was sure he could entertain me in other ways as well.

I instructed the Regulators that Beneto was to be let inside whenever he came to visit. Meanwhile, I tried to concentrate on my schoolwork, though I was much more interested in seeing my friend.

True to his word, Beneto came back to visit me practically every day. We played games, and he played his guitar, though his skill never improved. He "helped" me with my schoolwork, which meant he let me concentrate on the books for a short time before he suggested doing something else—which I gladly did.

The diamond of my happiness sparkled brighter. I don't think I have ever laughed as much.

After several weeks, though, my father came to see us in my rooms. His spies had reported to him how often Beneto visited the Watchtower, and he soon learned that this was the same student who had been my friend in the Alchemy College, the one who had shown insufficient "dedication and originality."

The Watchmaker strode into my quarters while I sketched out alchemical reactions on my worktable and Beneto played with his guitar. As he looked at Beneto, I could read disapproval on his face, though his expression remained as calm as stone, like one of the angel statues from my old village.

"Introduce me to your friend, Charlotte." The fact that he used my given name, rather than his endearment of "my angel," set the visit on a more formal level.

In a rush of words, I explained how we had become friends, although I left out any mention of kissing. Beneto set the guitar aside and came over to shake my father's hand. "I wanted to be an alchemist, sir, but that didn't work out, so now I am a musician. I will be a great guitarist someday. Your own destiny calculators predicted it."

"Did they?" His expression didn't change. "They are still prototypes and not guaranteed to be accurate."

Undaunted, Beneto picked up his instrument and began to pluck the strings like a miner trying to discover a rich vein of music. He worked at the chords, searching for a melody that remained just out of reach. "I am self-taught. It allows for more creativity, sir."

My father watched the young man blindly go through the chords, making error after error. He seemed unexpectedly upset. "Enough! The guitar strings would allow for a mathematical progression if you understood how to play, but this isn't music. It is discordant *noise*. And there's no place for it in the Stability. We should not encourage discord."

Beneto set the guitar aside, but the Watchmaker remained stern. "Charlotte has studies to complete, and she cannot afford the distraction of your company."

Beneto looked disappointed, but he got up to leave. I insisted, "I'll concentrate, Father. I work better when Beneto's here."

"The evidence suggests otherwise." He summoned the Regulators to take Beneto away. "You can see your friend some other time, if he wishes."

"Of course he wishes. He's my friend."

Beneto flashed me a defeated smile as the Regulators marched him out of my room. . . .

He had indeed been a distraction, but I found it much more

difficult to concentrate on my work over the next week, not knowing where Beneto was. My father sent Martin to sit quietly by the golden hearth in my room, but that wasn't the sort of company I was looking for. The alchemical reactions in my homework eluded me, the probability mathematics of the destiny calculators seemed like a random roll of the dice.

Exasperated, I would stare out the tower windows, regarding the neatly organized quarters that spiraled out from the center of Chronos Square. At night, the blue coldfire streetlights decorated the city map like constellations, and I knew that somewhere out there, Beneto must be thinking of me. But I could not leave the tower; when I asked for an escort to take me out into the streets, I was instead sent back to my room.

After ten days of missing Beneto, my father came to stand in my chambers with a satisfied, yet sad demeanor. "Friendship is not a stable thing, my angel. Your friend was an impoverished young man. He got into the Alchemy College on a scholarship, but failed in his work there. He sought out your friendship because of your wealth and position, nothing more. I am sorry to say he wanted your gold more than your company. He was not your real friend."

"That's not true!" I thought of Beneto's roguish smiles and his open laughter, our stolen and not-so-stolen kisses, but I also remembered how pleased he had been with the gold coins I'd given him . . . and how some of our golden utensils disappeared after we were served our meals.

"I doubted you would believe me, so I tested his resolve," said the Watchmaker. "One of my agents offered Beneto a large sum if he would stay away from you."

"Why would you do that?"

"To test him, and to make a point. Exactly as I suspected, your 'friend' snatched the coins, didn't even haggle, didn't ask if he could tell you goodbye. He simply left. You will never see him again. I knew he was a rogue."

I hung my head. "That's not true."

"I'm afraid it is, my angel. The pain will subside. Better that you learn this lesson about people when you are young and resilient."

I didn't feel resilient; I felt devastated. The tears flowed down my cheeks. "That can't be true."

"I wish it were not so." He gestured out into the corridor. "But I brought you a gift so that you can remember your friend—just make sure you remember the rest, as well."

Three workers brought in a statue, wrestling a life-size figure made of solid gold—as if my chambers needed more gold! It looked like Beneto, exactly as I remembered him, with the same clothes, the same unruly hair, his handsome features perfectly rendered, although his roguish smile was gone. The sculpted expression seemed concerned and confused, rather than flippant.

"Knowing your heartache, I had my sculptors create the likeness for you, just after he accepted the bribe and went away."

"But how . . . ? How could it possibly be so exact?"

The statue was such a precise reproduction it looked as if a potent alchemical reactant had saturated my friend and transmuted *him* to solid gold. But of course that was not possible. Even the Watchmaker could not accomplish such a terrible miracle.

Could he?

"My sculptors are very good," my father said.

He left the statue in my room and told the Regulators that I was to concentrate on my work, to be escorted to the Alchemy College and back for classes, and that I had no business wandering the streets of Crown City in search of diversions. "She has a much greater purpose than that."

So, I was trapped in my rooms with Martin, who no longer gave me any comfort, and the uncanny golden statue of Beneto, which looked far too real to be any work of art.

The Watchmaker understood many things about order, about civilization, and about humanity, but his own daughter remained a mystery to him. He thought that once he got rid of Beneto and locked me in the tower, I would simply follow the orderly blueprint he had drawn for my life. But my emotions did not run like clockwork, and my heart was not made of gold.

I stayed in my chambers, pampered and protected, but a prisoner nevertheless. The Regulators stopped me each time I tried to leave. Always loyal, Martin greeted me every day with a metronomic swishing of his tail before he curled up in the same spot on the floor, but my studies had no luster for me anymore. My life was tarnished.

I asked my father for a guitar, so I might struggle my way through the chords that had so vexed Beneto, but the Watchmaker said no. "You have more important concerns."

Proud of his many accomplishments, he wrote a chronicle of how he had saved Albion, reminding the people of the prevalent chaos before he rescued them. He gave me a draft manuscript of *Before the Stability*—a chronicle that featured me and described how my fever-struck village had been burned to the ground by frightened people. He thought I would marvel at seeing my place in history, that I would appreciate the breadth of what he had done.

I hated the book. I sat alone in my room, taking no comfort from the golden statue of Beneto, who remained bright, young, and unchanged. Even Martin was no longer the same.

When I looked at my reflection in the gold-framed mirror, I saw that my skin had grown pale, my cheeks sunken, my eyes hollow. When I used a golden brush on my hair, loose strands came out. I thought it was just a broken heart. My father was worried about me, and I said, "I want to go outside again, Father. I want to be alive. I want friends. I want love!"

"You have much more than that, my angel." He was not convincing, and the tighter he held on to me, the more damage he did.

I realized long before the Watchmaker did that my illness was more than just a broken heart. I was sad and weak, and eventually even he understood that I was *ill*, that I would not just cheer up. I could feel my thready pulse, my feverish sweat, my decreased appetite, my loss of hair. I was not just heartsick, I was *truly sick*. It was another biological misstep like the one that had taken the real Martin from me long before his time. Now *I* was the one much too young, and my own biology ticked away—ticked away, despite everything the Watchmaker had done for me, how he had saved me, protected me, preserved me . . . *fossilized* me.

No matter his plans for me to succeed him in ruling Albion, *I* was the one who was only immortal for a limited time, and when the Watchmaker finally realized that, he brought in an army of his best physicians, commanding them to diagnose me and discover what was wrong.

They pored through their physical textbooks, their anatomical blueprints. They drew blood, tested my skin with reactants, ran tests with greater precision than the most complicated experiments in the Alchemy College. And they finally found the culprit.

"It is slow poison," the female chief physician announced to the Watchmaker, while I lay in bed listening. "Your daughter has been building up an adverse reaction to the alchemical residue used to create your gold." She gestured at the golden furnishings and golden basins, the golden goblets, golden plates, golden knives, and golden forks all around my room. "It is a very rare condition, and its progress is inevitable."

"Then we must remove all the gold!" the Watchmaker commanded. "We have to cleanse her, purify her again."

"That won't help, sir. Nobody can cure the wasting disease."

My father stared at them, then he turned to me. His steely eyes were wide and shimmered with tears. For the first time in my life I saw him *helpless*. And that seemed to terrify him—as it terrified me.

Despite what the doctors said, he ordered all of the golden

trappings removed from my chambers, leaving me with wood, stone, and fabric. It reminded me of my original home in the old village, the one that had been guarded by impotent angel statues.

Distraught, the Watchmaker came to me with Martin following beside him. "I wanted to give you everything, my angel. I showered you with gold, but the gold was poison to you. My good works, my wealth, my prosperity, my Stability . . . I would give it all up to have you happy and healthy again."

I didn't believe that, but I let him say his words; it's even possible that he believed the promise in that fleeting moment. We all want what we cannot have, but *having* a thing diminishes our desire for it.

The Watchmaker sat with me while I rested (supposedly to regain my strength, though it merely dwindled instead). He put his head in his hands, and I saw him more vulnerable than I had ever imagined. With a chill, I realized that he would have quietly gotten rid of anyone else who saw *him* looking so weak. He was a dangerous man.

Of all the things he had removed from my room, my father left the golden statue of Beneto, somehow believing that I appreciated the thing, that it would give me strength. Instead, I begged him to take it away. "Bring me an angel instead," I demanded. "A statue, like the ones in my old village."

I didn't believe in angels watching from above, but I was desperate to take comfort in something. I needed to have hope, to place my faith in someone other than the loving Watchmaker.

Desperate to comfort me, my father brought in four statues of folk angels, carvings he had found in some distant villages that still clung to the old ways, even after the Stability.

According to legend, there were four angels, goddesses of light, of sea and sky and land, beautiful female figures with stone faces and empty eyes, petrified wings with perfectly carved feathers. How could such a being, no matter how ethereal, ever hope to fly when it was made of stone? I didn't pray to the angels, didn't worship them. They were not so much goddesses, but rather manifestations of the human spirit, and for *that* reason I drew strength from them.

As my gold sickness grew worse, I would open the windows of my tower room and stare across Crown City, feel the breezes in my face, hear the murmur of so many busy little people seeking out their destinies, some of them with implausible dreams, others who would never learn how to dream at all. Meanwhile, I was trapped in the Watchtower, prevented from leaving, even though they believed the Watchmaker's beautiful daughter was well and truly blessed, that I possessed everything a person could want.

I wanted Beneto back, I wanted my freedom, but those treasures were not allowed.

But so long as I remained within the tower, I could explore the rooms, wander to the highest chamber and down to ground level. Bureaucrats and alchemists saw me drifting about like a lost ghost, accompanied by the clockwork dog, then they ignored me. The probability calculators and the secret alchemy labs intrigued me, but those rooms did not have what I sought.

Inside a dusty, cluttered storeroom filled with relics from conquered villages that had accepted Stability only with great reluctance, I discovered an object out of place among the military paraphernalia, a tangle of wires, splintered wood, and a resonating box. It had been tossed there with offhanded scorn, forgotten for years, but I recognized it immediately.

Beneto's guitar. He would never have left it willingly. I had never believed my beautiful friend would abandon me for a few coins, and now I *knew* my father had lied.

I wept in the stuffy storeroom for an hour before I composed myself enough to return to the main rooms. I could not let the

Watchmaker know what I had discovered, and I knew I could not stay.

There must be a way out of this prison—any way out. . . .

Late at night, with the stars in the heavens and the city far below, I looked at the stone angels in my room, but I was not brave enough to pray to them. Then I climbed up onto the sill of my open window. My legs were shaky, my hands trembling, and yet I set my bare feet on the stone and stood there on my precarious perch.

I knew I would never get out of the Watchtower. My father would never let me leave. I closed my eyes and lifted my chin to feel the night against my face, and then I spread my arms, as if to fly. . . .

That was when I decided I had to escape.

I knew that if I waited, I would think too much about it. Fear would eat away at my resolve, and logic would take the place of optimism. Thanks to the Watchmaker, I'd been brought up to believe that all is for the best, that we get what we deserve. Did I deserve to die alone, locked in a room, wasting away from a disease caused by too much gold?

If I waited, if I planned, I would grow weaker day by day. The sickness would wring the life out of me. My hands would shake, my muscles would atrophy. It had to be now.

I stepped down off the windowsill and yanked the covers from my bed. I tore the sheets into strips, which I knotted together. I pulled down the gossamer curtains and twisted them so that they also added to the rope. I had no idea if the length was sufficient; I knew only that the Watchtower was very, very high.

It was long after midnight when I made my escape. Once away from my prison, I had no idea where I would go, how I would survive by myself in Crown City. At any other time I could have simply reached out a hand and picked up an incalculable treasure of golden objects right there in my room. Now, I would be on my own, left to my own devices.

But Beneto had lived on the streets, so I was certain I could do so myself. Besides, I didn't know how much time I had left. Tick-tock. Who does?

I secured one end of my makeshift rope to the sturdy bedpost, wrapped a loop of the fabric around my waist, and tossed the rest through the window and out into the emptiness. I climbed onto the sill, yanked hard to test the rope's stability, then began to lower myself.

I prayed that my muscles would be up to the task. My arms trembled, my hands clenched the knotted sheets. I pressed my toes against the rough stone blocks of the tower, finding footholds; I lowered myself farther, relying on the strength of the rope to hold me.

I worked my way down foot by foot, one storey, then the next. I passed darkened windows where officials were sleeping. I climbed beneath workrooms and storage chambers where the Watchmaker spent his days. The ground looked so close, yet so far away. I concentrated on the descent. I was so weak and so scared.

Coldfire streetlights cast an eerie glow over the city, which was now silent, everyone asleep. I usually saw the square crowded with people, raising their hands in celebration as their loving Watchmaker stepped out onto the high tower balcony to address them. Now, except for the orderly patrols of the Blue Watch, Chronos Square was empty.

I found another windowsill and had to hold on, to rest, but even that briefest pause made my adrenaline seep away. My whole body shuddered. I was dizzy. Black spots danced before my vision, and I swayed on my creaking, makeshift rope, but I kept climbing down. I reached the end of the bedsheets and came upon the much slipperier fabric of the strung curtains.

I was two-thirds of the way down the tower, and I despaired of ever reaching solid ground. I couldn't go farther, yet I had to.

When I gasped, my lungs were on fire. Was this some bizarre test?

Then a group of Regulators marched into the square on routine patrol in their perfectly orchestrated march. They kept their eyes straight ahead, following the path of best inspection, but one man glanced up and saw me. He pointed upward, and the other Regulators turned to see a figure dangling from the high tower, clinging to a makeshift rope.

I tried to scramble down as the Regulators picked up their pace, striding toward the base of the tower. I was too weak and too ill, though; even if I reached the ground, I could not outrun them. But I had to try.

My arms spasmed, yet I kept lowering myself, trying to be faster. The curtain fabric was slippery, my palms sweaty, and I began to slide. I clung tighter, swaying, swinging, dizzy and disoriented. I finally caught the wall again and anchored myself. Still nearly twenty feet to go. I was sure that I couldn't make it, but I had to go on.

Then high above me, halfway up the tower, one of my makeshift knotted bedsheets unraveled, snapped free. The rope broke, and I fell, and fell, all the way to the hard pavement below.

※

My story should end there, since you requested my life story for your book, and my *life* ended at that point—my life as I knew it, my life as a human being. But my father wouldn't let it go at that, and life has a certain persistence. Dying is not so easy when you are the Watchmaker's daughter.

When I awoke, I found myself in a plush bed, though I couldn't feel the softness, at least not the same as before. I was not in my private bedchamber, but in a different room, a familiar room—one of the Watchmaker's workshops where he dabbled in clockwork mechanisms, alchemical exotica, and the quintessence.

I saw my father's face leaning over me. He appeared to have

aged a decade, his face drawn, seamed with lines and new wrinkles that looked like a million cracks in his perfect façade.

How long had I been asleep? Or had the depths of his concern for me drained all those years from him in a heartbeat?

When I stirred, blinked, and focused on him, the weight of concern and despair lifted from him like a curtain rising on a long-anticipated play. "My angel, you're awake! You are strong and alive. As good as new."

I didn't feel new, I just felt . . . different. I remembered trying to escape, climbing down the makeshift rope, *falling* . . . and the hard courtyard too far below. How——? I realized that everything in my vision now had a bluish tint, an electrical aura.

"You are no longer sick," my father said. "I purged the poison and repaired the parts of you that were broken. You are fixed now. Everything runs like clockwork." He straightened and smiled. "All is for the best."

Martin ambled in and stopped beside the bed. He sat dutifully, wagged his metronome tail. With great effort I lifted my left hand, saw my fingers flex—and saw the thin hydraulic tubes, the fine clockwork gears and the faint glow of coldfire that ran through my veins that were no longer veins. I knew with instant revulsion exactly what my father had done.

"Noooo . . ." I tried to scream, but all that came out was a whisper.

The Watchmaker was insistent, exuberant. "In my years of studying the alchemy of life, I've learned the secret—and I bequeath that secret to you, Charlotte. You prayed to the angels, and they couldn't save you. But *I* did, using coldfire and quintessence . . . and love."

I struggled to sit up in bed, and my body moved on command, like a windup soldier. To comfort me, I suppose, the Watchmaker had brought in the four angel statues to stand guard inside his workroom. He had also brought the perfect—or eerily *too perfect*—golden statue of Beneto, my true friend.

"I gave you your life back," he said. "My greatest work."

I could not appreciate the sheer joy he displayed. He called me his daughter, but I was his trophy, his experiment. He called me his angel, yet he had made me into this only-partially-human thing. He had robbed me of my freedom, then my life, and now my humanity. Beside the bed, Martin the clockwork Dalmatian sat perfectly still, a statue of life.

Still smiling, the Watchmaker said, "With the quintessence inside you, you can live for a long, long time! Maybe not immortal, but close."

❖

I remained in the tower for many, many years after my fall, after I was rebuilt. I had more time now, and more determination. I learned everything my father could teach me, and I went well beyond a passing knowledge of alchemy. I had my own plans.

In all those years, the Watchmaker never told me his own story, where he had come from, what he'd done before he saved Albion. But he did tell me about the many possible worlds that were just like our own, sideways universes that were a reflection of this one, but with differences—sometimes hair-fine differences, sometimes major shifts. But he didn't want to talk about those other possible worlds. He had made Albion perfect, just as he had made me perfect.

The Watchmaker believed in me, but I didn't believe in him. I simply bided my time. And thanks to his quintessential modifications of my body, I had all the time one could wish for, all the time one could endure. . . .

Now that he had remade me, the Watchmaker wanted to believe that I would take my place dutifully, just like Martin the dog. He renewed his resolve that I was destined to follow in his footsteps, to take over and carry the heavy weight of responsibility for all the poor people of Albion, to ensure that his Stability would continue long after he was gone.

I knew that I could not win by resisting him, so I changed my tactics and I embraced what he tried to teach me. I cooperated, and used my cooperation as a weapon against him. I would be responsible for my own freedom, and I would achieve it in my own way.

Through vigorous study, I completed the advanced curricula of the Alchemy College. I learned the secret of creating gold from the baser elements, but I was not interested in that. Thanks to my father, the world had enough gold.

Previously, the high-order mathematical magic of the destiny calculators had been beyond me, a secret too slippery to grasp, but something had fundamentally changed when I became this quintessence-powered, coldfire-infused approximation of a human being. The destiny calculators were more than just estimates to me now; I grasped them with the strength of a lonely lover's embrace.

I had private tutors from the College, but I also had access to the original texts, which I pored over. I became attuned to the predictive algorithms that studied the branchpoints of decisions. I could map out the many possible histories that might occur, each one of them true. I simply had to forge the path along the branchpoints that would lead to the best outcome.

My tutors marveled at my grasp of the subject, but I was wise enough not to show them exactly how good I had become. Even for the Watchmaker, the destiny calculators were only approximations to guide his choices. For me, though, they were *exact*. Alchemy became child's play, and predicting my destiny and anyone else's became my philosopher's stone, my quest for gold.

And because I was myself partly machine, I predicted intuitively, and I predicted that if I ever intended to escape the Watchtower, I could never let my father know the extent of my abilities.

I scanned ahead, reeling out the tangled threads of fate and future, looking for my chance, never forgetting what the

Watchmaker had done to Beneto, to me. I secretly used multiple destiny calculators to verify my own predictions, and I determined exactly when I would have my best chance to get away. I waited, I shaped my life, guided as many events as possible, flying like time's arrow toward the bullseye of my freedom.

I had to wait seventeen years before the perfect opportunity arose.

The Watchmaker's advisers and his destiny calculators suggested turmoil in Albion, a weak link in the Stability. Some outlying villages with delusional nostalgia wanted to overthrow the Stability, and my father's primary flaw was that he could not comprehend why anyone would wish to do so.

But even though it had been a very long time for me, I did remember colorful days when I was just a little girl—my loving family, the harvest festival dances, the music, the kindly old woman who made pumpkin cookies. There was a sense of *life* back then that was closer to the heart than any perfect, untroubled existence.

The Watchmaker could not abide that, and he took his troops and marched off to the rebellious villages so he could realign his Stability.

It was the chance I had been waiting for. Freedom was a goal in itself, and if other people could live across Albion, then so could I. At least, I wanted that chance . . . a chance I'd never had.

Knowing through my own predictions that the opportunity was imminent, I had been spending more time with Martin, my once-beloved pet. I used the time to reprogram his mechanism.

The spotted dog had complete freedom of movement throughout the Watchtower, and the Regulators did not notice or question him, so I sent Martin to the storerooms to fetch me the tools I needed. The dog trotted happily up to the high clock room, with its gears and clacking mechanisms. With the paper clenched in his jaws, Martin delivered requisitions supposedly from one of the clock keepers, asking for rope and equipment to be delivered up there.

One step at a time—tick-tock. Martin cleared the way for me. He was a good dog after all.

Though I was forbidden from leaving the tower, even after so many years, no one bothered to prevent me from going *higher*. The Watchmaker was gone with his armies, and his remaining Regulators were on patrol at the outskirts of Crown City to maintain peace and order. I went to the high clock room, with its gigantic gears and the pendulum swinging endlessly, the clunking gear and catch pounding out the drumbeat of time.

Martin followed me and sat watching my movements across the wooden floor as I pulled out the coils of rope, the block-and-tackle, the well-oiled cargo pulley system, and the fabric sling I had fashioned for myself. I opened the ornate stained-glass window of the external clockface to smell the night air and the freedom that I had longed for nearly two decades before.

This time I was determined to succeed. The destiny calculators all but guaranteed it.

Before, when I tried to climb down my makeshift rope, I had been too weak—as were the knots—and even though my body was now repaired and enhanced with fine pistons and hydraulics, I chose a much easier and much safer way to make my descent.

The large turning gears of the clock mechanism kept perfect time, but in this situation I realized that the gears were also a perfect engine, a smooth and brute-force pulley that could lower me all the way to the ground.

I attached the rope properly, took a moment to say goodbye at last to Martin, shedding coldfire tears as I hugged his spotted fur, and then I wrapped myself in the sling, lowered myself out the clock tower window, and progressed one second at a time, one notch at a time . . . all the way down to the flagstones of Chronos Square.

I was free. I began to run.

With the Regulator presence reduced in the city, my chances

of encountering the Blue Watch were already slim, and with my superior predictive abilities, I could increase my odds. I eluded them.

211

At the time I thought my escape was a harrowing, dangerous adventure with tremendous risks, but I've long since realized that the Watchmaker may have surrendered to my desires. Though I had played my role, he seemed to know in the secret places of his heart that I would never forgive him for what he had done to me.

He *let me go*.

After I fled to the outlying villages, I eventually came upon Magnusson's Carnival Extravaganza, and the carnies embraced me even with my strangeness—or perhaps because of it. I became a part of the carnival, a featured attraction.

Since I understood the paths of the destiny calculators, using a deck of Tarot cards instead of the sophisticated machinery, I could predict the future—*a* future—and advise those seekers, telling them what they wanted to hear or, in rare instances, what they *needed* to hear. The Watchmaker had made me into a freak, and I would make no secret of that. Here, it was an advantage.

Cesar Magnusson welcomed me. He was a plump, bald, and lonely man with an extravagant handlebar mustache. Eventually, I grew to love him; not with the bright passion I had felt for my dear friend Beneto, but with a happy contentment that was good enough. He was only the first "Cesar Magnusson" to run the carnival, there have been many more in the long decades since.

The carnival has been my home for more than a century and a half. Even quintessence fades with time, but my eyes are open, and I see the world through this small booth. But that is all I need to see, for I have seen it all already.

With all of his Regulators and his reasonably accurate destiny calculators, the Watchmaker could have pursued me at any time. I know that. A woman with clockwork enhancements to her body and coldfire in her eyes cannot hide, and I did not try to. I know my father still watches me, but he has left me in peace.

The Watchmaker missed his perfect daughter, especially at first. I'm told that he despaired—but he did not surrender. Like me, he had all the time he needed. He decided to start over.

It took him years of hard work and intense research, but more than a decade after I had escaped into my other life, my father introduced Albion to his own new miracle, as if to prove that he no longer needed me.

He gave the world his Clockwork Angels.

CHAPTER 13

Even though the alchemy-treated paper in her book did the work of writing out the fortune teller's tale, the effort of simply *remembering* it all exhausted the ancient clockwork woman. *Charlotte*. The windup key on the side of the booth slowly rotated to a halt, and the fortune teller sat straight, resetting herself.

Her last words came out in a dry rattle. "I need to rest now."

But Marinda had the woman's story, a long tale that went on for many pages. As she read it, Marinda realized that this fortune teller with her two centuries of astonishing experiences could have filled the entire volume by herself. Once again, the truths were a burden rather than a revelation.

Marinda had been brought up to believe that the world worked in a certain way, but now she realized that many things were different from what she thought she understood. And it made her angry.

As the Magnussen Carnival Extravaganza continued in all its joyful glory around her, she glanced toward the tall tower where the Watchmaker lived, a vantage from which he could observe Chronos

Square, Crown City, and all of Albion.

And now when she saw the golden statue of the ragamuffin boy positioned near where the carnival had set up, Marinda simply stared. Now she believed the Watchmaker had placed it there on purpose—knowing that Charlotte was with the carnival . . . knowing the old fortune teller would see it.

After everything she had just learned, as well as previously reading of her father's experiences when he had tinkered with the Clockwork Angels, Marinda felt a glow of anger rising within her. There was much more to the loving Watchmaker than she had previously realized—and not all of it good.

That was when Marinda made up her mind: she would go to see the Watchmaker in person and find out what he had to say for himself.

When she returned to Chronos Square the next morning, the carnival had departed like a brief summer storm that freshened the air and then moved on. The square was empty, save for the early workers in their red coveralls using pushbrooms and buckets to erase the debris of the show.

Back in her lodgings the night before, Marinda had reread the tales of all the lives the Watchmaker had left his mark upon, and she skimmed his autobiography, which she had purchased from Underworld Books. Even though that official tome had a great many pages, it did not contain much truth, according to what she knew now. . . .

Near the Watchtower, she paused to study the golden statue, thinking of Beneto and the mystery of what had happened to him. Had the Watchmaker truly killed him? Given all the years that had passed, the boy would be dead now regardless, unless he had achieved some kind of divine alchemical immortality. She stared at the smooth golden face, saw the hint of roguishness, possibly a hint of fear in his expression. She vowed to find the truth—and acquire another tale at the same time.

Two members of the Red Watch guarded the reinforced door of the Watchtower like statues made of flesh rather than gold. Straight-backed and businesslike, holding her leatherbound book, Marinda stepped up to them. "I need to see the Watchmaker."

"Do you have an appointment?" asked the guard on the left, but it was a pro forma question, for he seemed to know the answer already.

"I have a mission, which supersedes an appointment." She held up *Clockwork Lives*.

The guards were unimpressed. The Regulator on the left said, "The Watchmaker sees no one without an appointment, mission or otherwise." Their faces shuttered over as if they had become genuine statues.

But Marinda did not relent. "Please tell the Watchmaker that I am the daughter of Arlen Peake, a man he will surely remember. Also tell him that I know the full story of his daughter. I have questions that only he can answer."

She waited, determined and defiant, but the two guards did not flinch. She stared at them, and they stared back at her and through her. "Say the name Charlotte, and he'll know I speak the truth. His personal scheduler will surely find a way to make an appointment."

Finally, one of the Regulators moved. He did not turn so much as *pivot* to face the door, which he opened and then closed behind him.

Marinda stood at the base of the Watchtower for an eternity, or so it seemed, but the slow-moving hands on the giant clockface insisted that only seventeen minutes had passed. Finally, at 9:12 a.m., the door opened again, and a Black Watch captain emerged, regarding Marinda coolly. "If you are who you say you are, the Watchmaker has an immediate appointment available."

Marinda straightened her skirts, held the book close, and didn't acknowledge the two guards as she walked past them through the door.

The core of the tower was a dizzying disappointment of stairs, and the Black Watch captain moved at a brisk pace, as if to test Marinda's stamina. She passed the test, keeping up with him as they climbed past administrative offices, living quarters, laboratories, workshops. Finally, they reached a private room filled with mystery and intimidation.

The Black Watch captain gestured her into the room. "Wait here." He retreated, but paused before he closed the door on her. "If this is a hoax, the Watchmaker will not be amused."

"And if it is the truth? Then what will he be?"

The Regulator hesitated, as if he had not considered such a possibility. "That, I cannot say."

Marinda took a seat and waited, alone, listening to the tick-tock of a plethora of clocks that covered the walls, worktables, and shelves. She couldn't tell if this might be a repair shop—like her father had once run in the Regulator barracks—or if the Watchmaker was simply fond of clocks, many clocks. Her father had spent days held hostage in a workroom like this while he attempted to repair the Clockwork Angels. As she sat here now, the textures, the smells, and the carefully arranged disarray of spare parts added keen details to the events in her imagination, and they also reminded her of her father's cluttered workshop.

She did not keep track of how long she waited, for she was at the Watchmaker's mercy, and he had all the time in the world. Marinda had no intention of giving up. She wanted answers, and she wanted his story, and—a goal that was beginning to grow less important to her, she realized—she wanted to go home and claim her inheritance.

Finally, the door opened and a gaunt man entered dressed in a black jacket and polished black shoes. For a person with such power and presence, the Watchmaker should have been a looming titan, someone who made the universe tremble with awe, but he just seemed incredibly ancient, much like the clockwork fortune teller, although better preserved.

His skin was like parchment, his white hair plastered neatly over his head. The wrinkles all across his face were like a road map of arcane places. At the Watchmaker's side came the faithful Dalmatian, tail swaying back and forth in clockwork arcs. When his master stopped, the dog stopped and sat.

In a certain light the Watchmaker seemed kind and paternal, like a beloved grandfather; although in another light, he looked mummified. A pale blue glow hung behind his eyes, but they were bird-bright as they bored into Marinda, assessing her. "You make preposterous claims, young woman."

Marinda rose from the bench to face him, braver than she ever imagined she would be. "I have learned some preposterous things, sir. That is why I've come here, to ask for your help and to ask for . . . clarification."

On impulse, she bent down to pet the spotted dog. "This must be Martin. He looks remarkably well preserved." She saw the surprised expression on the Watchmaker's face and explained, "When my father was very young, he fixed some of the dog's damaged workings. Surely you remember him? Arlen Peake?" She raised her eyebrows, waiting. "I am Marinda Peake, his daughter."

"So you say." The Watchmaker remained skeptical. "You mentioned the name Charlotte. What do you know of Charlotte? And how?" His eyes widened as he suddenly realized. "Ah, the carnival! You must have spoken with her. This surprises me, for she doesn't often reveal secrets to strangers."

"Not just secrets. She told me her entire life story, from the fever in the village when she was a little girl, to her friend Beneto, to how she fell ill from alchemical contamination, how she tried to escape from your tower, and how you rebuilt her into something not quite human. I know it all. And I know my father's tale as well, how you held him here in hopes that he could repair the Clockwork Angels."

The Watchmaker's voice was hard. "Explain yourself."

Marinda held out the volume of *Clockwork Lives* and told him what her father had done. The Watchmaker took the book and sat at a worktable strewn with unrepaired clocks. In a startlingly rough gesture, he swept the mechanical debris onto the floor with a crash and bong of bells and pendulums. He rested the book on the now-empty surface, studied the gears and alchemical symbols on the cover, and turned the pages.

He pored over the first tale, her father's tale, and his coldfire-imbued eyes flicked back and forth like the pendulum of a clock. His expression became even more serious as he turned the pages, uninterested in many of the other lives. He paused to read the astronomer's tale more closely, then finally found the last and longest one in the book so far, his daughter's tale. He dropped into an even deeper, threatening hush as he read.

Marinda swallowed hard as she waited, suddenly fearing what he might do to her now that she knew secrets he had thought were so well hidden.

Finally, the Watchmaker closed the book, let out a slow sigh that was part wistfulness and part disappointment, and looked at Marinda with his piercing, quintessential gaze. "And what is it you want from me?"

Marinda steeled herself, remembering her purpose. "I want a very small thing, sir. Just a drop of your blood—one drop, that's all. Your life story will fill pages and pages. How could *Clockwork Lives* be complete without the Watchmaker's tale?" She waxed more enthusiastic. "The truth will be recorded here, the absolute truth. For history, for legend—alongside your daughter's tale, alongside my father's. Just think of the benefit to history."

"That is indeed what I am thinking of." He clutched the volume as if he could crush it with the strength of his fingertips.

With a chill, Marinda wondered if he intended to keep the book. What if he refused to return it to her? She realized how much importance it had gained in her life. It was, currently at least, the *only* thing she had left of her father. She swallowed hard and looked at the Watchmaker as a storm of emotions rippled across his parchment skin. She had a deep instinctive understanding of the word "terrible" that she had never known before.

He flipped through the pages again, intent, lingered on the story of her father again, and finally a calm washed over the Watchmaker's face, and he handed the book back to her. "Yes, I remember your father. Very well." He called for the Black Watch captain, who appeared in the doorway so swiftly he seemed to be spring-loaded.

"I will give you my story," he said, but did not sound defeated. Feeling a swell of relief, Marinda opened her book to the next blank sheet; it seemed fitting that the Watchmaker's tale would immediately follow his daughter's. "But I will not give you a drop of my blood."

The Watchmaker turned to a shelf in the workroom, from which he produced a different volume. "This is my official autobiography, which I make available to all citizens of Albion." He held it out to her. "*This* is the story that I choose to tell, with the details and the truth as I choose to tell it."

Though uncertain, Marinda accepted the book. "But . . . that doesn't help me complete *Clockwork Lives*. My quest . . ."

"I will help you with that as well." He turned to the Regulator. "Miss Peake has set out to acquire interesting tales, and I know the best way for her to do so. Place her aboard a steamer and send her away from Albion with all due speed."

The Black Watch captain had the information at the forefront of his mind. "The *Rocinante* is due to leave the harbor within the hour, sir."

The Watchmaker gave Marinda an unfortunate smile. "As a

reward for your father's service, I will send you to the continent of Atlantis, where you can be free to gather all the stories you like— far from here, where you will not disturb any of the good citizens of Albion."

Marinda was horrified. "But—!"

He tapped the cover of his autobiography, which he had given her. "And don't forget your book, a gift from your loving Watchmaker."

The Black Watch captain took Marinda's arm in an iron grip. "Come with me. Hurry now, or you'll miss your ship."

Marinda could barely keep her feet as the Regulator marched her into the corridor, then down the spiraling waterfall of stairs. The captain told her in a tone that invited no disagreement, "The Watchmaker is very generous."

She realized that he could just as easily have killed her. Instead, he had contented himself with sending her out of Albion and out of his sight. "Generous indeed," she said.

CHAPTER 14

Outside the tower, the Black Watch captain was met by two equally officious Regulators, all of whom escorted Marinda away from the Watchtower under no uncertain terms. They were nothing like the three charming clockwork Regulators that her father had built.

She protested, she huffed, but the Black Watch had their orders. "We will take you to the port and see you aboard the steamer *Rocinante*," said the captain. "You will embark on a great adventure to Atlantis—and far from here."

"But what about my possessions back at my lodgings? I have clothing, a valise, some books." Nothing she couldn't leave behind, but her protest was due more to indignation than sentimentality.

"You'll be compensated." The Regulator captain narrowed his eyes. "We get what we deserve." The Black Watch marched her at such a rapid pace that she stumbled; if she asked questions or complained, she didn't have enough breath to keep up.

The port at the mouth of the Winding Pinion River was a

bustle of large ships and exotic people with exotic merchandise, many speaking in strange accents, quite unlike the bucolic drawl of a Lugtown villager. Porters with steamcarts moved out of the way so the group could pass without hindrance. The captain led them directly to a towering steamer with blue-tinted steam gushing from the stacks as the engines built power. *ROCINANTE.* Crewmembers shouted as they prepared to depart, unraveling thick ropes from stanchions.

"Hold!" shouted the Black Watch captain. "You have a new passenger, by order of the Watchmaker himself."

The broad-shouldered sailors paused before raising the gangway, looking curiously at one another. "Captain Titus!" one of the men shouted up to the deck.

Before long, a short man with a crew cut and a lavish walrus mustache leaned over the rail. "We are not a passenger steamer. Besides, I hail from Poseidon City—the Watchmaker doesn't give me orders." His accent evoked thoughts of rare spices and strange melodies.

The sea captain's intractability surprised the Black Watch and amused Marinda. She took the opportunity to yank her arm free from the man's grip.

The Regulator captain paused, reconsidered. "Then you can classify her as cargo, for which you will be well paid."

One of the other three Regulators held up a pouch heavy with gold coins. The sea captain frowned, pondered the wisdom of a clash with the Watchmaker, and decided that a fee was better than a conflict. "More cargo it is then, but I will accord her the courtesy of a passenger. Welcome aboard, miss." The man stumped down the gangway and snatched the pouch of coins from the Regulator before turning politely to Marinda. "I am Captain Titus, Miss, and I hope to grant you a comfortable passage to Atlantis." He ran his eyes up and down her prim appearance. "No luggage?"

She had only her leatherbound volume and the Watchmaker's

official autobiography. "Nothing but these books. I hope you can provide whatever else I'll need during the passage. It was an . . . unexpected trip." She shot a glare at the Black Watch captain. "This gentleman says he will compensate me handsomely for the possessions I've lost."

She held out her hand and stared at the Regulator until he reluctantly produced another sack of honeybee coins, smaller than the first. Without a backward glance at the Black Watch, she followed Captain Titus up the ramp and boarded the *Rocinante* for her next adventure.

Later, as the steamer pulled out into the open water, she made a point of tossing the Watchmaker's autobiography overboard—where it belonged.

Marinda had never thought of herself as footloose; in fact, she had barely considered what lay beyond Lugtown—and now she was a world traveler, though not by choice. Since her father's death, she had grown more and more accustomed to living out of pocket and seeing what each day would bring. It was an unusual and uncomfortable change.

As the *Rocinante* steamed across the open sea for the next two days, she got to know the crew. The sailors were casual and made friends easily—more so than Marinda did, in fact. Since she had no belongings, two of the female sailors sorted through their garments and found spare clothes they could give her, although she insisted on paying them from her pouch of golden coins.

She had no idea what the future held for her. She had been exiled from Albion for requesting the Watchmaker's story, and for knowing too much of it already. Although he had not forbidden her from coming back, she had no idea if he would notice when she returned . . . if she ever did.

As the steamer chugged across the placid seas, she struck up conversations with the crew and learned about Atlantis—true details rather than fanciful travelogues from her father's library. The sailors told her about the rough streets of Poseidon City, the fishing villages down the coast, the alchemy mines in the mountains, even rumored lost cities deep in the Redrock Desert. They also told her about the treacherous Wreckers, pirates who preyed upon cargo steamers like the *Rocinante*.

In exchange, Marinda told the wide-eyed listeners about her own encounter with the Anarchist and his bomb that had brought down the steamliner. "After surviving that," she said, "I'm not afraid of Wreckers."

Once she had established a measure of trust, Marinda explained her quest and began to gather their stories. The amazed *Rocinante* sailors watched the alchemy react with their blood to spill out their life stories.

Marinda had imagined that sailors from a distant continent would have epic lives, but for the most part these men and women steamed from Poseidon City to Crown City, then back again, and again. They were wary of the Wreckers, endured the occasional storm, and performed their daily chores. They made up mysterious stories about lovely angels beneath the sea, but never actually saw them. They could spin out exciting tales, but when the true story of their lives was written out in their blood, the tales filled only a few more pages of her book, in total.

As the days went by, Marinda liked to stand at the *Rocinante*'s bow, breathing the fresh salt air and looking at the watery horizon in all directions.

Captain Titus joined her at the bow. He had respected her privacy during the voyage, keeping his distance, although he was obviously curious about her strange situation. While he stood next to her, he was struggling to think of a conversational gambit. He was entirely professional, but she saw a deep sadness behind his eyes.

Marinda gazed out at the ocean and said, "How do you know where you're going? It looks the same in every direction."

Captain Titus stroked his long walrus mustache. "I have a dreamline compass, miss. Several of them, in fact."

"I wish we all did." They both stared off to the west. "You are from Poseidon City?"

He nodded. "I have a wife, a little daughter, a son. *Had* a son." He hesitated, then added quickly, "My wife and her brother manage an inn in the city, the Cygnus Tavern." When he reached out to hold the rail, his cuffs slid up to reveal his wrists, which were encircled with scabs and fading bruises. Self-consciously, he tugged down his sleeves to hide the marks.

Had a son? Obviously, he did not want to talk about his sadness, so she chose a safer, general question. "What are the people like in Atlantis?"

Titus acted as if he had never considered the question before. "Oh, the clothes are different, and the accents, and the foods they like to eat . . . but I suppose they are still just people inside. Some of them good, some of them bad, some funny, some angry, some you can trust, and some you can't." He paused. "What are the people of Albion like?"

She thought about the various lives she had acquired for her book. "About the same."

The lookout sounded an alarm on the fourth day of the voyage, but Marinda could see no imminent danger. Nevertheless, the sailors rushed out on deck, manning battle stations. Captain Titus emerged from the bridge house, carrying a spyglass. The lookout pointed urgently toward the sky.

Marinda shaded her eyes and peered into the cloud-flecked expanse, but could see nothing more than what appeared to be a large bird. "What is it, Captain?"

Titus frowned as he put the spyglass to his eye. "A Wrecker scout—can't be anything else." He handed Marinda the spyglass.

She pointed the tube toward the clouds, and when the bird-like speck came into focus she realized the object was much larger than she had imagined. It was a battered airship that looked as if it had been put together by rambunctious children in the dark. The vessel puttered closer, staying high above the *Rocinante*.

"They've spotted us, so we better demonstrate that we won't be easy pickings." Captain Titus flashed a hard grin. "I just spent a lot of money on new defenses while we were in Crown City. Let's see what they can do."

As the Wrecker scout circled, Titus barked orders. Working together, sailors pulled away tarpaulins to unveil a pair of gold cylinders mounted on the upper deck. "You've practiced and drilled with the alchemical cannons," yelled Titus. "Now it's time to see if we got our money's worth."

The sailors kept a wary eye on the airship overhead. The Wrecker pilot seemed to be taunting them. Two crewmembers loaded the breech of the golden cylinders with packets of sparkling powder, then mixed in reactant liquids before sealing the chamber. They swiveled the alchemical cannons upward and pointed them at the patchwork airship.

Marinda listened to the sizzle and hiss of the churning chemicals. The sailors backed away from the golden cylinders, covering their ears. Titus gestured for Marinda to do the same.

The two cannons roared, spitting blue-white gouts of weaponized coldfire toward the airship. When they exploded in the sky, Marinda couldn't tell if either one was a direct hit, but the Wrecker scout reeled away in urgent retreat, barely able to maintain altitude as it limped toward the horizon.

The *Rocinante*'s crew jeered at the fleeing pirate, and Captain Titus looked pleased with himself. "I suspect the Wreckers will leave us alone—for now." He tried to reassure Marinda. "We should be all right for the rest of the voyage, provided we keep a head of steam." He hesitated, then asked, "Would you join me for dinner, miss?"

She smiled. "Yes, I would—so long as I can bring my book."

<hr />

In the captain's stateroom, Marinda set *Clockwork Lives* on the table and glanced at the captain's interesting keepsakes collected from a lifetime at sea: a selection of colorful seashells, several sheets of paper on which he had been writing a letter, a framed chronograph of a sturdy woman, a tall teenaged lad, a little girl whose hair was in pigtails. His family, she presumed.

"I take it you don't often have the company of a lady on board, Captain?"

"I don't often have the benefit of interesting conversation either, and fortunately tonight I will have both." He flushed, as if embarrassed. To make sure she didn't think he was flirting with her, he said, "I have a wife back in Poseidon City, a woman whom I love dearly. Nineteen years, and our marriage has survived more voyages than I can count. I feel the call of the sea when I'm home . . . and when I am at sea, I feel the call of home. It's like a tether pulling me both directions."

She looked at the chronograph. "Your children?"

"Yes. My son Aiden . . . he also felt the call." His voice fell. "Sometimes it's a curse."

She was startled to find a pair of iron manacles half-hidden behind the letter on the writing desk. To hold an unruly sailor in the brig? "What are these for, Captain?"

He swallowed hard, self-consciously touched the hidden bruises on his wrists. "For protection."

"Protection? Against the Wreckers, you mean?"

Titus gave her a strange smile. "We have more to worry about than Wreckers. The Wreckers are new, and the sea is vast and deep."

She touched the cold manacles. "Then protection against what?"

"For my own protection—against myself." He slid the manacles out of sight on the shelf. "The call is much stronger than most people realize. The angels under the sea . . ." His voice trailed off in wistful wonder, and fear.

Forcing himself from the distraction, Titus went to the small table, which held a covered tureen and two china bowls. "Fish stew, fresh from the galley." He ladled a serving into her bowl, and another one for himself as she took a seat across from him. "I apologize that I can't offer anything fancier. As I said when you boarded, the *Rocinante* is not a passenger steamer."

She tasted the fish stew and offered an obligatory compliment, noting spices she had never tasted before. "You did, Captain. And this was not a trip I expected to take, either."

He looked at her with his wistful, sad eyes. "And why was the Watchmaker so anxious to get you out of Albion? I hope you will tell me your story."

"I'll tell you my story, Captain, all of it. But it comes with a price."

He paused with a soup spoon raised halfway to his mouth. "What price is that?"

She slid *Clockwork Lives* across the narrow table. "I'll need your story in exchange."

THE
SEA CAPTAIN'S TALE

On my first sea voyage, a man jumped overboard in the middle of the night. He was laughing the whole time until the waves swallowed him. That was how I knew something else was out there.

By the time the other sailors threw ropes and life-preservers into the water, it was much too late. They shone coldfire lanterns down on the placid waves, but the man did not call out for help—not once—and we saw no sign of him in the dark and moonless night.

Captain Macallan looked disgusted. He let the other sailors take out boats to perform a perfunctory search, calling out their comrade's name, but they received no response. Finally, the steamer sailed on.

"He didn't fall overboard, Captain," I said, jarring the man out of his disturbed thoughts. "He jumped on purpose."

The captain narrowed his eyes, measured me. "The angels got him," he said. "The angels of the sea."

Then he went back to his stateroom and locked himself inside.

I grew up in Heartshore, a small fishing village south of Poseidon City. My father was a fisherman, and I learned to walk on a deck before I walked on land. I fell asleep each night with the sound of the waves as comforting as my mother's breathing. The sea called to me, and when my father saw me gaze out at the waves, he clapped me on the back. "You're a born fisherman!"

But that wasn't enough for me. The fishing boats from Heartshore rarely lost sight of the coast, and my gaze stretched farther—beyond the horizon. Heartshore was a warm and lovely place, but I wanted adventure!

I set off to find my fortune when I was old enough to sign aboard a cargo steamer—which is not very old at all. I ran away from home and went to Poseidon City, where I loitered around the port until I found a steamer looking for a crew. I would receive almost no pay, but the captain promised "a wealth of experience." Only two days after I arrived in Poseidon, I was crossing the sea in a ship full of metals, minerals, and alchemical powders for export to Albion.

Sailors whispered about the angels beneath the sea, beautiful women who could play a man's heartstrings like a musical instrument. I suspected they were just stories meant to tantalize or alarm a gullible new shipmate. I had grown up with fishermen, after all, and I knew about stories that were never meant to be believed, no matter how well told. But the undersea angels didn't sound like the usual tall tales; in the sailors' voices I heard as much fear as wonder.

And then that man jumped overboard in the middle of the night. Maybe he had seen the angels for himself, or believed so with a fervor that verged upon insanity.

For the rest of that first voyage, I stared over the edge of the steamer, looking in vain. I would go out at night and listen, trying to hear their mysterious song. But the sea kept its secrets, and I heard no ethereal voices beautiful enough to drive a man mad.

Not that time at least.

——◆——

It was on my third voyage, far out at sea and heading back to Poseidon City, that I did hear the music—more urgent, more beautiful, and more compelling than anything I had ever imagined.

I was asleep in my hammock belowdecks, off duty, and I sensed the presence dancing on the edge of my dreams. I woke in the darkness to the decidedly unmusical snores of my shipmates. The only light came from a half-shuttered lantern in the corner near the piss pot. The songs I heard came from the other side of the hull, at the waterline—and I knew I had to see for myself.

I swung out of the creaking hammock, careful not to wake anyone. With the voices of angels ringing in my head, I crept out on deck. Something told me I needed to keep this a secret. The undersea angels were calling to me and me alone. They had chosen *me*—none of the other sailors. I needed to hear their music for myself. It was an experience that could be cherished but not shared.

The night was black, without a moon, and I saw a pearlescent glow on the waves, rippling at the stern of the ship. The music came louder inside my head, an aria sung by voices that could never have come from human throats. Leaning on the rail, I stared down into the water, where I saw swimming figures—beautiful sleek forms with feminine curves and pearlescent skin.

Seeing that I had answered their call, the figures bobbed just beneath the surface. I could make out one angel, her face crystal clear, her features achingly beautiful. Her wings were made of iridescent scales, and they flapped like fins and drove her along. The angel easily kept pace with the steamer's engines.

My heart felt as if it would burst out of my chest. My throat went dry. I *ached* for her.

She looked up at me, her eyes wide and bright, her smile

233

longing. She spread her gem-like wings as if to fly beneath the waves. She opened her arms to reach out for me. She wanted me! She *needed* me. She called to me to join her.

I felt a rush of hope, a sense of self-worth greater than I had ever experienced. It would be so easy just to swing over the side of the steamer and drop down into the sea. She silently promised me a kiss . . . and an infinity more. Tears were pouring down my face. I *needed* this!

"Hey, you! Lad, what're you doing? Get away from there."

My trance was shattered, the hypnotic manacles broken. The song jangled in my head as if a trapdoor had opened beneath an entire orchestra. When I felt strong hands grab my arm, I thrashed and struggled like a wild beast.

By the time I managed to look overboard again, the glow had vanished from the water, as had the angels beneath the sea. They were gone. They no longer wanted me—at least not tonight.

I had missed my chance.

———— ◆ ————

The ocean remained silent for the rest of the voyage, and when I explored Crown City, even the wonders of that fabled place seemed flat. The Clockwork Angels were just inferior artificial contraptions, not remotely as beautiful as the angels I had seen in the sea. . . .

In time, I became a true sailor instead of just a boy who wanted to run off to sea. I crossed the ocean over and over and again, growing wise in the ways of the tides and the weather. In a few years, with his appreciation and a heartfelt recommendation, Captain Macallan allowed me to transfer to another ship, where I would be groomed as first mate.

I kept longing for that elusive music, searching the sea and the wind for the songs of the angels. Though I sometimes heard it, the marvelous women never came close. They must have been haunting other ships and other sailors less prone to disappoint them. I yearned for them, but they did not answer me.

Eventually, though, I found another way to break that elusive call: The only thing stronger than the unrealistic longing of a fantasy love is a *real* love and a family, and ties that bound me to solid ground instead of the sea.

Each time my ship returned to Poseidon City, I frequented the dockside taverns, but I felt most at home at a particular inn with a flying swan on its signboard, the Cygnus Tavern. The common room was no different from other inns; the food and the ale no more special; but a young woman named Selise caught my eye, and I caught hers.

Selise and her brother Rickard ran the Cygnus Tavern together because their rotund old father had a heart condition that prevented him from doing heavy work. Selise was smart and beautiful, quick with a joke or just as quick with a barbed insult when a rude customer deserved it. Something about the set of her eyes, the curve of her cheekbones, made me think of angels beneath the sea—and when I realized that fact, I went from being smitten to being in love.

While I sat in the Cygnus Tavern like a mooncalf, Selise would find a way to brush my shoulder or stroke my arm when she thought no one was looking. Each time my ship steamed away to Albion, I held my memories of her like a jeweler polishing and re-polishing a precious gem, and on each trip back to Poseidon City, I spent the days thinking about when I would see Selise again. That proved to be a cure from the seductive call of the angels.

Finally, at the start of a long storm season, which the weather diviners claimed would be the most severe in decades, I decided to stay behind and give up the sea. I had saved up my pay, because with dreams of Selise to occupy me, I had little need to spend my wages on carousing, though I did occasionally buy exotic treasures that I brought back to Selise.

In Crown City, I had bought a ring of the Watchmaker's gold, and when I returned to Atlantis, I purchased the most beautiful fire opal from the quarries of Endoline. It seemed a perfect balance—a gem from Atlantis, a gold ring from Albion, since the two continents pulled me back and forth, with the ocean in between. I intended to give that ring to Selise as a memory of my life as a sailor, the life I would be giving up for her.

Before the hearth in the Cygnus Tavern, I went on bended knee and asked Selise if she would marry me. The late-night crowd of drunken sailors fell into a hush as they realized what I was doing, then let out a roaring cheer when Selise accepted my proposal. From behind the bar, her brother gave me an approving nod, since he had measured me a long time ago.

When the rough storm season came, I was settled in my new home, landbound, a happy newlywed working in the tavern along with Selise and her brother. I felt no regrets; in fact, I barely thought of my former shipmates at all until they came back into the Cygnus Tavern when they returned to port.

A year later Selise's father died, not unexpectedly, but in Nature's odd sense of balance, she discovered she was pregnant soon afterward. Selise eventually gave birth to a healthy, red-faced boy who could squall with hurricane force. We named him Aiden. Selise was a good mother, and I thought I was a good father. The baby grounded me and anchored me. I learned the joys and the exhaustions of being a parent.

My shipmates came and went all year long, telling their adventures, which I knew were mostly lies, but I listened with an increasing wistfulness. Those days seemed so far away. Before long, my baby boy and my wife, both of whom I loved so much, who anchored me, began to feel like genuine anchors dragging me down.

The sea called to me.

I fought it for a long time, strengthening my resolve when Aiden took his first steps, or said his first words, but each time I left the tavern to go out on errands, I took detours to the docks and just stared at the ships, the names painted on the bow, counting which ones I knew.

I watched the brotherhood of sailors as they laughed and joked, singing chanteys while they hauled crates, then went out to carouse in the town. They were alive and energetic, full of the moment instead of long-term plans. Back at the Cygnus Tavern, I saw only a horizon composed of everyday days.

Oh, how the sea called to me.

Rickard saw the different look in my eyes, the glances I gave the sailors in the tavern. "You are going to hurt her," he said to me in a low voice, and I was startled at what he had realized—what I, myself, had been unwilling to admit.

I held on as long as I could, but Selise already knew long before I found the courage to talk to her. "It will be just one more voyage," I promised her, a promise that I fully intended to keep. But Selise knew I wouldn't.

"Come back to me," she said. I could tell Selise was heartbroken, but she wouldn't surrender to tears. "As long as I know that, I can stay here. I have a home and a good business, my brother and his family to keep me company. I won't be the only sailor's wife in Poseidon City. That's how it is. Just don't make me a sailor's widow."

Several captains offered to take me aboard as part of the crew, and I chose my ship carefully. I kissed my wife and held her so tightly and for so long that I almost changed my mind. Almost. I hugged my three-year-old boy and swung him around so that his memory of me would be laughter and smiles.

Then I sailed off for Albion.

The sea was a calming influence on me. I had satisfied my hunger, and now I could relax, like sipping a glass of fine brandy after a delicious meal. The ocean was calm, and the passage both ways was uneventful—so uneventful, in fact, that when I brought my pay back to the tavern, I suggested that I make just one more voyage. I hadn't been gone that long—only a month—and I had barely gotten the taste of a sailor's life again. Selise was resigned but not surprised.

Then it became a third voyage, a fourth, and a fifth. I would stay home for a week in port, help as needed around the tavern, spend time with Aiden and Selise. The Cygnus Tavern prospered, and my family wanted for nothing.

On my seventh voyage, though, the angels beneath the sea called to me again, sang to me, and set their hook in my heart. That irresistible pull dragged me out onto the deck at midnight, stumbling, like a fish being reeled in. The songs swelled inside me, the voices like diamonds and honeydew. They sang to me of wishes that could indeed come true and of the tyranny of unfulfilled dreams. They moved me. How they moved me!

I tried to be silent as I went out on deck, for I wanted no interruptions, no sailor on the night watch to stop me as had happened before, but I felt as if I'd lost my sea legs. My knees were wobbly— though it didn't matter to me because when I joined the undersea angels I could fly with them beneath the water, maybe even sprout my own pair of iridescent wings.

I saw them swimming beside the ship, goddesses of light beneath the waves—wings spread, arms outstretched, mouths open and filled with promises. It would have been so easy to slip overboard and be with them. So easy . . .

Although the temptation was like a storm front, I chose to resist. I thought of my anchor, my Selise, my Aiden, my family, my home, the Cygnus Tavern. Under the onslaught of the angels, my lifeline felt as thin and fragile as spider silk, yet I clung to it nevertheless. I cherished Selise's face, remembered running my fingertips along her cheek, kissing her lips.

Yet the angels still called me.

I remembered my laughing boy, swinging him around in my arms to make sure he remembered me when I was gone. Was that how he would remember me forever, if I went with the undersea angels now?

No!

I tried. I fought. I felt drunk with desire as the song resonated in my head, in my heart, and in my soul. The angels in the water spread their arms. They sang. My lifeline stretched and frayed, and I knew I was lost. I could not resist.

Suddenly, another sailor was beside me, grinning like a madman. His eyes were wide, delirious. Laughing, he leaped over the rail into the sea.

In that moment the spell was broken. I watched the man disappear beneath the waves. The angels enfolded him, and for a moment their iridescent wings looked sharp and dark, like shark fins.

I came to my senses, yelling, "Man overboard! Man overboard!" But it would be no use. The angels had wanted me—or they had wanted *someone*, and they were satisfied with the companion, or the victim, they had received. I was shaken, heartsick, and terrified because I knew that if they ever made that call again—and oh how I wanted them to!—I would not escape.

After that ordeal, I hurried back to the safety of home. *Home*—the word meant something more to me again.

Those dark and tantalizing fears out in the sea had burned me, changed me, and when my steamer finally returned to the Poseidon City harbor, I could not get off the ship fast enough. I raced to the Cygnus Tavern, found my beautiful Selise and my laughing boy Aiden, swept them both up in a hug, and promised I would stay with them from that point on.

For months, I took solace in the daily routine of the

inn—working the bar, sweeping the floor, dealing with customers, performing chores. At night I held my wife and slept soundly, though occasionally I was haunted by nightmares—and sometimes seductive dreams—of the angels beneath the sea. But *Selise* was my angel, and the call of family was far stronger than the call of the sea.

I managed to keep that promise for more than two years.

I would carry Aiden on my shoulders, but as he grew older he insisted on walking beside me. We spent days at the docks watching the steamers, seeing the cargoes they brought in from distant Albion, watching the crates of exotic gemstones and alchemical minerals delivered from the mines inland.

I told the boy of my seafaring adventures, and Aiden was enthralled, just as I had been as a boy in long-forgotten Heartshore. I described Chronos City and the Clockwork Angels, careful not to mention those far more dangerous angels in the sea.

But as my life's pendulum swung back the other direction and the balance shifted again, the terrors of those feminine voices disappeared into memory. I never doubted what had happened to me that night, but the call of the sea tugged in the opposite direction, pulling me away from my home and out to that compelling expanse of ocean.

Selise saw the yearning in my eyes and in my heart, and she knew what I was thinking. She had never understood the pull on a sailor's heart, but she understood *me*, and she knew that I would be miserable if she didn't let me go. "I would rather have you part of the time than lose you forever," she said. "Find a ship, do a voyage or two until you get it out of your system, then come back to me and stay for a time."

Selise made me promise to stay home during the dangerous storm season, and I agreed to the condition, but I understood there were greater dangers out in the sea than mere storms. I knew what lay beneath.

Before I set off again, I prepared myself. When I signed aboard another steamer, I knew how to protect myself.

I had paid a blacksmith to craft me a pair of manacles.

I did not hear the singing of the angels again for two more years, by which time I was captain of my own small ship. And the next time the ethereal music throbbed in my head and in my soul, I locked the manacles around the rail and around my wrist. To keep me safe. The keys were in my cabin, and my first mate had his instructions.

In the pale moonlight, I gazed down at the painfully beautiful women with their iridescent wings, their beckoning arms, their beseeching expressions. They insisted that I join them—and more than anything else in my life, I wanted to do just that. I longed to jump overboard.

But the manacles held me back. I fought and struggled, unable to think straight, and when I reached out for memories of Selise and Aiden and the cozy Cygnus Tavern, the angels' tone changed. They became angry, *jealous*. They did not like to be defeated. I had failed them, betrayed them, tricked them—and I thought I had betrayed myself.

I thrashed against the manacles, bemoaning my helplessness, wondering why I had been so foolish. Then other sailors ran down the deck toward me, grabbed me and held me even as I struggled. My wrists were raw and bloodied.

But the singing fell silent. The frustrated angels vanished, leaving me alone.

When I came to my senses again, I embraced the memory with great satisfaction, reveling in the experience. The angels were like a dangerous drug, but my resolve and my love for my family was stronger than the pull of that addiction. The manacles had bitten into my wrists, but I was alive.

Though many sailors talked about the angels beneath the sea, and some claimed to have seen or heard the calling, no one had escaped them unscathed as I had.

—◆—

After time and tribulations, I found a satisfactory balance, a stable point between the pull of the sea and the pull of my family back at the Cygnus Tavern. It seemed appropriate when I learned that in ancient times Cygnus the swan was also a god of *balance*. What could be more fitting?

I would sail during the trading season, stay home during the storm season. I was reliable and competent, and eventually I became captain of a larger ship.

My son grew to be a sturdy lad who helped his mother and uncle at the tavern, but he also sneaked off to the docks to watch the sailors. Selise and I eventually gave Aiden a little sister, an adorable copper-haired girl we named Cythia—all blue eyes, sparkles, and freckles, as much of a joy to our family as our son had been.

When I sailed back and forth across the sea, the crew indulged my peculiar habit of staying out on certain nights manacled to the rail so I could stare at the water with my head cocked just so, listening hard into the whooshing silence. Some thought I was eccentric; others thought me mad.

Five more times over the years, the angels came to me, calling with more and more urgency, and though I wrestled with the manacles, I could not detach them. I endured, and I adored, and I recovered from the pain of bruised wrists with the euphoria of the music I had heard and the beauty I had seen.

I became the captain of the *Rocinante*, a majestic ship with a thick hull and a wide beam that could ride through any storm. Our fighters could fend off the Wreckers if need be. I had the respect of my fellow captains, and I had my quiet, perfect home at the Cygnus Tavern. The best of both worlds.

Cythia grew into a spunky girl who stopped clinging to her mother's skirts and learned how to get into trouble all on her own. Aiden became a headstrong young man with dreams of his own, so I was not surprised when, coming home from a voyage, I found Selise in tears and a shadow over the tavern.

"It's those stories you put in his head! You and the other men in the tavern." She clenched her fists and pounded my shoulders. "Aiden ran off to sea! He signed aboard a steamer to work as a cabin boy. He's gone!"

With a heavy heart, I held Selise as she let her anger rush out like the retreating tide. I had seen the look in our son's eyes, and I knew the call of the sea was strong in him. "He'll be all right," I reassured her. "Just as I was. It's in his blood. If you understand me, then you understand Aiden."

She was weak and shaken, and I knew she had been crying for days. "All that we can do is wish him well. It's what he wants." I made her a promise that I knew I truly would keep. "When he comes home, I'll take him aboard the *Rocinante*. He could work as a ship's mate with me. There's no need for him to be on a strange ship. We'll be together, and we'll both come home to see you."

She brightened, as if that thought had not occurred to her. I continued to hold her. "He'll be safe with me," I lied.

I learned the name of the steamer Aiden had joined —a good vessel and a good captain, so I knew my boy was in satisfactory company. It would probably take a voyage or two before I could find him, work out an agreement with the captain, and bring my son aboard the *Rocinante*, but it would happen.

As my ship headed back out for Albion, the air took on a sour smell as of something dead. A red tide—a poisonous bloom of algae that sucked all life from the water like a spreading bloodstain on the waves.

A pall settled over the crew, and I gave orders for the *Rocinante* to keep going at full steam, anxious to make our way through the ocean sickness as swiftly as possible. But the red tide went on and on, and we hadn't found the end of it even by sunset.

Late that night with a full moon overhead, I couldn't sleep. I felt an uneasiness in my mind as if the angels were singing to me again, but this time in an off-key dirge. I ventured out onto the deck, heading to the bow where I could be alone. The stars looked down as I fastened my manacle to the rail, just in case.

Before long, the sea took on a luminous character, the phosphorescence that preceded the appearance of the undersea angels, but this time it was a sickly red glow, filtered through the algae and the belly-up fish bobbing in its path.

The angels began singing, and I heard them in my heart. I tugged on the manacle chain and looked over the side of the steamer. The beautiful forms appeared, oblivious to the death around them, spreading their iridescent wings as they looked up at me with unearthly eyes. Their song was as powerful as always, but compelling in a different way—not as seductive, not as jealous. Not as angry. This felt . . . *victorious*, as if the angels were somehow satisfied at last.

I strained against the manacle, and the metal cuff bit into my wrist, but the pain didn't jar me out of the hypnotic trance.

The angels swam together at the waterline, glorious, yet also terrible. When they saw me gazing at them, they *laughed*, and the music broke off inside my head. Two of the angels swam away with a flash of their undersea wings, leaving only one behind.

I was baffled. I had withstood their advances so many times, and they would no longer try to tempt me. The last angel looked up at me. *We don't want you.* Her voice was an insidious whisper within my brain. *We don't need you.*

She began to stroke away from the *Rocinante* before she laughed again.

We have your son.

Then the angel dove beneath the water, leaving me there, chained to the rail and unable to escape the heartbreaking news. I sobbed until dawn.

———————◆◆———————

I still have the manacles, but the angels have stopped calling to me, singing to me. They are satisfied with what they took, and now the sea, for all its mysteries, is just an empty book.

CHAPTER 15

After Marinda read his tale, Captain Titus didn't want to talk about what he had revealed. Even though she felt close to him, and sad for him, he held his pain and his silence as a hidden cargo.

Nevertheless, for the next two days as the steamer moved toward Atlantis, she kept her ears open when she stood on the open deck, hoping and fearing she might hear that ethereal music. But all that came to her was the constant whisper of waves. . . .

On the foggy morning when she first glimpsed the shores of Atlantis, the reality sank into her. An entirely new continent, on the far side of the world, a wide ocean away from Albion—tears sprang to her eyes. She was gazing upon a sight that her father had longed to see, a sight that he had forced *her* to see.

At first you will hate me for this. And then you will love me for it.

Other boats and ships joined them as they closed in on the harbor, drawn like iron filings to the magnet of Poseidon City. Captain Titus found an available dock where the steamer could tie up and unload the cargo from Albion.

The crew crowded at the bow, waving to anyone on shore. One of the female sailors offered Marinda an extra change of clothes; another gave her a traveling bag to hold her meager possessions and her *Clockwork Lives*.

Marinda stood on deck looking at the strange skyline of the strange metropolis. Poseidon City had its own character: rooftops of black tile, swooping curves rather than precise angles, crooked streets, a haphazard motley of stalls, awnings, and shops. And she saw the people—countless people, each with a story. She just had to find the worthy ones to include in her book.

When the steamer had tied up, sailors began carrying crates from the hold, hooking up winches and pulleys for the heavier containers, eager to be off to their families or favorite taverns— wherever they felt most at home. Gripping her travel bag, Marinda looked down the gangplank and braced herself for this reluctant adventure that the Watchmaker had forced upon her. Her heart felt both heavy and filled with nervous joy.

Captain Titus startled her. "You'll be making your own way from now on?"

"Yes, I suppose so." She still had many empty pages left, but with a whole continent full of people, she was sure she could fill them. "It is still a long journey, but I'm not entirely sure where to go."

The captain stroked his walrus mustache, and she saw the scars on his wrists. He reached into his pocket and removed a small gold and crystal device about the size of a pocketwatch but of an entirely different design. "I would like to give you this gift, Marinda Peake. I don't know if it will be of use, but it may show you the way."

She took the device with curious wonder. "I've never seen such a thing."

"It's a pocket dreamline compass, a nautical model, but some say it is keyed to the heart more than to any magnetic fields. The inner dial tells you where you are, and the arrow points to where you should be. The readings are often inaccurate." He seemed embarrassed. "I've never been able to get it to work myself, but you might have better luck."

She smiled. "Thank you, Captain. It is a fine gift. I will keep it close."

"Keep *all* your possessions close, miss. Poseidon City can be a dangerous place. Watch yourself."

Straight-backed, Marinda stepped down the gangplank and said over her shoulder, "I've been getting very good at doing just that."

❖

Poseidon City was more rough-and-tumble than Crown City. Her senses were bombarded with overlapping voices in exotic accents, strange musical instruments that produced odd melodic noises that were far more distracting than soothing. Merchants shouted at her, offering wares that she did not recognize. The people wore bright clothes, headbands, gaudy scarves, and ostentatious enameled jewelry. Food stands presented skewers of fish and vegetables with piquant spices that stung her eyes.

The movement of the crowd had an ebb and flow, like a living organism that followed its own rules. She looked at the peaked roofs of the buildings, clotheslines raising their banners of laundry, men guiding overloaded carts of produce, women leading clusters of unruly children. As she looked down one street after another, she saw not a single clocktower, and she wondered how these people kept track of time . . . or if they did at all. The Anarchist would have felt right at home here.

At the end of the docks, she came upon a sturdy fishing boat that had just arrived and tied up; it was old, but freshly painted and well cared for. A lone fisherman carried crates and stacked them patiently on the dock. He was about Marinda's age with a weather-scoured face and sad brown eyes. Busy with his work, he didn't seem to fit here any more than she did. When she paused, he looked up and caught her gaze. "Smoked fish from Heartshore, ma'am? Preserved with sea salt and driftwood smoke." Marinda remembered that was the fishing village from which Titus had fled as a boy. "Are you a merchant, looking to buy a supply? I've got a fresh cargo to unload."

The rich smoky smell of the fish made her mouth water. She laughed. "No, I'm not a merchant, but I am hungry." She reached for her coins. "Could I buy a piece? For lunch?"

He opened a paper-wrapped package to expose dried golden fillets marked with brown grill stripes. "No, you may not—I was about to break for lunch myself, and I have all too many opportunities to eat lunch alone. Would you join me? My name is Hender."

"Marinda." She accepted the invitation with grace and stepped aboard his boat, where he made a makeshift seat for her from one of the crates, sliding it across the deck into position. He pulled up another seat for himself, and a larger empty crate served as a table. He spread the paper to display a stack of smoked fish fillets, far more than enough for the two of them.

Hender seemed embarrassed when he realized he had no utensils. "I didn't think this through very well, I'm sorry."

"One can either complain or make do," she said, "and I think we're resourceful enough to make do."

"I do have bottles of spring water. They're even cold."

"All the better." She was happy for this respite, which gave her a chance to catch her breath and catch her wits before she made her way into the sprawling city, which seemed far larger and much more chaotic than Crown City. This fisherman, who wasn't even from the big city, had put her at ease in an unfamiliar environment.

The first bite of fish melted in Marinda's mouth. She smiled back at Hender, complimenting the flavor. "From Heartshore, you said? I've heard of the town."

He was surprised. "Not many people have. No reason for it."

She looked at his eyes and realized that the sadness was an old sadness, something that had become a faint part of him and would always be there, like a faded scar. "I've come a long way looking for stories. Do you have a story to tell?"

Hender's brows drew together. "A story? What sort of story would a poor fisherman have?"

"A wife? Children? Adventures on the sea?"

His expression fell. "No children, and my wife has been gone for seven years now. I'm just a fisherman." He cocked his head and awkwardly changed the subject as he washed down another bite of fish with water from the bottle. "Your voice has a strange flavor, Miss Marinda. Do you come from one of the northern villages? A town that renders leviathan oil, maybe?"

"No, I just stepped off the steamer *Rocinante*. I'm new here—I come from Albion."

"Albion?" He gave her a distant, wistful smile. "I always dreamed of seeing Albion, and my Ana talked about it, too. Is it as marvelous as they say?"

She thought about how to answer that. "You sound like my father. He always dreamed of seeing *Atlantis*, and now I'm finally here . . . but people are people and places are places. They all have their own sort of magic, I suppose."

Hender's gaze turned to where a cargo steamer was pulling away from the dock and heading out of the harbor. "It's good to dream of other places, whether or not you ever actually see them. I think that's what hope means. Maybe someday I'll get to Albion myself." Her heart ached when she saw his expression.

But she couldn't think of Albion yet—she had just arrived here in Atlantis. "And I have a whole continent to see." She took out the dreamline compass that Captain Titus had given her, looked down at the incomprehensible dials. "This is supposed to tell me where I should go, but I don't know how to use it." The pointer wavered uncertainly back and forth, but kept pointing back at Hender; Marinda certainly didn't know what to do with that idea.

A troubled look crossed his face. "You can get just as lost relying on a compass if you don't have a good idea where to go in the first place."

She finished her smoked fish and enjoyed Hender's company for a while longer before she stood from the wooden crate that served as a makeshift chair. "Thank you, but I need to make my way, see some of the city, and find lodgings for the night."

"And I have to finish unloading my cargo and find a merchant to buy it. I appreciate the lunch—it was far superior to eating alone. I hope you find where you're going."

As she explored the streets of Poseidon, she kept her coins close and her wits about her. She saw groups of ill-clad youths on the street, and rugged sailors trying to achieve the greatest hangover in the least amount of time.

She passed several disreputable-looking inns, which made her think longingly of her quaint, cozy cottage back in Lugtown and her charming clockwork Regulators. But that was a long distance away and many months in her future. She still had her quest to complete, and she needed a place to stay in the meantime.

When she found an inn that looked marginally more acceptable than the others, Marinda booked a room. The innkeeper woman took one of her coins, held it up to the light, and admired the honeybee symbol. "Good Watchmaker's gold—you're welcome to stay here anytime."

The small room was furnished with little more than odd smells and disappointment. Taller buildings blocked light from coming through the narrow side windows, and even though it was midday, the interior seemed as dim as a cloudy dusk. Marinda left her travel satchel in the room, knowing there was nothing of value in it; she pitied any thief desperate enough to steal an extra set of dirty skirts and pants. Back home, a treasure of gold waited for her as soon as she could claim her inheritance . . . but here, this was all she had.

Marinda undid her tight and efficient bun, deciding to wear her hair down, since she was in another part of the world now and she didn't need to impress anyone she knew. It felt liberating to have her hair free and loose, and she was ready to face a new city. Then she set off, carrying only her leatherbound book, Captain Titus's dreamline compass, and her securely tied purse.

Marinda walked along the thoroughfares, careful to remember her way back to the disappointing inn. In Crown City, all the main roads were straight, like the spokes of a wheel emanating from Chronos Square. Here, though, the streets were as straight as shattered glass, with dog legs and hills and dead ends. Many dark alleys looked like the lairs of predatory spiders waiting to trap unsuspecting flies, and Marinda kept to the crowded thoroughfares.

Among the people, she saw few welcoming gazes, no friendly offers of conversation. Now she wished that she had talked longer with Hender. Preoccupied, she stepped in a puddle and frowned at her clumsiness. She stomped the splash of mud from her shoe, glanced into a narrow side street—and saw an unexpected sign above a hidden business, a set of stairs leading down and a shop window.

Underworld Books.

She blinked. The lettering was exactly the same as on the similar bookshop in Crown City.

Marinda paused in front of the display window, seeing familiar volumes: *Before the Stability*, one titled *The Myth of the Clockwork Angels*, a large art book filled with chronographs from Crown City; there was even an ancient-looking copy of the Watchmaker's official autobiography.

With a rush of excitement, Marinda hurried down the steps and yanked open the door. Inside the shop, the dusty air smelled of the weight of literature. In the back room she caught a glimpse of the large gold-framed moonstone mirror that she now knew was a doorway to many possible worlds. And sitting prim at her table with her hair pulled back in a tight bun, with round glasses and a smile that she reserved for customers, was the bookseller.

Marinda caught her breath. "Mrs. Courier! Do you remember me? Marinda Peake—from Crown City?"

The woman frowned. "No, I don't believe so. And I generally go by just Courier."

"I came to you at your other store. I talked with you." She held out *Clockwork Lives*. "I'm filling this book with tales. You gave me a drop of your blood."

She was surprised and disappointed by the blank look on Courier's face. "I'm afraid you must have me confused with some-one else."

Marinda placed her leatherbound book on the front table and opened to the page where the bookseller's tale began. "Look, your entire story. I know about the moonstone mirror. I know about Omar and how you hope to find him . . . just as he hopes to find you."

With growing astonishment, Courier peered down at the pages, ran her fingertips along the blood-written words. Her eyes widened behind her spectacles. "This is not possible! I assure you, Marinda Peake, I have never met you before." She read another page with avid interest, then shook her head. "This is indeed Underworld Books, and my name is Courier." She tapped the alchemically treated paper. "But this is not me—or at least not this version of me." When she looked up, tears welled in her eyes. "But you know me, you know my story." Her voice became quiet and dry. "I was never brave enough to write it myself."

"The alchemy wrote it," Marinda said.

This other Mrs. Courier sat down and pulled *Clockwork Lives* toward her, engrossed in her own tale, reading page after page.

When she finished, she looked up at Marinda with deep sadness. "Yes, that is my story—or almost the same as mine. A few details are different, but . . . I was hoping for a different ending. So hoping." The other woman handed back the volume. "As a bookseller, I believe in few higher callings than chronicling the lives of interesting characters. I wish you well in your mission."

Marinda was about to ask the bookseller for help, but a disturbance in the back room interrupted them—a clatter, a heavy footfall. A strange man emerged, staggering into the main room on unsteady feet. He had dark eyes, gray-flecked hair, and a drawn, astonished expression.

"Again," he said, "and again and again!" He looked around the bookshelves, confused.

Courier rose to her feet, aghast. Her hands were trembling, her mouth open. She couldn't speak a word, nor could she tear her eyes from the man.

The stranger glanced at Marinda, but she became invisible to him as soon as he saw the bookseller. He froze as if he had been alchemically transformed into a statue.

Courier spoke in the tiniest of voices, as if afraid that uttering the name might shatter the vision in front of her. "Omar . . ."

The man broke into a run. "Oh, my love, my love! You're here—you're finally here. After so long!" He threw his arms around the woman and smothered her with kisses. "Finally here! You're finally here." He kissed her neck, then her lips, and drew back just to stare at her face. The two of them had tears pouring down their cheeks. "We're both finally here!"

"I've always been here," she said, "but we were never in the *same* here."

They began laughing and weeping and talking all at once.

Knowing she didn't belong in this particular moment, Marinda quietly retreated to the door. Now, at last she had an end to one of her stories.

As her father had said, some lives were epics . . . and there must be plenty of stories here in Poseidon City and all across Atlantis; she just needed to find them. She walked briskly, head held high, holding her book. The people around her seemed less dreary; she saw fewer surly expressions, heard conversations rather than complaints.

A young man with a mop of blond hair and raggedy clothes walked along, apparently distracted. He stumbled, bumped into her, and caught his balance against Marinda, before he excused himself, embarrassed. She saw that his left wrist ended in a clean stump.

The sight distracted her for a moment, but when she felt an unexpected tug, she reached out with her hand as swift as a whip. Before the young man could bolt away, she grabbed his other wrist. He held her purse of gold coins in his hand, as well as the small blade with which he had sliced the cord.

The young man thrashed and struggled, but Marinda's grip was like the manacles Captain Titus wore. "Let me go!"

"No—you are a thief."

"I just bumped into you, that's all." His lie was bold and obvious. He held the coin pouch in his hand.

She stared at him. "You tried to steal the only thing I have left in the world."

He snapped back, "And what makes you think I have anything for myself?"

Holding up his stump, he tried to twist his other arm away, but Marinda wouldn't let go. "If you think that'll make me pity you, you're sorely mistaken. I'll find the city guard and have you locked up in a prison."

His face paled. "Wait, there's no need for that. You have your pouch—now let me go."

She saw something in his expression. Even though he was young, the pickpocket looked bruised and toughened, with plenty of hard-life experiences under his belt. "What's your name?"

"Guerrero," he said, as if it were a matter of pride. "But you'll never find me again." He struggled once more, but she refused to let go.

"I will release you and not call the authorities—but I have a price."

He looked suspiciously at her. "I don't have anything."

"Yes, you do, and you can easily give it to me—no harm done. I'll let you go . . . if you give me your story."

THE
PICKPOCKET'S TALE

When you steal, what is stolen from you?

It was a necessary lesson, but not everyone learns a lesson in time—or at all.

I had been warned not to break into the old man's house. The other pickpockets on the streets of Poseidon City were terrified of the place. "That old man is a *necromancer*," one of them told me when I mentioned my plans. "He's an evil alchemist. And dangerous."

I laughed bravely, making the other boy feel like a fool. It is easy to laugh bravely when you are safe and far away . . . and before you do a stupid thing.

"The Watchmaker in Albion is an alchemist, and he has more gold than any person can imagine. So I hope the old man is an alchemist." I narrowed my eyes. "You will all remember the name of Guerrero. Oh, you'll never forget me!"

My friends were not laughing. "We'll remember your name, when we tell stories about what happened to you."

I brushed them off and made my own plans to break into the necromancer's house and rob him blind. I had been wanting to do that for a long time.

<hr />

When I was just a boy, my father taught me how to steal, and he tried to teach me how to kill. He said I had great potential.

We were abandoned on the streets of Poseidon. My mother had died of a fever when I was but five years old—at least that's what my father said. He thought I didn't remember her, but I could recall my mother's face very clearly. I remembered a screaming fight, her shouting at my father, calling him worthless, and then she had stormed off. She left me there with him, and I never saw her again.

I don't remember her dying of any fever, but my father clung to that story with all the desperation of a broken man clutching his last few copper coins at the gambling table.

We lived on the streets, and I was always hungry. When I begged him for food, my father scowled at me. "If you want food, you have to hunt for it. Out in the wild there are predators and prey." He gestured to the crowded marketplace, the inns, the small houses of working people, larger houses of merchants in the hills that rose from the harbor. "Everything around you is for the taking."

He took me along the bustling streets, told me to keep my hands to myself but my eyes alert. "In the wild, a lion has to hunt his prey in order to eat. Do you want to be a lion, Guerrero?"

I didn't feel like much of a lion with my empty stomach and my dirty clothes, but I nodded.

So he taught me how to hunt marks in the city. I had heard him complain that I was an impossible burden on him, but he learned how to make use of me, too. He explained that some animals hunted alone, some hunted in packs. And we were a pack—him and me.

We would walk quietly together, studying the marketplace and the individual stalls. At first, because it was relatively safe, he would have me dart in and steal portyguls, pomegranates, or apples from Albion. I learned how to be fast and reckless. I could grab fruit and race away while the merchants bellowed after me (if they noticed me at all).

About half the time I got caught, and as I struggled and thrashed, sometimes dropping the fruit I had stolen, my father would come charging up, looking indignant and upset. "My boy, what have you done?" He would groan at all the onlookers. "Didn't I teach you better than that?" He would strike me on the side of the head, graciously return the stolen fruit, and drag me away from the fuming merchant. "I'll make him learn his lesson, believe me!" my father would growl, and we would get away with it.

And I did learn my lesson—I learned how to be more nimble and more adept at dodging pursuit.

If I escaped unscathed with my booty, we would meet in a prearranged alley. I'd hand him the fruit, and he would cut it into pieces, giving me my share, which was about a quarter of the take.

When my father needed to steal something more valuable, such as a stall vendor's daily money chest or a metalworker's jewelry, we used a different ploy. I would wander into the marketplace where jewelers sold gold chains or tourmaline pendants, pearls from the northern coast, fire opals from the alchemy mines. I'd wander in innocently, skipping along, then let myself grow confused. When I reached the proper spot, I would suddenly start wailing for my father. The "lost and panicked little boy" was an extremely effective diversion.

When the jewelers and the city patrol rushed to help the poor, terrified child, my father would snag a few gold chains or amethyst brooches. He showed restraint, taking only one or two amulets so the merchants didn't even notice they'd been robbed, at least not right away.

We learned the underside of Poseidon City, hidden places that no one saw and no one knew about, except for people like us.

There were abandoned buildings, empty basements, snug and sheltered alleys. Every night a different home.

"It's because we are free, Guerrero," my father said. "A new roof whenever we like, a warm home, and then we move on and find another." I learned later that we had to keep moving to avoid being caught. The justice of the city patrol was swift and meted out with clubs.

We would look at the lighted rooms above the shops, where families lived in their permanent homes. My father would laugh at how they were caged, and how we were free. But I thought the houses looked nice. Part of me longed to have a place like that of our own, but my father cuffed me when I mentioned it. "I didn't raise my son to be a fool. Worthless dreamers are *prey*, not lions."

But he started to gaze at the private dwellings as well, the mansions in the hills, and his eyes held a new gleam. We paid attention to the houses of the merchants, the landlords, the city's elite, and we resented the rich people who built extravagant dwellings and sprinkled gold on their food to flaunt how superior they were to people like us.

He grew excited when he learned that some of those mansions were unoccupied, filled with food and possessions that were left to gather dust while the landowners went to vacation in the countryside to lead decadent lives. Breaking into those houses was easier than stealing from marks on the street, with a far smaller risk of being caught. We would locate one of those empty homes, break a low window. I was still small enough and young enough to worm my way through the hole, then unlock the door and let my father in.

I remember that first house—I had never had such a feast! We ate salted ham, pickled eggs, cheeses, preserved fruit, honey, and smoked fish. My father found grime-encrusted bottles of wine so old he insisted they were valuable, so he opened one for himself and one for me, making me drink it. I don't remember much beyond feeling awfully sick and him laughing at me as I vomited on the rich merchant's sofa.

One looming house was set apart from the others on a steep slope—it looked ostentatious yet sinister, and as we watched night after night, we never saw more than one hooded light moving from room to room; occasionally, colored and stinking smokes wafted from rooftop vents. The house wasn't empty, but it seemed to exude mystery.

I looked at it with curiosity and fear, hoping my father wouldn't suggest we try to spend the night there. To me, the house looked haunted, or cursed. My father, however, looked at the mansion with avarice in his eyes.

We knew other street people like us—not friends, not colleagues, not even competition. They were a source of knowledge, however, and my father began asking them about the house. Most of them shuddered. "Dangerous, too dangerous! That man is a monster," said one. "A wizard," said another, while a third called the owner "an evil necromancer with magic prism eyes."

My father was not frightened, though. He stared at that mansion with an increasing hunger, and I knew he would not let go.

He obtained a large sharp knife—stole it, no doubt, although he said he purchased it—and he got a smaller knife for me. After he gave me the blade, he took me to where we could look up at the supposed necromancer's mansion. He said, "You're not ready yet, Guerrio. I need to teach you the next thing. You know how to steal, but it's long past time you learn how to fight," he said. "Because sometimes the prey fights back."

I was scrappy, but fighting was never the preferable tactic because sometimes the prey might win. Sometimes a lion was killed.

For my deeper training, we preyed upon weaker people in the streets. We would linger behind taverns and strike men who were so drunk they could barely walk. We rolled them and stole from them, but most had already spent the bulk of their money in the tavern. My father robbed several of them to show me how it was done, and then he made me do it by myself. In the garbage of an alley they were easy pickings, and I didn't see how this was preparing me to fight an evil necromancer (who was probably just an eccentric old man anyway).

Sometimes our targets yelled for help, and I learned to dodge and dash away, running with all my might before the city patrol came. Once, when I ran away with a disappointingly thin sack of coins, I bolted between buildings and emerged in a narrow side street with my father puffing to catch up. Unexpectedly, I ran into another gang of street kids who surrounded me—five of them—as if I had sprung a trap. They were predators too, hunting the weak, but these were a different kind of predator. Not lions. More like hyenas.

They reacted swiftly, viciously, when I burst in among them. Working together, they grabbed me; one snatched the stolen coins out of my hand, and another shoved me against a brick wall, knocking the wind out of me.

"We've seen you," said one of them. "Don't like you." He punched me in the stomach with the force of a battering ram. I doubled over, coughed and retched. They took turns hitting, slapping, slamming me against the bricks. I flailed, but could not land a blow. One punched me in the face, and blood poured into my eyes so I could barely see.

When I looked up, I saw my father come running up between the buildings. I knew I was saved. But as the boys kept beating on me, my father just watched.

After they had taken the few coins from me, I had nothing left for them to steal, and I provided little sport against five of them, so they eventually grew bored and went away, leaving me bleeding and groaning in the gutter.

My father stood over me, frowning in disappointment. I tried to speak through swollen lips, but there was too much blood in my mouth. I finally managed, "Why didn't you help me?"

He grabbed me by the arm and pulled me to my feet, despite my outcry of pain. I was sure several of my ribs were cracked. "You have to learn how to fight. Be a lion." My father wasn't sure I had learned my lesson, so he got even harder. "You have too many boundaries, Guerrero. We have to make them go away."

I think he was looking for the right opportunity.

Several days later, we attacked a staggering sailor who wandered the wrong direction away from a tavern. He looked like a poor mark, not quite inebriated enough to make him defenseless, and he was larger than the two of us together, but my father pushed me forward, made me try to pick his pocket. The sailor fought back; he bellowed as I grabbed his money purse.

My father rushed in to join the fight. "Stop him from shouting!"

I saw a flash of steel—his large blade—which he plunged into the sailor's side. The drunken man gasped and choked, initially in disbelief, and then the pain hammered into him. My father ripped the knife free and plunged it in again, higher, then withdrew and stabbed a third time. The sailor's screams were hoarse now, mere gurgles. He slithered to the ground as I backed away in horror, but my father wasn't finished; he was just building momentum. He pushed the sailor to the garbage on the ground and stabbed him more times than I could count. When the victim lay bloody and twitching, my father grabbed the money pouch and tossed it to me. When I caught it, blood got all over my hands.

"You . . . killed him," I said, stupidly.

Sneering, he yanked my arm, and we ran away from the corpse. "And what do you think a lion does to his prey? He *kills!* That's what you have to learn—be a hunter, not a victim."

When we were in an open street under a full moon sky, he grabbed me by the shoulder, turned me, and pointed up at the looming house of the necromancer. It still looked so tantalizing on the hill, a shadowy hulk with a glimmering light in one window. "*There!* Remember that. You have to learn to do anything for *that.*"

Our lives were focused toward that goal, but as he built the eccentric old man into a greater and greater nemesis, my father made my training harsher. Desperation leads to justifications.

Each day and with every scavenged or stolen meal, he reminded me that we were free, that we made up our own rules—but it was my father who made up the rules, and he forced me to do things that I did not wish to do.

After the third man he murdered in front of me, I realized that he liked using his large knife, and he egged me on, forcing me to draw my knife whenever we attacked, just in case I might need to use it.

On the last time, late at night, I was with him while he brooded, planned, and grumbled, searching for a new victim. A thin man with a small valise left a shop and locked it, turning down an empty, deserted street. He was a tailor, I believe, not our usual victim, but my father grabbed him, dragged him into an alley. The man yelped. "I have nothing." He flapped his hands, dropped his valise. "Take my papers, that's all I own."

My father didn't want to believe him. "Hold your knife, Guerrero. Be ready."

I drew the knife as instructed, not sure what my father wanted. "But he's no threat to us."

"Help me," the tailor wailed.

My father let go of the victim and shoved me toward him. "Kill him—you have to kill him, Guerrero!"

The thin man cringed. I had the knife, but I froze. My arms were shaking. "No," I said.

My father slapped me in the back of the head. "You have to kill him! He knows your name. He'll call the city watch."

But I'd had enough. I knew how to survive in Poseidon City, but I wasn't sure how much longer I would survive living with my father.

"Kill him! Be a lion."

I whirled with the knife and jabbed it at my father's face instead. "You want to feel my claws?" I darted the blade back and forth, as I yelled to the tailor out of the side of my mouth. "Run!"

He scrambled out of the street, arms and legs bouncing like a scarecrow blown away in the wind.

My father reddened, and he grabbed for his own large knife, but I slashed with my dagger. This time the blade bit more than just the air. I sliced across his cheek, leaving a bright red line. He had taught me to steal and tried to teach me to kill, but I chose to be a coward rather than a murderer.

I jabbed my knife at him again, and he backed away, shocked. As he pressed his palm against his bleeding face, I fled. My father had said it many times before, but now I felt the difference. Now I *was* free. Now I was truly a lion.

———

I survived on the streets, as I knew how to do so well. I used what I had learned from my father, and also the *opposite* of what he had taught me. I never spent time with him again. Didn't want to. Didn't need to.

I made friends, shallow ones because I didn't know how to do anything else. Some friendships lasted months, some only a few days, but they were like bright burning stars. I left them when it became necessary. Fundamentally, though, I was alone—and meant to be that way.

I learned how to get what I wanted. I fought occasionally, but mostly I escaped. I was swift. I was clever. I was a *survivor* instead of a victor, and that was enough for me. Whenever I found a safe, empty house, I would slip inside, take from those who had too much, and use things that would never be missed.

But as the years passed, I kept looking at the old man's house. My friends on the streets also avoided the place. They told stories that reinforced the fears my father had . . . but the wild and specific details were so similar that I realized they were simply repeating rumors my father himself had started. I laughed them off, because I knew the stories weren't true, and I knew what sort of man my father was.

In time, though, I realized I would have to prove it—as another way to be free of my father. The mansion crouched on the hillside like a hoarder hunched over some ill-gotten treasure. It was a sinister, intimidating place, and every night I saw that eerie glow wandering from window to window.

Then the necromancer's house went mysteriously dark, empty, silent—for weeks. I watched for several more nights. A chill went down my spine as I made concrete plans, for it is a frightening thing when a fantasy becomes an actual possibility. The necromancer had vanished, or died, or maybe been trapped in some terrible misfire of a spell.

I had to make my move.

I chose my night carefully, waited for the dark of the moon, when the necromancer's mansion was one looming architectural shadow. Holding my sharp knife and ready to fight, I broke in as I had done countless times at other homes, but this felt different. Infinitely different.

Dangerous . . . and tantalizing.

The gloom inside the mansion was oppressive, like a strangler's silence, but as I crept forward I could see that this strange and mysterious man, whoever he was and whatever his powers, was as inconceivably wealthy as my father had claimed. That part of the legend at least was true.

Urns were filled with gems, as if for mere decoration. Gold glimmered from all furnishings; mirrors hung on the walls with gilded frames and blank pearlescent faces that looked like moonstone, rather than silvered glass. There were statues and candlesticks, many made of gold, but others of even rarer silver or platinum. Chandeliers hung from the arched ceilings, sparkling with memories of light that came from nowhere within the mansion itself. A polished marble fountain was filled not with trickling water, but with long quartz crystal prisms that showed rainbows in a spectrum of black.

With so much fabulous treasure, how could I be afraid? I could just grab an armload of gems and gold and run grinning into the night. But I didn't. I should have known better.

Breathing fast, I climbed a wide river of stairs that flowed from the upper level. Though I resented him, my father had prepared me for this. If the evil wizard lunged out at me, I would stab him with the knife and dash away.

I moved cautiously, eyes alert, ready to run if I encountered some slavering monster or crimson-eyed litch intent on stealing my soul. I doubted I could fight a necromancer (if he *was* a necromancer, instead of just an eccentric old man).

When I reached the upper level I found an immense gallery with fountains and basins, empty frames on the walls that seemed to be waiting for portraits. And more mirrors, including one large looking glass on a stand. I heard a muffled voice, a desperate cry that seemed to come from far away.

The voice came from inside the looking glass.

As I stared, a figure appeared on the other side of the mirror, a kindly-looking old man with long gray hair and a voluminous gray beard. He was *inside* the reflecting pane, an image without an afterimage. "Help!" he said, but his cry was muffled through a thin pane of glass and however many dimensions there were between us.

I was startled. I wanted to grab coins, jewels, and golden candlesticks and run away, but curiosity got the best of me.

The old man pounded from behind the looking glass, and I heard only small vibrations. "Help! Please!" His eyes lit up when he saw me. "I've been trapped for so long."

A lion would not run, no . . . but would a lion *help?*

"Are you the necromancer?" I asked, holding up the knife as if to impress him.

A look of alarm crossed the old man's face. "Is that what they call me? A magician, a sorcerer? I always thought of myself as a researcher in the arcane sciences. I constructed this mirror with special alchemy, a recipe described in the most secret research from lost almanacs. The spell was designed for purity and hope, but something went wrong, and I became trapped in here. You must let me out. Only you can let me out."

I was afraid to take a step closer, remembering all the wild stories I had been so quick to discount. On the streets, I knew when to run from a fight. "Why should I do that?"

270

Desperation leads to justifications. The old man said, "If you free me, you could have all my wealth."

"You are in no position to bargain." I faced the mirror, straight-backed and cocky. "If you're trapped, I can take all your wealth anyway."

His expression became somber. "But could you live with yourself?"

When you steal, what is stolen from you? I hadn't learned that lesson yet.

I shrugged. "Probably. What does this mirror do?"

His voice remained distant. "It's a reflecting glass designed to trap evil, to drain it from the person who gazes into it. It's a cleansing spell, but I became trapped inside." He reached out to the edge of the mirror. "Just take my hand, pull me out."

The old man looked so desperate. His voice trembled. My father had painted him as a fearsome monster, and I felt I had to prove that he was wrong, as he had been wrong in so many other things. I was torn. Was I a lion? Was I prey? I steeled myself. I was *human*. And I wasn't afraid.

Hesitant and skittish, ready to jump away if necessary, I reached out to touch the mirror at the point where the old man's hand met the reflecting glass. "I can pull you out," I said.

As my fingertips brushed the surface, though, it was as if I had popped the membrane of a soap bubble. His fingers folded around mine—and then the mirror glass folded around my hand as well. The necromancer's grip became like a claw. "Or I can pull you *in!*"

He seized me, refused to let go. With a rushing astral wind, I felt something being drained out of me, as if an artery of my soul had been severed and the mirror was siphoning off the evil parts inside me.

"Let go!" I struggled, dug in my heels, but some part of me was gushing into the mirror, pulled through to the other side of the reflection. The mirror was designed to steal a person's *evil* . . . and it had stolen the entire presence of the necromancer. Now it was draining me. Would there be anything left on this side of the mirror?

I thrashed and yelled, not caring if anyone out in the streets heard the struggle. The necromancer held tight, dragging me farther into the mirror. My hand already felt dead, my bones and skin turned to ice. His grip was like a manacle far more secure than any wrist-shackles the Poseidon City guard used on a criminal.

I yelled and kicked. The tall mirror wobbled, but remained rooted to the floor. I could not break free, and I used all my strength to pull backward, to drag this evil man out into the real world again—or would that only be worse?

Dark rainbows flashed from the old necromancer's eyes, and a wicked grin stretched his wrinkled face as he tugged harder, trying to draw me the rest of the way into the mirror. I felt weaker every second, diminished. My entire existence was being drained away, flooding to the wrong side of the reflection.

As I fought and yelled, I heard another muffled voice and twisted my head to see a second mirror hanging from the wall, a golden frame around a silvered moonstone glass. *My father's face* was behind it—I could even see the scar on his cheek from where I had cut him. He pounded and cried out from far away, but he was lost inside the mirror—as I would be any minute now. My knees were already watery, trembling; my strength was waning.

"I am a lion!" I said in a ragged shout.

Somehow, I found the strength to lift my sharp knife. My hand had plunged inside the mirror, and the necromancer refused to release his grip. Crying out, not daring to think, I swung the knife down and hacked at my own wrist. It was the only way I could survive, before any more of my arm was pulled into the hellish looking glass. The sharp, bright lightning of pain gave me the strength to jerk harder, and the necromancer recoiled. But it wasn't enough. Another blow, and the pain was impossible, an explosion of brilliant agony through skin, tendon, bone. I don't know how many more times I chopped before I fell backward into the room, collapsing onto the floor with my wrist spouting blood.

I crawled backward, reeling, unable to think. The old man, still trapped in the reflecting glass, howled—and my instinct was to flee screaming into the night. But I had to stop the bleeding, and I struggled out of my shirt, wrapped the sleeve around my wrist, and pulled it tight, trying to cut off the flow.

When I got back to my feet, wanting only to lurch away, I knew I had one last thing to do. Tucking my bloody arm against my chest, I used my good hand to grasp the frame of the looking glass, throwing my weight against it until I wrenched it off balance. The evil mirror fell face forward and shattered on the floor, breaking the trapped necromancer into a thousand sharp shards on the floor. I don't know if it killed him or just imprisoned him there forever.

I was gray and sweaty, ready to collapse, but I had to get out of there. Dripping blood and cradling the severed wrist, I staggered away.

From behind the mirror on the wall, I saw my father's face,

furious then wheedling. He pounded on the glass. "Free me!"

But I didn't know how to do that, nor did I care to find out. If I shattered the mirror, it might kill him. Or maybe not.

Before I fainted, I drew a breath, swayed in front of him, and held up my bloody stump before the reflection. "You taught me, Father," I said in a voice made hoarse from screaming. "I am a lion."

When you steal, what is stolen from you?

I staggered down the steps and out of the necromancer's mansion, unable to think straight, foolishly neglecting to take so much as a golden candlestick or any jewels from the fountains. I fled the evil place, barely able to stand upright because the pain was so great, leaving the echo of my father with all eternity to reflect on what it really meant to be trapped.

In a way I was more free than ever before.

CHAPTER 16

Fascinated, Guerrero watched the words scroll his harsh life across the pages, though he didn't actually read the pages. "Quite a trick. And that spells out my story?"

Marinda closed the volume. She had let go of the pickpocket's hand, no longer concerned that he would run away. It didn't matter. "Maybe not the way *you* remember the events. This book tells the true story of a person's life."

Even though he'd almost been caught, he seemed cocky, amused, forgetting about the loss of his hand. "If you want a real story, go find Cabeza de Vaca! He's the greatest explorer in Atlantis. He goes from tavern to tavern telling his tales. He'll be happy to give you his story—but you'd have to buy him a drink."

"I've spent far more than that. Who is he?"

"He's been searching the continent for the Seven Cities of Gold. Some say they're just a myth, but he's convinced. He spent his whole life going to spectacular places and enduring dangerous adventures. He could tell you a tale or two." Guerrero nodded at

Clockwork Lives. "I'll bet his story would fill the rest of your book."

Marinda straightened. "In that case, I should find him. Where would I start?"

Guerrero laughed. "Ask in any tavern—everyone knows him." He darted into the streets and vanished down an alley, but Marinda already had his tale. Now she set her sights on another.

◆◆◆

Poseidon City had a great many public houses, but Marinda was methodical, and she decided that her job now—her actual profession—was to fill her book. For a single woman alone, walking into dockside drinking establishments might have seemed unduly risky, but she steeled herself and did what was necessary. Since her father's death, she had learned how to do many things she'd previously thought impossible.

Cabeza de Vaca proved to be as legendary as Guerrero had promised. Sailors, tradesmen, merchants, minstrels—anyone who wanted a warm place to drink—told stories about the great explorer. "Cabeza de Vaca isn't hard to find, ma'am," said one sailor. "He's like a cannon going off—always happy to tell of his latest adventures."

Indeed, everyone had heard of him—but no one knew where he was. The dreamline compass Captain Titus had given her was no help whatsoever in guiding her.

In order to acquire information, Marinda spent some of her coins, buying rounds of ale for the suddenly attentive sailors. Many were happy to repeat stories that the explorer had told—how he had explored canyons and mountain peaks, endured blizzards, survived avalanches, been chased by packs of wolves.

"I heard he's off in the Redrock Desert now," said one sailor.

His companions laughed as they shared their own stories of the man. "Remember the giant lizard he found sunning itself on a plateau? Cabeza de Vaca roped it and rode on its back as it galloped along the sand dunes until it finally died of heatstroke."

"Or how about the human skulls he found in that eagle's nest?"

One man with bags under his eyes leaned forward and tapped Marinda's book. "Why aren't you writing these down, if you're looking for stories? What would be better?"

"The real stories would be better. And for that, I need to find him."

"Oh, he'll be back. He returns to Poseidon City whenever he needs supplies or when he needs to raise more funds."

Another man interjected, "Or when he just needs a drink." They all laughed.

"Then I'll keep looking for him." Marinda left the tavern.

A man called after her. "At least he's easier to find than the Seven Cities of Gold." They all broke into loud chuckles.

She went from street to street, tavern to tavern, and she began to despair of ever finding Cabeza de Vaca. She studied the dream-line compass, but the dial was incomprehensible to her, and she doubted the device was designed to help a person find a particular man in a particular tavern.

Along the way she did acquire several tales from blustering braggarts who, when the blood was spilled on the page, had no real tales to tell at all.

She searched for days, and the story of her own inquiries spread around as well. As soon as Marinda entered a new tavern, the patrons knew who she was. "It's the crazy woman with the strange book looking for Cabeza de Vaca," they would say.

For Marinda, finding the man had become a quest in itself. For most of her life, her imagination had been a dormant seed despite her father's attempts to make it germinate; now she longed for a real and interesting tale. She needed to find out what Cabeza de Vaca really had to tell.

In her third fruitless week, Marinda turned down another street and saw a signboard for a tavern she had not yet visited, showing a swan and a constellation. A smile crept across her lips. The Cygnus Tavern—she knew she had to go there.

Music, laughter, and conversation came from within. She pulled open the door to find the usual wooden tables, the usual hearth glowing with a stack of ignited redcoal, the usual sailors from various steamers in port.

She looked around the Cygnus Tavern with a sense of distant familiarity, remembering Captain Titus's tale. Yes, this was exactly the way she had pictured the place! A man behind the bar poured a tankard from a keg and handed it to a man who could barely prop himself in his seat. *That must be Rickard*, she thought.

A girl of about six years with red hair and pigtails, freckles, and bright blue eyes ran about gathering dirty mugs and serving food— Cythia. And the woman carrying trays of mugs, looking harried and overworked—that had to be Selise, the wife of Captain Titus.

Marinda knew this place, knew these people . . . but they didn't know her.

Titus had shared his tale with her, although he hadn't known exactly what—or how much—he was sharing. Marinda doubted even Selise knew all those truths about him. Even the closest husband and wife were still secrets to each other. Maybe all stories weren't meant to be shared, she realized.

Marinda hesitated at the tavern doorway, but another sailor came in behind her, nudging her inside. Three tables had been pulled together to accommodate a larger crowd of sailors. Sitting on wooden benches, they leaned forward to listen to a broad-shouldered man with a square head, shaggy hair, an unkempt beard, and a squint in his left eye, as if a shard of something had lodged in there. His fists were like rocks as he thumped them on the tabletop hard enough to jostle the tankards.

"Three days with no food or water!" he said, his words slurred. "Wandering the desert until I came upon a trail, footprints in the sand." He took a long slurp and emptied his tankard. "They were my own footprints—I'd gone in a long circle! Cabeza de Vaca, the great explorer who managed to find his own footprints!" His listeners groaned; one of the sailors laughed.

Before she could bother with doubts, Marinda strode to the table. "Cabeza de Vaca? I've been looking for you."

The conversation stopped, and the sailors turned toward Marinda. One of them nudged a companion in the arm. "See, I told you. It's her!"

The man lifted his shaggy head, focused on her with some effort. "I've heard about you—what do you want from me?"

"Probably to pay for her children," one of the raucous sailors burst in.

Cabeza de Vaca ran his eyes slowly up and down her prim form. "If you say I fathered a baby, I'll probably deny it . . . though you are a pretty one. Or you could be, if you worked harder at it."

She frowned. "And why should I want to work at being pretty, if you're the prize I'd have to look forward to?" The other sailors guffawed at her retort. She lifted her chin and continued. "I want nothing more than your story. I've heard a lot about you, and if the reality is half as interesting as the tales, I want to include it in my book." She lifted *Clockwork Lives*.

"Half as interesting?" Cabeza de Vaca pounded another rock-fist on the jittery table. "I promise at least two-thirds as interesting!" More laughter. He lifted his tankard. "I'm happy to tell my stories to anyone who buys the drinks."

Marinda took out one of her gold coins, knowing it was sufficient for at least a full round. One of the other sailors had the good sense to flag down Selise and call for more tankards of ale.

Marinda nudged the closest sailor to slide down the bench and make room for her. "I need more than just your spoken tale." To the fascination of all the observers, she withdrew the golden needle from the book's binding. "I need a drop of your blood."

Cabeza de Vaca frowned. "What for?"

"A drop of your blood on these alchemically treated pages will give me your story. Or are you afraid to share it?"

The explorer lifted a large hand and extended a fingertip toward her. "I hope your needle's sharp. Got calluses from climbing cliffs in the Redrock Desert with my bare hands."

She jabbed him with the needle, which went straight in. Cabeza de Vaca yelled "Oww!" and drew back.

Marinda guided his finger above the empty page. A red droplet welled up, saturated with alcohol, but when it splashed on the page and spread out into words, the alchemical letters were neat, as always.

THE
SEEKER'S TALE

I had a dream, or perhaps the dream had me. I don't know which came first, or which was stronger—I won't know until the story ends.

An unending quest becomes a reason unto itself, a journey that means more than any destination. And I learned how to pass that dream on to others, even if I did not succeed for myself.

I grew up in a lakeshore village, Opal Lake, which was nestled in the foothills with the rugged mountains visible beyond. Farther still, I had heard of the unexplored Redrock Desert, but the desert and the mountains were so distant they might have been a different world entirely. I didn't bother much with daydreams then; I was busy enough with my everyday diversions. I would catch frogs in the tangled marshes or take a paddleboat to scoop mudfish, which provided more sport than food.

When I was fourteen years old, an old man with one missing foot changed my life, ruined my life. He infected me with an unattainable dream, a fever of the imagination. "Tell me, Cabeza," he said to me as he sat on a weathered tree stump on the lakeshore, "ever heard of the Seven Cities of Gold? Ever know anyone who's seen them?"

Old Fernando hobbled around with a crutch, swinging his footless leg beneath him; he wove frog traps from dried reeds and occasionally caught mudfish or crabs to sell. Mostly, the old man liked to talk.

"Seven Cities?" I asked. "I've never even seen one city."

"Not just any city, Cabeza." Fernando leaned forward, no longer interested in the reeds he was idly weaving. "Cities of *gold*. Lost cities. Towers and walls so beautiful they hurt your eyes when the sun shines on them."

"Gold? Here in Atlantis? You must mean in Albion—cities built by the Watchmaker? He makes all the gold."

The old man made a rude noise. "Not that kind of gold! And I don't mean any place like Poseidon City either. You don't think we were the first people to live here, do you? The Elder Race of man built those cities, all seven of them, deep in the Redrock Desert on a high mesa rising above a sparkling lake. They're so far away and so unattainable that no one has yet found them." The old man shook his head. "Although I tried." His voice became clogged with tears. "How I tried for so many years."

"But you never found them?"

He shook his head and looked down at his unfortunately abbreviated foot. "I gave it my best attempt, and alas I'm no longer able." He raised his eyes. "You, though . . . *you* could find the Seven Cities. Wouldn't that be more glorious than splashing in the mud and feeding marsh gnats?" To emphasize his point he swished his palm around his face, scattering the tiny bloodsucking insects.

I glanced at his stump. "Is that how you lost your foot?" One of my friends told me that a swamp alligator had bitten it off, but none of us really knew.

He nodded slowly. "Most grueling ordeal of my life, dragging a bloody stump for four days out of the desert, using only a mesquite branch for a crutch."

"So, it wasn't a swamp alligator then?"

He scowled at me. "There aren't any swamp alligators in the canyons of the Redrock Desert." He gazed toward the foothills. "Beyond the mountains, far outside of civilization, you will see landmarks and miracles. There's a shrine up in a slickrock grotto, a pool of purest water that seeps through time itself, a sacred place for the Elder Race. Any man who drinks of the water is said to become immortal. It was called the Fountain of Lamneth."

I had never heard of the Fountain, nor the Seven Cities for that matter, but I didn't have extensive schooling . . . and his enthusiasm was infectious.

Fernando set his reeds aside to lean closer. "I thought they were just silly myths at first, but every legend has a kernel of truth. *Someone* must have seen the Fountain of Lamneth at one time.

"I tracked the markings, traveled through a wilderness so deep that it didn't even remember the *idea* of human footprints. I saw rock writings, petroglyphs that told an ancient story and gave directions to intrepid dreamers like myself." The old man's eyes were shining, and his voice took on a greater intensity. I couldn't look away.

"At the end of a narrow, high-walled canyon, I climbed from one shelf to another on the slippery red rock. I could see the smooth grotto above, a beckoning doorway with a trickle of the purest water. The Fountain of Lamneth—it had to be! The rock wall was sheer, but I found handholds and hauled myself up using all my strength, arms, legs, fingers. It was precarious—but my whole life was precarious. I was all alone in that slickrock canyon, months and countless miles from the nearest human being.

"I was exhausted by the time I reached the ledge, lifting myself up on my elbows, barely holding on. I raised my head over the lip just enough to see that beautiful hollow surrounded by emerald vines and a carpet of lush moss. The drip of fresh water was like music, and I saw the pool shimmering like a moonstone mirror. The Fountain of Lamneth—one sip would grant me immortality. It was perfect. It was a miracle!

"Then a boulder broke from the side of the crumbling cliff, and I slipped, taking more rocks with me as I scrambled for any kind of handhold. I cried out into that endless empty wasteland where no one could hear me.

"I should have died in that fall, but somehow—a blessing and a curse—I was uninjured . . . except for my foot. A boulder had smashed it clean off from my ankle. I managed to tie a makeshift tourniquet before I fainted.

"By the time I woke, much of the bleeding had stopped, and I had nothing to do but go on or give up—and I could always give up later. I gazed one last time at that lost canyon, the high unattainable grotto where I had seen only a hint of the Fountain. . . . Some other seeker would have to find it.

"I dragged myself through the canyon and found a broken branch for a crutch. I followed the canyon to a larger wash and followed that wash until I met a stream, followed that stream to a larger stream, and finally a river. I kept going downhill out of the mountains until I came upon a village."

Fernando looked up, his eyes shining as if he had been transported to another world. He waved more gnats from his face. "You're young and strong, Cabeza. *You* could find the Fountain of Lamneth, or even the Seven Cities of Gold." He reached out to grasp my arm. "You can do it—no one else can."

I answered with a nervous laugh and told him that I had to go do my chores. But I didn't know how to resist those exciting stories. I didn't sleep at all that night or the next. On the third night, when I finally dozed off from sheer exhaustion, I dreamed of gleaming towers, majestic cities with walls of gold, architecture that made even fantasies ache.

I knew I had to find the Seven Cities. I had been infected.

————◆◆◆————

When I told my parents I intended to set off for the Seven Cities of Gold, they forbade me in the strongest possible terms—which is a very good way to inspire a teenager. In secret, Fernando told me everything he remembered about his route, about the intervening mountains, and the Redrock Desert. His stories painted a jumble of spectacular images in my head.

I secretly packed supplies, food, rope, packets of alchemical firestarter . . . and a great deal of encouragement from the old man with one foot. I could see the mountains on the horizon, and I knew the Redrock Desert lay beyond them. I would find the Seven Cities of Gold—and the Fountain of Lamneth, too, for good measure.

I sneaked away from home one night and trudged off into the dark, following the constellations, which seemed to lead me directly where I needed to go. By the next morning, my confidence had already begun to flag, but I knew that a quest is not something one undertakes lightly. Reaching my goal would require more than a half day of effort, so I stuck it out. Sore feet would be the least of my concerns.

But sore feet became sore legs and a sore back. My pack weighed as much as a boulder and I discarded all the luxuries I no longer considered necessary, bit by bit along the way. It took me five days to cross through the foothills up into the mountains—and I had not even begun the real journey through unexplored territory.

In two weeks, I saw not a single soul. At first, the solitude was exhilarating, then frightening, then simply oppressive.

As I wandered, occasionally I would look up in the sky and see a chugging steamliner plowing across the winds, delivering cargo to the mountain villages or scattered lake towns. But the airship captain flew too high to see me even if I tried to signal him. I walked onward, climbing and descending, following the fading vapor trails of steam the airships left in the sky.

I ran out of food. Since I had grown up in a comfortable village, I had few survival skills. I didn't really know how to hunt, and I certainly couldn't defend myself if I should come upon a giant bear.

I ran out of firestarter on the night of the first snowfall, and I huddled under my thin blanket, shivering against the bone-breaking cold. I cursed my poor planning and my gullibility. And I hadn't even reached the Redrock Desert yet! I was a fool.

The next day, trudging onward with numb feet and doubled vision, I topped a ridge and looked down into a cleft of rock, saw sheer cliffs with stairstepped quarries, mine shafts, even the terminus of a steamliner supply rail. A mining town built into the cliffs!

I nearly collapsed at the sight. I had not eaten in days. My throat was parched, my clothes tattered, and my satchel of belongings nearly empty. I reeled like a drunken man toward the quarry and the cottages built of stone. Three miners hurried out to catch me as I fell. "You look as if you've been chewed up by the world," said one.

"And then spat back out," said another.

They carried me to an inn where they gave me water and hot broth and bread that tasted like ambrosia—not that I've ever tasted ambrosia. The miners gathered around, all of them intent. They gave me a mug of mountain spirits, which made me dizzy.

"Where are you from, lad?"

"What are you doing out here?"

"What's your name?"

I lifted my large head, which was shaggier than usual after my tribulations. "I am Cabeza de Vaca from Opal Lake, and I am on a quest to find the Seven Cities of Gold."

The miners drew back, some chuckling, others amazed. "You've been out there, then? You've been to the Redrock Desert and come back?"

I hesitated only a moment, unwilling to admit my dismal failure. "Yes! Months of staggering around lost, but searching. All the things I've seen." I shook my head. "I can't even describe."

"Try," said one of the miners, and they all leaned close to listen.

So I told them what they wanted to hear. Remembering Fernando's descriptions, I talked about fantastic rock formations, stone windows, petroglyphs, and a mysterious grotto high in a canyon wall that held the Fountain of Lamneth.

"The Fountain?" one of the miners cried. "Haven't heard that one in a long time!"

Seeing the enthusiastic reception to my words, I told them even more.

The mining village was called Endoline, and the men and women worked a rich vein of alchemical minerals, extracting sunstone, bloodstone, dreamstone, green sulfur, fire opals, and many other rare substances, all of which were shipped by steamliner to Poseidon City for trade, mostly to Albion.

The Endoline miners tended me, cleaned me up, gave me fresh clothes, and let me rest there until I was more than recovered. When I regained my strength, the people were eager to re-supply me, stuffing my pack with a far more practical inventory of survival goods.

"Will you be going out again to find the Seven Cities?" they asked. It seemed important to them that *somebody* continue the search. "And when you find them, will you come back here and tell us?"

"Of course," I said. "I promise."

They advised me about the mountains and the desert, definitely more accurate directions than old Fernando had been able to provide. And so, with more caution than the first time, I set off toward the great mysterious expanse beyond the mountains.

———————◆◆◆———————

I lasted five days.

The desert was an inhospitable place, but I forced myself to go into the canyons that Fernando had talked about. Towering walls of rust-colored rock were marked with dark stains that I could not decipher. My feet were sore and my spirits were low. I was tired of being alone, but I had not yet found what I was looking for. I made up my mind to continue for one more day, because my food would not last longer than that. Then I would have to make it back to the mountains, or I'd perish out there, lost and alone.

In the distance I saw a large chiseled design on the side of a mesa, a pattern that looked like a flying owl clearly drawn by the hand of man, but so distant and so high that it had to have been carved there by the Elder Race. What mortal could have achieved something like that? I shaded my eyes and stared longingly at the distant cliffside and the rugged intervening terrain—and I knew it would take me several days to reach the base of the mesa. I did not have the food, or the stamina, to make it, and so with one last longing glance, I turned around and made my way back. . . .

Reaching the mountains, I followed the lines of roads until I found another mining village, this one named Broken Cliffs. Again, they welcomed me with astonishment. I staggered into their town. "I've been to find the Seven Cities!"

And the people gathered around me. "The Seven Cities of Gold? You come from the Redrock Desert?"

"Yes," I said and told them how I'd wandered the uncharted landscape, the grand designs I had seen on the slickrock cliffs. "A message from the Elder Race for seekers like me. I didn't reach the Seven Cities this time—but I will return."

My story fired their imagination, and I began to realize the value of what I was providing. I rested in Broken Cliffs for weeks, waiting for a cold snap to pass. The villagers were happy to replenish my supplies, give me warm blankets and wool clothing, and they also offered me vague directions and advice.

I set off again. . . .

I repeated the same scheme, over and over—for years. I ventured deeper into the Redrock Desert, always searching, going as far as my supplies and my blisters would allow. I became familiar with the various mining towns, which were much easier to find than the Seven Cities.

When I eventually returned to Endoline, I was delighted to find that the villagers remembered me. They had continued talking about my tribulations from the first time, and they had added fanciful perils, glorious visions, and remarkable discoveries that exceeded even my ability to describe. Then, as I returned to Broken Cliffs, Chalcedony Wells, and Quartzline, my own story preceded me. The *fact* of my quest had revitalized dreams of the Seven Cities, awakened curiosity and a sense of wonder in those who led painfully uneventful lives. What was wrong with that? I felt proud to give them such inspiration.

At one point, five years into my quest, I realized it was more efficient just to wander the mountains from one mining town to the next, telling my story without the bothersome step of arduous desert explorations. By then, I was familiar enough with the landscape that I could describe my adventures convincingly without having to suffer further. It was far less taxing that way.

Eventually, I returned to my old home of Opal Lake, a grown and hardened man full of adventures, ready to be received as a hero. I was disappointed to learn that old Fernando had died years earlier, as if relieved to have passed on his dream to me. The people of Opal Lake remembered me as the boy who had run off and never come back. My parents were glad to know I was all right, but they had grown accustomed to life without me.

I spent nights in the village telling stories by a bonfire at the lakeshore. I described the Seven Cities of Gold, and I told them

I had found the mystical Fountain of Lamneth, but declined to drink of the magical water, so as to maintain my hold on humanity. The people of Opal Lake needed the second-hand adventure, for they would never experience anything similar for themselves.

My mother tentatively asked if I intended to stay, and the crowd of listeners fell silent as the bonfire crackled. I looked at her and shook my shaggy head. By now I had grown a beard. "Someone has to find the Seven Cities of Gold, and I am determined that it'll be me. *Somebody* has to explore the world."

The villagers applauded me as a hero. They gave me the supplies I needed—food, fresh clothes, newly soled boots—and I departed, leaving only my stories behind.

At first I set off toward the mountains, but when I was out of sight, I circled back and headed instead toward the coast. I had more important things to do in Poseidon City.

————◆————

After all my years of questing, I had built up a vivid imaginary picture of what the Seven Cities of Gold looked like, but I really had no comprehension of what a "city" was at all. Opal Lake barely qualified as a village, and even the mining towns of Broken Cliffs, Endoline, and Chalcedony Wells had no more than a few thousand souls.

Poseidon City, though, was a cacophony of people, vehicles, smells, shadows, and streets—and an expansive audience hungry to hear about my epic journey. These everyday people sorely needed a dream of lost marvels.

I had spent enough time in the Redrock Desert that my face was weathered, and people said that my gaze had an odd quality of *distance*. Remembering what I had seen in the eyes of old Fernando, I cultivated an edge of exotic wariness, a hint of driven madness.

Since I had been infected by the quest, pushed to the far fringes of nowhere in search of that splendid mirage, I wondered just how much truth there had been in Fernando's tales. What if he hadn't actually lost his foot from a fall after glimpsing the Fountain? Maybe his foot had been amputated after something as mundane as an infected cut? But who wanted to hear that story?

I'd suffered through enough starvation and thirst in my search for the Seven Cities, and I much preferred to spend an evening in a tavern with a drink and a friend—preferably many friends, and preferably friends who would buy the drinks.

Poseidon City had ale far superior to anything in Opal Lake or the mining towns. With its countless workers, weary men and women who rarely, if ever, set foot outside the city, there was an infinite landscape of taverns and listeners. Apart from the stream of sailors who frequented the dockside inns, most of the taverns had regular customers who did not visit other drinking establishments. Therefore, I could go just a few blocks away, pull up a new bench, call for a tankard of ale, and tell the very same adventures to an entirely different audience. No one would ever know the difference.

My heart swelled when I saw their intent expressions, when they glanced toward the windows and considered mysteries that had never previously crossed their minds. I was doing a good service. Even though my stories were not true—well, very few of them at least—I didn't consider what I was doing *lying*. I was entertaining. I was *inspiring*. And if I could give these lackluster people a sense of wonder for the mere price of a tankard of ale—or two or three—then it was a good thing by far.

Once I learned which taverns were most lucrative, I began to dream aloud about my next expedition to the desert. I vowed that if I could just go farther, if I could just endure longer, I would find the object of my lifelong quest. Then, as my next step, I would forlornly look at my empty money purse and request funds for supplies so I could head out into the emptiness again and find that great dream of human history. . . .

I made a fair amount of money that way, but when I had completed the circuit of likely drinking establishments, I could no longer stay in Poseidon City and remain convincing. So, I used some of the generous contributions to buy actual supplies and booked passage on a cargo steamliner that took me out to Endoline again (no use walking all that way).

With a full belly, warm clothes, and plenty of supplies, I set off in a different direction, winding through a new set of canyons on an unpredictable course, going wherever the desert and my feet would take me. Maybe I was caught up in my own story.

After a week out there, though, I'd had quite enough. During my year in the city I'd grown better at talking than walking. Muscular thighs had given way to a rounded gut, so I looped back into the mountains, found another mining village, one I had not visited for two years, and plied them with my stories.

Eventually I returned to Poseidon City, having let the audiences lie fallow long enough. My most receptive crowds were in the dockside taverns because sailors were always new. Crews came and went, and most of the local listeners were tired of hearing about Albion or their absurd myths about angels beneath the sea. They had never heard my tales of the Seven Cities or the Fountain of Lamneth, though!

One day, before the taverns opened for the evening crowds, I came upon a place called Underworld Books. I wasn't much of a reader, preferring stories told from one person to another without the intervention of written words. But the proprietor of the bookshop seemed to have explored more exotic worlds than I had. She knew exactly what I might be looking for, even though I didn't know myself. She watched me from the door of her shop. "I know what you lack. You are a seeker."

I smiled, scratched my shaggy beard. "Ah, you've heard my story, then." I extended a large hand. "I am Cabeza de Vaca, the man who will find the Seven Cities of Gold."

"That is your intent, but you lack a map. I have maps. I have exactly what you need."

I was doubtful. "If maps existed to find the Seven Cities of Gold, then someone else would have found them by now."

"There are maps from different worlds," said the bookseller. "Some accurate, some not, but all could be useful, since the Redrock Desert doesn't change much from universe to universe."

I suspected she had cultivated this tantalizing tale to lure potential customers. Still, I realized that if I carried maps—as props—my own story might be more believable. I patted my tattered trousers. "I have little money. I'm a weary traveler who generally lives off the land."

"I think not." She frowned at me. "And I think you would be a much more effective seeker with my maps."

Maybe she glimpsed the sack of coins I kept hidden under my shirt, but I knew she told the truth. So I purchased the maps at a price that I thought was too high, but the bookseller's penetrating gaze seemed to peer right through me, and she would not lower her price.

I marveled at the maps she provided; they would indeed be quite beneficial, for not only did they sketch out the rough topography of the desert, they also showed the intervening mountains in greater detail, the roads, the mining villages, even some population clusters that I had not visited before, places that had never heard my stories. All in all, a good trade.

Eventually, I set off to the wilderness again, telling everyone I would continue my quest until I found the Seven Cities, and they all bought me another round of drinks.

With the maps I could travel deeper into the desert, go places I had never seen. This time, I felt the quest more strongly than I had experienced since I'd listened to old Fernando spin his tales on the muddy shore of Opal Lake.

The maps also showed me easier ways into the desert, and by

now I had gotten more proficient at choosing my supplies, and I also knew how to locate rock potholes that held rainwater or hidden springs surrounded by tamarisks, so I could actually stay out there longer.

That time, I ventured deeper into the arid wasteland than I had ever gone before, and finally I saw a shimmering mirage, something I had never expected to find. A gleaming expanse of a distant lake that lay like a moonstone mirror at the base of an enormous mesa that rose from the desert like an island in the sky. Exactly as the legends had foretold! The Seven Cities must be up there, the Elder Race separated from base mankind in their high fortress.

I froze like a starving man holding a spoon of food up to his mouth, afraid to take that first delicious bite. It was there, within a day's journey—two at the most! I could traverse the shallow lake and climb those cliffs. I could find the Seven Cities of Gold at last.

But what if the cities were a disappointment when I found them? What if the gold was tarnished, the majestic cities no more than abandoned huts that were crumbling into dust? Maybe it was better that I didn't risk that.

After all, my dream was perfect as it was.

Because it was late in the afternoon, I camped. The sun set behind the mesa, and red rays sent a firestorm of flares reflecting from the broad lake in the distance. That night I slept restlessly and dreamed of the finish line, the long unfulfilled quest that had sustained me for my entire life.

What would I do with myself if I finally found my goal?

<hr>

Next morning, I packed up my camp and headed into the sunrise on the trail ahead, *away* from the mesa, leaving the prize in the shadow behind me.

No, I was not ready to find the cities—not yet.

Long afterward, I kept telling my story to many people who

listened breathlessly, and the tales grew in the telling, thriving like a garden. My search itself became a thing of legend—and that was something I chose to perpetuate, because it was good for *them* to have their legends, too, to have their unattainable dreams that I could provide. In my mind, that was a far more satisfactory experience than actually finding the Seven Cities.

Life is but a candle, and a dream must give it flame. Who was I to extinguish the flame?

CHAPTER 17

As the alchemical letters petered out on the page, Marinda skimmed the story as fast as she could, ignoring the background hubbub of the Cygnus Tavern. Cabeza de Vaca, well into his fourth tankard of ale, had been happy to receive the fresh one Marinda bought for him in exchange for his tale.

Selise stepped up to the table carrying a tray of tankards. The explorer swayed a little on the bench. His eyes were bleary, and he was barely able to discern the letters in Marinda's book; he certainly had no idea what the words said.

"Did you get what you needed?" He ended his sentence with a belch.

The other sailors were fascinated by her book, the golden needle, and the loquacious drop of blood, but none of them could read the tale of Cabeza de Vaca as fast as the alchemy chronicled his life.

But by now Marinda could, and her annoyance bordered on anger as she read the story of his scam, which seemed worse than the tale she had gotten from the pickpocket. Cabeza de Vaca was like a vampire thriving on the blood of dreams and the generosity of those who believed in him, who paid him to be a surrogate adventurer for their own lackluster lives.

As the seeker leaned forward and tried to read the pages, Marinda slammed the book shut. "It's your own life story. You, more than anyone else, should know what it says."

"We all know his story," said one of the sailors.

"Do you?" Marinda asked.

Selise set the tankards down on the table, and Marinda paid her with one of her gold coins, realizing that her funds were dwindling rapidly.

With a calculating glint in his bloodshot eye, Cabeza de Vaca leaned close, as if he intended to intoxicate her with his breath. "I could offer you an opportunity, miss. I know where to find the Seven Cities of Gold, and I'm going to make another expedition. I'll be successful this time, but there are certain expenses—supplies, new boots, a rough map. Would you help support my expedition? Just a few coins will do—I see you have some left in your pouch."

"Not enough," she said.

"Or maybe you could accompany me. You're pretty enough, especially if the nights get very lonely. You could be part of history—think of it. You and I might discover the Fountain of Lamneth. We could be the ones."

"I don't think so."

As the sailors took their tankards of ale from Selise, Cabeza de Vaca looked around. "Which tavern is this, by the way? They all look alike . . . Ah, Cygnus—yes, that's the one. There used to be a lad here who always listened to my tales. I would talk and talk, and he paid closer attention than the rest of you did. He wanted to see the world, and I strongly encouraged him. . . ." Cabeza de Vaca scratched his shaggy head. "*Aiden!* Yes, that was his name. He said he was going to leave someday and set off on his own, just like me." He picked up his new tankard and glanced around the room. "I wonder whatever became of him."

Selise froze, holding her half-empty tray. The color drained out of her face. With a loud crash, she dropped the rest of the tankards on the floor.

Cabeza de Vaca laughed at her. "Clumsy tonight, aren't you? That reminds me of another adventure I had—"

At which point, Marinda remembered the groundswell of the pain and loss she had read in Captain Titus's story, saw the agony on Selise's face now. The explorer's obliviousness to the consequences of his tales infuriated Marinda. Impulsively, she seized his tankard and threw the ale in his face. As he sputtered in surprise, she rose, keeping her voice hard and cold. "You don't know how dangerous stories are—especially when they're not true."

Holding the book close, she stormed out of the Cygnus Tavern.

CHAPTER 18

Despite his personal flaws and counterfeit quest, Cabeza de Vaca's tale had filled several pages in *Clockwork Lives*. But about a third of the volume remained empty, pristine sheets of alchemically treated paper demanding blood.

Poseidon City was not an inexpensive place, however. Frugality would be enough to extend her means of subsistence for only a limited time. She had to pay the expenses of her unexpected life here—not just everyday lodging and food, but what she had to spend to acquire the life-tales of interesting subjects. Unfortunately, those turned out to be bad investments more often than not.

Now, more than a month since the Watchmaker had sent her away from Albion, Marinda's funds were dwindling more rapidly than she was able to fill the empty pages in her book. And even after *Clockwork Lives* was completed, she'd still have to pay for a passage back to Albion, which would not be cheap.

Unlike Cabeza de Vaca, who was more salesman than explorer, Marinda would not find gullible patrons to fund her quest. And she had to survive in a land without friends.

She didn't give in to desperation, though. First, she sought out Underworld Books, since Courier was the first—and perhaps only—friendly face she had encountered in Poseidon City. But although she returned to that section of town, walking up one street and down another, searching the narrow alleys and dim byways, Marinda never found the mysterious bookshop. It was as if once reunited with her long-lost Omar, Courier had closed up Underworld Books, and it had simply winked out of existence.

She thought again of the fisherman Hender and the village of Heartshore he had talked about. She believed it would be nice to see him again, but she doubted Heartshore would be a place bursting with stories. . . .

One other family in Poseidon City was familiar to her, however—even though they did not know Marinda, as such. So, she brushed out her hair, put on her best set of remaining clothes, and went back to the Cygnus Tavern on a quiet afternoon and introduced herself to Selise and Rickard, while the redheaded girl in pigtails played with the cat. Two of Rickard's children scrubbed spilled food and ale from the wooden tabletops.

"My name is Marinda Peake. I traveled from Albion aboard the *Rocinante*." She looked at Selise, seeing that she had the woman's interest.

Rickard interrupted, "The *Rocinante* is not a passenger steamer."

"That's exactly what Captain Titus said, but the Watchmaker was very anxious to expedite my passage out of Albion. I got to know the captain rather well on the voyage. He told me many things about your family, the tavern . . . and Aiden."

Selise's face fell, and her brother looked angry. "What do you want from us?"

Selise suddenly remembered Marinda. "Oh, you're the one who threw a tankard at Cabeza de Vaca."

"Because of what he said—those stupid stories and the damage they do." Marinda lifted her chin. "I was hoping I might find a job, at least a temporary one?"

Selise glanced at her brother, then made up her mind. "If my husband told you about us, then you're welcome here. There's always work to do."

◆◆◆

The Cygnus Tavern couldn't afford to pay Marinda much, but they did allow her to move out of her seedy inn into a small room in the back of Cygnus, which saved her the cost of daily lodgings and the annoyance of nightly bedbug bites.

She was glad to feel useful again, and she seemed to have more energy. Selise clucked her tongue at Marinda's plain clothes from Albion and the serviceable work outfits the sailors had given her on the ship, and instead found some hand-me-down clothes that fit her. "Here, these are much prettier." And they were. Cythia even enjoyed helping her brush out her hair; no one had ever done that before.

This was far from a quiet, perfect life, but at least it was a life.

Her one request was that she be allowed to ask tavern patrons for their tales to include in *Clockwork Lives*.

"You're a writer, then?" Selise asked her. "A storyteller?"

"I'm a collector of stories. I can't go home again until I've filled this book."

Selise finished washing a set of tankards, inspected a chip, and set that one on a drying cloth among the others, confident her customers wouldn't see the flaw. Rickard wrestled a barrel of fresh ale onto the rack, used a small mallet to strike loose the bung, and inserted a new spigot. He looked up at her. "So you'll be wanting my story then, and Selise's?"

Marinda felt a chill. Thanks to the sea captain's tale, she knew Titus's family far more intimately than they suspected, but she did not—could not—tell these people the painful secrets she knew, or how she knew them. "Stories are very personal, even intrusive. Better if I ask a stranger that I'll never see again. And I like to think that you are friends of mine."

Selise accepted the explanation. Rickard poured part of a tankard from the fresh tap, tasted it, and smacked his lips. "And a worker shouldn't necessarily know everything about her employers."

Instead, Marinda tended the customers for weeks, watched the sailors come in every evening and helped chase them off well after midnight. She rarely needed Rickard's help when a burly seaman became too intractable flirting with her. The sailors would have preferred a bustier, more lively barmaid, but she retorted, "We get what we deserve."

She would ask amenable patrons for a drop of blood, but disappointingly, for all their talk and travels, they rarely had lives that deserved to become legends. After a time she did fill a dozen more pages—with dozens more lives.

Optimistic and curious, in the evenings before she went to bed, she occasionally took out her dreamline compass and studied the pointer, which seemed to drift inland, westward, maybe toward the Redrock Desert. Or perhaps that was just because of Cabeza de Vaca's wild stories. . . .

Even so far from Albion, she discovered that most of these people spent day after day ticking off the calendar as if it were a list of duties instead of a journey to be enjoyed and fulfilled. Was it living or just existence? Most of these people accomplished little, strived for little, and went nowhere. Even old men had far too little to tell after a lifetime of living.

She remembered her father's original words: *Some lives can be summed up in a sentence or two. Other lives are epics.*

Why didn't these people do something else? Didn't they want to leave their mark, have an impact? Then she was ashamed at being so judgmental, recalling her own life in Lugtown. Why hadn't *she* wanted to do something else, before her father forced her on this adventure? The thought had never crossed her mind. Why had *she* been content with a humdrum existence? Why did Marinda think that a *quiet* life was equivalent to a *perfect* life?

One morning after she finished cleaning up from the previous night's customers, she flipped through the tales she had recently acquired, pages and pages, all of them small and uninteresting. If she stayed in Poseidon City for another month or two, Marinda could keep adding words, person after person after person—but that wasn't exactly what her father wanted her to do, was it? She didn't intend for *Clockwork Lives* to be a tedious almanac of brief information. She wanted these tales to be special. She wanted the *people* to be special.

She started thinking that she would have to look beyond Poseidon City. Atlantis was an entire continent—why should she limit herself?

A few weeks later, Cabeza de Vaca returned to the Cygnus Tavern, regaling his avid listeners with imaginary explorations, and Marinda knew full well that he had not been on any long journey. The seeker didn't even seem to remember where he was until he sat up straight and frowned at Marinda in the middle of a particularly loud and ridiculous tale. "You're the one who threw ale in my face! You stabbed me with a golden pin."

"You gave me your story." She narrowed her eyes. "So I know the truth—unlike these other people."

For the rest of that evening, the shaggy man talked in a more muted voice, and his stories were at least somewhat more realistic.

After hearing Cabeza de Vaca again, though, Marinda made up her mind. She would travel to the mountains herself and see what stories she could find in the alchemy mines.

CHAPTER 19

Miners sometimes came to Poseidon City on furlough, and occasionally a workhorse steamliner would convert a cargo car into a crowded passenger vessel to haul a group into the city and then back to the mountains. After Selise made sure that this was what Marinda really wanted, Rickard arranged for her passage out to Endoline.

Marinda bade farewell to her surrogate family at the Cygnus Tavern. She had a little more money now in her purse—enough to survive and enough to gather a few more stories. Epic ones, she hoped.

She made her way to the outskirts of Poseidon City, where parallel steamliner rails extended toward the foothills; traveling airships used them to align themselves for landing.

Though the rail terminus was not at all like the Mainspring Hub in Crown City, it was still a bustling depot where long trains of levitating cargo cars touched down, carrying harvested minerals labeled with arcane symbols, many of which matched the markings on the front cover of Marinda's book.

Unlike her father, though, Marinda was no alchemist, and all the elements were mysteries to her. She asked the depot workers how she could find an airship flown by someone named Commodore Pangloss. They directed her to a crowd of well-muscled men and women who were obviously no strangers to hard labor. Though they had signed on as passengers, the hearty people helped unload the crates, clearing one of the transport cars so they could be on their way.

Marinda carried her dreamline compass, the traveling bag, and *Clockwork Lives*—all her worldly possessions. By now she had learned how to create and take her world with her, and she expanded her horizons with every place she visited, every life she acquired.

The airship was polished, freshly painted, and well cared for; obviously, the Commodore took great pride in his motivator car. He was a dark-skinned man with a bald head and an enormous black beard that looked as if it had exploded from his chin. He had a bear-like build, broad shoulders, and sturdy legs; he also had a twinkle in his eye and a smile as he supervised the unloading of his cargo. He went out of his way to meet the passengers. "I like to know the cargo I take aboard my steamliner," he announced to them all in a resonant voice. "And I make a point of knowing the people, too."

He gave Marinda an appraising look, since she seemed out of place among the miners. He thrust out his hand. "Commodore Pangloss, madam. Welcome aboard my steamliner. What brings you out to the mountains? Family? Work?"

"Curiosity," she said.

The Commodore laughed. "A valid reason if I ever heard one! We stop at several settlements along the way. I fly a smooth ship, and it'll be a comfortable passage. Are you heading out to Broken Cliffs? Odyssey Canyon? Or all the way to Endoline?"

"Endoline, I think. I may as well experience to the limits if I'm going to experience at all."

He laughed. "Have you ever been aboard a steamliner before?"

"Yes, but it was an . . . unsettling experience. Back in Albion." She did not tell him about the unfortunate ending of her last steamliner trip.

"I thought I detected an odd accent in your voice."

Some of the workers shouted for help, and Pangloss ran to study the alchemical markings on the crates about to be loaded. "Keep those boxes separated—never place reactants close to each other!" He glanced back over his shoulder. "Sorry, madam, I have work to do. Maybe we'll chat more at one of my stops."

He lifted a stack of books bound together with a leather strap. "I have plenty to keep me company during the voyage—including a new volume of *The Adventures of Hanneke Lakota*." Marinda was delighted to hear the title. He took the books with him as he strolled down the line to inspect cargo containers and the inflation of his levitation sacks. When he was finished, he shouted up to the motivator car. "Mr. Hardy! Are we ready to depart?"

A young man popped out of the lead car, wearing a porkpie hat and a grin. "Yes, Commodore! I stoked the fires. Pressure's building up."

Pangloss tossed him the package of books, and the young man caught it nimbly. "All aboard!"

By now, the returning miners had swept out the empty cargo bin, loaded their own duffels aboard. Some set up plank benches against the walls; others had even brought folding chairs in their travel packs.

Marinda climbed aboard and saw that she would have far fewer amenities than on Captain Pennrose's steamliner. The people crowded together were friendly and welcoming. Her own travel bag was woefully uncomfortable for use as a cushion, and one of the other miners, who had a much plumper duffel, offered it to her while he took turns with his brother sitting on a folding chair.

Ready for departure, Commodore Pangloss slid the compartment door shut. The walls of the cargo compartment had enough slats for daylight, and some of the travelers had brought along self-contained coldfire lanterns—miner lamps—for additional illumination.

The pistons chugged, steam burst from the main boiler, and the airship groaned forward. Marinda felt the movement, sensed the steamliner picking up speed, heard the big steel wheels grinding and then skimming along the coldfire rails. Finally, with a lurch, they were airborne. Some of the miners chuckled, while others held on and tried not to look queasy.

When the airship leveled off, Marinda stood up to peer through one of the wide slats in the wall of the compartment. As cold breezes whistled through, she looked down upon a landscape that was different, yet strikingly similar to the rolling terrain of Albion. She watched the tiny trees below, the sinuous texture of grassy hills, the random spiderweb of roads.

During the flight, the miners kept up a low buzz of conversation, mostly talking about work and rocks, and more rocks. Marinda introduced herself, striking up a conversation with any of the miners who seemed friendly. That in itself would have astonished the original reserved woman from Lugtown. By now, though, Marinda would have surprised that former version of herself many times over.

She kept *Clockwork Lives* stashed in her travel satchel, and she listened for anyone who might have lived a significant life, something better than the short uneventful summaries she had spent so much time collecting in the Cygnus Tavern. She didn't want any more small stories. The book deserved better.

The miners told her about the mineral wealth buried in the mountains for those who knew where and how to look. They explained at great length about the blends of chalcedony, the dangerous beauty of reactant ferrocerium, and of the rich vein of redfire opals that had just been found in a spur canyon near

Endoline. In a more hushed voice, they whispered about the all-too-rare inclusions of valuable quintessence that were hidden like liquid pearls in the deep mountain. Brightening with nostalgia, Marinda told them about the agate quarry in Lugtown and how occasionally—but only occasionally—one of those thunder eggs contained a spark of quintessence, for which the Watchmaker paid handsomely.

Even though the riders came from different villages, these men and women had remarkably similar life experiences. Throughout the voyage to Endoline, Marinda listened to their conversation, but also told her own adventures from Albion, across the sea, to Poseidon City. She sensed that they were amused and entertained, but they did not necessarily believe her. Apparently, Marinda was a less convincing tale spinner than Cabeza de Vaca.

The steamliner stopped at several villages along the way to unload cargo and passengers. Commodore Pangloss and his young assistant conducted business in each town, unloading and loading cargo, then setting off again. Marinda explored briefly, but always decided to move onward. Although Pangloss seemed a gregarious person, he preferred the company of his books and his young assistant in the motivator car.

She rode all the way to Endoline with the last group of miners, and she arrived in a noisy town so deep in the canyons and surrounded by high peaks that the shadows stayed until late morning and returned in early afternoon. The stone cliffs had been excavated in stairstep tiers for the quarry, and large, dark tunnels were bored into the mountain. Glowing orange fires from cast-iron basins filled with ignited redcoal made the place seem like an encampment of fireflies.

When the steamliner landed, the remaining miners sprang out of the half-empty passenger car, bidding Marinda farewell. It was a small enough place, but before she could disparage the town, she remembered the stuffy travelers on the weekly steamliner in

Lugtown, who had thought the same thing about her own village.

Taking her satchel of belongings, she stepped out into Endoline. She looked at the ore cars, the steep zigzag roads cut into the rock, and the stone buildings clustered near mounds of rock tailings. She hoped that all those mysteries the miners claimed were buried within the mountain might lead to an epic story or two.

⧫

She paid for a room at one of the three inns using some of the Atlantis currency she'd received for working in the Cygnus Tavern. After the seedy inn she had endured in Poseidon City, she found these lodgings quite acceptable.

Miners gathered in the inn's common room throughout the day and night, muscular and gritty men and women who clung to small pleasures. Because they worked underground by the light of cold-fire lanterns, they had a fluid definition of a "day," without regard for how the rest of the world observed time. She thought such an idea would have driven the Watchmaker mad.

After she had settled into her room and changed into fresh clothes, she returned to the common room with its blazing redcoal fire and the tables crowded with weary miners.

Commodore Pangloss and his young companion were there, but they had just finished their meal. After paying the innkeeper for their dinner, they headed back to the steamliner. On his way out the door, Pangloss noticed Marinda and touched his smooth forehead, as if tipping an imaginary hat.

When she sat alone at a table, just observing the other miners, many of them gave her a sidelong glance, but such things no longer bothered her. She may have "fit in" at Lugtown, but she now felt more at home with herself no matter where she was.

Late in the evening, a wiry, dirt-streaked old woman came in and set herself apart from the others. The rest of the miners had well-mended work clothes, sturdy flannel shirts, thick canvas pants, but this woman looked as if she had crawled out of more than one avalanche and hadn't bothered to wash her clothes afterward. She had rampant hair and a gaze that could bore through rock.

She chose a table near the redcoal hearth and sat by herself. The innkeeper served her a polished stone cup of the local "strong mountain spirits" and left her alone.

Marinda watched her, intrigued. A month ago, anxious to fill her book by any means possible, she would have gone up to anyone she met, asking to add their tale to *Clockwork Lives*, but she had collected too many uninteresting stories that way, and she wanted this volume to hold a different quality of lives. She needed *Clockwork Lives* to be not a book that was put away to gather dust on a shelf, but a book that demanded to be *read*.

For now, she simply observed and listened. . . .

For the second and third day, she explored Endoline, watched the miners go in and out of their tunnels, work their shifts, load ore carts, and wait for the next steamliner to pick up their mineral harvest.

Some of her traveling companions welcomed Marinda, and she was happy for the conversation, but her attention was drawn to the lone woman with the wild and unruly appearance who came in night after night but didn't seem to want any company. Marinda's companions glanced over at the old prospector, then bent closer across the table. "That's mad Anrika. If you're collecting bizarre stories, she'll tell you things that might set the pages on fire!"

"Has she been through terrible experiences?" Marinda asked.

The other miners chuckled. "*She* believes so. We take Anrika's claims with a very large lump of rock salt."

Marinda had heard tall tales and exaggerations before, and she had no interest in chasing wild imaginings. Despite all the bluster, the talespinner's drop of blood usually wrote an unsatisfying story.

But this tough woman intrigued her. Unlike the braggart sailors who talked about their unbelievable experiences at sea, or Cabeza de Vaca, who looked for any ear to fill with his ridiculous tales, mad Anrika made no effort to tell her story. As far as Marinda was concerned, that gave her a measure of reliability.

Finally, on the fourth night she took her own cup of mountain spirits—which she ordered as a courtesy, though she would nurse it for hours—and sat next to a surprised Anrika. "You have seen things," Marinda said. "You have a story to tell. I would like to hear it—if it's true."

When the old prospector looked at her, her blue eyes seemed like shattered crystal. "Oh, my story is true, but I've stopped telling it because no one believes me." She snorted. "I've got my work to do."

"And what is your work?"

The prospector stared searchingly at her, as if assessing the likelihood that Marinda would respond with scorn or laughter. She lowered her voice. "I'm going to find the heart of the quintessence. It's in the mountains somewhere. I heard the voice of the world down in the tunnels, and I tried to follow it. I can feel the throbbing pulse of the earth. *Quintessence.* I know it's there, if I could just find it again. I came so close. I almost touched it once . . ."

Anrika scowled and took a drink from her stone cup. "Ahhh, you won't believe me. The other miners think I'm a fool for digging tunnels that go nowhere, following my senses instead of the veins of redfire opals or refractive topaz. But I will find it—I'll dig deeper and deeper. Just because they can't hear the song, doesn't mean it is silent." Marinda saw a fire deepen in Anrika's expression. "You won't believe me any more than the rest of them do."

Marinda slid her book forward. "I know how I can believe you. With this book, *you* will write your story through a reaction of alchemy and blood. I'll draw out the events and chronicle them on the pages. If you're telling the truth, it will all be proved right here. It only takes a prick of your finger."

She turned to an empty page. The old woman flipped to the preceding page filled with blood-written letters. She looked proud and determined. "I'm telling the truth. How do I convince you?"

Marinda slid out the golden needle from the binding. "With this."

The old woman extended her finger. "Then let me prove it to you."

THE
ALCHEMY MINER'S TALE

When I was a girl of ten, I fell into a cave—a deep, dark hole. It was a miracle, though I didn't know it then.

My father, an alchemy miner, was less lucky. Three years earlier, he had died in a mine cave-in. The mineral blends that made this area's geological harvest so lucrative also made the rock unstable and unpredictable. The alchemical minerals were buried deep inside the mountains, waiting to be discovered like a hidden treasure . . . or a ticking time bomb. When exposed, reacting elements could respond violently to air, light, or moisture. My father was buried deep in the mountain, sealed off in a collapsed excavation shaft.

In a time of such tragedy, the people of Endoline drew together, taking care of their own. My mother had many options before her, with the help and support of the whole town. Instead, she chose to silence her sadness by leaping from a cliff. Apparently, it was more important for her to show her grief for my father than to show her love for me.

As an orphan, I was left to fend for myself. I learned how to survive on the kindness of the townspeople, and I spent most days exploring and receiving an education in things that truly mattered. The mountains around Endoline were full of rugged cliffsides and deep notches, with many places to get into trouble. I would wander wherever I wanted, with no one to tell me I shouldn't.

One morning, I decided it was a good day to chase lizards sunning themselves. I wasn't sure what I'd do if I caught one, but they moved faster than my darting hands anyway. I scampered along the rocks, climbing, sliding, pursuing a particularly large spotted lizard, which vanished into a clump of scrub brush. There, in the underbrush, I discovered a hole in the hillside like the eye socket of a giant skull. Forgetting the lizard, I crawled closer to peer into the shadows. As dirt crumbled around me, pattering down into the unseen depths, I wormed my way forward, smelled the dusty breath of the Earth. I leaned closer, sniffing, peering ahead to see what I could see.

Then the ground gave way beneath my hands and knees, collapsing inward, and I became just one piece of debris in a building avalanche. I flowed with the dirt and rocks down a steep incline into darkness. I flailed, clutching at loose stones, trying to swim with the rockfall, and then I was airborne, flying blind—until I struck bottom. A boulder smashed down only inches from my head. A blanket of dirt cushioned me, and I slid to a halt.

I lay gasping, in shock, feeling the aches sweep over me, dreading that I would realize the much sharper pain of a serious injury—but that didn't come. Eventually I caught my breath, got to my hands and knees, and stood, careful not to hit my head or impale myself on some rock shard.

The darkness was as absolute as the silence. I could breathe, I could move, but I couldn't see where I was. I had been swallowed by the gullet of a mountain giant, and it would be days before anyone in Endoline even noticed I was missing, if they didn't just assume I had run off. I would have to solve my own problem—but I was no stranger to doing that.

I explored gingerly, tiptoeing in a random direction, making sure of my footing. I swept my hands in front of me in the inky blackness. I had no idea the extent of this dark chamber. One misstep, and I could plunge off a precipice or start another avalanche—and thus finish the job I had so ineptly started by chasing lizards in the sun.

The falling boulders must have buried the opening or knocked me into some side chasm. I saw nothing, heard nothing, and I realized it would take a very long time for me to die down here. I wondered if my father had felt the same dark abandonment during the mine cave-in, or if he had been killed instantly. I would never know.

I shouted as loudly as I could—but not for help. I knew no one could hear me down here. Rather, I used the sound of my voice to test for echoes, listening to the reverberations to get a sense of the chamber around me. It seemed large.

Hours passed. I tried to imagine how this cave had gone undiscovered for so many years when the miners of Endoline had explored the mountains thoroughly, but sometimes a person doesn't notice what is obvious, right in front of her.

Outside, the sun continued its passage across the sky. I circled my grotto, my prison, and could find no way out. Finally, in late afternoon the sun dropped to a certain position. At exactly the right angle, light struck the newly collapsed cave opening, which was now cleared of scrub brush, thanks to my fall.

In my deep darkness, I noticed a change in the quality of light, glimmers that twinkled like stars appearing in the dusk. I looked up in amazement, sure that I must be hallucinating, that the blackness was poking needles of temptation into my eyes. But the twinkling grew brighter. Shards of light formed never-before-seen constellations in the grotto around me.

I clung to stories that now seemed all too real, mystic lights that were said to be a miner's friend: the souls of those who had died inside the mountain, glimmers of hope that could lead a lost person to safety. In that brief moment, with all the geological wonders illuminated around me, I was absolutely sure these lights must have been fragments of my father's soul, guiding me to safety.

As the setting sun moved bit by bit, the light intensified, bounced through a zigzag of obstacles. Crystal flares reflected, ricocheted about. Like thousands of minuscule mirrors, the mineral shards gathered more illumination and filled my grotto with a visual symphony.

All around me, I suddenly saw fantastic rock sculptures, forests of stone columns, and underbrush of crystals and gems—a light show that no human had ever seen. I drank in the glorious sight, filled with wonder. I wished I could spend hours just staring at the treasure around me, but I saw the light changing, knew it would last for only moments more as the sun continued setting. I had to move.

I glanced around quickly, memorized my surroundings. In an instant, I absorbed them, like taking a chronograph with my mind.

I saw where the cave-in had occurred, the tumbled boulders piled in a debris fan at the base of a sheer dropoff. The loose rocks formed a ramp, and I was sure I could get halfway up it. There were also cracks, handholds in the wall above.

The light was fading already. I raced forward, climbed on the uncertain boulders, pulled myself up one, then another, listening to pebbles and larger stones patter into the deeper grotto.

I climbed, racing against time and light. I made it to the top of the rockfall before the brightness diminished. I looked ahead, memorizing potential handholds. I sprang to the most difficult one, caught it with my bloodied fingertips, and hauled myself up, skinning my knees, using my toes to lift my body higher.

Then the light drained away like a door shut on the myriad reflections, and the grotto plunged back into blackness.

But a few small crystal flares still sparkled like bright stars, and I gasped as I realized that the tiny lights were exactly where I needed them to be, like illuminated dots showing where to place my hands and feet. I climbed, out of breath. My throat and lungs were burning. More rocks fell, and I caught myself, holding desperately with one hand until I gained another foothold. I could not let myself lose momentum.

I reached the top of that steep dropoff, and I hung there wheezing, my muscles shaking. I wasn't out yet, but I was closer.

When I recovered myself, I realized that the blackness had a faint undertone of gray, and I headed toward it. I finally saw a thin slice of dusk outside. I climbed and clawed my way to the opening, and fresh air and freedom. When I at last emerged, I was covered with dirt. I feasted on the fresh air, then looked back into the dark hole of the cave.

I had been deep inside that mountain, and I knew I had nothing to be afraid of. That was when I made up my mind to be a miner.

———◆———

There is a language in stone, in the mountains themselves, and I spent my life learning to speak it, learning to read it, and learning to listen to what the rocks were saying.

The alchemical minerals mined from Endoline fed not only the demands of our own land, but the insatiable needs of the Watchmaker and his alchemist-priests in Albion. Though the miners had tunneled into the mountains for centuries, new deposits were discovered every year. Pulsing seams of redcoal, inclusions of fire opals, veins of tourmaline or dreamstone, chalcedony, black amethyst. I learned them all, knew how to identify them by feel, by reflective index, by phosphorescence factor, and by their varied reactions when scratched with an alchemical stylus.

I worked the tunnels and shafts alone, which suited me and the other miners just fine. I had always been eccentric. With my coldfire lantern, pickax, and sample hammer, I would worm my way into cracks and crannies, unexplored tunnels, fissures in the cave walls. Though I'd never been properly schooled, I learned the instincts of geological science. I knew that all substances were fundamentally composed of the four primary elements—fire, air, water, and earth—mingled, assembled, and transformed in varying combinations.

But I knew there was more, the elusive fifth element, the *quintessence*, the indefinable substance that engendered life itself, the element of the human soul. As I explored the mines, I remembered the crystal flares that had saved me when I was buried in the cave. I realized that what I had seen was no more than reflected light on gemstone fragments, but I knew there was more to the universe than natural science. I sought to understand the myths of twinkling lights deep in the tunnels. Many times over the years, I saw those sparkles in tunnels so deep and so far from the open sky that they could not possibly have been the wandering reflections of sunlight. I knew better.

As I explored alone, holding my coldfire lantern high, I would see glimmers in the distance, taunting me and leading me. They vanished if I followed them for too long, but I did not feel abandoned, because I knew they would come back if I had a great need.

I came to realize that if these mountains were so rich with precious minerals, then maybe the mountains also held a vein of quintessence hidden within the rocks.

I would place my bare hands against the rock walls, turn off my coldfire lantern, and stand there in the darkness, breathing evenly, feeling the stone . . . and feeling the soul of the mountain. I could sense vibrations, a throbbing, like a heartbeat. I was familiar with the smell of damp dusty air, the never-changing chill of the underground, but sometimes I sensed lines of warmth in my palms. I followed them, but couldn't find the source. Nevertheless, the heart of the quintessence was waiting for me somewhere down there.

Though I remained aloof from the others, the mining company

was satisfied with me, since I found many valuable inclusions and accessible veins of exotic minerals. The riches meant nothing to me. I grew bored with fire opals and dreamstones; they didn't have the quality I really wanted.

I followed the glimmering lights in the dark, shaft after shaft, using my pickax to break through thin walls, clear rockfalls, and open passages into a labyrinth of natural caves, which were likely connected to the one I had discovered as an incautious girl.

When I entered the natural caves —as opposed to the brute-force tunnels dug by miners—a new subterranean world opened for me. My lantern unleashed a chain reaction of crystal flares in the walls like a meteor shower deep underground. Maybe it was the ghosts of myriad miners rejoicing that someone had discovered them? Or stray fragments from the reservoir of quintessence lead-ing me onward?

As I followed one flash, another glimmer would lead me down a side passage; more sparkles guided me deeper, and when I paused, absolutely still, I could hear the mountain breathing, panting with excitement as if anticipating what I was about to discover.

The glimmering lights lured me along, and I followed them without reservation, without caution, and without common sense. I became hopelessly lost in that maze of tortuous caverns and pas-sages. But I grew more and more hopeful of finding what I had sought for so long.

The air thickened, and when I touched the stone walls I yanked back my fingers. The rock was hot! When I switched off my lan-tern, the tunnels had a dull red glow at the edge of my vision. That glow drew me onward like a traveler with the hope of a warm fire on a cold, snowy night.

The sound of breathing grew louder around me and the heart-beat of the mountain became distinct, like drumbeats through the rock—and the tempo increased.

As I wound my way forward, the lights became a flurry around me, a storm of bright stars. All the ghosts of fallen miners? Their souls gathered like sparkling raindrops blown in the wind, circling and ready to rejoin the reservoir of the original quintessence.

The drumbeat/heartbeat was louder, hammering harder. The vibrations shook the floor, the walls, the ceiling. I turned a sharp corner and saw where part of the stone had slid away to expose a window of glory filled with a fantastic ocean of heavenly light. The most dazzling vein of fire opals could never be more than a pale shadow of this amazing shimmer, composed of something entirely beyond earth, air, fire, and water.

A pool of the fifth element!

It was so breathtaking I wanted to immerse myself in it, to drown in it, to be there forever. My hands and my face stung, burned from proximity to the quintessence.

The rumble inside the cave grew louder, and the ceiling cracked. The walls shuddered; boulders slid down. Dust and pebbles rained all around me, and I had no choice but to retreat. I had already been buried in a cave once. Tumbling rocks slid across the narrow passage so I could no longer see the quintessence whose intense purity had nearly blinded me. I cried out in dismay.

As the tunnel collapsed, I stumbled away. Darkness enveloped me, for I had shuttered my coldfire lantern. The pulsing red glow faded into shadows, and then blackness. The roaring collapse diminished into echoes, until the throbbing of the excited mountain calmed again.

I found myself in a safer section of the caves, but I had no idea where. I went to the rockfall, pounded uselessly against the piled rocks. The quintessence had shown itself to me, given me a taste of that purity, and now I would starve for the rest of my life—unless I could get back there.

I sat for a long time, knowing that either I could just die there with some measure of contentment, or I could survive and try to find it again.

I chose to live.

The fabulous light had changed my vision somehow, and I could see the ethereal glints more clearly than before. I surrendered my faith to those glimmers of lost miners' souls, or whatever they were. I followed them. I did not worry about crevasses or dropoffs because the glimmers would not lead me astray. The memory of the quintessence kept me going, and eventually, miraculously, I found my way back into one of the carved mine tunnels. When I finally returned to the open air, I was surprised to see that my hands and my face were burned raw from the flare of the quintessence.

I had to find it again.

The flickers of light had saved me for a purpose, and when I rejoined the other miners in Endoline, they marveled at my burned face and hands, and the indefinable mad sparkle in my eyes.

"I discovered the heart of the mountain," I said. "The source of the quintessence is there, deep in the unexplored caves—and I've seen it!"

Nobody believed me. I had been odd for most of my life, after all. But I didn't need to impress anyone or convince anyone. I had faith in myself, and that is all the faith a person really needs. Finding the quintessence was the only thing that mattered to me now.

I resigned from my work, which only reaffirmed what some had said all along—that I was flighty and unreliable, that I had no business being in the mines. I spent a year searching the caves without success, then another year, then a decade, then another decade. I relived that moment when I'd seen the glorious light, the crux point of my existence.

But I know *exactly* what I was meant to do with my life. I will keep hunting for the quintessence, and I will find it again someday.

Then all the elements will be complete.

CHAPTER 20

When the words finished spilling and spelling out on the page, the old miner leaned back in her chair. "Read that. You'll see the truth." Anrika glanced at her goblet of mountain spirits, finished the rest in a gulp, then levered herself to her feet. "I need another drink."

At the table in the stone-walled common room, Marinda read the alchemy miner's tale, caught up in the story. Each major tale in *Clockwork Lives* conjured such vivid images for her. In a wistful moment, she remembered the look in her father's eyes when he would read books aloud to Marinda, but she hadn't felt them in the same way, hadn't understood them in the most basic sense— not until recently. Yet another detail that had changed in her quiet, perfect life.

She was still reading when Anrika came back with her drink. The old woman sat in silence, sipping and watching as Marinda turned pages. "That is the truth," she said again.

"I believe you. I've already seen and experienced much more

than I had thought possible."

A group of miners at a nearby table broke into laughter. One man called, "Anrika, today we found something in shaft twelve that might interest you."

"I doubt it," she responded in a rude tone that made Marinda realize she had faced such mocking before.

"A goblin infestation!" said the miner. "We heard them snickering."

"And they stole Mikhail's lunch," another miner spoke up. "I didn't know goblins liked boiled goat!"

Anrika ignored them. Having just read her tale, Marinda was annoyed that the townspeople would laugh at the old woman's dreams. She herself had only begun to see the magic in the world—and then she realized that she likely would have disbelieved, too. Back when she was in Lugtown, she'd never had time for imaginings or quests. But now it was important to her.

She straightened in her chair, looked at Anrika instead of the other miners. "Take me down there with you. Maybe we can find the quintessence together."

Anrika narrowed her eyes. "I've been searching for years. Why would you be able to find what has escaped me for so long?"

Marinda reached into her pocket and withdrew the small gold-and-crystal device that Captain Titus had given her. "Because I have this."

The prospector raised her eyebrows. "And what is that?"

"A dreamline compass. It's supposed to help me find where I should be."

"Does it work?"

"We'll see—if you let me accompany you tomorrow. I can help complete the story."

Anrika finished her drink of mountain spirits. "I'll meet you at dawn."

Marinda awoke in the pre-dawn darkness, then dressed in the sturdy set of pants one of the *Rocinante* sailor women had given her. She left the quiet inn to find a nervous-looking Anrika standing in the crushed-stone streets of Endoline. The old prospector carried a pickax and two coldfire lanterns, one of which she handed to Marinda.

Having left *Clockwork Lives* safe in her room, she felt oddly undressed, but she did not intend to carry a book through winding and possibly treacherous caves and mine shafts. She held up the dreamline compass. The pale blue coldfire light glistened off the crystal face, and the dial lazily bobbed back and forth. "Let's go find your quintessence."

Anrika guided her away from the tailing mounds and well-lit shafts near the main town and then out along a steep hillside. The narrow path looked as if it was traveled only by wild game and one eccentric prospector. Anrika led her to an opening, then gave her a sidelong smile. "This is the same cave I discovered when I was a little girl. Over the years, I broadened the entry, added planks as a ramp, even installed homemade ladders."

Once inside the caves, the old woman maintained a careful, steady pace. Even with the light of the lanterns, Marinda thought the walls seemed too close, and darkness swallowed everything but a small bubble around them. She followed as Anrika passed side passages, climbed down ladders, led her deeper into the mountain. "I'll take you close to where I know it has to be, and then you can help guide me—if your gadget works."

Along the way, the prospector stopped and unshuttered her lantern to flood coldfire light into a breathtaking grotto of stalactites, crystals, mineral flowers. "See this? It's just a fraction of what we'll see when we find the quintessence." Marinda wanted to drink in the marvelous sight, but Anrika was impatient to move on.

More cave passages spiderwebbed out in various directions, and as time went on the old prospector seemed more pensive, considering options. Her voice took on a hushed quality. "It's here, so very close, hiding behind one of these walls . . . but there are still so many other ways to go." She turned to Marinda. "Any suggestions?"

When she held up the lantern, her weathered face was bathed in an eerie, pale glow. Marinda held up the dreamline compass, looked at the dial and the pointer—the arrow pointed clearly and steadily in a distinct direction. "Let's try this way. . . ."

Grinning with anticipation, Anrika hurried along, while Marinda followed, holding a lantern in one hand and the compass in the other. They traveled down and deeper, winding along, and Anrika grew visibly more excited. "Your compass is taking us in the right direction. Did you see the lights?" She slammed down the shutters on her lantern, gesturing for Marinda to do the same. When they were plunged into darkness, Anrika laughed. "Yes, there! It just flashed—did you see it?"

Marinda searched the infinite darkness, trying to find a diamond of light, a fleck of a soul fire leading them on, but she missed it.

"It doesn't matter." The old prospector opened her lantern again. "It's this way. If you listen hard, you can hear the heartbeat, and if you keep your senses open, you can *feel* it." She hurried ahead with the pickax over her shoulder.

Marinda still consulted the compass, watched the wandering pointer, and called to Anrika when the old woman overshot a passage. "I think we're supposed to turn here."

Anrika seemed to be concentrating in a fugue state, then nodded. She turned down the side passage where the compass pointed. "Yes . . . yes, you're right."

They entered another grotto, where reverberating echoes implied the enormous size of the chamber. Their coldfire light shone out, dwindling in the black distance—and then the phosphorescence came back. Marinda gasped as she saw towering fungi, a toadstool forest deep underground, each pale form rising as high as a tree. "Look!"

Anrika gave only a sidelong glance to the mammoth mushrooms. "I wager the quintessence makes them grow like that. We've got to be close to the source—sense the life throbbing through them!"

Marinda could smell the powdery scent, the moist, mildewy overtones in the fungus grotto, and she heard a metallic trickle of running water that seeped through cracks. She wanted to embrace more of these marvels—had her father even imagined such a sight?

Then uneasiness rippled through her. "Shouldn't we be more careful marking our route? Are you going to be able to find your way back?"

"No time for that now. And if I become part of the quintessence, why would we ever want to go back?"

Marinda felt cold. "That wasn't what I—"

"Where does your dreamline compass tell us to go now?" Anrika seemed urgent.

The dial spun, wavered, spun further. "It isn't locking on. . . ."

The old woman held up her coldfire lantern, glanced again at the towering mushrooms, then grinned. "That must mean we are so close that all paths will lead us there."

She bounded off, with Marinda following, afraid of where Anrika was going, but more afraid to be left alone in the deep dark.

The tunnel wound deeper, and Marinda could hear the passage of air, an oppressive sound that was like breathing. Vibrations penetrated the soles of her shoes. When she touched the rock wall beside her, it was warm and trembling.

The old woman extended the lantern in front of her. "It's *here!*"

Marinda's dreamline compass was spinning in random, excited circles.

Abruptly, the tunnel was blocked by a flat stone wall, but the cave still throbbed around them. Anrika stared at the obstacle as if her sheer defiance could make it dissolve. She set down her pickax and leaned forward. She pressed both palms to the stone, then she laid her cheek against the wall. The prospector backed away, grasped the handle of her tool. "Keep clear!"

Anrika was an old woman, but strong, and she swung the steel-tipped implement at the offending wall. Sparks flew from the tip, and rock chipped away. Marinda heard an increase in the thrumming sound all around them, as if the old woman had awakened something.

Anrika swung the pickax again, smashing it against the rock. Marinda retreated another step, holding up her coldfire lantern to provide light. Though she was uneasy, she also felt caught up in the thrill. Marinda could not deny the power in the air, the throbbing energy all around them.

"But—what are you going to do with so much of it?" Marinda remembered the quicksilver droplets the Lugtown quarry workers occasionally found in cracked thunder eggs, but she had only known of the tiniest quantities.

"It is life itself," Anrika said. "The wellspring of the essence of the world."

Her dreamline compass whirled, sparked, and then gave out with a silent sigh, spinning down into dim uselessness. Marinda held it, shook it, but the compass no longer responded.

On the third blow, the rock wall cracked—and a slash of lightning emanated from the splintered stone. Anrika reeled backward. With renewed strength, she chopped a fourth time, which exposed an unearthly pool like a celestial mirror that reflected angelic light.

It was an astonishing, incredible sight, pulsating with a glory Marinda had never before beheld. She understood now what had drawn this woman on an irrational quest for so many years of her life.

Anrika began laughing—laughing as if her sanity had just

crumbled along with the stone. "It's real, and I can be part of it!"

The storm of light forced Marinda to shield her eyes. The heartbeat hammered and shook the tunnel now, and the roar she heard was not just in her ears, but a groan of breaking agony from the cave itself.

Anrika stood silhouetted in front of the purifying light, reveling in it. "This is where I need to be!"

The ceiling began to come down. "We have to go!" Marinda yelled as she scrambled backward.

The old woman turned, her lips drawn back in a wild grin. "You need to go—but I stay *here.* This is where I belong."

She dropped the pickax and stepped forward with both arms extended—and plunged her hands up to her elbows in the pure quintessence. Laughing even louder, Anrika sounded as if her voice would tear out of her throat. When she glanced back at Marinda, the quintessential glow had reached all the way to her eyes, shining out like blazing stars. "It's glorious, *glorious!*" She forced a last shred of control into her voice. "But you have to go—*run!*"

"How will I find my way back to the surface?" Marinda said, looking at the burned-out dreamline compass. "I'm lost!"

"Follow the lights. They will help you. *I* will help you if I can."

The cave was rumbling, the mountain stirring, but Marinda couldn't tell if it was from joy or anger. Anrika leaned deeper into the wellspring of light, her face filled with an uncontainable satisfaction; her entire body was luminous, such a bright and dazzling form that even angels would have shielded their eyes. With one final cry of happiness, Anrika was absorbed into the pool, a silhouette of pure light that coalesced into the rest of the reservoir.

The cave shuddered and twitched, as if in an involuntary response, bringing down rocks to shelter the raw, exposed nerve. Marinda had to back away, and then she began to run.

She staggered up the winding passage, ducking as rocks began to fall. The coldfire lantern shed grotesque shadows and distractions around her, but she kept going as far as she could remember the way. Pebbles and rock shards pattered down from the ceiling, and she emerged into the cavern of gigantic mushrooms. The mammoth fungi were like an eerie prehistoric forest, absorbing sound and reflecting back pale phosphorescence, but now they swayed as if in a hurricane. A jagged boulder from above smashed down and crushed one of the enormous toadstool caps, sending out a shower of spores and rock dust.

Marinda kept running, gasping, her throat on fire. She had no inkling which way to go. The labyrinth of underground passages was impossible to navigate; her dreamline compass had failed, and Marinda had no reason to believe that any glimmering souls of fallen miners would help the daughter of an inventor from a small town in Albion.

She ran, trying to keep ahead of the rockfalls, peering into the dark and hoping she didn't plunge into an unseen crevasse. Then, in a moment of near hopelessness, she saw a tiny sparkle. It might have been no more than an imaginary glint, but she followed it anyway. Even a guess was better than inaction.

Anrika had possessed a sense of the mountain depths with an instinct developed after a lifetime of exploration. But Marinda had to trust this.

From behind and below, dazzling white light spilled out like a flood, closing in on her.

She saw another glint up ahead, and when she encountered an intersection of tunnels, she glimpsed a sparkle down the left one. With nothing to lose, she didn't question, simply ran.

A light sparkled ahead, like a flaring breadcrumb, and she heard a whispering voice that came to her clearer and louder than the rockfall. *This way. Almost there!* It sounded like Anrika's voice, somehow alive in these tiny fragments of light.

Marinda clutched the coldfire lantern, climbed up broken boulders, and emerged in an upper passage, surrounded by darkness beyond the coldfire light.

Another sparkle. *This way.* The voice sounded even clearer now, and Marinda didn't care whether it was delusion, desperate hope, or truly the voice of the fallen prospector.

This way!

She was taken by surprise when she came upon the first ladder. How had she gotten here? It didn't seem possible! Marinda climbed, struggling to balance the lantern. She dropped it, and the lantern tumbled down and smashed on the stone floor, spilling pale blue light that was quickly engulfed by that other intensifying glow.

Behind her, she heard a crack and a roar as more of the cave collapsed in on itself, and she knew that the old prospector was surely dead, buried in the released quintessence. Or had become part of it, as she had wished.

The tunnel walls ahead sparkled urgently, beckoning Marinda like a thousand glimmering diamonds. It was not her imagination. *I will lead you—but I cannot protect you!*

She made her way with all possible speed, climbing ramps and ladders, ducking under low ceilings, worming her way through tight passages, afraid she would be crushed at any moment. She lost track of time, of her breathing, of all sense of direction.

She listened to the continuing rumble, took heart in the ghostly voice that emanated from the walls and floor of the cave.

Unexpectedly, she staggered blindly out into the open air, off balance, catching her breath. Anrika's ethereal voice was gone now, no longer needed. The mountain's deeper bass sounds built to a crescendo. She turned to look into the cave opening, seeing a last glimpse of the searing quintessential glow and the dust that boiled out from the avalanche.

Marinda heaved deep breaths and somehow remained steady on her feet, both saddened and amazed at what she had just experienced.

After decades of searching, Anrika had found what she'd been looking for. And now Marinda had an amazing story to tell—one that she would make sure the Endoline miners believed.

CHAPTER 21

Θ

When she made her way back to town, Marinda was exhausted and strangely exhilarated. The shockwaves from Anrika's discovery had thrummed through the core of the mountains, and the miners had evacuated the deep shafts with no casualties and remarkably few injuries. Back in the inn, Marinda was bedraggled and alone—all the men and women from the mines knew that she had been with Anrika, and now she'd come back by herself.

As Marinda held a goblet of the mountain spirits in her trembling hand, she told her story to eager listeners, leaving out nothing. She spoke with an intensity that challenged them to disbelieve her, and when they saw the look of surprise and fear that was etched into her face, none of the miners—not even the ones who had mocked the old prospector—dared to raise any doubts.

They believed her and, by extension, they finally believed what Anrika had been saying all along. "Treat her with respect," Marinda said with a warning tone in her voice. "Someday, maybe a glimmer of Anrika's soul will guide one of you out of the darkness."

Marinda remained in Endoline for two more weeks, while she tried to think of what to do next. She had no desire to wander off into the wilderness of the Redrock Desert in search of lost cities. She already had one quest, and that was quite enough.

The miners treated her with a semblance of awe. Misunderstanding her quest to gather tales, some thought she was a newsgraph reporter from Albion. She convinced three of them to give her their stories in a drop of blood, but they were small, simple tales that filled less than a page each. But she would find other worthy stories; she knew it.

Some miners invited her into the tunnels so she could chip away fresh fire opals from a thriving vein, or see a seam of redcoal like alchemical lifeblood that pulsed through the rock. At the quarry she watched slabs of construction stone being cut and stacked for delivery to Poseidon City.

But she felt she was done here in Endoline, and it was time for her to go. She had almost no money left and no plan. So, she packed her things and was ready the next time Commodore Pangloss's steamliner arrived in Endoline. The hearty man remembered her when she stepped forward and asked if she might take passage back with him.

"So, is your curiosity satisfied, then? You've seen what you meant to see and experienced what you meant to experience?"

"That, and more, sir."

He sighed and seemed sad. "My assistant has gone off into the Redrock Desert, and I don't know if I'll see him again. But dreams are not easily swayed by logic. . . ."

Marinda lifted her chin. "I'm hoping you could take me back to Poseidon City—at a reasonable rate, since my finances are dwindling."

When he grinned, his great dark beard swelled like a

thundercloud on his chin. "I can let you ride for free in one of the rear compartments—if that is a reasonable enough rate." He watched alchemical cargo being loaded aboard one of the back cars, then turned back to her. "But I'm not going back to Poseidon City, Miss Peake. I'm on my outer run now, heading from the mountains back to the coast, serving the fishing villages. I'll be off to Leviathan's Reach, Seacliffs, then Heartshore—"

The last was all she needed to hear. "I have always wanted to see Heartshore!"

He was taken aback. "Truly? Never heard anyone say that before. More curiosity?"

She thought of Hender. "Curiosity, yes . . . and other things."

As she rode aboard the steamliner, Marinda realized with a sense of satisfaction that more and more of her book was complete. The end actually seemed possible now. She had already seen many places and met many people, and Marinda was confident that she could fill the rest of the volume, collect the last of the stories her father had asked of her.

But even when she finished *Clockwork Lives*, she didn't have enough money to buy passage back to Albion. She had been so focused on completing the task, and the end had seemed so distant for so long, that she hadn't considered what would happen afterward. She would have a full book, but no easy way to get home.

But after all she had been through, she wasn't about to give up. She could find work, scrimp, pay her expenses and save a few coins, but she would likely take years to save up the passage back across the ocean. Still, even though she was not an adventurer like Hanneke Lakota, Marinda had done more in the past year than in her entire previous life. And that was what counted.

She thought about her cozy cottage back in Lugtown: the quiet, perfect life that was all she had ever wanted. Yes, she could have married someone, maybe had three redheaded and freckled children of her own. Or, she could have done any other thing she chose, since she was smart enough and competent enough—but Marinda had never *chosen* to do anything. She understood what her father had wanted for her.

Her memories of Lugtown had been softened by the distance of nostalgia, but except for the memories that came with it, life at her father's cottage was not altogether different from the way people lived in Endoline, or Poseidon City, or elsewhere.

No matter where they were, others would dream of faraway places, places they were never likely to see—according to the fisherman Hender, that was called "hope." She needed her own dream, and it had to be something more than just to go home to a place where dreams were no longer a part of her life.

Marinda held out hope that Heartshore was as pleasant a place as she imagined it would be. Recalling soft-spoken Hender as they had sat on their crates for a lunch at a makeshift table, she thought maybe a place like that was what she needed, at least for a while, before she went on another quest, or found the means to go home.

Maybe there, for a time, she could start a new quiet, perfect life—on her own terms.

Due to the Watchmaker's Stability, all the villages in Albion were constructed according to a plan that had been studied, designed, and approved to be the most efficient and satisfactory type of human habitation.

In Atlantis, the people built their towns with preoccupied chaos, adapting streets and buildings as the needs grew or changed. Endoline branched outward from the quarry and the various mine entrances, its layout shaped by the topography of the mountains. Poseidon City was a riot of crowded structures and confusing streets.

Heartshore was a fishing village, plain and simple. The heart-shaped harbor that gave the town its name was just a divot in the coastline; docks and piers extended into the water, and tortuous wooden staircases wound up the sheer bluffs to the headlands and the main town above.

The Commodore's airship touched down on the headlands above the sea. The people came forward and quickly unloaded the supplies, while Pangloss was anxious to be on his way again, because the sea breezes had picked up and he was worried about rough skies.

Marinda disembarked and bade him farewell. They had talked frequently during his stops along the way, and the bearlike man was sad to see her go. "And you're sure this is where you're meant to be?"

"No, not at all," Marinda told him, as she looked out to see some of the fishing boats toiling back to the docks below. "But it's where I am now."

The people of Heartshore greeted her with curiosity rather than suspicion. The tiny fishing village received few visitors who didn't already have business there; tourists had no reason to come, and so there were very few lodgings available.

She needed a place to stay, but by now she had little left of the money she had earned by working in the Cygnus Tavern, and only a few of the gold honeybee coins for emergencies. After she asked several people about a home or a room where she could live for weeks, possibly months, possibly longer, someone said, "Umberlin owns an empty shack out on the point you could probably have for a song."

"I can't sing very well."

"Then a small coin. He's not picky."

Umberlin was an old man who painted boats when boats needed to be painted, and otherwise sold leviathan oil for heating and light. "I was told to see you?" she asked. "I'm seeing the world with my own eyes. I came from a small town in Albion, then Crown City, then I took a steamer voyage across the ocean to

Poseidon. I visited the alchemy mines in the mountains, and now I'm here."

She knew her voice had an odd Albion accent, but old Umberlin reacted as if she had spoken in an entirely foreign language. He looked at her skeptically. "I suppose someone needs to see the world, just to make sure it's all still there."

"I need a place to stay for a week or two . . . possibly longer. I don't have much money, but enough to get started."

"That problem is the same all around the world."

Umberlin had to be reminded, twice in fact, that he did have a small unoccupied house he could sell or rent. It had been empty for so long that he was surprised to recall that he owned the place. "Oh, yes! Been abandoned for years, not much more than a shack. It'll take some fixing, though."

"I'm not too particular." She didn't even need to see it, because the home would be whatever she made of it.

One exotic honeybee coin from Albion was enough for Marinda to purchase the shack outright. Satisfied with her purchase, because it was a clear start, Marinda was about to go find the house when she saw that the rest of the fishing boats were returning to the harbor with their day's catch.

With more anticipation than she admitted to herself, Marinda hurried down the steep zigzagged stairs to reach the shingle beach and the extended docks where all the boats would tie up. As she walked down the dock, fishermen emptied their nets into large bins where the flopping fish would be sorted and cleaned. Dock workers helped the boat crews untangle the fishing nets.

Marinda kept her eyes on the sea and finally recognized one of the boats. The lone fisherman threw a thick rope around the dock stanchion, pulled it tight, and glanced up at her. Marinda knew Hender immediately, and she smiled at him, but she wasn't sure he would remember her, even though she looked so completely out of place. They had only shared a quick meal and a little conversation in the busy Poseidon City harbor.

But he lit up. "It's Marinda Peake, the woman from Albion! I never expected to find you in a place like Heartshore. Poseidon City wasn't exciting enough for you, so you had to come here?" She could tell he was pleased to see her.

"Maybe there are different kinds of excitement." She raised her eyebrows, then stepped closer to him. "I'm here for a while, or longer than that. And I've learned that when I need something, it's best to ask." She helped him unload his fish, and he appreciated that she wasn't squeamish about getting her hands slimy. She met his eyes. "If I stay in this town, I need to find a trade, at least until I can figure out what to do next. I hoped you might have some suggestions?"

As Hender kept unloading his catch, he looked deep in thought. "What can you do?"

"Whatever I can learn to do. And I'm willing to learn quite a few things."

"Then you should learn how to mend nets, first thing. It's winter work, but I'm running short and I have three you can repair right now. I'll put them to use before the start of storm season. Several of my comrades are in the same position, and we could increase our haul if we had the extra nets right now."

"Then that's exactly what I'll do," she said. "I will divide my efforts between mending nets and repairing my new home."

"Your new home?" Hender paused to regard her, deep in thought. "Then you do intend to stay—for a while at least."

When she told him about the shack she had bought from old Umberlin, he looked alarmed. "Too close to the edge of the point for any sensible person, especially in storm season, but I suppose it's stood there intact for years. It'll last a little longer."

"Especially after I repair it," she said.

"You have your work cut out for you." Hender's smile lifted the curtain on the distant sadness in his eyes. "Could be, I might even find time to help."

———❖———

The shack was like a trembling waif that could collapse into splinters and planks if Marinda sneezed while inside. It stood near the end of the point, and erosion had washed away the cliff to within fifteen feet of the front door.

When she first arrived, the shack was a home for pigeons and drafts. With a broom she chased out the pigeons, then used driftwood and lumberyard scraps to patch the drafts. It was not a palace by any means, but in time, with hard work and patience, Marinda could turn it into a home that might be almost as nice as her cottage back in Lugtown.

She mended the fireplace with field stones, cleaned the chimney, and lit a warm redcoal fire on her first night. She purchased the supplies she needed from the small Heartshore mercantile and illuminated the main room with a lantern that burned distilled leviathan oil; the small bright flame smelled of ambergris.

As promised, Hender delivered three frayed nets and provided rope scraps, patiently showing Marinda how to tie off the holes or replace hopelessly tangled sections.

In the following days, she found the work soothing; she would sit alone in her shack during the day, sometimes with the shutters open and salt breezes playing inside. At night, she would light her oil lamp and read through *Clockwork Lives*, reliving what she had seen and done and what others had seen and done. The book was three-quarters finished, but still had room for more stories. Significant ones.

Hender often helped her with repairs, easily finding excuses to seek out her company. They would work together outside in the blustery wind, hammering down loose shingles on her roof. He also brought a few fish from his catch, insisting that she have enough to eat, and she insisted just as strongly that they eat together, so as to minimize the number of solitary meals that each of them had had all too often. Hender seemed happy to have the company. He had told her back in Poseidon City that he had lost his wife some years earlier, but she did not pry for details.

He was very curious about Marinda's own story, though, curious as to what had brought her to a place like this. She had not yet shown anyone in Heartshore her book, had not plied the fishermen for their tales, because that wasn't why she was here. But after a fine dinner and relaxing conversation, Marinda sat with Hender by the sweet-smelling light of the leviathan lamp. Finally, feeling very comfortable with him, she brought out *Clockwork Lives* and told him about her father's will and all the journeys those tales had shown her.

Hender flipped to the end of the book. "You still have dozens of blank pages."

"Once I had hundreds. And I want it to be a good book. It's no longer enough just to fill the empty pages with simple, uninteresting lives."

Hender nodded. "I can respect that."

They sat in a heavy silence for a long moment. He opened his mouth and closed it. Marinda thought he was going to ask if he could read the tales, but instead he surprised her. "Would you like to have my story? It's not much, but I would be honored to be included." He had avoided the subject in their first meeting but now he seemed interested in sharing with her.

Although Hender seemed to be a quiet and devoted man, she guessed that a drop of blood from his fingertip would spell out another short plain tale like so many others. But she didn't want to disappoint him. "I can't turn down the offer. I'll be happy to take one more step toward completing my quest."

She removed the golden needle from the binding. As she took his fingertip, Hender flinched, not from fear of the pinprick, but from fear of what the alchemy would reveal to her.

But he braced himself, nodded, and let her gently take his life.

THE
FISHERMAN'S TALE

I was born to be a fisherman, and never had any doubt what I was meant to be. There's nothing wrong with understanding what you can do, what you *should* do, and being content with that. We each measure life with our own yardstick.

Like so many others in Heartshore, I went out each day to follow the unmarked roads on the sea; I caught fish, brought them back, unloaded my nets, tallied the haul, went out again the next day, and then came home—as regular as the tides.

I married Ana, a girl I had known since childhood. She and her mother would light smoky beach fires of greenwood and kelp and set up long racks where they would smoke fish all day long. Many fishermen did this themselves, but Ana's family used a special seasoning that was the best I'd ever tasted. Ana's smile added even more spice. She and I were friends, and we grew close.

In such a small village, it isn't hard to *know* the person who's meant for you. Our transition to a married couple was as smooth as the change of the seasons. One evening, a year into our marriage,

Ana and I strolled along the rough shingle after the tide had gone out. We liked to take beach walks together; we would talk about small things or just communicate with a comfortable silence as we looked out at the gray water.

Ana stared for a long moment. "You've gone far away out to sea. Have you ever seen Albion?"

I laughed. "I never sail my boat very far from the coast, and Albion is an entire ocean away! It takes a big steamer days to cross so much water. My little fishing boat would never make it that far."

"I know," she said wistfully. "But I like to think about another continent on the other side of the world." She bent over to pick up a black rock that looked out of place among the stones on the beach. It had rounded edges from being washed and tumbled through the waves. "I wonder if this came all the way from Albion."

I smiled. "Unless stones learn how to talk, we'll never know."

She picked up another stone, a typical one, and turned it in her fingers. "And this one is from our continent." She flung it as far as she could out into the waves, and I watched it splash. "Someday the currents and tides will take that one to the shores of Albion . . . and some other fisherman's wife will pick it up and think about me."

"Someday," I agreed. It was a good answer for many things. "Someday we might see Albion ourselves."

In the distance we saw a splash—large dark figures swimming slowly, rising up to crest, then diving deep again. I extended my arm. "Look, leviathans."

Ana grinned. The large black beasts were slick, their hides studded with fearsome-looking spines, but they had a gentle disposition unless attacked.

We watched the majestic and powerful creatures swimming in the distance. Some armored steamers hunted the leviathans, killing them on the waters and butchering them aboard factory barges to render the sweet-smelling oil. Most of the leviathan hunters lived in an isolated village far to the north, shunned by many of us who didn't like the messy business they conducted. Yet we purchased barrels of leviathan oil, nevertheless.

Ana held onto my arm. "My mother says it's good luck to see leviathans."

"But bad luck to hurt them," I said.

That was when she told me we were expecting our first child.

⊷⊶⊷

We lived in a comfortable shore house partway up the headlands, precariously balanced among the sandstone terraces of the cliffs. Ana loved the view and would often step outside just to stare at the sea. Each day as I set off in my fishing boat, I knew she would be there, waving at me.

With our house balanced on the slope, Ana had to climb a steep staircase down to the beach or up to the main village, and I worried about how she would manage as her pregnancy progressed.

But three months in, Ana lost the baby in a series of cramps and pain and blood. She was so weak, I was afraid I would lose her too. I kept my boat tied up for days and stayed home to care for her until she recovered. Ana was distraught at having lost the baby, but one of the midwives in town comforted her, told her things that I didn't know how to say, gave her medicines that helped her grow strong. I assured Ana we would try again. We were young, and we had time.

How could I possibly know that we didn't?

I had lost a week of the best fishing season while I tended her, and so my year's catch was much diminished; I didn't have enough fish to preserve and sell in Poseidon City. If Ana and I wanted to start a family, we would need the money in order to build a larger home in the main town.

So I went back out on the water every day, trying to make up for the lost time.

The weather took a sharp turn with the season, and the winter storms were coming. Every fisherman possessed a quicksilver weather glass that had a sympathetic affinity for atmospheric pressure, sensing changes that were too far out at sea to be seen from shore. My fellow fishermen knew that the oncoming weather was going to be bad, so they tied up their boats and hoped that the harbor would provide shelter from the worst battering.

But I looked at the quicksilver weather glass, sniffed the air, and told Ana that I would go out one more time. She was worried about me, still pale in her recovery after the miscarriage. "You'll be careful?"

"Always," I said, kissing her. "I never go far from shore, and I can outrun the storm if I need to. Besides, a storm always stirs up bigger fish. I'll have a catch the likes of which no one in Heartshore has ever seen!"

"Just promise you'll come home," she said.

I promised.

When I headed out of the harbor, standing at the bow with my face to the wet breezes, the rest of the fishermen stayed behind, shaking their heads. A few other boats had gone out, too, lingering near the shore where they could run back to safety if the wind whipped up and the seas grew too rough.

But I knew that the larger schools of fish would be farther from shore, so I headed out into deep water, thinking of the payoff, not out of greed but of necessity. If I wasn't going to catch a full load of fish, then there was no point in taking the risk.

I cast out all four of my nets and trawled for several miles, then pulled them up, pleased with a good haul of green snapper and spotted whitefish in the first three hours. My dreamline compass told me where the coast was, but even when I couldn't see the shore through the mists or distance, I could feel the weight of a continent out there . . . and I could feel Ana. It warmed my heart to know she had stood outside our house and watched my boat head off until it dwindled to a tiny speck on the sea.

The air thickened, and the waves grew rough; I was sure hurricane winds would strike the coast like a blacksmith's hammer before evening. I emptied the fresh fish into the cargo locker and dropped my nets one more time, thinking that a final catch and a full hold would be enough to calm Ana's worries.

Something changed in the sea around me, though—and it had nothing to do with the weather. I didn't understand what it was. There seemed to be a fear down below, and the fish just . . . vanished in the water. I leaned over the side of the boat, but I couldn't see much through the murky, churning waves. Nevertheless, I *felt* it—and a chill went down my back.

I used the steam winch to haul up the nets, but they were all empty. I smelled a bitter tang in the air and looked back toward the invisible shore, thought of my home and my wife. Determined, I dropped the nets again, using weights to take them even deeper. I would try a final time before heading back to Heartshore.

I added redcoal to the boiler to feed the chugging engine. The skies became a bruised gray, but my fishing boat toiled along, trawling the deep waters.

Then the entire vessel lurched as if seized and shaken by some giant's hand. My engines groaned and vented a despairing gasp of steam. The net ropes went so taut they were like the thrumming string of a musical instrument, and the winches shrieked with the effort of holding them. The boat tilted at such a steep angle I could barely keep my feet on the deck. Seawater sloshed over the rail, and one of the lockers of freshly caught fish scraped along the deck boards and thumped against the side.

The boat lurched again, tilting the other way. The net ropes went slack, then pulled in another direction. The pulleys creaked; the ropes twisted and strained. I fought my way to the engine controls, operated the gear mechanism, and began to reel in the nets. I feared what I had caught down there, but I also had to know.

As the net strained, the underwater *thing* bolted, and I nearly lost my footing as the boat was dragged unwillingly across the waves—hauled for miles like a bobbing toy. The engines howled in protest. The steam pressure rose beyond tolerable levels, and I desperately vented it. If my engines exploded, I would be stranded at sea with the dire storm closing in. The groaning winches struggled to raise the nets, but they were no match for whatever I had caught.

Finally, in the water ahead, the creature breached the surface— a black-skinned leviathan, hopelessly tangled in my nets, its long spines caught in the ropes. When the leviathan's jagged back sliced through the choppy water, I saw that it was ancient and huge, its hide crusted with barnacles.

The monster saw my boat, seemed to know that *I* was responsible for its pain and terror, and it rounded in the water, tangling itself further in the multiple nets. The ropes and the winches went slack as the huge thing headed toward me, churning the water into froth.

Standing on the wet deck, I yelled for it to stop, begged in every way I knew how, but the beast surged forward and rammed my boat. The shuddering crash nearly threw me overboard, but I hung on to the ropes. One of my fish lockers tumbled into the sea, but I didn't care. Two of the leviathan's wicked-looking spines impaled my boat—which left the creature hopelessly caught and unable to extricate itself.

A basso rumble of despair came from beneath the water as the monster's tympanic membrane groaned in a voice that I had heard only from a great distance. In awe, holding a rope to steady myself, I looked overboard—and saw the leviathan's eye: a shining, milky disk as wide as the span of my arms. It stared up at me, angry, confused, or perhaps sad. Its hide was scarred with lacerations along its skin, probably from an encounter with the sea hunters.

I was no butcher who would kill leviathans for their oil. I could smell the sharp scent of its ambergris wafting upward. The leviathan's wide mouth opened, showing millions of hair-fine teeth for eating the tiniest creatures of the sea.

I sawed at the ropes with my fisherman's knife, cutting the nets free. When the strands came loose, the leviathan struggled, rocking my damaged boat back and forth, but even the loose ropes remained wrapped around the beast like strangling bonds.

The monster thrashed its long fins and began to move the boat again. I realized to my horror that if it tried to dive, I was doomed—the beast would either shatter my boat, or drag it beneath the waves.

"Please . . ." I said, and the leviathan's troubled eye stared up at me.

By now the dark clouds had closed in like an angry mob to watch our helpless tableau. The waves swelled, and the wind howled loudly enough to drown out the creature's mournful sound. The two spines that pierced my hull were wedged tight, surrounded by splintered wood.

In its struggles, my boat lifted up and crashed down, but the leviathan could not free itself. Storm swells buffeted us, and cold rain slashed down as I stood on the deck shouting, "I didn't mean to! I wasn't trying to hurt you."

I remembered my promise to Ana that I would come home. I had to find a way out of this.

I studied the scars on the leviathan's hide, saw raggedly healed cuts, gashes caused by boat hooks and grappling chains. Yes, this one had fought off sea hunters, maybe more than once. It had a right to its fear and mistrust, and I knew that it could easily smash me to flotsam if it decided to do so.

The storm became a furious roar, and even without the damage to my hull, I wasn't certain my fishing boat would make it back to Heartshore. As the waves lashed us back and forth, the leviathan was trapped and weakening as well, both of us caught in an accidental death embrace.

I had to do something, and I thought of only one way we could both be free. A painful way. But we might survive, one or the other, or both. I knew that I had to do it, and I could only hope the leviathan would understand.

As the storm battered my boat, I fought my way through the horrific wind to the small wheelhouse and retrieved my hatchet. I held the stout handle and said "I'm sorry" one more time, hoping that the leviathan would grant me luck for freeing it—*good luck*, so I could make it back home.

Saltwater crashed over the edge of the boat and flooded the deck, but I dropped into the dim fish-smelling hold where the tusk-like spines had pierced my hull. I could hear the leviathan straining, moaning its sorrowful song, but the spines remained inextricable.

I raised the hatchet, telling myself again that this was my only chance. Hoping the blade was sharp enough, I swung the hatchet with all my strength and bit into the first tough spine. The blade cracked through the outer shell and dug deep into what must have been a nerve. The leviathan exploded into a frenzy, lurching my boat like chaff.

But I could not stop now. I struck again, chopping deeper and deeper, hacking through the spine. The leviathan fought back, but I flailed five times with the hatchet before the severed tusk clattered to the bottom of the hull where it lay sloshing in the water that poured in. The beast wrenched its body, and the stump popped free. As seawater gushed in through the splintered hole, I could not hesitate.

I steeled myself and turned to the second spine, striking hard with the hatchet. The leviathan nearly capsized the boat in its frenzy, but I grappled with the curved tusk, blow after blow, chopping until finally the second spine fell free. With a wild lurch, the leviathan tore itself away from the boat, and seawater flowed in.

After clumsily fashioning the best makeshift patch I could manage, I staggered up to the deck, not letting myself feel triumphant, for this was only the first step in the ordeal that lay ahead. In a slowly sinking boat, I faced the impossible hurricane force of the storm.

Not far off, I watched the freed leviathan breach the waves, twisting as it threw off the frayed remnants of the nets. It leaped out of the water, as big as a house. Lightning flashed around it, and I could see the disheartening stumps where I had amputated two of its majestic spines. The leviathan crashed back into the water, sending up spray and foam, before it dove deep.

But my boat was now free as well. When I made it to the engine house, I activated the pumps again. The boiler's heat had not died down entirely, and I salvaged some scattered redcoal, which I added to the furnace. When the engines began chugging, the boat finally moved, making headway.

But in all the lurching chaos, my dreamline compass had been smashed completely out of alignment. I had no way of knowing where the shore was; I had only my instinct.

So I set course and prayed.

The sky was black, choked with wind and rain. The waves hurled my boat upward, then dragged it down like flotsam. The vessel fought its way through the swells. I had no idea how many miles away the leviathan had dragged me when it had first been caught. My hold kept taking on water, so I climbed down through the hatch and began to bail with all my might. I let the boat chug onward, unguided.

I had no sense of time, no day or night—there was only darkness, rain, and waves. My floundering vessel struggled along, covering distance, but I had no way of knowing if I was heading toward shore and home . . . or if I'd gotten disoriented and was unwittingly heading into open sea, never to see land again.

I felt the call of home, knew that Ana was back there, and I kept hoping. I set course in the direction of my heart.

The storm went on forever. My boat listed to the side. Although I tried my best to patch the holes in the hull, water still gushed in. I shut off all feeling so that I could at least chase away the despair.

I went out on deck to hold myself against the wind and the rain, staring into the unseen. I couldn't stop thinking of Ana, who would be shuttered in our home listening to the howl of the wind, imagining me out here, and I vowed I would make it back. Somehow.

Then something struck my boat again, something large and heavy against the lower hull. Nearby, a black sawblade shape arced through the water, then nudged the boat again—the leviathan . . . but it was not an attack. Instead, the creature shoved the boat, turned the bow, and pushed me on a new heading. Had I been traveling the wrong direction? The leviathan moved me along, and I had no choice but to trust it.

I held on, and water spray gushed on either side of the bow. The great monster lifted my hull to keep the damaged part above the waterline—and I was moving again! Toward shore, I hoped. Surely this great creature of the sea would know.

The leviathan pushed me onward for hours, all the way through to the ragged edge of the hurricane. Clear dawn broke before the creature swam away, leaving me in calmer waters and the exhausted remnants of the storm.

And the shore.

Far ahead, I could see the thin shadow line of the coast. Adding the last scraps of redcoal to my laboring engines, I headed toward the mainland, trying to get my bearings. Finally, I saw a familiar promontory and knew that I was about ten miles south of Heartshore. My boat was riding low, and I hoped I could make it the rest of the way. Whatever happened, I knew I could beach the boat and stumble home overland.

When I reached Heartshore, I saw how hard the disaster had struck the harbor. I had been in the thick of the hurricane, but the storm had reserved some of its fury to batter my village. Many docks had been splintered and uprooted, thrown up onto the beach. Three fishing boats were capsized in the harbor. The town above the headlands was stunned and recovering. The villagers had come out to pick up the pieces, sort through the debris, and rebuild their lives. They looked just as bedraggled as I did.

Even after the ordeal I had been through, I felt jubilant. I had promised to come home, and I'd made it. After I secured my damaged fishing boat to a splintered piling, I bounded out onto the shore. I needed to let Ana know that I was safe.

But she was not. When the hurricane came to Heartshore, it had hammered in with massive waves and titanic surf. Five homes, including our beautiful little house on the headlands, and my Ana, had been swept away, washed out to sea at the height of the storm.

Even though I had come home, I now had to chart a different course with my life. Far off in the distance, I heard the leviathans singing.

CHAPTER 22

After she turned the last page of the tale, Marinda's heart ached. She looked up at Hender, who was pale and exhausted just from the thought of having his story told. "I am so sorry," she said.

He reached out, touched her hand, then closed the book for her. "You said you were collecting tales, and that's the only one I have. It may not be a happy story, but it's a true one." He paused, rebuilding his strength. "That was seven years ago, though. Now I am just a fisherman. Not a grand or adventurous life, and maybe not what I should be doing anymore, but I suppose that's enough."

He looked up at Marinda, and his face was lit by the warm glow of the leviathan oil lamp. "I thought it was the end of my story, but now you've come to Heartshore. Maybe there's more to the tale after all." He offered her a smile that made her feel warmer than the redcoal fire in the hearth.

She thought of the blank pages remaining in her book. "Maybe so."

Hender came back to her shack the very next day, carrying more frayed nets. "Bon Selden is willing to pay a premium if you can repair these in a week. We're getting close to the end of the good weather, so he needs them as soon as possible. I told him you could do it, and I'd be willing to spend some evenings working with you, if you need my help."

"I don't need the help, but I would certainly appreciate the company. We'll have them done in a week," Marinda promised. "You've been so generous in everything. . . ."

He smiled. "Speaking of which, I brought more lumber to repair your window frames before storm season comes."

Hender regarded her for a moment, didn't answer any of the questions she was thinking. By his expression and his silence, he seemed to be letting her know that although he still remembered and appreciated his long-lost wife, he had chosen to live his life in a forward direction—just as Marinda had. He was not unsatisfied here in Heartshore, but the horizons were close, and his dreams were kept quietly sleeping, waiting to be awakened.

"Yes," she said, "we have a lot of mending to do. And what do I owe you for the lumber and the labor? Another fish dinner?"

"That—and also tell me more about Albion. True stories."

Even with layers upon layers of repairs, Marinda's little home on the point was a work in progress. But at least it was shelter, and it was enough. The structure was small but livable, and she had arranged a workspace in the main room to mend the nets that Hender brought her over the next few weeks.

This was not the same as her cottage back in Lugtown, the place her father had built and where she had spent so much of her life. And she missed the three powered-down clockwork Regulators that had been gathering dust for so long. But Heartshore felt like a good place, too.

She had set off to fill *Clockwork Lives* with the stories her father wanted her to experience. Marinda didn't regret what she had given up in her years of taking care of him, but at least she understood what Arlen Peake had needed to show her. She knew that she could finish the book, and if she ever got the money to go back to Lugtown and present it to the solicitor, he would release her inheritance. She would have her father's treasure in Watchmaker's gold, she would have her cottage, and everything she could want.

But she wasn't sure she wanted a quiet, perfect life anymore.

Regardless, it would be a very long time before she could save up enough to buy passage to Albion. Going home seemed to be a dream as unattainable as finding the Seven Cities of Gold, but this place in Heartshore was her home and her life now—at least the current chapter of her life.

The villagers accepted her, perhaps even more than the people of Lugtown had. Maybe because Marinda was trying harder to be part of the community in Heartshore, and she knew now that life was what she made for herself. She had this home that Hender had helped her repair; she had work to keep her busy, and she enjoyed his company. On quiet nights, she could sit by herself—or with Hender—and relive all the lives that had left their mark upon the book's pages. As she drifted off to sleep, she could recall her own adventures and how they had brought her here to this town on the southern coast of Atlantis.

As the month passed, the Heartshore fishermen finished their last catches and prepared to tuck in their boats for the storm season. Villagers attached sturdy shutters, repaired roofs and windows to get ready for the weather. Marinda did what she could to make sure her shack would get her through winter—until Hender pounded hard on her door one morning. When she opened it to greet him, he stood before her with a look of deep concern on his face.

He said unceremoniously, "You have to leave—it's for your own safety. The storm is coming, and this house is too close to the edge of the headlands, too unstable. Everyone in the village is retreating." His face paled. "The quicksilver glass and the sympathetic weather gauge—I haven't seen a measurement so severe since . . ."

Marinda completed the sentence. "Since the leviathan storm."

He nodded. "I can look at the sky. I can smell the wind. And I just know. The hurricane will be upon us by the end of the day, Marinda. Trust me."

She trusted him.

He looked at the cliff dropoff only fifteen feet from the back of her house. "I know you've worked hard—"

She held up a hand. "*We've* worked hard, and we did what we could. But where will I go?" She gestured back at the small dwelling. "This *is* all I have."

"You could stay with me until the storm blows over."

She smiled. "I can't think of a place I would rather be."

In less than half an hour Marinda had gathered all her possessions, not much more than her clothes and the net she was repairing. And her book.

The wind was already blowing wet and cold by the time they abandoned her shack and went to Hender's house. The rain had already started by the time they closed themselves inside, barricaded the door, and settled in with each other's company.

She had never been here before, because he always came to see her. This was exactly what a single fisherman needed and nothing more, plain, warm, efficient. Marinda imagined this was not at all like the home he'd had with Ana . . . not like the home Marinda and the grocer might have made with their three potential children.

Many possible worlds . . .

Mounted to the wall, Marinda saw a pair of long, curved tusks. She touched them in amazement. "From the leviathan?"

He nodded. "I could've sold them, but they mean too much to me . . . just like your father's book means too much to you."

She felt very comfortable and welcome here, and a happy tension built in the air between them, like an altogether different kind of storm. With a redcoal fire in the hearth and the light of sweet-smelling oil lanterns, Hender stood close to her. "The house feels less empty than it ever has." Even as the clouds darkened outside, they laughed, accidentally touched more often than they expected, and worked together to make a dinner of smoked fish and potatoes.

When they were finished and sat quiet and satisfied together, he said, "Tell me about Albion again—since I can never see it for myself."

She had told him about her life in Lugtown, but now she unpacked *Clockwork Lives*. "I can do better than that." She had not let others read all the entries before, but stories were not meant to be held close as secrets; for a story to serve its purpose, it had to be shared. "I already took your tale for my book, but you can read the others here, my father's tale, the astronomer's tale, the bookseller's tale . . ."

Hender's eyes lit up. "Will you read them with me?"

For hours into the night as the worsening storm battered the house and all of Heartshore, they read together, and after the first story he kissed her. He and Marinda held each other all night and stayed warm, unbothered by the wind and fury outside.

———◆◆◆———

By the next morning, the storm had blown itself out, leaving the Heartshore harbor awash in debris. Marinda inhaled deeply as she and Hender stepped outside; the air smelled fresh and clean, as if some of the world's shadows had been washed away. She felt happy, thinking that her hoped-for life had gotten just a little more perfect.

They went down to the harbor where people were picking over

the wreckage. She carried the leatherbound book, thinking that as they went out into the village and the harbor, she might find a last few stories after all. Her own story—and Hender's—had certainly changed in the past night. Maybe if she took another drop of his blood it would add a happier ending to his tale.

One of the docks had detached, and two storage sheds had been leveled. Several sturdy boats, including Hender's, were severely damaged. Marinda felt sad for Hender when he looked at his tilted boat, the splinters, the leaking hull, the broken keel, but he stood stoic and resigned. "It was worse seven years ago, and we all rebuilt then." He sighed. "Same life, same destination. But I don't think my boat can be fixed."

He didn't seem to have the energy for it, but she took his hand. "I've never shied away from work. If that's what you want, we can make it." More than ever, she wished she could take him back to Albion and show him the things he dreamed about, but that was even more unlikely now. She believed she would be here in Heartshore for a long time.

When they left the cluttered harbor and went up to the head-lands and out toward the point and her shack, he stopped and stared as if the ground had become unstable beneath his feet. He opened his mouth, but couldn't seem to find the words, so instead he just squeezed her hand. Marinda felt a river of ice go down her spine.

A large section of the cliff had washed away, sloughing down into the sea—taking Marinda's precarious shack with it. It was gone.

"You were right." She stood next to him. "You saved my life, you know."

Hender held her close. "I didn't want you to go back to that ramshackle home anyway. I'd rather you stay with me."

"That is a perfectly acceptable option," she said with a smile that seemed discordantly bright so close to all the wreckage. Still carrying *Clockwork Lives*, she went to the edge of the dropoff and looked down to the shore below, where the outgoing tide had left a sprawl of rocks and debris from the collapsed cliff. The path down to the beach had entirely washed away.

She was surprised to see wreckage down there, an exotic patchwork craft with a sleek painted hull, draped with deflated gray levitation sacks. "Hender, there's a ship washed up on the beach! What sort of boat is that?"

"Not one of ours—nothing from Heartshore."

"Is it an . . . airship?" She bent over to get a better view, but he held onto her arm. "If there are any survivors, we have to help."

He turned and looked along the headlands, searching. "I know a place where we can make our way down to the beach. Come on— no one from the village will have come this far up the coast yet."

They hurried along the wet heather and grasses for half a mile until he found a shallow slope where they could pick their way down to the waterline. On the rocky shingle, they walked back to where the damaged airship had collapsed at the tide line.

As they approached, Marinda saw the patched air sacks, the battered hull painted with gaudy designs, bent smokestacks, rudders for sailing in the air rather than the sea. It took her a moment to make the connection, but she remembered the flying scout ship she had seen from the deck of the *Rocinante* when Captain Titus gave her his spyglass—the airship he had frightened away with a blast from his golden alchemical cannons.

As they poked around the wrecked vessel, they discovered a dark-haired man slumped over the stern rail, half buried under the deflated levitation sacks. He had crawled halfway out of the ship before he collapsed. He was bleeding—severely.

They hurried forward to help the man. His shirt was soaked with blood and he could barely breathe. When Marinda rolled him over, he groaned. "He's still alive! We need to help." She touched the man's face, saw that he had several wicked-looking scars on his cheeks. His eyes were swollen. She remembered the hapless victims of the Anarchist's bomb aboard Captain Pennrose's steamliner, and how helpless she had felt then.

Marinda tore the man's shirt and pressed it against the wound.

Hender helped her. "He's lost so much blood."

Marinda had assumed the man had been injured in the storm, but when she turned him over, she saw the wounds, a small neat hole in his back, a more ragged exit hole in his chest. "Could it be from a bullet?"

Hender helped her prop the man up, lifted his chin. Blood continued to ooze from the wounds, even as Marinda tried to staunch the bleeding. A rattle came from the stranger's mouth, and when he coughed, a red bubble formed at his lips.

"We have to get back to town, bring a doctor!" she said.

Hender shook his head. "He won't last that long."

Something caught Marinda's eye in a deck brace beneath the dying man—a smooth, round object. She reached in and plucked it out. "The bullet went right through him." She held it up, wiped off the blood.

The bullet was made of gold.

The dying man gasped, choked, and looked up at them. His eyes focused momentarily, seeing them and the wreckage of his ship. He managed to utter two last angry words, "Damn you!" Then he collapsed as the life melted out of him.

"Who is he?" Marinda said, baffled. "How did he get here?"

Hender stepped back from the body. "We'll never know."

But Marinda instantly made up her mind. "Yes, we will." She took out her book. "We'll get the full story."

THE
WRECKER'S TALE

The Watchmaker came to destroy us, to eradicate us from existence—in exactly the same way we had set out to destroy him.

It was a deceptively sunny day with calm seas when the
Watchmaker's war zeppelins and armored battle steamers converged
on our floating city. They fired upon us with explosive projectiles
from gold alchemical cannons; marksmen shot off rounds of precision bullets, mowing us down on the decks. Then the uniformed
Regulator infantry—red, blue, and black—swarmed aboard our
clustered ships.

But we were the Free People of the Sea! What could we do but
fight in the only way we knew how? Recklessly, independently, and
with all our heart and soul.

We were slaughtered.

The Wrecker city was an island of lashed-together ships we had
preyed upon, like a predator building a home from the bones of
his victims. Our floating settlement kept accreting as we seized one
ship after another, after luring them to their doom on the reefs.

Because we were free, we lived in no fixed position, and no one should have been able to find our floating island. But the Watchmaker can be relentless.

On that particular day, the Anarchist was with us on one of his infrequent visits—and he would be an extra prize for the Watchmaker. Those two despised each other, and the Watchmaker was willing to crack open the world itself in order to destroy his mortal enemy.

Even though the Anarchist reflected my personal philosophy of life, I did not sympathize with him, nor did I follow him. None of us did. Among the Wreckers, it is every person for himself. In fact, I suspected the Anarchist might have been using *us* as cannon fodder to provoke the Watchmaker into this climactic attack.

If so, then damn him—yet another instance of someone coming to take everything I had.

My sister, Xandrina, should have commiserated with me, but her heart was even harder than mine. She often said, "If someone can take a thing from you so easily, then it was never really yours in the first place." She had once stolen a gold pocketwatch from me— one of the first pieces of booty I had ever collected. Xandrina never admitted she was the thief, but I knew it was her. And she had made her point.

You have what you have, and you take what you take.

Now the Watchmaker and his forces were making their own point, one that I doubted any of us was going to survive.

As the battle surged, the Anarchist stood on a raised deck and yelled with a feral energy. He hurled alchemical bombs in fragile clay pots that shattered, and the explosions flung screaming victims—uniformed Regulators as well as colorfully garbed Wreckers—in every direction.

More battle zeppelins converged in the sky, and cannons fired on us from above, while other blasts hammered us from war steamers approaching across the water. The air was filled with shouts of defiance, cries of pain, and one voice that I recognized—Xandrina. "Caraldi! Fight—or do you want to let them take everything from us?"

I thought of the sack of hoarded gold coins I kept in my cabin, and I vowed to defend it. I grabbed a long, curved machete, while other Wreckers took blades from the armory closets. I squeezed the machete's grip as if it were the thin neck of a shipwreck victim.

I had fought to the death before—many times. That was what we did once we lured a treasure-filled cargo ship onto the reefs. No mercy—that was understood. But we didn't normally fight against such a well-armed opponent.

More explosions. More gunfire. More screams. "We are the Free People of the Sea!" someone yelled, a rallying cry.

Charging forward like an angry bear, I careened into the nearest Blue Watch soldiers before they could use their rifles. With my machete, I chopped an arm off, beheaded another.

I heard Xandrina shriek. With her colorful skirts flapping and her scarf torn loose, she ran toward the Watchmaker's soldiers with a large knife. "We are free! You can't take that from us."

Two Regulators cut her down in a volley of gunfire, and golden bullets tore her to shreds.

If someone can take a thing from you so easily, then it was never really yours in the first place. Xandrina had never really been mine; I knew that all along.

More Regulators died, but I didn't. Not yet at least. I might have lost my sister, but my gold was still safe. Our island of conglomerated ships was smashed apart. Flaming wrecks drifted free, and the Wreckers aboard seemed to believe they could get away—but the Watchmaker's gunship steamers bombarded them until nothing remained but flotsam of splinters and blood.

The Anarchist was laughing, his hair wild. He lobbed another of his exploding pots, which blasted a hole in one of our own decks. I had never understood the man. Not at all.

A swarm of Black Watch dropped onto the main deck, and when I saw a trim man in a different uniform walk through the smoke, an old man who exuded confidence and rigid power, I knew that we had lost—every scrap of all we ever had.

The Watchmaker himself had joined the battle.

———※———

Xandrina and I came to the Wreckers as a gift from the sea—a gift, as it turned out, that no one really wanted or cared for, yet they kept us anyway. The Wreckers cling with a claw-like grip to what they have, even if it's only two small orphan children pulled out of the sinking ship smashed upon the reefs.

I don't remember anything about my life before that night; Xandrina was two years older than me, and she claimed to remember, but she refused to tell me. "It doesn't matter, Caraldi. You've lost that past, and you'll never get it back. Better that you forget."

That was one of the key lessons of life among the Free People of the Sea—not to dwell on something that you've lost, for soon enough you are sure to lose something even more dear to you.

I was "born" that night of the shipwreck, as was Xandrina. I remember the storm, the shouts of terror, the awful roar as the steamer's hull was gutted by the submerged reef . . . then people swarming aboard—not crewmembers, but a motley group of gypsies wearing slickers, carrying nets, clubs, swords.

I remember blood and butchery. I remember a woman trying to defend us—it might have been my mother or just a kindly sailor. I have no memory of her face, but she was taken from me as well. I didn't understand what was happening, just knew that there seemed to be a lot of blood everywhere.

Then two of the strangers stood before my sister and me: a bald man with wild eyes and one ear, and a stocky woman with wild hair and both ears. They each held long, notched blades. They stared at us two children, trying to decide what to do.

Xandrina looked at me, but it was a dismissive glance. She faced the woman with wild hair. "Kill him first," she said.

The woman was taken aback, but the bald man let out a guffaw, and he lifted his blade. "No sense playing favorites. Kill both at the same time."

The wild-haired woman sheathed her blade and grabbed Xandrina's skinny arm, then she snatched me up, too. "We'll take them as another prize from the raid."

"No profit in keeping brats that ain't ours. More mouths to feed and more troublemakers to watch."

"Some of these people had guns—we'll lose a few fighters tonight," the woman said. "These kids can make up for the loss. We can raise them to be Free People of the Sea."

As the woman dragged us out onto the deck, the bald man gave me an extra shove. "Just don't let them bother me." Then he stalked off to continue his rampage. The woman hauled us out into the rain and placed us, shivering, into a boat that was already overloaded with everything the Wreckers could carry from our sinking ship. . . .

In the dark, windy night, they returned to their city of stolen ships, unloading spoils as the rain petered out. My sister and I were dumped unceremoniously on the decks as well.

"How many killed tonight?" the woman shouted to no one in particular.

"Ours, or theirs?" someone answered.

"Theirs don't count."

"Two of ours. Make that three—Devon lost an arm in a bad way, and he'll probably bleed out."

"We took these two replacements from the ship." She nudged us into the crowd. "Better start training them as soon as possible."

———◆◆◆———

The wild-haired woman accepted no responsibility for us, though. If Xandrina and I thought she would become our surrogate mother, we would quickly learn that was not the case.

The young are resilient, and it took very little time to strip away the veneer of our original lives and what others would call civilization. Xandrina fit in among the Wreckers faster than I did. She was not afraid to ask questions and bold enough to take what she wanted. If someone complained, she laughed. If someone resisted, she fought back; sometimes she won, sometimes she lost. She made certain that her little brother didn't starve, but she rarely gave me food without extracting some kind of price.

You have what you have, and you take what you take.

I grew accustomed to days filled with singing and dancing, and raucous music with no recognizable tune, as seemed appropriate for such a carefree group. The Free People of the Sea had few inhibitions, and emotions that ran high. An outburst of joy and laughter could swiftly change to rage or jealousy. Brawls came and went with the frequency of summer storms.

Sometimes the arguments turned into fistfights, often with the loser dunked overboard while the spectators laughed. Other feuds were settled with knifings or throats being slit in the dark. Occasionally, bodies were dumped over the side of the great floating raft.

The Wreckers refused to choose any leader, but somehow they functioned with their own set of customs and laws that no one had ever codified. That may have been why the Anarchist considered them so close to his own heart.

Friendships shifted, as did lovers. Few attachments went deep, and even when the women had babies, they didn't reveal the identity of the father, and no one asked. The children were raised with a communal mindset, out of not shared responsibility but shared disdain. Every person had to fend for himself, and even Xandrina drifted away, preoccupied with learning how to steal from the Wreckers themselves. More often than not, she was successful.

I was less nimble at it, though, and I would be caught, then roughed up. I suffered many a bruise, split lip, or blackened eye for my clumsiness. And the other Wrecker children would steal anything of mine they could get their hands on, leaving me with nothing again.

We were all expected to help harvest the ships we lured to destruction, and for that, we had to be tough, even from an early age. When I was considered old enough—though I never learned who determined that, or how—it was decided that I needed to learn how to fight and how to be ruthless.

Two men grabbed me by the arms one morning and dragged me to the center deck of one of the ships in our floating island. Another boy, rail-thin and with flickers of fear in his eyes, was herded forward just as roughly. I had seen him before, but I didn't have any feud with him.

Both of us were brought to a hatch, and another Wrecker opened the heavy trapdoor to reveal the rank-smelling hold below. While the other boy struggled, I listened, so I would know what the Wreckers expected of me.

A woman—I think it was the wild-haired one who had saved us on that first night—held up two stout wooden sticks, each as long as my arm, then she tossed them down into the hold. I heard them clatter on the wooden deck eight feet below.

"Fight," said a bearded man with a tight black scarf around his head. "However long it takes. When one of you wins, call out and we'll haul you up."

People gathered on the deck; some had climbed to observation platforms, cheering us on. It had been more than a month since our airship scouts had spotted any victim ships for us to attack, and they were bored. The Free People of the Sea always needed new amusements.

I looked up, surprised to see Xandrina among them, dressed in calico clothes patched together from dresses found in stolen steamer trunks. She raised her hands and shouted as loudly as all the others, but I wasn't certain she was cheering for *me*.

While I was distracted by my sister, the man in the black scarf knocked me over the lip of the hatch and down into the cargo hold. I didn't even have time to yell as I fell, flailing. I struck the deck, which knocked the wind out of me. Only a second later, the skinny boy came tumbling down on top of me.

From above, faces peered into the cargo hold, and then the heavy hatch slammed shut, plunging us into blackness. My heart pounded, but I didn't freeze. I remembered the two stout wooden sticks the woman had tossed into the hold. The rules of the game became clear enough—even if the Wreckers did not stand by their rules. In the last flash of light as the hatch closed, I spotted the sticks, noted where they were.

I realized that the skinny boy hadn't yet thought of this.

I was already moving as the darkness sealed shut around us. I seized the closest stick, knowing how sturdy it was, how much damage it could cause.

Too late, the skinny boy scrambled around, feeling blindly, making too much noise. Knowing exactly where he was, I could have spun and struck out at him, but I realized the smarter move would be to get the second stick. I remembered where it was.

Without the foolishness of caution, I slid across the deck in the darkness, waving my stick like a blind man's cane, and I heard it clack against the second wooden club just as the skinny boy found it. I grabbed the other end, and he pulled back. We wrestled, then I slid my stick briskly down the second one like a flint striking a spark on steel. I smashed the boy's knuckles, and he yelped, releasing the club. I grabbed for it.

Now that I held both sticks in my hands, I moved forward like a dervish, slashing at the darkness and feeling a meaty satisfaction as I struck the other boy's shoulder. I think the first blow was hard enough to break his collarbone; I know the second one was.

He wailed and roared, and even though he had staggered away to hide in the darkness, his whimpers let me pinpoint his location. Another blow caught him on the side of the head, or maybe in the face. I couldn't see. He collapsed, sobbing, and I backed off.

His yells were enough to encourage the Wreckers on the deck above; I heard the stomping of feet.

The boy dragged himself away, and I paused, but this wasn't enough for what the spectators were expecting. I waited awhile, then went hunting for him again. The boy was easy to find, and I rained down blows on his hunched back, and backed away again for a brief rest.

How much more did I have to do? I was sure there was more to this test than just to see which boy could beat up the other.

After giving him ten minutes to recover his dignity, or at least his breath, I pummeled the boy again with both sticks. Sobbing, he begged for mercy, but I was positive that *mercy* was not a lesson the Wreckers would ever teach. The best I could do was let the boy live. Two more blows rendered him unconscious, and I decided I had done enough.

After I shouted up, the hatch was raised, and someone dropped down a ladder. I climbed to the deck and emerged into the bright light, blinking and grinning, washed by a wave of cheers. I held up both bloody sticks.

"Caraldi doesn't even have a scratch!" a woman yelled, evoking a round of laughter.

I glanced back down into the dark hold. "That boy will need help. He's not moving very well."

Some of the spectators grumbled uneasily. Two Wrecker men descended into the hold and carried up the bloody, limp boy.

I felt dizzy, even a little sick when I saw the damage I had inflicted on my opponent. His face was swollen, his lip split, several teeth knocked out. His left arm hung limp, and blood oozed from several contusions on his head. In the darkness, I hadn't been able to see his wounds. I was surprised to discover my own brutality, but the others found it praiseworthy.

Xandrina came up to me, smug. "I knew you would win. I'm glad I bet on you."

But the man in the black scarf wore a disappointed expression. "The loser in the duel has been found lacking. He'll be no good to us. Get rid of him."

I was suddenly worried. "Are you just going to throw him overboard? No one told me what—"

"No one should have needed to tell you. He'll be set adrift, without food, water, or shade from the sun. He won't last long, but that's not our problem. You took care of that, Caraldi."

They dumped the boy in a small lifeboat they had taken from one of their wrecked ships; they had plenty to spare, after all. Though the boy moaned, he still wasn't conscious. I didn't know if he would ever wake up, but when he did, the currents would have taken him far from the floating Wrecker city into the open, pitiless ocean. Three men lowered the lifeboat over the side of the raft city and released it. They didn't even give him a set of oars.

The man in the black scarf looked at me. "That was no mercy. Better if you had just killed him—I hope you learned your lesson."

I had. Afterward, I made certain to kill all the other opponents they made me fight.

———◆◆◆———

I fell in love, or at least that's what I called it.

The girl's name was Faara. She was lithe, with brown eyes and long black hair. We were at an age where bravado on my part and demure glances on her part were enough to cement our attraction. Her lips trained me in the art of kissing.

Though the clustered ships were crowded with people, Faara and I discovered private corners, unoccupied lower staterooms, or sheltering stacks of crates in a quiet cargo hold that gave us many opportunities for stolen kisses, and I became another kind of experienced thief.

Neither Faara nor I knew what we were doing, but growing up among the Free People of the Sea had taught us to learn for ourselves. We practiced, we fumbled, we groped, and soon enough we became better at what we were doing—then, *quite good.* There are times when instinct takes over and even the most woefully uneducated people understand how to make the pieces fit together. And that was quite a delightful discovery.

Faara enjoyed our lovemaking so much, though, that she decided to practice with other boys as well. Such was the way of Wrecker relationships, and she certainly wrecked ours. One young man, Bello, stole her from me entirely, and there was nothing I could do. Heartbroken, I begged her to stay with me, but Faara just laughed, as did Bello, who swept her off to another deck.

Another thing stolen from me. Another thing lost. Xandrina came up to me, showing no sympathy. "If something can be taken from you so easily, then you never really had it in the first place."

My mood was foul and bitter—which prepared me perfectly for my first Wrecker raid the following night.

By day, our scout pilot took one of the battered airships into the sky. She would cruise the expanse of ocean and follow the primary shipping lanes, while others studied the imminent weather, hoping for the right combination of opportunity and storms. I had flown some of the runs myself, but never found a proper target.

Cargo steamers were frequent, but many of them had defenses, and the Free People of the Sea were not a navy. We were hand-to-hand fighters, but only when we had ensured our advantage through trickery. A successful hunt required the perfect combination of timing, bad weather, and a gullible captain.

As a storm rolled in and a vulnerable steamer approached, we made our preparations. When I saw Faara clinging to her new lover, kissing Bello and wishing him luck, I very much wanted to kill somebody. I was ready for the raid.

When black clouds smothered the stars and rain whipped the waves, Xandrina was given the honor of climbing a makeshift derrick we had built on our floating island of ships. She ignited the suspended sphere of contained coldfire so that it hung there, a dazzling beacon in the night, a tempting ray of light to draw in unwary sailors lost in the storm.

The wind blew so hard I was afraid Xandrina would lose her grip and be flung from the scaffold to her death. But she could take care of herself. Someone had to ignite the beacon, and that someone was her.

The Wreckers gathered with lanterns doused. We donned our rain slickers, armed ourselves with swords, daggers, and clubs. Sharpened grappling hooks would be used to snag sacks of valuable minerals and rope-lashed crates from the dying ship, and they could also serve as weapons in a pinch.

The coldfire sun beckoned from the derrick, offering false safety. The laboring steamer chugged toward the reefs in search of sanctuary, then, like a beached leviathan, the vessel lumbered onto the rocks, where it lay trapped, its hull torn open.

With a wild shout, the Wreckers took boats and rafts, while others lashed themselves together with ropes, forming a human chain across the reefs so we could gut our catch. We swarmed the wrecked steamer, using hammers and crowbars to rip open the hull and get at the cargo inside. Others climbed up to the tilted deck. I had a machete and a sturdy iron cudgel; I could use either with equal proficiency.

The small cargo steamer had no more than twenty crew aboard. The doomed sailors fought valiantly, knowing they were going to die—and we knew they were going to die as well. We overwhelmed them by sheer numbers. The rain lashed out, drenching the deck and washing away the bloody stains of the dead men and women we threw overboard.

Near the stern, Bello had just killed a cabin boy and stood over the scrawny body, digging in the pockets. He pulled out a gold pocketwatch and held it up to show off his prize.

Since I was dressed in my rain slicker and hood, Bello didn't recognize me. I took two steps forward and smashed his face with my iron cudgel, turning his grin into a pulpy red smear. Then, because a job worth doing is worth doing well, I used my machete to hack his neck. After he dropped to the deck, I plucked the gold pocketwatch from his twitching hand. My first prize in a raid!

"If someone can take a thing from you so easily," I said to his corpse, "then it was never really yours in the first place." I thrust the watch in my pocket, slid Bello's body overboard into the churning, foaming waves, where it joined the dead crew members. . . .

The Wreckers celebrated that night, and the sharks fed well. We stripped the steamer of everything we could carry, and when the weather calmed, we added the ship to our ever-growing floating city. I claimed one of the new cabins for myself, and I even took back Faara as my lover, but I realized I didn't want her as much anymore, so I discarded her within a month.

Although the Anarchist was not one of the Free People of the Sea, he thought he belonged among us. Since we had no discernible leader, no one would tell him to go away, and we listened to his rants. Some Wreckers said he had been one of us for a time, and now he was back to inspire us.

He was a dark-haired man with a goatee and eyes so dark they seemed to have black lenses. He railed about the tyranny of the Watchmaker in Albion, the cages of precision with which he trapped his citizens. None of us would ever live like that, since we were free people, but the Anarchist was a *freedom extremist*. He was so passionate about his cause that he worked himself into a frenzy when he lectured us. When he suggested that we could help his cause by raiding more cargo ships and stealing more of the Watchmaker's gold, that was an alliance every Wrecker could embrace.

The Anarchist taught us how to make explosives with the alchemical materials we seized. He provided secret information about shipping routes, as well as stolen manifests that identified which steamers carried the most treasure. The Anarchist didn't rule us, or control us, even though he believed he did—and he was welcome to his delusions.

It was a tumultuous time. It was exciting. I amassed my own private treasure of gold coins, and after I killed two people who tried to steal them from me, the others left my spoils untouched.

We had everything we wanted: food from the larders of the ships we seized, supplemented by all the fish we could catch. The Wreckers were feared, and we were powerful. Occasionally, we would send boats to Poseidon City and, in disguise, we would buy any treasures we wanted . . . but having the treasure was a reward in itself, and I was happy enough with my gold.

But thanks to the provocations of the Anarchist, the Watchmaker had substantially increased his patrols. We knew he was hunting for us. Our scout airships regularly searched for new targets to hit, while remaining vigilant for any surprise attack.

Not vigilant enough, however.

When the Watchmaker's forces finally found us, they descended like a storm upon our floating city. I knew this kind of overwhelming response was not merely to enforce the law—this was personal and malicious. This was because of the Anarchist. Damn him!

As my existence was ripped apart by explosions and gunfire, I saw so many things taken from me again. Regulators swarmed our decks in much the same way Wreckers would swarm aboard a steamer on the reefs. This time *we* were being ransacked, and the Watchmaker would show us no more mercy than we showed our victims.

War zeppelins and battleship steamers closed in. Heavily armed Black Watch dropped onto our decks, opening fire. Troops killed Xandrina.

We could fight, but I knew we would all die. *I* would die—unless I could get away. I would not stay and fight for the Free People of the Sea, any more than they would have stayed and fought for me, but I refused to lose everything again, not all my hard-won treasure.

So I concentrated on escaping. One of our scout airships was still anchored to the deck nearby, its levitation sacks flabby but ready to fly. We should have sent out multiple patrols, alert for the Watchmaker's armada. Only one of our scouts had come back to raise the alarm, and that barely in time.

I knew how to fly the thing, and I prayed that I could get away. I was covered with blood. I had been fighting in a daze, and I had killed at least ten Regulators—certainly, I had done my part.

As the battle raged, my fellow Wreckers threw themselves into the fight with reckless lack of planning. It was obvious they didn't even realize they were doomed.

I killed another Regulator, slicing him open with my enormous machete so that his red uniform took on a deeper color of crimson. Then I bounded across the deck to my cabin, sidestepping fallen bodies. I kicked open the door. I would not leave my gold behind.

From all the pursers' lockers I had raided and the captains' vaults I had emptied, I had amassed sacks of honeybee coins from Albion and coins of various mintings from Atlantis. I had jewels, I had rings, and I simply couldn't leave them all behind. My sister was gone, but I wouldn't let the Watchmaker steal this last thing of mine—at least not all of it.

I couldn't carry my entire hoard, though; one heavy sack of coins would have to do. I hefted it, felt an ache in my arm, and was surprised to see several bleeding cuts and one shallow, stinging furrow where a bullet had grazed my arm. Outside, the gunfire and explosions continued. I gathered my strength and burst out of my cabin, charging straight to the anchored scout airship.

The Watchmaker directed his forces. The battle was still raging, but the tide had turned. I would not have much time—or much chance. The sky was already filled with war zeppelins. I could only hope that one small scout ship would prove too insignificant a target for them and I could slip away even in a hail of gunfire.

As I ducked and dodged, I looked across the decks and saw another Wrecker scout airship puttering away into the sky, heading toward Albion. Several Regulators raised their rifles and shot at the levitation sacks. My heart sank, but even though this was risky, I had no other chance. Once I got aloft, I would head in the opposite direction, toward Atlantis, where my gold would be good, and I could live a good life.

We get what we deserve.

Ducking low, I made my way to the tethered scout ship, wincing at the whine of ricocheting bullets. I reached the vessel and hacked at the ropes with my machete. Cut free, the ship immediately began to rise.

I tossed my sack of gold coins up into the small cabin, where it landed with a thud and acted as ballast, but not enough to keep the vessel from rising. Before it lifted too high, I sprang up to grasp the rope ladder dangling from the side, and I began to climb hand over hand.

As the ship rose higher from our embattled Wrecker city, I reached the top of the ladder, grasped the edge of the hull. I would wring all possible speed out of the burbling coldfire engine and fly away.

I heard shots from below, turned to see a group of Blue Watch pointing their rifles toward me. Holding the edge, I tried to swing myself onto the airship's open deck. Golden bullets spanged off the hull, and several of them punctured the levitation sacks—but they were small holes, and the levitating gas would leak out slowly. I was sure I could get away.

Just as I hauled myself over the rail and onto the deck, one of the bullets struck me in the back. A hot, ripping pain skewered me from behind, knocked me forward as if I had been hit with a sledgehammer. My legs went numb, and my knees collapsed under me, but I crawled to the piloting house, reached the controls. I shoved the accelerator lever forward, a simple mechanism, and the airship hobbled off through the sky, somehow dodging the battle zeppelins. Their cannons fired a constant barrage of alchemical projectiles, primarily aimed down at the cluster of Wrecker ships.

The pain was astonishing. I saw the ragged hole below my shoulder where the bullet had exited, and blood flowed out, soaking my shirt. Damn the Watchmaker and his soldiers! Damn the Anarchist for causing this! Damn the Wreckers for letting us all become such easy victims!

The pain continued to roar inside me until, much worse, it became cold and numb. I worked the piloting controls to the best of my ability and set course for the coast of Atlantis, as near to Poseidon City as my bearings could manage.

The wound continued to bleed, and I felt myself growing weaker by the hour, but I refused to believe I was dying. I had my treasure in gold, and I had escaped the battlefield. I could not accept that the Watchmaker had stolen my life as well.

I gritted my teeth. My life was *mine!* And I would not give it up, not to the Watchmaker, not to anyone. But I did surrender to unconsciousness. . . .

When I finally awoke, I could barely move. I saw that the airship was moving sluggishly. The levitation sacks were leaking from numerous bullet holes, and the coldfire furnace was burning low, but I had escaped the Watchmaker's armada and the Wreckers. According to my bearings, I had nearly reached Atlantis. If only the engines would last long enough, if only *I* would last long enough . . .

The airship rocked, buffeted about by strengthening winds, and I dragged myself up to look out the main window, hoping I might glimpse the coastline. I had lost so much blood that my body seemed a distant thing. But I would cling to my last threads of strength. I would make it, damn them all! I was close to the Atlantis shore.

With my eyes focused forward, I saw that I was heading directly into the cloud wall of a tremendous storm.

CHAPTER 23

As leftover storm breezes skirled around them, Marinda and Hender huddled next to the crashed airship and the dead Wrecker. Shoulder to shoulder, they read the pages of Caraldi's tale and learned the terrible things he had done without remorse, without mercy. Now they understood the bloodstains, the wounds, the golden bullet, even all the old scars on his body.

Hender said, "I doubt any airship could have survived that hurricane."

Marinda did not feel sorry for the man, now that she knew who he really was. "We get what we deserve." Nevertheless, they agreed they would bring the townspeople to the wreck and give the man a decent burial, a *human* burial, whether or not he was a decent human being.

After reading the tale, she realized that the Wrecker depredations were now at an end, thanks to the Watchmaker's assault. Ships crossing the sea no longer needed to worry about pirate attacks. And surely the Anarchist hadn't survived the battle? It didn't seem possible . . . but that edgy man had also found a way to parachute from an airship high in the sky, shortly before exploding his bomb.

Hender dragged away the gray fabric of the levitation sacks that lay like a shroud over the scout ship's hull. Marinda helped him, and they both saw the sack of treasure at the same time. It was so full of gold that the seam had split, spilling countless coins on the deck.

She stood amazed. "The Clockwork Angels say that good work leads to good fortune . . . but sometimes good fortune happens all by itself."

"Just as bad fortune does," Hender said. "And we have had enough of that already."

Together they lifted the sack of gold, careful to hold the split seam together. Even so, dozens of coins pattered onto the rocky beach with a musical metallic sound. They both laughed.

"This will be enough to buy a new fishing boat," Marinda said. "And we can make repairs to your house, make it a fine place for both of us to live. If . . . that's what you really want."

"After I lost Ana, staying in Heartshore was never what I really wanted, but I just . . . did." Hender suddenly seemed more alive, standing taller, straighter. "There is certainly enough money for you to go back to Albion."

Marinda saw the light in his eyes, the hope. "And for you to see if Albion lives up to my stories. This will be more than sufficient to buy passage *for two*, with a fortune left over. We can both go—I'd be glad to have you with me. I'll show you what I know of Crown City and Albion."

"I've always wanted to see it, but never thought it might be possible." He was smiling. "We could go to your cottage in Lugtown. I love Heartshore, yes, but there's too much here for me that even storms can't wash away. Either way, I will have to start again—and I'd rather start with you."

Even in her excitement, though, she paused. "Yes, Albion . . .

but I can't go home yet—not quite. I'm not finished."

The Wrecker's tale had filled many pages toward the end of *Clockwork Lives*, but the last section remained blank. Judging from her previous experience, in order to fill it she might have to talk to a dozen people or more, depending on how brief and uneventful their lives were. "Not until my book is full."

Standing next to her, Hender turned the pages with callused fingers. On the stormy night, he had read the whole volume with her, and now he said, "I know what you've endured in order to gather these tales, Marinda—all the places you've gone, the adventures you've lived." He leaned closer. "Have you put *your own* story in here?"

She blinked. The thought had never occurred to her. Her father had sent her on this quest to meet other people and to witness other lives, but also to understand how much of her life she had given up for him. Were her own experiences worthy of inclusion in *Clockwork Lives*?

They were now.

The two of them went around the crashed airship to take shelter from the sea breezes. Leaning against the tilted hull, Marinda removed the golden needle from the binding of the volume. After she found the next blank page, Hender took her hand and used the needle to prick her index finger. He squeezed out a drop of blood, which fell onto the anticipating page.

Together, they watched in pleased astonishment as the tale of her own adventures—in the quest of finding other adventures— filled all the remaining pages in the book.

We are secrets to each other
Each one's life a novel no one else has read

Marinda and Hender spent months in the indirect journey back to Lugtown, with a side trip to Crown City and many parts of Albion that she herself hadn't seen before. What they saw and did on the way would have filled another entire volume.

The two were in no hurry to get home, although they were glad enough when they did. They arrived just before the beginning of winter, and when Marinda returned after more than a year away, Benjulian Frull was astonished to see her. She had far too many tales to tell and she wouldn't rush it—a story like hers deserved to be told well with an attentive audience. She would have time to do so, all the time in the world, and she knew that at least some people in this sleepy village would be willing to hear . . . maybe even one of Camberon Greer's redheaded boys.

In the solicitor's office, she opened the leatherbound volume, proud to display the pages crowded with blood-written words, numerous lives and experiences distilled into the quintessence of humanity. He was delighted.

"You fulfilled the terms of your father's will!" said Frull. "And I am truly pleased to release the gold ingots in his account in the Watchmaker's Bank. I'm sorry it was so difficult for you to earn your inheritance."

Marinda had thought about it a great deal, all the journeys, all the ordeals that she now thought of as *adventures*. And she had found Hender, a man who shared her desire for a quiet, perfect life, but who also had dreams of seeing the world. She and he were true counterparts; together they discovered a contentment, a synergy that neither could have achieved alone.

"My father was right," she said. "I couldn't understand why he would do such a thing to me. But now I do. Now I love him for it."

Back again at the sealed and preserved cottage, Marinda set about the work of putting her household back in order, and the first, most important step was to activate the three clockwork Regulators, which had been such an important part of her life.

Marinda and Hender polished, lubricated, and charged Zivo, Woody, and Lee, and when they awakened the three diligent contraptions returned to duty as if no time had passed at all. The refurbished Regulators served just as faithfully, but even more efficiently, in their earnest attempts to help.

Now that the cottage no longer seemed so empty, Marinda took a new interest in the books her father had left behind on the shelves. She had hardly bothered to look at the titles before, and now she was surprised to see that old Arlen possessed a copy of *Before the Stability* and even an early edition of the Watchmaker's official autobiography. Marinda decided she would read that on a quiet winter night, for amusement if nothing else.

To her greater delight, she also found a worn volume of *The Adventures of Hanneke Lakota*. Unobtrusive on the shelf, with a plain spine, the book had been hidden in plain sight. Marinda had never touched it, and Arlen had never asked her to read from it. With wide eyes and trembling fingers, she withdrew the book and stared at the imprinted words on the cloth cover. Had her father journeyed to other worlds himself, or had he visited Underworld Books? Had Mrs. Courier sold him this precise volume?

As she opened the book now, she discovered an inscription on the title page written in a firm hand that she recognized as her father's. *My sparkling daughter, if you are reading this, then I know you discovered what I hoped you would. If this book means to you what it means to me, then you know more of my story and you have created a story of your own. I dedicate this adventure, and all adventures, to you—because you were the best part of my own tale.*

As she stood there, reading it again and again with words blurred through tears, Hender came up to her, read over her shoulder, and gathered her into his arms.

———◆◆———

Seeing a stranger with Marinda, a man with an odd foreign accent and no explanations for his presence, created something of a stir among the people of Lugtown. Those who had the ability and the imagination made up their own stories, and Marinda was content to let them do so. For those who expressed concern, she merely answered, "All is for the best." And that was enough explanation for them.

With gold from both the Watchmaker and the Wrecker, Marinda and Hender were among the wealthiest people in Lugtown, but boredom was unacceptable to them. Just like Courier and Omar, they decided to open a small bookshop, the first the town had ever had, just down the street from the solicitor's office. They carried a selection of books, not all of them Watchmaker-approved, but their biggest challenge was to convince the people to let their imaginations thrive. One story at a time, though, they would open a few eyes.

In a very special spot at the end of the shelf, she placed the finished volume of *Clockwork Lives*, to be read by anyone who was ready.

The bookshop also sold blank journals. Although the empty volumes did not possess the same alchemical magic as *Clockwork Lives*, that did not stop Marinda from wanting to fill more and more pages with her own adventures. With ambitious planning, she and Hender kept ten as-yet-empty volumes for themselves, and they could always get more once those were full.

The bookshop was open only in winter, because they had other things to do for the rest of the year. . . .

As Albion's winter set in and the two enjoyed their quiet, perfect life in the cozy cottage, Marinda and Hender were happy.

But they were happiest of all when they spent time by the light of a coldfire lamp, studying books and maps and legends. They would make plans, choosing where they wanted to go and what they wanted to see for their next big adventure . . . come springtime.

MANY POSSIBLE WORLDS

by Kevin J. Anderson

When you create an entire universe and fill it with interesting characters, how can there possibly be only one story to tell?

When Neil approached me with the basic story and lyrics for *Clockwork Angels* in 2011, I got to work fleshing out the detailed plot, developing the characters, and doing the important "world-building," which is my particular forte.

As we passed the chapters back and forth, our imaginations went off on tangents, caught up in interesting ideas that didn't fit into the main story of *Clockwork Angels*, or characters that we wanted to know better (but in stories of their own). While working on the novel, we would make comments that "someday" we'd get around to those other tales, maybe as stand-alone short stories. In particular we had a story idea about the mysterious bookseller Mrs. Courier hunting through countless parallel universes to acquire interesting new volumes for Underworld Books.

Clockwork Angels: The Novel came out in a beautiful edition from ECW Press, became a bestseller, won some awards. Rush went on an extended tour for the album. I had my own book tours and then subsequent novel deadlines. Two years passed, and we kept thinking about that "someday." We loved the Clockwork universe, and we loved the characters. We definitely wanted to visit them again, but there was no hurry. The stories and ideas would keep gestating.

Finally, in summer 2013, my wife Rebecca and I were going to visit Matt Scannell (a mutual friend of ours and Neil's) of the band Vertical Horizon for a concert at the Sky Sox baseball stadium in Colorado Springs. Rebecca and I had hoped to spend the afternoon with Matt ahead of time, but the band kept encountering glitches and difficulties with the show setup, the stage itself, the sound systems. Matt's growing frustration was plain when he sent probably the funniest text I've ever received: "Whatever your expectations are for tonight, lower them."

We finally got to chat with Matt backstage just before the concert. After all the headaches of the jinxed concert setup, Matt wanted to talk about something much more fun—*Clockwork Angels.* He loved the book and eagerly wanted to know if we were going to do more work in that universe. I reassured him that we had several interesting tales of peripheral characters, people we wanted to explore more. "But we don't want just a collection of random stories," I said. "I'm still looking for a framework to connect them all, a unifying story. I just haven't figured it out yet."

When it was time for the show, Rebecca and I went to our seats with the kids and our two young grandsons (their very first concert!). The event was for a great cause—to stand up against bullying in schools—but the setup was problematic, with the stage out in the middle of the baseball field about a million miles away from the seats, so Matt could not interact with the audience as he usually does. The sound system still had some glitches—but *we* were having a great time, particularly with the baby grandkids swaying and laughing to the music.

Meanwhile, the wheels were turning in the back of my mind,

and as song after song played, I was still searching for some unifying Clockwork story. Then, as I was listening to Matt sing "Save Me from Myself"—which is itself a song comprised of a group of interconnected stories—I got it. Genuine stadium-level Eureka! lights going on over my head.

At first you will hate me for this. Then you will love me for it.

I suddenly thought of Marinda Peake caring for her ailing father, then inheriting a mysterious alchemical book that could write stories from a drop of blood . . . and her mission to fill that volume with stories before she could get her own life back. It was exactly the frame I was looking for. The clockwork gears in my head kept spinning overtime for the rest of that concert.

Afterward, when Rebecca and I went backstage again, I was bursting with excitement. Because of the technical problems with the show, the band members were not entirely happy, but oblivious to their mood (in typical Kevin fashion), I gushed to Matt about how his song had triggered the perfect way to connect all the Clockwork tales. He listened with complete focus as I told him about it, and when I finished, he stood there with obvious tears in his eyes—and I knew *that* was what he would remember about this concert.

We still weren't ready to plunge into the project, though. I had several major books to complete by deadline, Neil was recuperating from the long tour . . . but my mind did occasionally wander back to the Mrs. Courier story and other ideas I had for the strongman, the fortune teller, the pickpocket. Every so often, Rebecca would ask when I was going to get around to writing the next Clockwork book, and I would answer, "Someday."

I finished and delivered *Mentats of Dune* and *Hellhole Inferno*, two large science fiction epics cowritten with Brian Herbert. Then I tackled *Blood of the Cosmos*, an 830-page science fiction opus in my "Seven Suns" universe. When I'm writing such a big story with so many characters and storylines, it's the only thing I think about day after day until the book is done. In late June 2014, I finished the last chapter of the last draft and sent it off to my editor—and I felt like a marathon runner crossing the finish line and stumbling to a halt, not sure what to do now. That novel was finished, my brain was exhausted, and I needed a recharge. But I was still pumped up with creative adrenaline.

I live in the beautiful mountains of Colorado with countless trails I love, spectacular scenery, and many National Forest campgrounds deep in the wilderness. As soon as I sent off *Blood of the Cosmos*, I packed my camping gear in the back of the car and picked a campground near several interesting trails in the Cache la Poudre canyon. I drove off to spend two days in the wilderness by myself absorbing the scenery, with no deadlines at all—just letting my imagination rest . . . or roam.

I went on a six-mile hike along a rushing river, climbing up into a spectacular gorge. Even though I had no intention of writing anything at all, I always carry my digital recorder just in case I want to preserve some notes. Lulled and inspired by the majesty around me, I began to think about the *Clockwork Lives* frame story. Before I knew what was happening, I started world-building, developing the sleepy town where Marinda Peake lived, and a woman who wanted nothing more than to have a quiet, perfect life, but is forced to become a reluctant adventurer—the opposite of young Owen Hardy in *Clockwork Angels*.

When I thought of her town in the Watchmaker's Albion, I thought of her eccentric inventor father . . . and then I thought of her runaway mother and how she could fit into one of the stories, then a brash steamliner pilot, and the clockwork gypsy fortune teller, and a sea captain's tale, and an alchemy miner on the continent of Atlantis.

Some of the stories came out with fully developed plots, while others were still just ideas, but the people were very vivid in my imagination, some of them familiar from *Clockwork Angels*, others completely new characters. One idea led to another, then another. It was like an imaginative bag of popcorn popping.

During that hike I dictated twenty pages of detailed notes for *Clockwork Lives*, ready to send to Neil. By the time I had them transcribed the following week, however, I was heading off on another long-planned hiking trip to complete a spectacular twenty-mile loop in the Flat Tops Wilderness near Steamboat Springs, Colorado. Since I didn't have time to polish those notes for Neil, and I found myself on a long trail with twelve hours of hiking ahead of me, I decided to go for it. Instead of giving Neil just the notes, I dictated the first four complete chapters. What better way to show him in full detail what this book was going to be like?

A week later, without any forewarning, I sent him forty finished pages. "Surprise!"

Fortunately, it was a pleasant surprise, and he loved what he read. At last, we were off and running, plotting how the stories would fit together, the overall arc of Marinda's journey, filling the gaps and deciding which other tales we might like to include from *Clockwork Angels* characters who had caught our attention. The stories themselves were individual gems, some of them exciting, some horrifying, others just fascinating to us. For me, though, the heart of the book was Marinda's story and how all those tales became part of a larger tale.

"Someday" had become "now," and I began writing in earnest. The draft of *Clockwork Lives* was coming together nicely when, in a novelistic sort of serendipity, Vertical Horizon came around again to play another concert, and once more Rebecca and I went to meet Matt at the venue beforehand. (No technical difficulties this time!) His first question was, "So what about those other *Clockwork*

Angels stories?" I smiled and said that it was definitely in process. As we talked more about the frame story I had thought of during their previous concert, I came up with the perfect nugget, two lines that are the core of the novel:

Some lives can be summed up in a sentence or two.
Other lives are epics.

I wrote that down on a scrap of paper and stuck it in my pocket. Those became the first two lines in the novel.

As Neil and I completed each section, each tale, each chapter, we grew progressively more pleased with *Clockwork Lives*. Over the past quarter century I've written a great many books and I'm always proud to see them published, always glad to tell my stories and do my best, but in this case all the pieces fit together so *perfectly*, and the message itself of the individual tales and of Marinda's story occupies a special place in my own heart. Neil is convinced *Clockwork Lives* is one of the best books I've ever written—and so am I.

We hope you enjoyed it.

Clockwork Lives owes a great deal to the music of Rush and Neil's bandmates, Geddy Lee and Alex Lifeson, as well as to Pegi Cecconi of SRO. Nick Robles, who did such a magnificent job on the artwork for the *Clockwork Angels* graphic novel, also provided enthusiasm and imagination with his illustrations, sparking many ideas to make these stories even better.

Kevin would like to thank typists Karen Haag and Mary Thomsen; test readers Steven Savile, Tracy Mangum, and Diane Jones; and of course Rebecca Moesta for accompanying me for all the journeys of this great adventure.

We both owe immense gratitude to the supportive and energetic people at ECW Press, from our intrepid editor Jen Knoch, to art director Rachel Ironstone, publishers David Caron and Jack David, as well as Erin Creasey and Samantha Dobson.

Kevin J. Anderson is the bestselling science-fiction author of over 125 novels. His original works include the Saga of Seven Suns series; the Terra Incognita trilogy; *Resurrection, Inc.*; *Hellhole*; and many others. His novel *The Dark Between the Stars* was nominated for the 2015 Hugo Award for Best Science Fiction Novel of the Year. He has written spin-off novels for *Star Wars*, DC Comics, and *The X-Files* and, with Brian Herbert, is the co-author of 15 novels in the Dune universe.

Neil Peart is the drummer and lyricist of the legendary rock band Rush and the author of *Ghost Rider*, *The Masked Rider*, *Traveling Music*, *Roadshow*, *Far and Away*, and *Far and Near*.

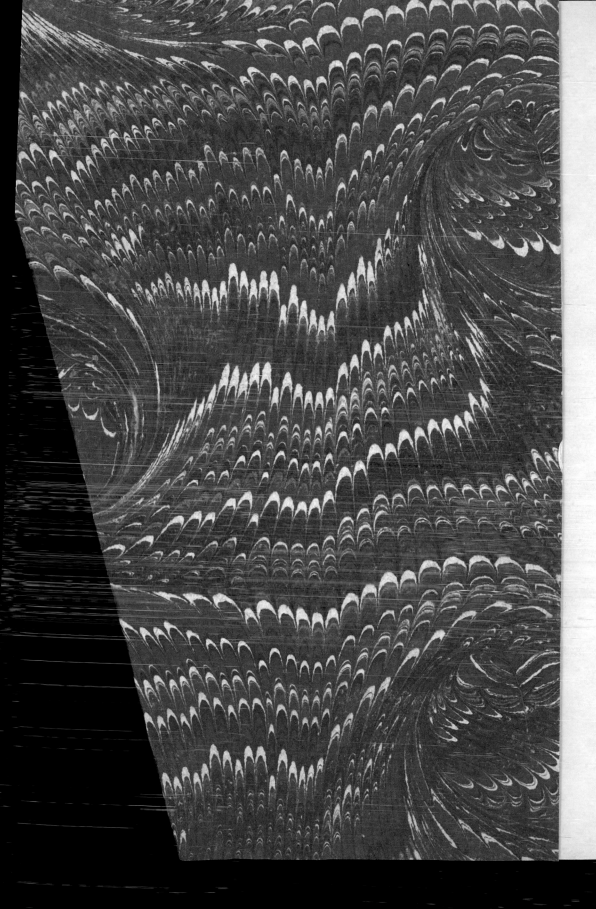

Published by ECW Press
665 Gerrard Street East, Toronto, Ontario, Canada M4M 1Y2
416-694-3348 | info@ecwpress.com

This is a work of fiction. Names, characters, places, and incidents either
are the product of the author's imagination or are used fictitiously, and any
resemblance to actual persons, living or dead, business establishments,
events, or locales is entirely coincidental.

Library and Archives Canada Cataloguing in Publication

Anderson, Kevin J., 1962–, author
Clockwork lives / written by Kevin J. Anderson and Neil Peart.

Issued in print and electronic formats.
ISBN 978-1-77041-294-1 (bound)
ISBN 978-1-77090-808-6 (pdf) — ISBN 978-1-77090-809-3 (epub)

I. Peart, Neil, author II. Title.

PS3551.N373C57 2015   813'.54   C2015-902728-4
                         C2015-902729-2

Editor for the press: Jennifer Knoch
Cover design and illustrations: Nick Robles
End-papers: © Jill Battaglia/dreamstime.com
Author photos: KJA © T. Durren Jones; NP © John Arrowsmith
Printed and bound in Canada by Friesens   5   4   3   2   1

We acknowledge the financial support of the Government of Canada through
the Canada Book Fund for our publishing activities, and the contribution of the
Government of Ontario through the Ontario Media Development Corporation.

Get the ebook free!

At ECW Press, we want you to enjoy this book in whatever format you like, whenever you like. Leave your print book at home and take the eBook to go! Purchase the print edition and receive the eBook free. Just send an email to ebook@ecwpress.com and include:

- the book title
- the name of the store where you purchased it
- your receipt number
- your preference of file type: PDF or ePub?

A real person will respond to your email with your eBook attached. Thank you for supporting an independently owned Canadian publisher with your purchase!

Published by ECW Press
665 Gerrard Street East, Toronto, Ontario, Canada M4M 1Y2
416-694-3348 | info@ecwpress.com

This is a work of fiction. Names, characters, places, and incidents either
are the product of the author's imagination or are used fictitiously, and any
resemblance to actual persons, living or dead, business establishments,
events, or locales is entirely coincidental.

Library and Archives Canada Cataloguing in Publication

Anderson, Kevin J., 1962–, author
Clockwork lives / written by Kevin J. Anderson and Neil Peart.

Issued in print and electronic formats.
ISBN 978-1-77041-294-1 (bound)
ISBN 978-1-77090-808-6 (pdf) — ISBN 978-1-77090-809-3 (epub)

I. Peart, Neil, author II. Title.

PS3551.N373C57 2015   813'.54   C2015-902728-4
C2015-902729-2

Editor for the press: Jennifer Knoch
Cover design and illustrations: Nick Robles
End-papers: © Jill Battaglia/dreamstime.com
Author photos: KJA © T. Durren Jones; NP © John Arrowsmith
Printed and bound in Canada by Friesens   5   4   3   2   1

We acknowledge the financial support of the Government of Canada through
the Canada Book Fund for our publishing activities, and the contribution of the
Government of Ontario through the Ontario Media Development Corporation.

Get the ebook free!